AGAINST ALL ODDS

OTHER TITLES BY BRITTNEY SAHIN

Stand-Alones

Until You Can't

The Story of Us

Falcon Falls Security

The Hunted One

The Broken One

The Guarded One

The Taken One

The Lost Letters: A Novella

The Wanted One

The Fallen One

The Wrecked One

Dublin Nights Series

On the Edge

On the Line

The Real Deal

The Inside Man

The Final Hour

Becoming Us

Someone Like You

My Every Breath

Hidden Truths Series

The Safe Bet

Beyond the Chase

The Hard Truth

Surviving the Fall

The Final Goodbye

Stealth Ops Series

Finding His Mark

Finding Justice

Finding the Fight

Finding Her Chance

Finding the Way Back

Chasing the Knight
Chasing Daylight
Chasing Fortune
Chasing Shadows
Chasing the Storm

Costa Family

Let Me Love You
Not Mine to Keep
The Art of You
The Best of Us

AGAINST ALL ODDS

BRITTNEY SAHIN

This is a work of fiction. Names, characters, organizations, places, events, and incidents are either products of the author's imagination or are used fictitiously. Otherwise, any resemblance to actual persons, living or dead, is purely coincidental.

Text copyright © 2025 by Brittney Sahin
All rights reserved.

No part of this book may be reproduced, or stored in a retrieval system, or transmitted in any form or by any means, electronic, mechanical, photocopying, recording, or otherwise, without express written permission of the publisher.

Published by Montlake, Seattle
www.apub.com

Amazon, the Amazon logo, and Montlake are trademarks of Amazon.com, Inc., or its affiliates.

EU product safety contact:
Amazon Media EU S. à r.l.
38, avenue John F. Kennedy, L-1855 Luxembourg
amazonpublishing-gpsr@amazon.com

ISBN-13: 9781662526756 (paperback)
ISBN-13: 9781662526749 (digital)

Cover design by Caroline Teagle Johnson
Cover image: © Francesco Carta fotografo

Printed in the United States of America

AGAINST ALL ODDS

CHAPTER ONE

Seraphina

Miami, Florida

After nine and a half months, I should've been used to the horror show that was my life. And yet, each day proved to be another disturbing glimpse into how the other half lived. *Evil.* The yin to good's yang.

My boss had his dinner knife against a man's throat while his guests partied downstairs. This was sadly just another Saturday for me. That didn't change the fact I had no desire to sit in Ezra's office and watch someone get tortured, even if the man was a criminal.

I quietly sat on the couch, wrapping up the request from Ezra to run some numbers. Ankles crossed, MacBook on my lap, I looked up, catching Wade checking me out. He was one of Ezra's most trusted bodyguards, and any minute, Wade would take over the interrogation so my boss wouldn't get blood on his suit. He had guests to entertain, after all.

I considered trying to hide the view of my cleavage from Wade, but if Ezra caught him gawking, it'd be his neck, and I wouldn't mind seeing Wade on the other side of a knife for once.

To say I was off-limits to everyone with a pulse in Miami was an understatement. And why had my boss deemed me as such? Easy. Ezra wanted me. Rather desperately, in fact. His wife was the only reason I was safe from him making a move, but it still made him crazy that he couldn't have me, so he ensured no one else could. That worked in my favor since I sure as hell didn't want any of his colleagues or clients to come near me.

I rolled my eyes at Wade, hoping he got the message, then focused on my screen, my report now complete.

"Sir?" I spoke up, dying on the inside a little each time I had to call him that.

Ezra moved his ice-blue eyes off his target and to me. The man was the forty-year-old poster boy for if two perfect high-cheekboned celebrities had a baby. "You have an answer for me?"

"I do, and the numbers don't add up. I triple-checked them." Bad news for the man on his knees with the knife to his throat. "I forwarded the report to you." I closed the laptop and stood.

Wade took note of my legs, because he seemed to have a death wish tonight.

"Mind if I step out and get some air?" *Before I stab you both in the eyes with my high heels?*

Ezra lowered the knife. "Since when does a little blood bother you?"

"It doesn't." *Not anymore. You've made me numb to it.* How messed up was that?

Numbness meant you didn't feel anything. Anger was how you dodged the pain when numbness failed to prevent you from feeling it. And detachment, well, that was a result of living your life bouncing around between the two.

"You plan on telling me why you need that air? Or will you just keep staring at me with your tits hanging out of that dress for Wade to see?" Ezra's voice was rough, scraping over my skin, nearly prying goose bumps free.

Did I need to remind him he had his assistant buy the dress with the demand I wear it tonight? I opted to bite my tongue over that. I had a job to keep and a neck I rather liked attached to my head. "I'm not feeling well."

A harrumph I had no idea how to read was all he gave me. Fantastic. Now I had three jobs: accountant, party host, and mind reader.

Ezra's attention returned to his friend, whom I'd now marked for death by verifying that the numbers were wrong. Lev Markovich may have known Ezra most of his life, but that didn't change the fact that Ezra would make an example of him. For the last two weeks, Lev had been skimming money, underreporting earnings, and pocketing it for a rainy day.

One thing would always hold true: Numbers never lie. Not unless they were manipulated, at least, and I had no choice but to be honest if I didn't want to end up at the bottom of the Atlantic myself.

Did I want Lev to die, even if he was a shit human being? *I mean, maybe.* Not for this reason, though. There were plenty of others that I believed warranted his death.

Ezra removed the gray tape from his soon-to-be-dead friend's mouth in one quick movement, and Lev immediately barked out, "She's lying. Setting me up." He then switched over to speaking Russian, and dammit, I needed to understand what he was saying, especially if he was going to try to throw me under the bus.

My boss—and I used that term loosely—was born in Kyrgyzstan, same as Lev, but they both moved to the States when they were younger. Aside from English and being fluent in his native languages, Russian and Kyrgyz, Ezra also spoke another three. He may have been an evil asshole, but he was a smart and linguistically gifted one.

"You can leave," Ezra told me, which I assumed meant he wasn't falling for Lev's bullshit. "Send Vanessa up here in your place. I'll need someone to clean up the mess after."

"Yes, of course. Thank you, sir." I quickly extracted myself from the room before Lev could spew more garbage at me, then sought out Ezra's personal assistant. Afterward, I went to the third floor to take refuge on the veranda attached to one of the guest rooms. I tossed the laptop on the bed and went onto the balcony, escaping outside.

I bent over the railing, my mind racing in a hundred directions, worried Lev would become a new problem for me.

When the fresh air failed to soothe my soul and fill my lungs with oxygen, I opted for plan B. The bodice of my strapless red dress packed both my breasts *and* my ability to breathe inside it. I unzipped it halfway down my back, feeling immediate relief.

At the throat-clear behind me, followed by the, "You okay, ma'am?" in a deep voice, I lowered my hands to my sides.

My first inclination would've been to switch over into defense mode, but since when did evil "ma'am" me? Not unless this was the devil's new game of seduction? Rope the innocent into submission with a raspy voice. *Am I even still good?* Did I qualify after nine months in evil's lair?

"Miss?" Another peculiar word to hear from someone at one of Ezra's parties, since he didn't exactly mingle with the best of people.

"I didn't realize anyone was out here." *Not supposed to be.* "Needed air."

"Opposed to the air inside?" There was a hint of humor to his tone, but I also realized he sounded closer to me, which meant I needed to zip up and face him. It was never a good idea to keep your back to a man in this house—you were bound to get stabbed in it.

"Yeah, the narcissists inside were using it all up. None left." I had no idea how the insult would land. The pendulum could swing either way.

He laughed. A deep, rich one that fell over my body in a shockingly erotic way. That was unexpected, and an oddly pleasant reaction I had to shake off.

"Anyway." I remembered my zipper and went back to work trying to get it up. The odds of success weren't in my favor, given I'd needed Vanessa's help earlier.

"I'd offer an assist, but that'd probably be out of line for me to do." Well, this guy's batting average with winning me over kept going up and up.

Had he wandered into the wrong house and bypassed security? There were always eight guards rotating the perimeter every half hour and two parked out front like the men outside Buckingham Palace, minus the scarlet tunics. So it was doubtful this mystery man had slipped by anyone.

"I've gone to war with zippers before. I'm good. There are worse enemies to have." I finally remembered to speak. *Bravo.*

I had a habit of having conversations with myself, often forgetting no one else was privy to them. That was what happened when you had to play pretend for as long as I had. You couldn't voice your real thoughts, or you'd wind up on the other side of cutlery.

"Well, of course, unless you catch your fly on your . . . you know . . . That'd be a battle I wouldn't want, if I were a guy," I said when he remained so quiet I wondered if he'd abandoned me.

"Doesn't sound pleasant, no." The husky quality of his voice disturbed me because it was far too soothing. He was also distracting me from what had happened in Ezra's office.

But also, since when did men at Ezra's parties have sexy laughs or voices made of silk?

"So, I take it that means you've never been in that kind of battle." Small talk truly was an art form, and I'd spent over nine months polishing up my skills. I'd never been the best at it before, but when you get thrown into the deep end of the pool, you learn to sink or swim.

"Not with a zipper, no." He cleared his throat, and I read that as a polite request not to ask for a follow-up about what other battles he'd been in.

I let go of the zipper and clutched the front of my dress so it wouldn't fall forward. "I'm going to have to ask you for help," I relented.

"Wars are rarely fought alone." The somberness in his tone caught me off guard, and I shuddered as he gently anchored one hand over my shoulder.

I closed my eyes, shocked to find myself enjoying his touch. Heat spread through my body, firing up my nerve endings, challenging the numbness I'd grown accustomed to.

"There. Victory," he announced as I continued to try to wrap my head around the feeling of safety this faceless stranger provided.

"Something tells me the taste of victory is that much sweeter when it's been a hard-fought battle," I mused, letting go of my dress top. "If only zippers were our greatest problems, right?" There was a tug of pain in my chest at the truth I'd allowed to fall from my lips.

"I should let go of you now, I suppose." Yet his hand remained on my skin like a brand that didn't burn, and there I was, liking it.

Maybe I missed the touch of a man? Skin-to-skin contact with someone who didn't make me cringe or cause my stomach to revolt. So I gave in, caving to the feelings, and whispered, "A few more seconds won't hurt." I kept my eyes closed, playing pretend for a bit longer as the pad of his thumb made small sweeping motions where he held me.

While numbers didn't lie, neither did vibes. And even with my back to him, I could tell he had good ones. I'd sell myself on that idea, at least. Give myself one more minute.

When he finally let me go, I blinked back to reality, remembering an important detail that killed the moment I shouldn't have been having in the first place. "No one is allowed on the third floor."

"I apologize. I wasn't aware." His sexy, gravelly voice lured me into turning around.

When our eyes met, I realized the battle had only just begun. Forget the zipper. I was about to go to war with myself, unsure whether or not I should give in to the kind of temptation I thought I'd said goodbye to long ago, and for good reason.

My mystery man dragged his thumb along the underside of his chin while studying me with the same unmistakable desire he no doubt saw in my eyes. And not in the way Ezra and Wade looked at me. No, this was different. This was something *more*. It was as confusing as it was surreal.

He brought his knuckles over to his stubbled jawline next, swiping the back of his hand along his skin as if in a daze, further stoking the flames of this need taking hold of me.

This feeling, this . . . whatever it was happening to me, had me stepping closer when it should've sent me back.

Staring into his eyes made me realize I missed more than just the touch of a man. I missed my life B.E. Before Ezra.

My family.

My friends. (I only had two good ones, but that'd been enough for me.)

I missed laughing, too.

Hell, even crying during a movie.

"Who are you?" I needed a name. I needed to know who he was and how he was capable of cracking through my walls designed for self-preservation.

"Not sure how to answer that." The small smile that settled on his lips felt genuine, but it was also powerful enough to continue doing what I'd thought was impossible: open up my heart.

These feelings were as dangerous as they were unexpected, and it took all my strength to try to redirect. To remind myself why I'd left my life behind. "Well, um, a friend or associate of Mr. Sokolov's would know better than to come up to the third floor."

"You're right. I'm neither." His honesty was the breath of fresh air I'd come outside for.

My bottom lip took asylum between my teeth as I waited for him to fill in the blanks I hadn't asked for while I studied him. To investigate the way darkness didn't blanket him like the other men I'd been around. Not that there was a halo above his head, either, but there sure as hell was something drawing me to him aside from his devastatingly good looks.

Based on the slight crinkles around his eyes and the few fine lines across his forehead, I'd guess he was in his mid- to late thirties. And speaking of those eyes . . .

They were the most beautiful shade of blue green I'd ever seen in person. They reminded me of the waters off the coast of Aruba.

His eyes also told a story of a man who really had seen his fair share of battles, and maybe that was why I felt connected to him. Maybe he had a tough past too, and so we could relate on some unspoken level.

He reached for my wrist, and a shaky exhalation escaped my lips at the feel of his hand on me. He held my arm between us and skimmed his finger along the phrase tattooed on the inside of my forearm.

The featherlight touch emboldened me to take another step forward, lulling me into a false sense of safety that could never truly exist inside Ezra's home.

"You are your only limit," he said, reading the words inscribed there, the pad of his thumb softly moving over my skin.

I blinked a few times, trying to pull myself back together but failing. "Who are you?" I had to try again; the need to know was too strong.

"I'm just . . ." He gently guided my arm to my side, though his fingers remained softly around my wrist.

"Just what?" The words broke from my mouth like breaths of dying air, desperate for one last moment of life before they were extinguished forever.

When he didn't answer, my attention found a new home—on his body, which was close enough to mine that it wouldn't take much for us to be flush against one another.

Broad chest and shoulders. Strong arms. Corded forearms exposed with his sleeves rolled to the elbows. If I removed his dress shirt, I bet I'd find a rippling wall of hard abdominal muscles.

He let go of my wrist and cupped his mouth, probably as shocked as I was at this thing happening between us. Unidentified flying objects made more sense right about now than the magnetism drawing two strangers together.

His hand left his mouth, taking a detour up into his hair. Golden brown and thick. Medium length and slightly wavy, flipping up a touch off to the sides. I had to resist the urge to dive my fingers through it.

"Your name, please." If I knew his name, surely I'd find out he was a bad guy. Then I could break the spell. Lose this odd connection. Tuck my old life away into the past, where it had to stay to keep me safe. Return to my current status quo of numb, angry, and detached.

His forehead tightened, and those lines of defiance told me his lips were going to be a steel trap in not providing a name. "I don't think that's a good idea unless you tell me you don't work for the Sokolovs."

I nearly answered with the truth, but the rational side of my brain returned, restoring a hint of logic to the chaos swirling there. "I'm one of Ezra's accountants." Those words burned going down like cheap tequila.

"Accountant." No question mark in his tone. More like he was testing out the word to see how it sounded, and he didn't like it. No disdain for math, but maybe some for my boss. "Any chance you'd consider a career change to work for someone else?" He maintained that rigid, tense posture as if also holding his breath in the hope I'd say yes.

If only it were that simple. "That almost sounds like a job offer."

Without hesitation, he offered, "I'd create a position for you, if you'd take it."

"It'd never work," I admitted, my throat thickening.

"Why not?" He didn't sound offended, more so saddened by that fact.

"I never mix business with pleasure." One step closer. Just one more would be safe without going too far, without throwing everything I'd worked for away for one hot night. "I get the feeling that'd be a hard-fought battle I might lose with you," I confessed. "And I'm not in the position to fail at anything right now." *Even if I want to taste defiance on my tongue in the form of a kiss from you.* "You should go. If Mr. Sokolov finds us . . ."

"And you don't mix business and pleasure with him, I take it?" There wasn't jealousy there, more like he was searching for reassurance that Ezra had never laid a hand on me.

"Of course not—and also, he's married." Maybe he really didn't know much about the host of the party, which had me even more curious as to what he was doing here.

"Marriage doesn't mean anything to a man like him." His tone had quickly gone from silk to leather with that statement. "Has he ever hurt you?"

No, but he will if he finds us here alone. "Do you think I'd tell a stranger if he had?"

He surprised me by reaching for my cheek, a rough hand on my smooth skin somehow the perfect match. "You should leave him," he said instead of pressing, more than likely formulating his own opinion with my nonanswer.

"It's complicated." In so many ways. In every direction that pointed north, south, east, or west, in fact. *I'm trapped for as long as it takes.*

"I'd happily help you uncomplicate things."

I couldn't believe I was standing there wanting to reveal all the *whys* I was an accountant to an evil man. "I don't even know you."

"I think you recognize I'm not like the other men here." He let go of my face but didn't back away. He was so close I could smell his cologne, and whatever he was wearing was delicious to my senses. Earthy and sensual. As masculine as his aura.

I was seconds away from letting muscle memory take over. Touch him and let him touch me back. Kiss him and let him give it right back (and probably more).

Time to back away. To break the spell and the moment for good. *You'll die if I don't.* "I can tell you're not like the others, but you can't help. I'm sorry. Thank you, though."

His jaw hitched, working to the side as if fighting a much tougher battle than my zipper. An internal one as to what to do with me.

I didn't take him for a quitter, but in this case, I had to let him know there was no choice. We had to say goodbye.

He closed his eyes and released a deep breath, the battle waging on.

Mere inches separated our breaths from tangling, our bodies from touching. The temptation was too great, so I staggered back.

"Ryder." He dropped the name on me in a low, deep voice while opening his eyes. "My name's Ryder."

Ryder. Talk about a fitting name for a man like him.

"Do you have a good memory?" he asked before I could respond, and I nodded. "Memorize my phone number. If you change your mind, you call me. Or text. Whatever you can safely do." He gave me the digits, then repeated them three more times, and I knew I'd never be able to call him, but I committed the number to memory anyway.

"Goodbye." I was shocked at the physical pain that one word caused. *You're just a stranger.* I'd probably need to hit myself over the head with that reminder in the days to come.

Ryder repeated his number one more time, then gave me a hesitant nod and echoed my goodbye.

I tightened my hands at my sides as I forced myself to watch him walk out of my life.

The fact I nearly let tears obstruct my vision sent me back to the edge of the balcony. Planting my forearms on the railing, I leaned forward and bowed my head, resisting the wild and ridiculous urge to chase after him.

After a few minutes had gone by, and I'd managed to lock up the emotions that didn't serve me well, I opened my eyes.

Of course Ryder was in my line of sight, because why wouldn't he be? Testing me, right along with my willpower.

His profile was to me as he lit a cigar. He was the only one outside, even though the storm had stopped an hour or so ago. He must've sensed my eyes on him, because he turned and looked up at me.

We maintained eye contact for what felt like a minute. I simply stared at him as he puffed on his cigar, trying to grasp how he seemed to hold the keys to unlocking all these feelings I'd sealed off with dead bolts and barbed wire.

I didn't trust myself to not surrender to my impulses, so I forced myself to retreat inside.

I barely made it two feet into the bedroom before I slammed into a new problem: Ezra was in the doorway, blocking my exit.

"What's wrong?" I backed up those two steps I'd taken, recognizing that look in his eyes. Definitely not lust, but anger. Shit, what'd Lev say? I'd forgotten all about him after meeting Ryder.

Ezra dragged his hand up and down the column of his throat while observing me.

"Whatever he said to you is a lie," I blurted out.

He tipped his head, breathing hard, as if rage was festering and about to boil over and burn me. He stalked even closer, erasing the space between us. "I learned something interesting. It's amazing what people admit with a knife to their throat."

"Oh yeah?" I tried to pull off nonchalant when I was anything but. "What?"

He backed me up against the wall by the balcony doors. Then parked his hand over my shoulder and caged me in. "DEA arrested Lev two weeks ago. Gave him a choice: go undercover for them or rot in a cell forever."

Shit. I had to keep it together. "Let me get this straight—not only was he stealing from you, he was working for the DEA?" Maybe he risked skimming from Ezra to fund his escape from both him and the agency? "Did you kill him?"

"Of course." He shifted closer, letting me feel the erection in his dress pants. "But as for you . . ." With his other hand, he reached up and unexpectedly forced my hair down from its pinned-up position.

I hid the wince of pain so he wouldn't get off on it. "What about me?"

"Lev said the DEA has someone else on the inside looking to stab me in the back." Fisting my hair, he tugged, drawing my chin up and my mouth closer to his. "I really hope he's wrong about it being you."

He pushed away from the wall without letting go of my hair and produced his favorite weapon of choice.

"Like I said, it's amazing what people confess with a knife to their throat." He pressed the blade against my sensitive flesh. "Tell me, has my favorite accountant been a bad girl? Have you been deceiving me all this time?" The knife pinched my skin but didn't draw blood. "Are you working for the DEA, too?"

CHAPTER TWO

Ryder

Just before

I lit the Italian Toscano cigar I had on me, the vanilla aroma hitting my nose as I pocketed the lighter. I needed an excuse to stand outside the party while I waited for my teammate, Alex, to join me. Also, I needed to cool off after my confrontation with the woman in red.

I held the smoke in my mouth for a moment, allowing the flavor to spread, then exhaled while slowly turning around. The reason I was now in need of a smoke—and I wasn't even a smoker—was staring down at me from the balcony.

Who the hell are you? I puffed on the cigar, trying to recalibrate. I had to remember why I was at the party, and it wasn't for her, even if I now wanted it to be.

I couldn't wrap my head around how she'd wound up entangled with a man like Ezra Sokolov.

She doesn't want my help. I had to keep beating that reminder into my brain so I wouldn't take control of what felt like a dire situation for her and storm the house. Steal her away from a corrupt man.

I'd been up on the balcony to get a better aerial view of the property while waiting on my team's target to arrive, and out she'd come. The woman of my dreams.

My three teammates had been in my ear, heckling me over the wireless comm. I'd been so taken aback by her, I'd forgotten they could hear us. I'd muted my comm a few seconds too late into my conversation.

Thirty-eight rotations around the sun. That was how long I'd been on this floating rock of a planet, and not once in all that time had I ever felt such a strong connection to anyone, let alone a stranger.

Fuck, I'd even broken protocol and given her my name, ignoring the fact she knowingly worked for a criminal. It'd taken all my energy to walk away from her, to not resort to my basest instincts to throw her over my shoulder and save her anyway.

She doesn't want my help. There it was again. Not landing. Not fucking sticking. Not with those brown eyes still laser focused down on me, just begging for me to go back inside and do something insane. At the least, taste her lips. Then, if she'd let me, take away her problems.

When she backed away, breaking contact, it felt like I'd been sucker punched. If it wasn't for realizing Alex was en route to me, I'd have gone inside to find her. Ask her one more time to walk away with a total stranger. You know, because why fucking not?

"You good, boss?" Alex circled me, placing both the $10 million house and myself in his line of sight.

"Stop with the *boss* shit," I muttered, both joking and also serious.

"Just getting used to how it sounds. Rolls right off the tongue, doesn't it?" His cocky wink would've ground the gears of our former team leader, who quit two weeks ago.

I returned his obvious razzing in a very mature way—by rolling my eyes.

"You didn't answer me, though." For a man who could intimidate most people into submission with just one scolding look, you'd never know he had the biggest fucking heart of us all. And that made him a serious pain in my ass, caring too much about me, right along with shit I didn't want to talk about.

Two women I didn't want to discuss with him now dominated my thoughts: the one he'd heard me speaking to upstairs before I'd muted him and the one who'd put me in a bad mood before the op started tonight.

I looked around the patio by the rectangular infinity pool, ensuring we were still alone. Checked the balcony again. No sight of her.

"And of course I'm fine." Despite the fact I had walked away from the woman in red upstairs and would probably never see her again.

Lightning never strikes the same place twice. My mother's words about extraordinary things never happening more than once weren't metaphorical for me right now. Because I'd felt a bolt of something shoot straight through my veins, and it lit me the fuck up. And I wanted to be hit again and again.

I undid the top two buttons of my dress shirt, unsure if there was any air in my lungs left after that woman had quite literally stolen my breath.

"Why wouldn't I be good?" I hissed, agitated that I was agitated. *Make it make sense.* I grimaced at the realization he'd answer my rhetorical question.

"Our comms are muted this time." He winked again, the fucker. "It's safe to talk."

I didn't need the reminder he'd eavesdropped on the start of a conversation that centered around a zipper, which had somehow morphed into me remembering my days in the army. Real wars and battles that hadn't lost their hold on me, not even two years after I'd left the military.

"The target is still a no-show, so we have time. Go ahead, take advantage of that four-year psych degree my mother forced me to get before I joined the army." He opened his palm, requesting a cigar, and I gave him the other one I had for the sake of our cover stories, along with the lighter.

"You worried I can't handle this new role of mine?" *Maybe you should worry. Hell, maybe I should.* I thought back to the mystery woman upstairs. The woman with the most seductive and tantalizing mouth of all fucking time. A mouth I still wanted to claim.

"You popping your Delta One cherry tonight isn't why I'm asking if you're okay," he said dismissively while handing me back the lighter. "You also know I'd follow you anywhere, brother. Reed feels the same."

Reed was Delta Three, and he was more the quiet, doom-and-gloom fucker on our team. Alex, on the other hand, was a glass-half-full kind of guy who could also cut through any situation with whatever tool needed to get the job done, whether it be humor or a machete. As for me? I didn't know how to define myself anymore.

"Not so sure what I think about Leo, though," he continued when I kept quiet, pointing the conversation in a new direction that I'd much rather go than continue to dance around his concerns about my headspace.

Tonight may have been my first op spearheading our unit as Delta One for our security company, but to me, we were equals. Hell, most of us had left the army with the same rank anyway. But as for our new teammate, Delta Four, we didn't vibe, which didn't bode well for our future in operating together.

Leo had joined a week before our team leader quit. He'd hired him as a favor to a general without consulting any of us first. So that'd been quite the fuck-you before walking out on us to work for a bunch of war profiteers. His new agency was far different from our company, Delta Shield Security.

We weren't beholden to anyone, not even the private and wealthy do-gooders funding us. We were also small and tight knit. Currently, it was just the four of us. We were a precision strike team. Mostly hostage rescue and tracking targets. Quick in-and-out jobs, usually for Homeland Security, paid for by their "discretionary" budget, without anyone knowing we'd been on the ground. Case in point, now.

"If Leo doesn't fit in," I finally began, fine with sharing my thoughts on this since our comms were muted, "we'll find a replacement for him."

"And fuck the general's wishes?" Alex smirked.

"Without a second thought." Turning to the side, I eyed the floor-to-ceiling glass windows that gave us a clear view of the guests, hoping to catch sight of the woman in red.

On that note, I really needed to wrap up thoughts of her. I still had a mission to complete, and she wasn't it. I also had three guys I was in charge of, which meant I couldn't lose focus like I'd done on that balcony.

Reed and Leo were still on overwatch, safely from view, keeping an eye on the guards to ensure a clean exfil when it was time.

While Alex and I had arrived using aliases and walked through the front door, Reed and Leo had come by way of a Zodiac. They currently had the inflatable motorboat hidden by the boathouse near the far edge of the property.

"This is Four," Leo announced over our wireless comms. "Property sweep is complete. We have thirty more minutes until they check again."

Based on our recon before the mission, there were eight armed guards who swept the one-and-a-half-acre property every thirty minutes to ensure it was clear. That gave us a generous half-hour window to exfil if we wanted to minimize the chance of engaging in direct combat, which meant tonight's op was low risk.

After responding to Leo, Alex grumbled, "I hate being in here unarmed, even if it's just a party. I'd rather be in a mirror maze with clowns popping out at the end than here with these fuckers."

I laughed. "I swear, man, you and clowns."

"What can I say, *It* did a motherfucking number on me as a kid." He puffed on the cigar around a smile. "So that's saying a lot if I'd rather deal with clowns than these assholes."

He was a genius at trying to divert my attention from my problems. If only I could think of clowns right now. Not about the woman upstairs. Or the fact I'd learned this morning my ex-girlfriend was four months pregnant by a close friend of mine. I hadn't even known they'd been dating until today, for fuck's sake. But talk about a way to start my Saturday, waking up to notifications on my phone from my buddies texting to see if I was good. You know, considering Lainey and I had only broken up *three* months ago.

I'd always wrapped up, so I doubted the baby was mine. Still, I'd had to make an awkward call today and ask her to promise me I wasn't the father. She'd provided the details about her unfaithfulness, which I regretted hearing—and led me to believe I wasn't the dad.

"All these rich pricks playing dress-up as businesspeople." Alex jutted his chin toward the house, talking rather skillfully with a cigar between his teeth. "They're the real clowns, I suppose."

"Nothing I hate more than two-faced people." I showed my cards with that remark, letting the truth out that I hadn't successfully hit control-override on my thoughts like I needed to do.

"Too bad we can't take all of these pricks down tonight." Alex with an attempt to redirect again, and I appreciated it. Maybe he ought to have been Delta One tonight. "But we're on American soil, and these guys are alleged businessmen, so I guess we have to be on our best behavior."

Businessmen, my ass. The house was full of finance bros who used their day jobs as a cover to launder money—not to mention the much uglier sin they helped with, which was drug trafficking.

And she, the mystery woman, worked for Ezra. Why? After learning that, now more than ever, I was on the same page as Alex, wishing we could at least take down Ezra. But since we were there on behalf of Homeland Security, we couldn't.

We'd accepted an assignment to find an individual who helped move money for a terrorist cell, and we'd tracked him to Florida. He was supposed to be attending this party as a guest. Without legally acquired evidence, the government couldn't arrest him for questioning, which was where we came in. *If he ever shows up.*

I looked inside the house again, checking for our mark, and when I didn't see him among the crowd, I let my thoughts drift back to her. The *her* who refused to leave my head.

The storm may have ended an hour ago, but I peered up at the dark sky, waiting and hoping for lightning to strike again, preferably in the form of the woman in red coming outside to find me.

I put out my cigar, continuing to reel from my encounter with her. Upstairs, those deep-brown eyes had me feeling like I'd been in quicksand. Sucked in to the point of no return, and I'd about lost control. I nearly forgot I spoke multiple languages, and it took time to remember a word in any of them.

Stunning was an oversimplification for her in that fitted red dress. A gorgeous body, and legs for fucking days.

When I'd set a hand on her golden-tan skin, inhaling her sweet perfume, it was the first time my pulse had raced in recent years when it wasn't mission-related from adrenaline.

I had the feeling if I were to peel back a few more layers, I'd find out she was just as beautiful on the inside, too. Gut feeling, at least. Then again, maybe I wasn't the best judge of character. My girlfriend did cheat on me with my friend, so there was that to think about.

"You good, boss?" Alex sent a wrecking ball through my thoughts, as he should've.

"You already asked me that," I reminded him.

"Well, the target arrived. I see him inside, so I'm just making sure you're—"

"I'm fine." I unmuted my comm and let the other two know we had eyes on the package.

"Ready to be gift wrapped and delivered to you," Alex said, since he'd be the one to go in and snatch and grab the mark without anyone ever knowing we were there. Then we'd take our hostage to our safe house nearby to be interrogated.

"This is Three. We still have twenty-five minutes to exfil before security makes their rounds on the perimeter again."

That was more than manageable. I faced Alex, nodding at him with silent orders to move on the target and complete his part of the mission.

It was time I put the ex who'd destroyed my faith in relationships out of my mind, right along with the one woman who oddly had me feeling as though somehow she could be the one to restore it.

CHAPTER THREE

Ryder

The mission had gone smoothly. Textbook perfect. I couldn't have asked for a better outcome. Alex had successfully removed our target from the party and passed him off to Reed and Leo before another perimeter sweep happened.

Easy fucking day—or in this case, night. Now for the hard part: walk out the front door, turning my back on the woman my gut told me needed help. That wasn't in my nature to do.

Okay, so maybe it was more than that. It was the fact I also wanted her. To know her lips. Her body. Her mind.

I didn't even give a damn that she knowingly worked for a criminal. It didn't matter to me. If she was willing to walk away from that life, then I'd move heaven and earth to help make it happen.

I tore my hand through my hair, contemplating my options now that the mission was nearly complete. The only part left to do was actually fucking leave.

At the sight of Alex inside the house—which meant he'd managed to discreetly slip through a side door—I headed in to meet him. The man was a master at getting in and out of places unseen. Growing up, Alex had learned a thing or two from his father, who was a Vegas escape artist with his own headline show.

I slid open the glass door, and the booming electronic music slapped me in the face. I kept my head down, turned away from the security cameras, and started for where Alex was waiting for me. In my peripheral view, a flash of red caught my attention, and I wound up colliding with a couple dancing. I held up my palms in apology before searching out my new favorite color.

When I determined it was her, it was as if someone hit the pause button on my life and everything around me stopped. The music. The dancing. All of it.

The woman in red. The gorgeous accountant. The woman I couldn't have.

Two guards strong-armed her out the side door with a 9mm trained on her.

My blood heated, and my hands converted to fists, becoming weapons at my sides. I was seeing red again, but in a much different way.

"You okay?" Alex asked, and I nodded toward the side door.

"The woman from the balcony needs help." Had Ezra found out she'd been alone with me on the balcony? Was she being punished because of it? "You got my six on this?"

"Of course." He discreetly tapped his earpiece, and I was thankful we'd told the guys to hang tight until we made a clean exfil before they took off, because now we needed them as backup.

We went outside, and I let Reed and Leo know there was a change in plans.

Maintaining our distance so we weren't exposed, we managed to catch up with her and the two men as they led her down a lit-up pathway. If they were heading toward where Ezra's yacht was docked, they'd run into our men.

"This is One. The two armed tangos and the woman are now on approach," I warned Reed and Leo over comms, low enough so I wasn't overheard. "Hide the hostage, and get behind your rifles and await my orders."

"We can make a clean exfil before they arrive," Leo said. "We're not supposed to let anyone know we're here. Why are we going to engage?"

I staggered back a step, not the direction I needed to go, but did I really need to spell this out for him? "We're not letting a woman die."

"This is Three, *lima charlie*," Reed responded, letting me know he heard my orders loud and clear and wouldn't be pushing back. "I'll advise when I have them in view."

"I disagree with this. We'll kick a hornet's nest by opening fire on these men. This is not our mission." Fucking Leo. So help me. He was outwardly telling me to fuck off, and this situation was already complicated enough.

"Your team leader just gave you an order," Alex hissed. "You damn well follow it."

"We're not in the military anymore. That shit doesn't work. I will not engage unless I'm fired upon." Leo was proving at the wrong damn time that he wasn't cut out for our team.

"I have them locked in," Reed, the voice of reason in my ear, let me know. "I can't see you two, which means you should still be safe from their view."

Good. "The second the first tango doesn't have his weapon pointed at her, take him and the other guy out."

Reed confirmed he'd heard the order, and I stopped walking when she tripped and fell forward. She took me and the guards by surprise when she pivoted and swept her leg around, knocking one guard off-balance. The second his weapon was no longer on her, Reed took the shot, using the suppressor so the noise was slightly less audible.

After Reed nailed him in the head, he let us know: "I can't get a clean shot of the other guy. She's in my line of sight."

I didn't hesitate and rushed to take down the second mark myself before he knew what was happening.

The second tango, sidearm in hand, was in the process of doing a three-sixty while ducking his head, searching for the direction the shot had been fired from.

I closed in on him from behind, threw my forearm across the front of his neck, and squeezed. CQB it was, then. I bent his arm, snapping it back with my other hand, and he barked out something in what sounded like Russian before dropping his pistol.

"Take her to the others," I yelled to Alex, unable to put eyes on her, too busy dealing with the guy trying to escape. I released my hold on him, only to shove him forward, knowing Reed would handle him.

Two rounds in his chest, and he was down.

I spun around, finding her staring at me with wide eyes alongside Alex. Her hair hung wild and messy around her face, covering one eye.

"We need to go. More will come." I stepped over a dead body to get to her. "Now," I said while offering my hand, "will you please come with me?"

CHAPTER FOUR

Seraphina

For nine months, I'd prided myself on how courageous I'd been. Told myself I was a badass and could handle anything for a just cause. I'd convinced myself of that up until now, up until this moment, minutes away from being tortured for answers and killed.

My mother used to always say to me, *Whatever will be, will be.* And my chance encounter with Ryder tonight just proved that. I wasn't meant to die. Not now, at least.

"Are you okay?" Ryder stared at me, the pale moonlight glinting off the water beside the dock where we stood near a rubber boat.

Four men were already seated inside. One was motionless, dressed in a suit with a bag over his head.

"Say something so I know you're not in shock. That you can hear me." Ryder's voice cut through the fog in my mind, pulling me back to him.

Shock? I was feeling that, too, I supposed. *I'm not dead.* That fact was as wonderful as the face of the man before me now.

With the dock lights illuminating him, it was easy to see every hard plane of his body, right along with his worried expression.

"I'm the opposite of dead," I said around the lump in my throat.

"Alive is a much preferable condition to be in, I agree." My hero's brows stitched together before he quietly knelt before me, directing me to hold on to his shoulders. "You can't walk on the boat in these things." His play-by-play of what he was doing and why it was needed helped, since I was still skipping through a tumultuous state of emotions.

Ryder removed my heels like a gentleman postdate, not like a man who'd saved a woman from nearly being assaulted and killed.

Because yeah, I knew exactly what would've happened on the yacht after Ezra took over for Wade and the other asshole. I'd more than likely not have been able to convince Ezra I was innocent, then no telling what he'd have done to me before taking my life, knowing I'd never be able to narc on him to his wife if I was dead. So a million *thank-you*s to this man and his friends would never be enough for saving me from that fate.

Ryder tossed my shoes on the boat while standing, then slipped a hand around my waist, preparing to escort me down into the floating escape device as I whispered, "Thank you. For everything."

He gave me a small nod of *You're welcome*, then helped me onto the boat.

"Seven minutes until our window is closed on a clean exfil," one of the men announced, turning on the small engine that'd be our saving grace to get us out quicker than paddling. "They'll discover those bodies soon."

While seated, I unscrewed the backs of my earrings and tossed the diamonds in the water. Now we couldn't be tracked by Ezra.

I'd always known the risks of my work, but I had no choice but to live in the land of denial while convincing myself I was invincible. It was the only way to survive.

"Trackers?" Ryder asked.

At my nod, he untucked his shirt from his pants and swiftly worked the buttons free, then removed the starched material, exposing his rock-hard body.

He quietly wrapped his shirt around my shoulders and guided my arms through each sleeve before sitting beside me.

"Move out," he ordered, hooking his arm around my back to keep me from going over the side.

I clutched the front of the shirt as reality caught up with me. Not the fact I'd almost died, but that my time with Ezra was over. I had a backup plan, but I'd honestly never expected to have to use it.

Instead of focusing on the *Weekend at Bernie's*–looking guy sitting across from me, with his covered head bobbing forward, only staying upright because of the support of the men squeezing him in, I closed my eyes.

I listened to the soft hum of the engine as we moved farther and farther away from what had been my hell.

I didn't open my eyes until Ryder announced, "We're here." I didn't know where *here* was, but I already knew it'd be better than where I'd been before.

Eyes now on my valiant hero—who had stolen my breath earlier, then stolen those guards' chance to steal my life—I allowed him to take my hand, and he held on to my shoes in the other.

"You'll be safe staying with us," he said, like a promise I so wished I could accept, as he helped me off the rubber boat.

Once on solid ground, the earth damp beneath my bare feet, I pulled my hand free of his touch, worried I'd never want to let go if I didn't do it now.

He cleared his throat and gestured toward the house sitting a hundred feet away in total darkness. I trusted these men even if they were strangers and had a hostage with them. Enemy of my enemy had to be my friend and all mentality. My mantra these days.

Barefoot, I followed Ryder up the path and into the home. He flicked on the lights, walking us into what was once the living room. No furniture. Only duffel bags, a few rifles, and two laptops.

I tightened Ryder's dress shirt around me like a robe as I watched two of the men drag the limp body into the hall and out of sight. I situated my back to the empty wall, waiting for instructions. Like how to breathe, walk, talk, and do all the things I'd been pretty great at up until three letters marked me for death: *DEA*.

Focusing back on the man who'd chosen to save my life, I tried listening to what he was saying to the other guy, but they were talking too low for me to make out much. Probably discussing what the hell to do with me.

With Ryder still shirtless, my gaze traveled over his strong back muscles as they pinched together. While he had no tattoos anywhere I could see, he was marked by something else—scars. A few here and there to indicate he'd been hurt, maybe even shot, at some point in his life.

He dropped my shoes onto the floor alongside him and rested his hands on his hips, talking in a hushed tone with the other guy.

Curiosity propelled me to go ahead and cut to it. "Are you government?" I asked.

Ryder's hands went to his sides, and he slowly turned to face me; his friend took that as his cue to leave.

"We're private contractors, of sorts." He closed the space between us, swallowing it up in three long strides. "Why was your boss planning to hurt you? Was it my fault? Did he find out we were alone together?" Worry crowded his face. Then guilt and a little blame. All the things he didn't need to feel or think.

I quickly shut it down. "Nothing to do with you." I eliminated the last bit of space between us while releasing hold of the shirt.

"Then why?" His determination to get to the truth that I wasn't ready to give was about to be a problem.

The less you know, the better. "Ezra was upset about something." That was probably too vague. He thought I willingly worked for a criminal, so why would he trust me?

The problem was, I still didn't know exactly why he'd been at the party or what he wanted with that unconscious man. All I knew was that I was unharmed and alive because of him.

Ezra had to be looking for me, though. Losing his mind that I got away, knowing how much I knew about his business. He'd hate more than anything that I'd bested him, and he'd never want anyone to know that truth. That I'd deceived him for over nine months.

"And you don't want to tell me why, I take it?" Ryder broke through my thoughts with an appropriate follow-up to my response.

"No." Simple, but hopefully an effective answer.

"If I hadn't been there, would you—"

"Have died?" I finished for him. "More than likely, but I guess God had other plans for me and sent you."

Ryder closed his eyes, his jaw visibly straining. As much as I wanted to unleash the truth on him, then let those big arms of his swallow me up into a hug, that wouldn't eliminate my problems. It'd only land him in the middle of them.

Ryder opened his eyes, his expression softening. "We should talk, though, don't you think?"

Talk. Such a big word for four letters. "Sure, would you like to know my favorite book? Movie? Pastime? Or maybe how I help myself fall asleep at night?" I let a small smile pull at the edges of my lips, hoping my mild teasing to evade the seriousness would buy me a little time. Like time to imprint the harsh reminder in my head as to why I shouldn't open up.

"I'm fairly decent at deflecting myself." He caught me off guard when he reached between us, drawing his finger under my chin, urging my eyes on him. My heart raced as he tipped his head, eyeing my mouth as my lips parted in auto-response. "Tell me your name." The rough texture of his words nearly slipped past my defenses.

"Maybe later?" *Don't press, please. I just might spill every ounce of truth inside me.*

Brows tightening, he continued to study me to the point I was worried he'd be able to read my thoughts without me ever opening my mouth.

Despite everything that'd happened tonight, like the almost-being-defiled-and-dying part, how in the hell was my desire managing to push through, turning into an achy neediness in my stomach?

But when he wet his lips, I wet mine.

And when he stared at my mouth, I eyed his right back.

His blue-green eyes laid siege to mine next, so I fought to stake claim to his.

We mirrored and echoed one another, silently locked into this moment.

Almost dying wasn't causing this, right? No, it'd started up on the balcony, and it'd grown into something so tangible I could reach out and touch it as if a feeling had actual mass.

"Ryder." His name had come out like two puffs of erotic air instead of as two syllables. "I, um . . ." *Need you to stop making me feel like this, or I'll never do what needs to be done.* I kept that to myself, not ready for him to actually stop doing the thing, because the thing felt so good. I could only imagine what would happen if he touched me beyond the finger beneath my chin.

He leaned in closer, so close we just might do it—lose our minds and kiss one another. It'd be a hell of a way to say goodbye.

But what if, afterward, I couldn't walk away? I couldn't let it be the kiss of death.

I flinched as the "anxious me" I'd kept buried inside my hard shell of "badassery," which I'd worn like a suit of armor, reminded me that everyone died. They always did. So I immediately jerked away from him.

The hard wall of his chest inflated as his gaze pierced right through me. When he let go of a deep breath, a resigned sigh I doubted was from defeat fell from his mouth. Then he quietly went over to a bag in the center of the room.

He knelt, looking for something inside it, and I used the opportunity to pick up my shoes as I waited to see what he planned to do.

A few seconds later, he stood and faced me, holding clothes. "Maybe change first; then we can try the talking thing? We'll start with your favorite book, then get to why Ezra planned to kill you."

That'll be quite the transition. "Sure."

He frowned, more than likely reading the lie on my lips. The hard work of pretending to be someone else for three-quarters of a year vanished in his presence. I was simply me. The badass, the anxious one, and everything in between. Mostly just safe, but safety was a short-lived experience I couldn't get used to, since it would inevitably end.

"Second bedroom down the hall on your left has a bathroom in there. I need a few minutes with the guys; then we'll do the talking thing."

He handed me the clothes, and I cradled them under my arm, careful not to drop my heels.

"I'll walk you there," he said, as if worried I might find my way to a different door, like the exit. An uneasy smile crossed his face. "Don't want you getting lost."

Once I was inside the bedroom, he remained in the hall and parked a hand on the doorframe.

"Thank you again for saving me." I nodded lightly, unable to meet his eyes this time, so I kept my focus on his rippling abs, doing my best not to get choked up over the fact I'd never see this man again. "I won't ever forget what you did for me."

CHAPTER FIVE

Ryder

I needed to walk away. Give her a few minutes of privacy. Maybe she wanted to use the bathroom—or, you know, get out of that dress—and I was still stuck in her doorway, unyielding. Unmoving. Worried that if I left, I'd discover she was a mirage and I'd hallucinated her.

I pushed away from the doorframe, doing my best not to act like a creepy fuck, just staring at her after what she'd been through. "I won't let him find you. I'll protect you." The words punched from my mouth like commands, my tone a bit gruff at the reminder of her boss's plans for her tonight. Thank God I'd been there; that was all I could focus on right now.

"I'm not your responsibility, but thank you." She semi-smiled, eyes falling to the clothes bundled against her chest.

You're going to be stubborn, then? She was a stranger, but based on our interaction on the balcony, I had a feeling I shouldn't have expected anything different. It'd be another battle with her to let me intervene. I wasn't sure what that even looked like. Kill Ezra in cold blood? Kill every dangerous man she may have had ties to?

The moment the curtain of her dark lashes lifted and her eyes landed back on mine, I knew I would if I had to. I'd go back to Ezra's right now and take him down if that'd fix things. I didn't care that she'd chosen to work for him. There had to be a good reason for it—but hell, even if there wasn't, I couldn't seem to find it in me to give a damn.

"I won't let anything happen to you." I needed her to hear me. Understand me. Acknowledge *my* stubbornness.

Her gaze dropped down the column of my throat to my chest, then moved lower and lower. My abdominal muscles tightened. Her eyes on me had me feeling as though she could brand my skin, mark me as hers with just one look. Fucking A, I'd be okay with that.

"I should change," she whispered in a daze.

Then eyes on my face, not my crotch. Which was where she was presently killing me with her focus.

Hand back on the doorframe, I leaned forward, waiting for her to look at me. "Promise you won't go anywhere?" My chest hurt from asking that, but my gut told me I needed to.

There were her eyes again, laser focused on mine like a challenge. "Am I your prisoner?"

I grunted. "Of course not." But what I really wanted to say was, *Yes, until I know you're safe. A hostage-for-your-own-good kind of thing.* But I couldn't, could I? "Just promise me." I set a hand over my chest, my heart flying beneath my palm. "I'm a stranger, yes, but I won't hurt you. I just want to help."

"The contract work tonight . . . is that for a government agency?"

Ah, there it was. She was scared I'd turn her in. Change my mind about her if I decided she wasn't such a good girl, since she had, in fact, worked for a very bad man.

Maybe I needed to barricade the bedroom door. Bolt the front and back ones, too. Fuck, what was I even thinking right now? Free will was a thing. I just didn't want her to have it if it meant she'd try to leave, placing her life in danger.

"I'm beholden to no one but myself." That was the truth, and I didn't blink or flinch when I shared it, hoping she'd believe me. "I'm a man of my word, and I'll keep it."

"You don't know me; why would you want to help me?" She'd asked me something along those lines on the balcony, and now here we were again, but at least we were on safe ground.

"Because I can. Because I want to." I let my hand fly from my chest to my side before I did what I really wanted to, which was hug this woman who seemed to need it.

Eyes cast between us, she lightly nodded. "You were military at some point, yes?"

"Army," I admitted, unsure if this would be a nail in my coffin or not. It was for some women I'd met in the past.

"My brother was going to be in the air force." Her tone was soft, as fragile as fucking glass. "I have to change," she quickly tacked on before allowing me to digest her tone, mood, and the fact her tan skin was losing some color. "I promise I won't take off."

"Make that promise, and look me in the eyes when you do it." Fuck, that was harsh. Probably rude. Very much authoritarian. I also couldn't take it back, because I needed to believe her, or I'd be coming into the bedroom with her, standing outside the bathroom while she changed. Never let her out of my sight.

She pinned me with a hard look that told me she didn't appreciate me telling her what to do. "Sounding more and more like prison to me." She loosened her hold of my clothes but didn't drop them. "Been there. Done that." Lifting her chin, she angled her head, daring me to do it again, to give her orders.

I wasn't one to retreat, but as much as I wanted to command her to let me help, I wasn't actually an asshole. I wasn't like Ezra. She had to make the choice, even if it was the wrong one.

"I hope you let me help you." I softened my tone that time, patted the doorframe twice, then gave her my back.

"Ryder," she called out, and I stopped. My muscles tightened on reflex. "I really am grateful."

She left off the *but* that I heard loud and clear. It cut through me like shards of broken glass. Jagged and painful edges digging deep into my old wounds.

At that, I walked away, listening to the door close. I kept going until I found the others gathered around the reason we were at this house in the first place. The man was still unconscious, but they'd tied him to a chair and removed the bag from his head.

"What happened back at the house was unacceptable," I said to Leo the moment he made eye contact. "You defied orders."

Leo fake-laughed. "I thought we were equals. Wasn't that part of the speech you gave when you took over as team leader?" He squared up his stance, ready to engage. The second person tonight who wanted to go up against me, but it was the first person who had my pulse still racing, worried her stubbornness would get her killed.

"You were okay with an innocent woman dying." The woman I was willing to risk everything for.

"She works for a criminal. Not fucking 'innocent,'" he snapped out, doubling down. "You all broke ROE tonight, not me. Killed two men without being fired upon first."

While I'd questioned some of the lives I'd been forced to take in the army, not for a second did I regret the ones taken tonight.

"They were going to execute her," Alex said, echoing my thoughts while coming up alongside me. "We don't let women and children get hurt. Not ever, for any reason. Mission comes second if someone is in danger."

"If you can't get on board with that, then you're off the team." Chills racked my skin as I thought back to how close she'd come to dying tonight.

"I'm not cool with this cowboy shit. Not going to prison because you go around killing people on American soil." Leo looked around the room at us, shaking his head.

"Fine. There's the door." Alex motioned toward it. "Please let it hit you in the ass on your way out."

Leo maneuvered around Alex and stepped in front of me. "I'd rather eat shit than work with you all. I'm out."

"Make sure he leaves and doesn't go near her room," I told Reed once Leo was gone, and he nodded and followed after him.

Once it was just Alex and me, he said, "We need to get ahead of the story. I don't trust that Leo won't call the general, and then he'll call the director."

"Just tell Director Hernandez we encountered two armed tangos when exfil'ing, and she was caught in the cross fire, so we took her with us." I turned to the side, putting eyes on our hostage. "Let him know the mission was completed as planned. We'll get the intel we need from him."

"She's going to be hunted by her boss. The security cameras inside his party will be checked so he can narrow down his list of possible suspects who helped her get away. I kept free of the cameras, but did you?" He cleared his throat. "I'm sorry to even ask you that, I'm sure . . ."

I'd been distracted when seeing her manhandled on the way out that side door, but I hoped old habits died hard and that I'd run on autopilot and dodged them anyway. "Have Reed hack the security cameras and double-check, just in case," I tossed out, ensuring we covered all our bases no matter what. "See if he can get a read on what Ezra's planning to do next. No sound on the cameras, but he might find something useful."

"And what do *we* plan to do with her?"

Good question. "Hell if I know." I just hoped that when I checked her room, she would still be there. That was hurdle number one.

She'd been out of sight for at least three minutes, and I was worried that was two and a half minutes too long. After Alex took off, I wasted no time going to her room.

My heart beat up into my ears as I knocked, as I waited. As I confirmed what I already knew.

The door wasn't locked, so I opened it, and discovered she was already gone.

She hadn't used the door but had gone out the window. The screen was on its side on the floor. My sweats and tee were still there, but her heels and my dress shirt were nowhere in sight.

Unable to stop myself, not thinking clearly, I took off for the front door since I was too big to fit through the window.

I searched the property. Looked around the neighborhood. Covered as much ground on foot as I could before standing in the middle of the street, dropping my head between my palms.

A stranger had just ripped my heart out. I wasn't sure how that was possible, but the splintering pain in my chest was brutal enough to tell me it was.

I finally made my way back to the house, steered clear of my teammates, in no mood to talk, and quietly went to the bedroom.

I picked up my discarded T-shirt and put it on before fixing the screen in the window.

"You can't help someone who doesn't want it."

I turned to see Alex in the doorway, and my shoulders slumped. "Yeah, I know."

"You still want me to have Reed keep tabs on Ezra and see if he puts a hit out on her? Maybe we'll get a name."

"I don't just want him watched—I want him killed." That was a gut reaction I more than likely couldn't follow through on, because Leo was right. I couldn't murder people without consequences, even if they were evil. Hanging my head, I squeezed my eyes closed. "But for now, just keep an eye on him and his movements."

"Roger that."

When I forced my eyes open, I found myself alone with my dark thoughts.

I shouldn't have left her room. I should've followed my instincts and never let her out of my sight.

It took me a few minutes to pull myself together and remember I still had a mission to finish. A man who had information to help DHS locate a terrorist cell. Lives to save. People who needed me, since she didn't even want me.

Two hours into our interrogation, my phone vibrated from a text. When I read the message, I immediately left the room and went out into the hallway.

UNKNOWN: I'm sorry. I know you want to help, but this isn't your fight. I also don't want you getting hurt because of me.

I wasted no time in responding, shocked she'd actually remembered my number and reached out. Did she have a burner? She wouldn't risk going home. No way. So how'd she get a phone at zero two hundred in the morning?

ME: You don't need to worry about me. I can take care of myself. But I am worried about you. Let me help you. I'm not above begging, not about this.

UNKNOWN: You're sweet. Despite being a bit of a control freak about my safety, especially since I'm a stranger . . . I can still tell you have a big heart. You saved me after all, a woman who works for a criminal. Says a lot. But this is my problem, not yours.

UNKNOWN: And your job makes things complex too.

ME: I won't turn you in. You don't have to worry about that.

UNKNOWN: Thank you again for saving me. I just wanted to say that and apologize for lying and leaving. Please don't involve yourself anymore. Don't go after him.

UNKNOWN: You know the "him" I'm talking about.

UNKNOWN: I need him alive. For a bit longer.

UNKNOWN: I can't explain more. I have to go.

What in God's name was she talking about? Was she really telling me not to kill the man who planned to murder her?

UNKNOWN: Please respect my wishes. I'm sorry, I have to go now. I'll be tossing this phone. Don't respond.

UNKNOWN: P.S. Maybe one day when it's safe, I'll bump into you again. Goodbye. -S

I stared at her message, coming up with as many *S* names as I could in the space of seconds. None of them sounded right.

I had a dozen messages I wanted to send but settled on one, assuming she'd stick to what she said she'd do and get rid of her phone. It hurt not to fight for her, but maybe Alex was right: I couldn't save someone who wasn't ready to be saved. No matter how much I wanted to.

ME: You know how to reach me if you need me. Take care of yourself.

Bubbles immediately popped up, sending hope up into my throat. Then they disappeared, and I didn't hear from her again.

CHAPTER SIX

Ryder

Washington, DC; three days later

I stared at the text thread with Alex and Reed. So much for celebratory drinking, which was our norm after an op ended.

My team had turned over the target package to DHS at the Pentagon today after extracting the intel needed from the asshole guest at Ezra's party. Now active-duty Tier One operators could be dispatched to take out the terrorist cell. Mission success.

ME: Really letting me drink alone, the both of ya, huh?

REED: The city is too crowded. There's a parade or something. I need to be armed to be around a clusterfuck of people. Staying at my hotel. Sorry.

ALEX: I was on my way, man, but I bumped into Beth in the lobby. Ironically, staying at the same hotel as us. You know I can never say no to her, and she wants to talk.

REED: Sure that's what she wants to do.

ME: She fucks with your head every time you see her.

ALEX: Don't Freud me. That's my job.

ME: I hate you both for bailing.

REED: You'll forgive me after I find something on your mystery woman.

ME: Don't stop until you do. I'll head back soon.

ME: And, Alex, don't let Beth get into your head. I'm serious. DON'T. That's an order.

ALEX: Roger that.

I closed out the group text, ignoring the fact my ex's name was below it with eight unopened messages. I had no plans to read any of them. Not enough scotch in the world for that.

I deleted the unopened FUCK YOU one from Leo beneath her name. I didn't need to see what else was written after those inspiring words. He was pissed that we'd gone around him to the director before he could try to throw us under the bus. As far as I was concerned, he was yesterday's news, just the way Beth needed to be for Alex.

I pocketed my phone and hung my head. I hunched forward, sitting there alone with my scotch, my posture slacking. There was a lot on my shoulders, like the fact I'd yet to find the woman in red or learn her real name. *Anna*, which I'd pulled from Ezra's work records, was sure as hell not it.

Her digital footprint left something to be desired, as in it was fake. I was probably one of a few who'd be able to detect that bit of truth. Clearly, Ezra's background check before hiring her nine months and now fifteen days ago hadn't produced any red flags.

Something or someone had to have tipped him off that she wasn't Anna on Saturday night to make him upset enough that he wanted to kill her. All that protected him from being skewered alive by me was her text request to not do so. But why couldn't I kill him? I knew that answer as much as I knew why she'd faked her name and identity to work for him in the first place.

Nothing added up, and I'd been trying to do exactly that—piece the story together. I had Reed hack into Ezra's home-security cameras, which proved to be a waste of time. Ezra must've realized he'd been breached and destroyed the footage.

Since our pictures weren't floating around online with kill orders, I'd successfully ducked the cameras while at Ezra's party. So at least we didn't have that problem hanging over our heads. Just the problem of finding the woman who'd cut and run, leaving a dull, achy pain in my chest.

I'd resorted to digging into Ezra's background as much as possible as a way to get to the truth about her, hoping I'd be able to figure out how she got mixed up with the likes of that asshole. All I presently knew was that Ezra hadn't outsourced help to find her, or I'd have heard about it. I made sure Reed kept his finger on the pulse of underground activity to see if a hit had been placed on her.

"I'll take the check, please." Time to head back to my hotel room and focus on trying to track down a woman who didn't want to be found. And if Anna was hard for me to find, she'd be even harder for anyone else to locate. Maybe if I had her real name and something meaningful to connect her to, that'd change things.

The only thing keeping me semi-sane was that I didn't think Ezra knew her real name, either. I had an old friend in Florida keeping tabs on Ezra and his movements just in case.

"Ryder Lawson, that you?"

I paid the bill and stood to face whoever had recognized me. Hudson Ashford was there, alongside another guy. "Hey, man. Been a minute."

Hudson went in for a quick one-armed hug. "I thought you moved. You back?"

"I'm not back, no." Fuck that. I'd never live here again after what went down with Lainey. "Here on business. What about you?"

"For work as well. I live in New York, but I rolled out a new project this year, and it's been bringing me to DC a lot lately." Hudson gestured to the guy at his left, who had an Italian Mafia look going for him. "He was army like you."

"A long time ago," the man responded, and I was right: There was a hint of Italian there that couldn't be missed. I'd become pretty damn good at keying in on accents and foreign languages through my time spent serving all over the world.

"Wouldn't have pegged you for army." I smirked, accepting the man's hand. "I thought you team guys ran in packs, only with SEALs."

"You mean when they're not busy writing books?" His buddy confirmed he bled army with that jab.

The SEALs had become a bunch of writers ever since they took down Bin Laden. You'd be hard-pressed to find much about Delta Force in a book or online.

"I'm Enzo Costa, this guy's brother-in-law."

Shock powered my hand back to my side. "You're married?" I hadn't seen Hudson in years. He'd left the military long before I did, but our paths had crossed here and there. His father was also the governor of New York, from what I remembered. Somehow I'd missed the news he was now hitched.

"I know, it came as a surprise to me as well." Hudson smiled, eyeing my naked ring finger. "How about you?"

I removed the shades hooked at the front of my shirt. "Very single. Like single-fucking-single." Chills hit my back. I turned and followed the eerie feeling with my eyes as it guided me to the bar's entrance. *Of all times.* Not the woman in red, but a woman who hadn't gotten the message after I'd sent her calls to voicemail and ignored her texts.

Lainey waved me over with a slight nod.

I turned to face Hudson and Enzo. "I'm being summoned. I've gotta bounce."

"That woman has *government* or *girlfriend* written all over her, I can't tell which," Enzo commented. The man was a good read of people.

"Sort of both." I shook my head. "Ex, though." Important clarification.

"Well, good luck with that." Hudson slapped a hand over my shoulder and patted twice. "Good to see you. If you're ever in Manhattan, look me up. I'm working on something you might be interested in."

"Oh yeah?" I checked the door, finding Lainey gone. Waiting for me to be a good soldier, follow orders, and step outside, more than likely. Some things never changed. "And that is?"

Hudson looked around the packed bar, probably not interested in discussing his new project in the presence of others, even if the place was a vet hot spot. "Let's just say we're hoping to curb the flow of a certain something from entering our country."

Drug trafficking it is. And that brought me back to thoughts of Ezra and my belief that he was a trafficker.

At this point, I knew more about that man than I wanted to. Like what time he got home on both Sunday and Monday nights. When he'd left his house today. Who he'd met up with for lunch in Miami three hours ago. Hell, I was on the verge of knowing when the man took a dump.

But maybe Hudson could assist in . . . *what?* Committing murder? That was where my head kept going, at least. Eliminate the threat to my woman in red so she could get her life back. "I'll be in touch, then."

We said our goodbyes, and they headed for a table, meeting up with a few others, and I went outside in search of a problem I was in no mood to deal with.

Lainey was in the back seat of a black Suburban, waiting for me with the door open. "Get in."

I rolled my eyes before hiding them with my sunglasses. I got inside and pulled the door shut, and she ordered her man up front to drive. The privacy divider lifted, and she turned in her seat to face me. I zeroed in on the file on her lap.

A new mission, from her? Was she out of her mind? I wasn't going to accept assignments from anyone until I knew Anna was safe.

"Did you track my phone?" I stared at her, unable to detect any signs of her pregnancy yet. She looked the same as she did when we went our separate ways after selling the house we co-owned in Arlington. All my things were still in a storage unit; I was currently a man without a home, drifting around between missions. Hotels had become my sanctuaries.

"I did, but that was because you weren't answering me. I tried to catch you before you left the Pentagon, but I'm pretty sure you learned some of Alex's Houdini skills and disappeared on me." She leaned back in her seat, her brown hair pin straight, resting just above her shoulders in her blue blazer. The woman was classy and beautiful, but now that I'd met Anna—who was an I'd-kill-anyone-just-to-share-the-same-air-as-her kind of gorgeous—well, she paled in comparison.

"And yet, you didn't take the hint and came looking anyway." I punctuated my words with venom. I clearly hadn't forgiven her for what she'd done. The wounds were only three and a half days old, after all.

"We agreed we'd be friends. That one day we'd be able to work together again. Well, that one day is now." She nudged the folder at me, but I didn't take it.

"That 'one day' chance was shot to hell once I found out you were pregnant with Jeff's baby, don't you think?" I lifted my chin, closing my eyes, hating to think about the past, but she was the one sucking me back into it. "Just tell me something: Was the pregnancy why you asked to break up? Or was the 'we should only be friends' reason legit?"

"I didn't know about the baby when we broke up. I couldn't forgive myself for cheating, and I told myself if we were meant to be together, I'd never have done that, so . . ."

I expected to feel something at her words. Anger. Sadness. Resentment or regret. Instead, I felt nothing. "I was on an op for you in North Korea, risking my neck for recon work while you were fucking him in our bed." Okay, maybe I felt something: betrayal.

Lainey had been my team's liaison with Homeland Security whenever we worked ops for them, but after our split, I'd requested that someone else do it until I adjusted to the breakup. The director stepped in himself.

Damn Director Hernandez for letting her come to me like this with a case, knowing I didn't want to work with her. Lainey had probably held something over his head as leverage to make this meeting happen.

And yeah, maybe I had assumed one day we'd be friends again and could work together. That we could put the past behind us since we'd been friends before dating. That was, until I found out she'd cheated on me and was pregnant with Jeff's baby. My ride-or-die-in-boot-camp friend. *That* fucking friend. His betrayal stung far more than hers.

"It shouldn't have happened—not while you and I were still dating. But that doesn't change the fact I still want what we agreed to. To be cordial and work together. Maybe you can forgive Jeff one day, too. I know he'd like that."

Are you crazy? "Not happening."

"We really were better suited as friends, and you know that. We should've stayed that way instead of becoming a couple. Admit it, you never really loved me. You didn't fight for me when I told you we should go back to being only friends, and that was before you knew the truth about—"

Yeah, don't finish that sentence. Not a good idea. I forced myself to look at her, my shoulders lurching forward at the sight of my hard-ass ex's eyes brimming with unshed tears.

"It's the hormones." She pulled a tissue from her purse and blotted under her eyes, and I did my best not to cave at the sight of her becoming emotional.

I waited for her to pull herself together, which didn't take long, and I considered her words. I'd known Lainey for years. Hell, we'd moved in together as friends while I'd still been active duty. Only when I left the military did we start dating. But was she right? Did I not love her? Was that why I kept finding excuse after excuse to wait to propose, even though I'd purchased the ring and had it hidden in my gun safe?

I never had the urge to kill for her. Protect her, yes. As a friend and a good human being, sure. But here I was, wanting to tie Ezra down to a table and run an electric saw through his body, to remove each limb one at a time, because of a stranger. A woman I couldn't stop thinking about despite her rejection.

"I'm not that forgiving," I said, not quite as decisively as the answer deserved. "So no, I'm not taking a mission from you. I'll pass. Find another team." I almost offered up a few other security-company names, including Hudson's since he was in town, but I kept my mouth shut.

"Well, it has to be you. Or, at least, I think you'll want it to be when you hear what I have to say." She urged me to take the folder again as I tried to stubbornly stand my ground and not accept it. "You're one of the best trackers out there. I need your help. Please."

"No," I gritted out, hoping the driver would pull over soon so I could get out.

"The director told me what happened last weekend on your op with DHS. You know, the reason you're in DC now?"

Her words had me slowly lifting my gaze to meet her green eyes. "We gift wrapped the target package for you to send a Delta or DEVGRU team to handle the terrorists. So if that's a thank-you, you're welcome, and we're done here."

"There's been a new development unrelated to that terrorist cell *but* connected to your op in Miami, and that's why I'm pushing through this awkward conversation and confronting you now."

That had my attention and a chill cracking down my spine. *Just tell me Ezra's now my target. Please, God, tell me that much.* "What is it?" I reluctantly took the folder.

She lifted her chin, eyes on the file. "There's a woman we need you to help track down for us, and I believe you two already met."

I closed my eyes as shock bolstered through me so fast I barely had time to play catch-up and understand what she'd said. *Anna. The accountant. The woman in red. The reason I haven't slept in days. S.* "Go on."

"The director mentioned you saved Ezra's accountant from the party that night. We didn't think it was relevant, not until we were pulled into a meeting this morning with the FBI and DEA. They combined resources two weeks ago to create a task force to get to the bottom of who's running this new criminal enterprise. They believe the Sokolovs aren't at the top of the food chain, and they're only answering to someone else. As of today, DHS is now part of the task force to find out who's in charge."

"Considering we abducted a guy at Ezra's party who was working with a terrorist cell, it's safe to say this group is doing more than selling drugs," I grunted. "But get to the point about Anna." She was all I cared to hear more about right now.

She ignored my sharp tone and continued, "Our DEA contact revealed they had two people on the inside with the Sokolovs. Neither knew about the other. They weren't supposed to, at least. One man, Lev Markovich, they forced to turn or serve time, and his body washed up on shore last night." She paused to let that sink in, and I waited for her to continue, my pulse flying. "We also found out that accountant you saved was deeply embedded in the organization, and she's missing."

I finally opened my eyes at that. Now it made sense. Her name, her fake social media, even her reason for taking off. That was why she was being dragged to the yacht or boathouse, and also why she couldn't risk opening up to me. I didn't blame her. Someone may have fucked her over and exposed her identity. She didn't know who to trust. "So, Ezra found out last weekend they were both working for the DEA."

"Looks that way." She eyed the file. "Anna Cruz's real name is Seraphina Torres."

Seraphina. A name I hadn't come up with, but it was perfect for her.

I stared at Lainey, trying to digest this. I was already doing the job they were trying to hire me for. "Was Seraphina an undercover DEA agent, or someone they forced to work for them like they did with Lev?"

"Not an agent or someone they turned. It's complicated, but yes, she worked indirectly for the DEA."

Indirectly? Complicated? I needed more than that.

"So," she went on, setting a hand over her stomach, a reminder of what she and Jeff had done, "unless you're secretly keeping this woman hidden after you rescued her, we're hoping you can find out what the hell happened to her and why she never made contact with her handler afterward. You know, before she winds up dead, too." Eyes narrowing on me, she asked, "Now that you're familiar with the target, are you in, or do you want me to reach out to someone else?"

Assigned by my ex to find the woman of my dreams.

What fucking luck.

I finally opened the file, and this time, without hesitation, declared, "I'm in."

CHAPTER SEVEN

Ryder

If I considered myself mad before, I was seething angry after having read Seraphina's file. Now that I knew her life, even if only in bullet points, I could figure out *why* she'd taken such risks to work for Ezra Sokolov.

She was brave and clearly had a death wish. That terrified me, especially since she didn't have the full weight of the US government behind her and was being hunted by them instead.

I was also mad at myself for letting her go. For not holding her hostage. For not convincing her to come clean to me. Most importantly, I was mad as a motherfucker because I couldn't save the dead, and what if she already was? What if there were crickets on Ezra's end because he'd found her shortly after she'd texted me, so he didn't need to dispatch a team to search for her?

"Fuck." The word snapped from my mouth, drawing Reed's eyes.

He was sitting in the armchair by the window in my hotel room, reading over the file. He'd remained eerily quiet while absorbing every last detail inside.

Seraphina, born and raised in California.

Seraphina, top of her class at Stanford, graduated with two degrees, one in mathematics and the other in accounting with a specialty in forensic accounting.

Seraphina, thirty-two as of last month in August, never married and no kids.

Seraphina, Seraphina, fucking Seraphina. Her name kept playing in my head like song lyrics you couldn't forget. I wanted to hear her name. Hold on to it. Taste it. *Live* in it.

Seraphina, whose life got flipped upside down when—

"This is heavy." Reed's comment jarred me loose from nearly spinning out, and that's what I was doing.

Losing my damn mind.

This wasn't like me. I didn't do this. I compartmentalized. Adjusted course. Always stayed in control.

I didn't obsess. I didn't overthink. I didn't want to smear another man's blood all over my hands the way I wanted to do with Ezra's, who I had every intention of going after once I tracked down Seraphina.

"She's resilient." Reed blinked a few times, setting aside the folder. "Maybe that's not even a strong-enough word."

"*Crazy*? How about that?" Now I was mad at her. For risking her life like this. For not letting me risk mine.

At the knock on the door, I assumed it was Alex, so I went over and swung it open without checking first. You know, top of my game and thinking clearly. "You send Beth on her way?" I asked him, stepping aside so he could get in.

He didn't budge, remaining in the hall, eyeing me. "You said it was urgent, so yeah, I did. But this better not be some bullshit to prevent me from making a mistake."

"At least you admit spending time with her would be a mistake," Reed said from behind me, and I was with him on that.

"Just tell me what's going on." Alex shouldered past me, not convinced I hadn't set him up to stop him from a casual hookup with that demon of a woman I hated.

"We've been tasked with finding Anna," I cut to it, shutting the door behind him. "She was an informant for the DEA. And her real name is Seraphina."

"What?" Alex spun around, nearly colliding with me.

"Told you it was urgent." I rolled my eyes, then pointed to the file.

"Lainey assigned us to the case, of all people," Reed added, standing to offer Alex the file so he could play catch-up. "I'm sure she strong-armed the director on that."

"You're kidding me, right?" Alex looked back and forth between the two of us. "You're telling me we're going after the woman you can't stop thinking about? That's our new mission from DHS?"

"Who said I—"

"You didn't have to say shit. We're both well aware you're obsessed." Alex focused back on the file as Reed dropped into the armchair by the window. "Never seen you like this. And now your ex is asking you to find this woman."

I ignored his comment because he wasn't wrong: I was beyond obsessed. I was two levels above that. "Just read it. Let me know what you think."

"Are we assuming someone blew her cover at the DEA?" Alex asked.

"Maybe." *Lev's, too, more than likely.* "But the very small handful of people who knew their real identities are denying culpability. No links to Ezra or evidence to prove they're lying."

"Well, I still don't blame her for breaking protocol and not reaching out to her handler after we rescued her," Alex said.

Unable to stop myself, I took the file from him, needing to look at her again. It wasn't like I hadn't already spent the last three days staring at the few photos of her as Anna on social media like some sick fuck.

The DEA had pulled two images from the CCTV footage outside a twenty-four-hour storage center only ten minutes away from the safe house we'd been at.

Seraphina had my shirt on over her red dress, and I'd never be able to rip the image of her wearing it from my mind.

"Since you didn't let me finish reading, fill me in," Alex grumbled, finally catching my eyes. "Go on." He rolled his wrist, motioning for one of us to talk.

Reed waited for me to speak, probably curious whether I'd be able to hit control-override and return to normal operating mode. You know, be a Tier One guy again.

I couldn't believe it, but all it took was a woman I'd spent a handful of minutes with last weekend to bring me to my knees when Al-Qaeda, ISIS, and the Taliban combined never could. Nor the US military-industrial complex, if I was being totally honest. They'd tried. Oh, how they'd tried.

"Well," Reed said, picking up on the fact I couldn't speak right now unless it was a string of curses, "Seraphina was undercover, working for Ezra as his accountant. Because it was too risky to check in often, she only did so once every two weeks. Her mission was to figure out who was heading the overall operation, as well as learn as much as she could about their trafficking routes and who they were working with overseas."

"Guessing she never did identify the head of the snake?" Alex asked him.

"Not that we know of," Reed answered. "She was supposed to make contact with her handler yesterday, and when she didn't reach out, he started digging into what might have happened. Then Lev's body also turned up."

"My guess is they killed Lev the same night we were at the house, and they'd been planning to kill her next." *But we stopped them. Thank fuck.* "Her handler at the DEA found footage from Saturday night of Seraphina at the storage unit she kept." I held up the photo taken of her that night, my stomach squeezing at the sight of her in my shirt all over again.

"So that's where she went after going out the window and disappearing on us." Alex folded his arms, staring at the image.

She texted me that night. I never told them. Not sure why I kept it to myself, but I did. Like it was my own dirty secret, buried deep, right along with all the things I'd imagined doing with the woman. God, I needed help. Probably therapy.

"She left the site with a backpack." I showed Alex the other image. She'd changed before taking off from the storage unit, wearing a ball cap, sneakers, jeans, and a black tee. No longer in my shirt. Did she throw it away there? *That's irrelevant, dammit.*

"I assume her handler gave her a backup alias and passport if her cover was ever exposed." Alex looked at me for an answer that time. "And she didn't use it, or we wouldn't be the ones tasked with finding her now."

I closed the file and set it down. "Right."

"She must have had her own contingency plan she kept from the DEA. Another alias to use to escape the city—and more than likely, the country—if she was ever in trouble. There must be someone out there she trusts who's helping her," Reed surmised. "My question is . . . if someone's really dirty at the DEA, why'd they sit on information about her and Lev?"

"Maybe it's not someone that's DEA," I pointed out. "The joint task force with the FBI was only recently created. Intel may have been shared with the Feds that they already had people on the inside."

Alex lifted his chin, eyes on the folder. "I'm guessing that information wasn't in the file. A possibly corrupt FBI agent on their task force working for Ezra."

"Right." Who the hell were we supposed to trust at this point? Made sense Seraphina wasn't so sure, either. "Could also be that Lev was only aware there was a second insider, and he fed that information to Ezra in hopes of saving himself."

"Yeah, can't exactly trust a criminal to do the moral or right thing," Alex remarked.

"Well, regardless of who may have sold her out, we need to find her ASAP. I want a location within forty-eight hours." My gravelly tone was probably as rough as the look on my face.

"You always were an overachiever." Alex cocked a brow, smirking. He strode over and gave me the firm nod of reassurance I needed. "We've got this, boss. Don't worry."

I didn't bother to correct him on the *boss* stuff. Not this time. I may not have deserved that term with how unraveled I'd become at the idea that Seraphina was alone, with the likes of Ezra and his men searching for her, but oh-fucking-well.

"After we find her, are we really turning her over to your ex?" Reed asked me. Something I hadn't wanted to think about yet.

"I don't know." Defy orders, or defy whatever logic was currently guiding both my head and heart? "But one thing's for sure: I'm not letting her out of my sight this time. Even if I have to personally escort her to the Pentagon myself."

"See. Told you. Obsessed." Alex's smile stretched. "And it's a good fucking look on you, boss."

CHAPTER EIGHT

Seraphina

Puebla, Mexico

This was the point of no return. It was plan B, a plan I'd hoped I wouldn't have to execute—but there I was, doing it.

I'd be placing a target on my head. Hopefully, not tonight but, if things went in my favor, soon enough. A matter of days, at the most.

As the taxi closed in on the fight club, goose bumps covered my skin. I skimmed the little ridges on my forearm, unable to read the quote there without any lights on, but I needed to remind myself of the words branded there: **You are your only limit.**

I closed my eyes, trying to fight the quiver in my lip, the chills slipping over my skin, and the tremble coasting along my spine about to crest into something more monumental. It wasn't like I hadn't spent nine months under Ezra's thumb. I could do this.

"*Aquí*," my driver let me know, and when had we stopped?

I didn't have a purse on me, just my cash and passport strapped under my shirt. Not even a phone. In preparation for this ride, I already had the money needed for the taxi in my pocket.

I swallowed and opened my eyes, preparing myself to get out. "*Gracias.*" After paying him, I visualized that I had a spine of steel and a body as hard and strong as Ryder's for protection, then opened the door.

There was a long line to get in the club. Not a woman in sight, so that was extra comforting. *Not.* Keeping my chin up as if I belonged there, I bypassed the line in a hurry and went straight to the bouncer at the door.

Surprise lifted his brows, and he lowered his iPad to his side. "Anna Cruz?" Good, so he was expecting me.

I was there to see Ángel, the owner of this place, *La Madriguera*, which simply meant the Den. "*Sí.*" I nodded, and he opened the door for me, and a few men groaned in displeasure that I'd skipped the line.

Once inside, I was escorted by another man through the crowd to a booth off to the side of the octagon where a fight appeared to be wrapping up.

Without looking up at me, the man I was there to see gestured for me to have a seat. He was alone with a bottle of the good stuff, eyes on the eight-sided cage at the center of the fight club. The match was now over, and the two fighters exited the ring.

"Thank you for agreeing to this meeting." I sat across from him, hoping it was dim enough in there that he wouldn't see my pulse visibly fluttering at the side of my neck like it surely was. I needed to come across as strong, as if I had an army of a hundred men at my command.

Beauty was in the eye of the beholder, but so was strength. If he saw it in me in spades, that'd be enough to will it to be real.

"You have ten minutes until the final fight begins. Use your time wisely." He slid a bottle of Don Julio 1942 Tequila Añejo over to me. "But first, maybe loosen up and have a sip."

Assuming that wasn't a polite request, I accepted the bottle and filled two of the glasses.

Ángel nodded his thanks, lifted his drink, and reached across the table. "*Salud.*"

"*Salud,*" I returned as he eyed me cautiously.

After a few quiet moments passed, he prompted, "Tell me about yourself. What is your background?"

I wasn't sure why he was asking that, but I toyed around with how much to divulge and gave him a nonanswer. "Mmm. A little bit of this and a little bit of that."

At his continued indifferent stare, I did my best not to fidget or come across as uncomfortable.

He'd more than likely already done his homework on "Anna Cruz," and this was an honesty check. He'd probably discovered I was an accountant for Ezra Sokolov as well.

"Tell me more. Details."

"Puerto Rican and Mexican on my father's side. A Colombian and Italian mother." The real me shared the same background as my fake one. Made things easier. "Throw in a random two percent German according to an ancestry test, and that's me," I added with a nervous laugh.

"American?" The scrutiny continued.

I needed to turn things around, and fast. Get him laughing or something. Ease the tension between us. "So, you didn't even google me, huh? Mildly disappointed."

His lips twitched into a semi-amused smile. I'd take that as a win.

"But yes, I was born and raised in San Diego."

Since he was allegedly an expert at reading people, I supposed there was no point in totally lying to him. From what I'd learned about him, he was known for being able to accurately predict every winner at this place based on his judgments of the fighters.

He sat back in his seat, hands going to his lap. He had a bit of a Vin Diesel, from the *Fast and Furious* franchise, look going for him, including the same deep voice that my brother would've appreciated as a fan of Diesel's. "And how'd your 'a little bit of this and a little bit of that' parents meet?"

Why do you care? Do you know the truth? Was that possible? I did my best to smile, even though my heart was galloping far too fast. "On vacation in *México*, actually. They were staying at the same resort.

Love at first sight." And why did an image of Ryder just infiltrate my thoughts? "Anyway." *Enough talk of my family.* I finished my drink, and he offered to refill my glass before I could object.

Swishing the liquid to coat his glass, he shared, "I have to admit, my curiosity is why you're sitting here across from me. You went to a lot of trouble to have this meeting, refusing to take no for an answer. I admire your determination."

"Some call it being stubborn. I prefer your word."

He smiled again while quietly scrutinizing me. He was probably calculating the risks. Crunching the numbers. Trying to determine if I was worth the gamble. I needed him to believe he had a winner on his hands.

"So, *Señorita* Cruz," he began, dragging out my last name a bit, "tell me, not just how I can help you but *why* you think I should." Glass to the table, he smoothed a hand over his clean-shaven jaw, never losing hold of my eyes.

Here goes. "*El enemigo de mi enemigo es mi amigo.*" I thought back to the day I'd used this line, but in English, and here I was, having to say it again.

"An enemy of my enemy is my friend," he translated, narrowing his eyes. A long pause had my stomach flipping before he asked, "And what common enemy do we share?"

One more sip of tequila was needed, because it wasn't every day I asked for a meeting with someone with ties to the cartel, one of the most dangerous in the region. Hell, his family, the Moraleses, were in charge. "The men who've been causing problems for your family's business are my enemy."

"I am not part of the cartel anymore. I parted ways with my family a few years ago, and my guess is you know that, or you wouldn't be sitting across from me right now." He motioned toward the packed club; it was shocking we could even hear each other talk over all the chatter everywhere. The noise also happened to cocoon our conversation, trapping it between us. "I run legitimate businesses now, as you can see."

Good answer, and the one I'd been counting on since he was why I was in Mexico in the first place. Plan B fell apart without him. "I commend you for walking away. That couldn't be easy."

His eyes flew to his drink as if I'd hit a nerve. "These men here are also my family now. I'm trying to keep them off the streets. Stop them from joining the cartel. Help them channel their frustrations differently, even if it means using their fists to make money. The food still must be put on the table, *sí*?"

"I understand." And in truth, I really did, but that didn't stop the jittery feeling in my stomach as I waited to learn if he'd help me or not.

"I'd do anything to protect them." His shoulders arched back, signaling strength and maybe a bit of defiance regarding his family. "And I mean anything."

Okay, well, good. I'd be needing him to *anything* his way on over to my side.

"It's not always easy to keep these men away from the strong overreach of my family's business, if you understand what I am saying?"

"I think I do." His family was known to disembowel and hang people who told them no. So, you know, not the best enemy to have. Possibly worse than the Sokolovs, which was saying a lot. "I have information that can help protect you and these men. I don't have the intel I want to share on me now, but—"

"If you plan to ask me to arrange a meeting with anyone in the cartel," he interrupted, "they will not let you walk away, even if you can help them with this common enemy you seem to have."

"I know." I gulped down the rest of my tequila, feeling its warming effects in my chest. "I have a plan for that, don't worry."

He continued to study me like I was a test he already had the answers to but wasn't sure if he trusted they were really the right ones. I could understand him being cautious and leery. If he didn't question me, then I'd be worried.

"These competitors of *mi familia* really pissed you off." It was a statement, not a question, but I nodded my answer.

"May I ask you something?"

"You want to know why I walked away, *sí*?" He added more tequila to my glass, and hopefully I'd be able to walk away on my own without someone carrying me. How many shots had I taken? These weren't one-ounce pours, that was for sure.

"I guess my curiosity's getting the best of me as well."

With his chin, he gestured for me to drink up. So I did. Such a great idea to drink more tequila . . . said no one ever.

"Are you familiar with the Battle of Puebla? Americans like to party on Cinco de Mayo, but I don't believe most know the significance of it."

"Yes, I know a little of the history. The French occupation here ended that day." I wasn't quite catching the relevance to why he left the cartel.

"We won that day, thwarted off foreign aggression and didn't give up. We were determined—or, as you prefer to say, stubborn." His shoulders relaxed for the first time since I sat across from him. "One day it hit me that my family had become the occupiers. Destroying and ruining lives here and turning their backs on what our ancestors fought for . . . freedom." He finished his drink, angling his head while staring at me. "So I walked away, and I've been fighting hard to keep these young men here from getting sucked into their world as much as possible."

"And the cartel doesn't come after you for this?" Blood was blood, but still, no cartel I knew about had the best of reputations.

"We have a mutual understanding. I don't bother them, they don't mess with me." He glanced around the club. "These men, though, I can only do my best to try and protect them. Show them the right way." As he finished speaking, a man in a suit walked over to the table and leaned forward to talk to him, speaking in Spanish, but I understood enough despite his hushed tone.

Ángel's expression quickly changed to one of disappointment before he gave him orders. From what I'd translated, the contender against the champion in the final fight was a no-show.

"You think the cartel got to him, don't you?" I asked him once we were alone again.

"More than likely we lost him to the cartel, *sí*."

He really did care about his city, his country, and his people. That much was obvious, and it made my heart hurt for him. I also couldn't help but admire him. He'd been born into the life, and he'd chosen to walk away, which took courage.

"I'm sure someone will step in to fight for him. Many have bets on the champ, and they'll be upset if the fight is canceled." He stood, so I took that as my cue to do the same, hoping I'd still be steady on my feet after how much tequila I'd had in such a short amount of time. "You're welcome to stay and watch the last fight." He adjusted the sleeves of his black dress shirt. "But keep in mind the crowd is a bit rough. They're not used to seeing a woman here."

"I can handle myself, don't worry." Thanks to my father, who may have been an accountant and raised me to be the same but had also taught me how to defend myself. Maybe not up against an entire club of fighters, though.

"I have a feeling you can." Ángel reached into his pocket for his phone, then asked me for my number. "I'll call tomorrow, and we will discuss this information you have that could be advantageous to us both."

"Thank you, I appreciate that." I set a hand on the table at my side for support, discovering the tequila had, in fact, done a number on me. I was a bit of a lightweight when it came to alcohol in general.

"On second thought," he said, frowning, "I think I'll have Javier keep an eye on you and walk you out when you're ready to go."

"That's not necessary." *I mean, probably not.*

"It's not necessary but needed." He made a quick call, and the same man who'd come to the table earlier reappeared. "Find a replacement?"

"*Sí, un americano. Un gringo,*" the man responded. "*¿Está bien?*"

Ángel looked over at me for a moment. "The night for Americans in my club, so it would seem." He nodded his okay to the man, then told him to find Javier and have him come keep an eye on me.

The guy turned to the side, waving at someone. I assumed it was Javier, but when I followed his gaze toward a side door opening, I about fell over. Because holy shit . . . it couldn't be him.

You found me. Why? How? I was shocked to see him and also . . . relieved.

"You okay?" Ángel asked, and I blinked and looked right past him, too transfixed on Ryder walking over to the vinyl-coated chain-link fence surrounding the canvas mat.

He was shirtless. His hard, toned body drew my eyes as he exchanged a few words with a man I recognized from his team in Miami. As if knowing he was being watched, Ryder slowly faced my direction.

The moment eye contact was made, I stepped back, colliding with the table behind me.

A tingling sensation spread throughout my arms and moved into my chest, leaving a feeling of safety swelling there that I wanted to latch on to.

I finally remembered to answer. "I'm fine," I said, then ripped my eyes away from Ryder and took a seat again. I did the opposite of what I should've done and poured myself a shot and tossed it back in the hope that it'd help me get a grip. The man I couldn't stop thinking about had found me, and I didn't know what to do with that knowledge.

Ángel offered me his hand, and I took that as my cue that he wanted me to stand and head closer to the fight, so I accepted.

"So, um, who do you think will win?" I asked as Ryder went inside the cage with the other fighter. "Your champ or this American?"

Ángel focused back on the cage as we neared it. "The *gringo*."

Ryder began loosening up, rolling his shoulders forward and back. The man was a block of steel. Carved, cut, and hopefully as impenetrable as he looked. "Why him?"

"He's going to fight in jeans," he said with a laugh. "Which means he wasn't planning to fight tonight, but he's willing to do it anyway. That takes *cojones*. And my guess is, he isn't fighting for money, but for someone or something else."

Yeah, apparently me. "Well then," I said, unable to look away from Ryder preparing to fight, "I think I'll stay and watch. You know, to see if you're right."

CHAPTER NINE

Ryder

A few minutes before

"Did she really just go in there?" Reed parked and immediately went for his phone at my orders to google the name of the place we were outside of now. "What in God's name is she doing at a fight club?"

"She skipped the line, so they either let her in because she's a smoke show or because they were expecting her." At Alex's words, I pivoted inside our rental SUV to face him.

I grunted something. I wasn't even sure what I mumbled as he slid farther back in his seat.

"What'd I say?" He smirked.

Not a good idea to piss me off when this woman was doing a bang-up job of giving me an ulcer by going inside a place packed with enough testosterone to fuel a war.

"Ah, so only you can think she's hot? Enough said. Copy that, brother." He went for the door handle but didn't open up. "Are we going in, or what? We didn't chase her all the way down here to sit around in the parking lot, did we?"

"Of course we are, but we need to know what we're walking into first." I twisted back around, realizing my rage was misplaced. Alex was trying to lighten my mood before I lost control and went inside unhinged, without a plan.

The man knew me well. The problem was that nothing would work to calm me down when Seraphina had slipped from our reach for the second time tonight.

We'd found her hotel just as she was getting into a taxi. I didn't think she saw us hovering in our SUV by the valet service, which meant she had no idea she'd managed to evade us again by hurrying inside the club before I could stop her.

It wasn't like I could jump out and yell her name, not with twenty-plus men standing outside the club. She didn't need that kind of attention, and neither did we. A more subtle approach to getting inside was needed.

"Well, fuck." Not inspiring words from Reed. "Based on what I can tell, this place is cartel owned."

"Cartel?" I hissed, seconds away from that ulcer now. "Tell me you're fucking with me like Alex was."

Reed shook his head and handed me his phone, letting me read the bad news myself.

The cartel here were competitors with Ezra Sokolov. "This makes no sense."

Although my team had quickly narrowed our search to Mexico within a day of Lainey assigning us the case, Seraphina had not been sloppy in covering her tracks.

We were damn good at hunting people down, but due to my extreme sense of urgency, once we landed in Mexico City, I called in a favor. A former Delta operator. Someone who colored much farther outside the lines than I did.

I knew Carter Dominick, who'd once gone rogue from the CIA to avenge his first wife's death, would have ten times the contacts and resources here in Mexico. I'd been right to play the phone-an-old-friend game. He'd found her for me here in Puebla, right down to the hotel she was staying at.

But we were a few seconds too late, and now, dammit, I had to go into this club unarmed. I removed the Glock tucked at the back of my jeans and handed it to Alex.

I needed to breach the club somehow so I could first protect her. Then I'd confront her about what in the hell she was doing down in Mexico in a cartel-owned club.

"If there are cameras inside, I can try and hack them so we have eyes on the place." Reed, finally saying something I wanted to hear. "Hand me my computer," he requested of Alex.

"In the meantime, I'll try and bribe my way inside." I opened the glove box and retrieved our comms, which looked like hearing aids but were really wireless transmitters. "Stay in touch." I positioned the device in my ear, then handed one to Alex. "You're coming with me, I assume?"

He nodded and accepted the comm, then stowed his Glock next to mine, and we went outside into the parking lot. We walked past the line, and my frustration grew when money didn't seem to entice the bouncer.

"Now what?" Alex cursed as we walked alongside the line to get to the back. "We just wait?"

Tearing my hands through my hair, I contemplated our options. Waiting outside for her wasn't one, because what if something happened to her while she was alone inside? I tapped my ear, unmuting the comm. "Tell me you have eyes on her."

"I do," Reed confirmed.

"And?" I set my hands on my hips, trying to slow my heart rate down and focus.

"She's sitting with someone who . . . Hold on." I could hear him typing before Reed announced, "She's with Ángel Morales, the owner. Just the two of them at a booth. Drinking tequila."

I closed my eyes, trying to come up with reasons why this woman would be here. The only conclusion I could draw was that she'd lost her mind, because I refused to believe she'd chosen to go to the cartel for help over the DEA. *No. Damn. Way.* But the dark corner of my mind reminded me that people weren't always what they seemed. My former friend sleeping with my girlfriend in my bed was a sharp reminder I'd have to carry with me.

"Based on what these men are saying in front of us, it's too full for more people to get in," Alex let me know. Thank God one of us was fluent in Spanish.

While I spoke four languages, I was seriously regretting never having learned Spanish. I opened my eyes, catching sight of a man in a suit outside talking to those in line. "Wait, what's that dude saying?"

Alex stepped around me. "Morales is searching for a new fighter. The main contender up against their champion didn't show." He turned to face me and issued a quick, "Don't even think about it."

Too late. I'd already made up my mind. "If it's our only way to get to her, I have no choice." I lifted my hand, waving the man over. "Translate for me, and don't fucking argue. I'll be fine."

The guy in the suit made eye contact, thankfully acknowledging me, and he started our way.

"Have you ever been in a fight like this?" Alex challenged, opting to be the voice of reason I didn't want to hear, because Seraphina was inside a cartel-owned club, taking shots of tequila with a Morales, of all people. And the Moraleses weren't the most likable fuckers on the planet.

"Of course I have," I grunted.

"CQB is different. This is MMA stuff." I didn't need that reminder, and I'd be fine. "Plus, you're getting old. These kids all look to be in their twenties."

I continued to ignore his parenting, lowering my arm once the man came over. "I can fight," I let the man know, hoping Alex would correctly translate.

"I speak English." The guy looked me up and down, his brows drawing together. "You're old."

I rolled my eyes and stepped back to peel my black tee over my head, letting him know age was just a motherfucking number. My body would tell a different story.

His gaze flitted over my chest, abs, and arms, which I'd had to work twice as hard to keep at thirty-eight than when I was twenty-eight.

"Maybe," was all he said. "Come with me. The both of you."

"You sure about this, brother?" Reed asked. Great, the two of them were ganging up on me.

Thanks for the vote of confidence. I kept that thought to myself as we followed the man past the line and around the bouncer who'd snubbed our money.

The second we were inside, a prickle of awareness fell over me that she was in there.

"Names," the man in the suit prompted.

"Alejandro." Alex provided his given name, and I offered my middle one, David, since Ryder was too uncommon.

"Stay here. Don't move," he ordered before walking away, disappearing through the crowd gathered around the empty cage at the middle of the joint.

"I don't like this." Alex shot me a worried look. "Maybe I should fight instead."

"You're a lover, not a fighter," Reed jabbed. At least I wasn't the only one he thought shouldn't step into the fight. I felt slightly less insulted.

"Fuck you very much," Alex returned in a semi-amused tone despite the gravity of the situation.

"I gotta go dark," I let Reed know, making a pass with my hand by my ear to remove the device and hand it over to Alex.

"You're clear to fight," a different man said on approach, gesturing us his way. "No shoes. Keep the jeans on."

Wasn't planning on taking them off, but thanks. We followed him over to the cage, where I stripped down to only my jeans.

A flood of heat rushed through my body and rolled over my skin at the feeling I had eyes on me. *Where are you?*

I turned to locate her, to find the woman who'd done a number on my sanity this past week.

That ulcer I'd been expecting to happen didn't. Just a heart attack instead.

I palmed my chest, feeling the dull, sharp ache there the moment we locked eyes.

The loud noises, the distinct chatter as people placed bets . . . then *everything* stopped when she pierced me with her brown eyes.

She dropped back down to sit, stealing my view of her.

"Don't let her out of your sight while I'm in this ring," I ordered Alex.

"You think she's going to be a flight risk? Take off again?" he asked instead of confirming he'd heard my order. He was glancing around the room—and knowing him, probably contemplating an exfil plan to get us out unseen.

"No, I don't think so, but she's clearly going to be a serious pain in my ass." *Already is.*

"Well, I say we cut and run with her now instead of you getting into that ring." Alex pinned me with a hard look. "I think I have a plan to get us all out of here."

"Your Houdini shit won't work for the three of us with all these people in here." I shook my head. "I've got this, and after I win, I have a feeling the owner will offer us a seat at his table, where she is. This is the best play."

We could get to the bottom of why she was there while also keeping an eye on her. *But* if she refused to go with us, then we'd need an escape plan. One thing at a time. First: not get knocked out in the ring.

"And you're also forgetting something else that matters." I expelled a deep breath, trying to ignore the feeling of being caught up in a storm without protection. "I'm highly motivated to win. Her life might depend on it, which means I'll fight in this ring like mine does." And based on the size of the man in that octagon, it might.

"Send you with a rifle downrange against twenty fighters, and I have zero doubts you'd come out unscratched. But you can understand this is different, right?"

"Okay, now I really am insulted by your lack of belief that I've got this." I slapped a hand over his shoulder. "Remember the quote we used to tell the new guys about to pop their cherries for the first time in battle? *When we have a cause to fight for, we can fight like demigods.*" I let go of his shoulder. "Now, quit your worrying about me and remember who the fuck I am: your boss." I sent him the typical wink he'd offer me, relieved to finally see him smile.

"Hell, maybe it's the other fighter I should be concerned about. You have to be careful you don't accidentally kill him. He's just a kid."

Well, that so-called "kid" was a twentysomething-year-old looking to make bank—but yeah, I got his point. I was older and had a kill count longer than my arm. Those deaths weren't on me, though. Well, that was what I told myself to sleep at night.

"Just take him down to the mat quick. You're a good grappler. Choke hold him so he taps out." At least he'd stopped lecturing me on my age and my lack of MMA experience.

"*But* if he does kill me in there, be sure to get her to safety, all right?" I joked, but he didn't seem amused, so I circumvented him to climb up into the ring before he switched back to parenting mode.

Once I was inside the cage, I had a better vantage point of Seraphina. She was now walking alongside the man I assumed Reed had pegged as the club owner, a Morales, and they were heading straight for the ring.

I bounced around on the balls of my feet, ignoring the champ, realizing I didn't even have a mouthpiece or a cup.

Seraphina clutched the chain-link fence, staring straight at me with parted lips.

I took a breath and a beat, then forced myself to look away from her so she wouldn't distract me, and I focused on the champ.

The second the fight was announced, the guy smiled and flicked his wrist, inviting me to come at him. And so I did.

CHAPTER TEN

Seraphina

The crowd went wild when the champ landed a hard punch at Ryder's ribs during the second round. He did some type of spinning kick next, sending Ryder against the fence, right along with me. I clutched the thing, trying to stifle my gasp of panic.

Ryder wasted no time going at him, ducking under his arm, missing a swing. But another three-sixty kick took him down on all fours. He lifted his head, spit out blood like it was nothing, then locked eyes with me.

"Get up," I mouthed, unsure if sound came with the words. My heart was flying so fast, I didn't think I could take much more of this after watching the first round.

While Ryder had held his own—much to the surprise of everyone there, based on their bets and their shouting at the champ in Spanish to "finish him already"—Ángel didn't seem tense or shocked.

I wanted to take his cue and relax, but that was a little hard to do, especially with Ryder still on the ground. *Still* staring at me.

While it felt like he'd been down there forever, only a few seconds had passed. But why wasn't he getting back up?

And then I understood it.

Why he hadn't budged.

The second the champ came for him, Ryder sat back on his heels in one fast movement, somehow catching the guy's leg between his forearms with precision, and he twisted his leg, taking him down.

Ryder caught him off guard, as he'd clearly planned to do, and, well . . . damn, that was impressive. But the fight was far from over. I needed to survive another round and a half, and my deodorant wasn't strong enough for my anxiety.

I looked across the other side of the cage to where Ryder's friend stood holding on to the fence, shaking it while yelling out instructions from his corner.

Ryder and the champ were now in some type of hold up against the cage, battling with elbows and knee shots to the body. I wasn't sure who was even in the dominant position from this angle.

"You know him. This is no coincidence there is an American in that ring tonight." Ángel's words pulled my attention to him. He had a hand casually propped up on the fence, observing me instead of the fighters.

"Why would you say that?" I probably should have gone with a solid and firm no instead, but apparently I'd forgotten the art of lying even though I'd done such a great job of it while working for Ezra.

Ángel looked back and forth between me and the action in the ring. "You're nervous about the result. You hold your breath every time the American takes a hit." He narrowed his eyes at me. "I thought maybe you just don't like fighting, but you are unaffected when the champion takes a beating. Well, more like relieved."

You really can read and judge people. I'd need to keep that in mind.

He faced the cage again, clutching the chain link. "You didn't know he'd be here?"

No point in lying. "No, I didn't. I barely know him, but he saved me from . . . well, the enemy. One of the enemies, I should say." *Not sure how or why he's here, but here he is.*

"Well, that makes much more sense now why he's in that ring. He realized it was his only way to get inside my club. Determined like you, I see."

Stubborn, that was for sure.

He shoved away from the fence, retrieving his phone from his pocket.

"Now that you know this, what will you do? Stop the fight?" I was okay with that as long as he wouldn't hurt or punish Ryder for this.

"Why would I do that? I just bet a lot of money on him winning." He held up his phone, showing me an electronic bet he'd made only a few seconds ago. "Now that I know why he's fighting, I'm even more confident he'll win." He gestured with his head to the exit. "I need to make a call, but I'll be in touch tomorrow around noon. Looks like you have an escort and won't need Javier."

"Wait—um, you don't want to see what happens?"

"I need to see if there's a chance I can still save—"

"The fighter who didn't show?" I finished for him, and he gave a resolute nod. At that, he left my side, and I was uncertain what to make of the exchange. He didn't seem pissed, so that was a plus, I supposed.

Once he was out of sight, I rounded the cage, getting jostled around in the wild crowd on my way to join Ryder's friend.

I made it over to him just as Ryder forced his opponent to tap out, which meant I wouldn't have to survive watching a third round.

Shock waves surrounded the ring as Ryder turned his attention on me.

"Seraphina," Ryder's friend said, barely loud enough for me to hear above the mix of cheers and boos, which was good, since I was there as Anna.

You know my real name? "Sera. You can call me that." I faced the cage.

"Alejandro, but you can call me Alex," he added as Ryder helped the defeated fighter up to his feet.

"Good fight," I overheard Ryder tell the champ while accepting a hand towel from the ref to pat down his body, which was glistening with sweat. He tossed the towel and started for the exit. He climbed down the steps, pointing at Alex. "Told you not to doubt me."

"Last time I'll be doing that," Alex said before deferring to me with a nod as if Ryder hadn't already noticed me.

Ryder stared deep into my eyes. The look swirling around in those blue greens of his said it all. He was both upset and curious about what in God's name I was doing there.

"Hi." That was the best opening I had for now.

"Hi," he echoed.

"What are you doing here?" I whispered, ignoring the crowd still going wild all around us. Some had lost a lot of money, from what I was overhearing. Bet on the wrong man.

"I could ask you the same thing." He lifted a hand, pushing his hair away from his face while keeping his eyes pinned on mine, as if worried that if he blinked, I'd disappear.

"It's not what it looks like," I rushed out, feeling defensive for some reason.

"It sure as fuck better not be." Ryder dipped closer, bringing his mouth to my ear. "Because how it looks is that you're in a club owned by the cartel, and you were taking shots with a cartel member."

"Looks are deceiving. You should know that by now," I murmured once he pulled back to locate my eyes.

He shook his head, more than likely preparing a speech but then realizing this wasn't the best place to lecture me. On that note, we needed to leave.

"Nice job in there," I forced out before swiveling around to make my escape, assuming he'd remain on my ass and follow me out. And he did, but he didn't speak or try to slow me down.

The line out front had dispersed, but a few people lingered, which made me uncomfortable. It'd be a bad idea to have a confrontation with Ryder in the presence of others.

When I turned to face him, he was in the process of covering up, pulling his shirt over his head. Thankfully, his face didn't look banged up. That was lucky.

Ryder quietly accepted his shoes from Alex next, and once he had them on, I asked, "What do you want? Why are you here?"

"We came here for you—and let me be very clear, we won't be leaving Mexico without you."

Direct and to the point. But the *why* still hung heavy and unanswered in the air between us. "You'll resort to kidnapping, huh?" I locked my arms across my chest.

"Hostage rescue isn't kidnapping." He motioned toward a black SUV not too far away. Was that my cue to get in?

Ha. He was crazy. Crazy for fighting to get in the club, and as crazy as I was for being here alone in the first place. "Do I look like a hostage to you?"

"No, just like someone who's lost her damn mind." He stepped forward, still breathing hard from the fight—or maybe because he was pissed at me.

"Look in the mirror," I remarked, not willing to back down. "You followed me to Mexico and stepped into a cage to fight someone to get to me." I freed my arms from their position to point at him. "Between the two of us, I'd say you're the one who's lost his mind."

He came in front of me, so close he had to lower his chin to look at me since he was a half a foot taller. "Maybe. I. Have." The grit in his tone sent a shiver up my back. "But you're coming with me whether you like it or not. Willingly or over my shoulder."

I scrunched my nose, searching for ammunition to withstand the intensity of his gaze, which had me wanting to do something I hated doing: Give in. Surrender. Let him take all my problems from me so I could breathe a little easier.

"Dammit, woman." He cursed again, then shocked me by doing exactly what he'd said he'd do. He picked me up. "I guess over the shoulder it is."

CHAPTER ELEVEN
Seraphina

Ryder's big hands slipped around my waist, and he lifted me from the ground with little effort, which was saying a lot since he'd just been in a fighting ring and had to be both sore and tired.

I told myself the reason I wasn't yelling or resisting as he literally threw me over his shoulder, my ass now probably level with his head, was because I'd draw attention to us. Not to mention he had been heroic in trying to get to me, taking my safety quite personally.

"Excuse me," I said in a low voice, "but your arm is right under my ass, mister."

"It won't be for long, *miss*." He maneuvered me inside the SUV, ensuring I didn't bop my head on anything, and set me on one of the captain chairs in the back. "There." He went so far as to reach around for the belt, his face coming close to mine as he buckled me in.

"Nice way to restrain me," I tossed out flippantly, despite the fact I was secretly happy to have him here. Well, minus the not-leaving-Mexico-without-me part. I'd have to work on that.

"Would you like me to get my cuffs?" He rested his hand on the side of the Tahoe, his arm extended, which made it impossible not to see his biceps tightening in the light of the parking lot just behind him.

"Don't make me call your bluff." I mean, at this point I should've stuck out my tongue at him since I was acting all of five. Being tossed over his shoulder like a kid in trouble must've been why I was reacting like this.

I'd survived under Ezra's thumb without snapping, but facing off with a man I barely knew had me coming close to—

"Ohhh," Ryder said, cutting off my thoughts while leaning in, "please test me. Call my bluff." His deep, husky tone sent tingling sensations throughout my body, and I opted to blame the shots of tequila this time, knowing damn well he'd inspired the same response back in Miami when I was sober. "Now, are you going to be good and behave, or what?"

I faced forward, noticing the quiet guy behind the wheel next to Alex.

Right, we had an audience. Not to mention there were still a few guys hovering in the parking lot. We didn't need one of those guys trying to fight Ryder to "save me."

"If you're going to be a pain in my ass—"

"That's exactly what I just said about you not even, what"—he looked toward the front—"ten or fifteen minutes ago?"

"It's you who came here uninvited and is manhandling me," I said as Alex twisted around to look at us both, smirking.

"I didn't manhandle you," Ryder grunted. "But please, go on and tell me what you planned to say before I cut you off." He pushed away from the Tahoe, and with the way he was staring at me, like a bull ready to charge, it took me a minute to remember how to speak in any language.

"My hotel. I have stuff in my room I need."

"That's where we were planning to go, but you'll be accompanied every step of the way. No disappearing on me again. After you get your things, you'll be staying with us." He left off the *whether you like it or not*, but it was implied.

"And then what?" I really wished I hadn't had so much tequila in such a short time period, which was impacting my overall executive decision-making skills. It was a coin flip whether I'd mouth off to him as a result or bend to his will. The first was needed, the second was more likely. Chances were, I'd settle somewhere in between and piss him off just enough to keep him at arm's length, a safer place to be.

"We'll discuss next steps tomorrow after you sleep." He slammed the door shut before I could answer, then circled the vehicle and hopped in on the other side. "Roll out," he said, spinning his finger in the air.

I stifled the urge to tell him to buckle up. I wasn't ready for him to know I cared about him, even if I did. It didn't have to make sense. It was just a fact. Just like it was a fact that everyone, at some point, always died.

"And who says I'm tired?" I blurted out a few delayed seconds later.

"Maybe *I'm* tired. I did get punched in the face for you."

I fake-laughed. "Who asked you to do that?"

"You went inside a cartel-controlled club with all men in there, and you expected me to stand in line and survive off hope alone that you'd be okay by yourself?" He dropped a few heated curses while running both hands through his hair.

I glanced out the window instead of at him, unsure if I should continue engaging with a man who had, in fact, taken down the champ on my behalf, even if he didn't need to. What didn't make sense to me were all the *why*s. Why he tracked me down. Why he cared. Why a stranger made me feel safe even after he'd lifted me from the ground and strapped me inside this vehicle.

"I was safe. Fine. Perfect." *Maybe. Sort of.* "You getting punched in the face and ribs was not needed."

"'Safe'?" He hit me back with a laugh of his own. Fake or not, his came across far too sexy. "You and I have very different definitions of safety."

I looked back over at him, knowing what he could do with those eyes of his even in the dim lighting. Like turn them into weapons, wield them with unrelenting force. Tip the scales in his favor so I'd do whatever he told me to do. *I'm already halfway there by being in this Tahoe.* "You know, you were such a gentleman in Miami. Look at you now. All alpha and broody."

He leaned across the space between our chairs, and instead of growling or barking at me like I'd expected him to do, he adjusted my seat belt, ensuring it was in the right place. "Cartel-owned club." He enunciated his words that time with extra emphasis, clearly enjoying pissing me off. "What the fuck . . ." Lovely dramatic pause there. ". . . were you thinking?"

"I thought we were talking about this after you get your beauty rest?" I snapped back, hating that he was right. I was tired. Grumpy. Grouchy. All the things. Mostly angry, because while I had no clue why he was truly here, it was fairly obvious he'd never approve of why *I* was here.

When he didn't respond, I glanced at him, finding his elbow resting against the door with his fist tight to his chin, eyes on the window. At the sight of his chest lifting and falling with deep, steady breaths, my shoulders waned as guilt tripped me up.

"Ángel is no longer cartel, and I wasn't there as myself but as . . . well, Anna." I finally let those important details sail free, reminding myself he was clearly acting like this because he believed Ángel was a threat and he'd been worried about me enough to enter that cage.

"Anna, Seraphina, or Jane Doe—it wouldn't matter, because he's a Morales. He was born into the cartel." He wasted no time in proving I was right about his current state of mind. Unhinged with worry and anger.

"It's not the challenges that define us, but how we respond to them." I may have been paraphrasing—or outright butchering—the quote I'd heard at some point in my life, but it was still true.

He lifted his brows, giving me an *Oh yeah?* with that look. He reset his attention on the window and asked in a low voice, "And Ezra, can he change?"

Nope. He's evil. I was sure of that. Not all people were capable of redemption. Those born without souls, for one, and yes, after working with Ezra, I knew that he fell into that soulless camp. I voiced those exact thoughts, then added, "Ángel's going to help me. Calling me tomorrow around noon." *I think. I hope.* "So I'm all set. You being overbearing is not needed." Partially appreciated, but I wouldn't dare admit that. Too much tequila-infused pride. "I don't know why you found me, and—"

"I have orders." His back hit the seat, hands going to his jeaned legs as if unhappy with himself for admitting that.

I had to replay what he said to ensure I'd heard him right. Realizing I had, my heart left my body and became roadkill. "Excuse me?" I reached over and parked a hand on his arm, urging him to face me. "Who? DEA?"

"It's classified . . . but no, not the DEA."

Who else would be hunting me aside from them or Ezra?

"Your case fell into my lap. Quite literally, in fact." Letting go of a deep exhalation, he added, "I took it so it'd be me coming for you and not someone else."

"And you plan to turn me over to them? Which agency? Also, did you already forget you told me over text Saturday that you wouldn't turn me in?"

"When did you two text?" the quiet guy from behind the wheel said, breaking his silence while exchanging a quick look with Alex.

"Just drive," Ryder said in a clipped tone, but at least his anger wasn't pointed at me that time.

So, you didn't tell them we talked over text, huh?

"And as for you, I'll do whatever I think is right," Ryder added, conveniently ignoring my questions.

I settled back in my seat, feeling like I'd been swallowed whole. I couldn't let him screw up my plans. I'd come too far. There was no way I'd tuck tail and go into hiding now. "And how do you know what's right?"

"Easy." He glanced at me from over his shoulder. "Whatever keeps you safe."

CHAPTER TWELVE

Seraphina

I wasn't ready to back down quite yet, even though I could see my hotel up ahead, so I raised a rather valid point that maybe he didn't understand as a man. "You ever consider maybe a woman doesn't feel safe driving off with three men she doesn't know?"

"You're right. That would've been inconsiderate of me not to think about." He casually glanced my way. "*If* we were strangers, and *if* we didn't save you from a club with over two *hundred* men in there who may have done God-knows-what to you had we not shown up."

I opened my mouth, prepared to argue, but he shook his head as a quiet request not to, and I turned my attention to the ceiling.

"And the eye roll of the century goes to you. Congratulations."

Oh, this man was playing with fire.

I whipped my attention his way, my ponytail flying over my shoulder at the movement. Before I could come up with something smart or sassy to say back, I realized we were at a stop and Alex was opening his door to get out.

"Take her to her room to pack," Ryder ordered. "Make it quick. Don't let her out of your sight."

"Afraid to be alone with me, huh?" I asked as Alex opened his door, then mine, and the SUV lit up inside.

Now I could clearly make out Ryder's expression, which meant he'd made up the whole eye roll thing. No way he'd seen the fact I *may* have rolled my eyes.

"I need to cool off. I need air. Space. To be away from you for five minutes." His blunt honesty sent me to my feet outside the SUV.

"Yeah, in that case, I need a lot more than five minutes." I hated how I nearly lost my balance and had to hold on to the door for support. My legs were Jell-O, and that was doubtfully inspired by tequila, and instead, by this man.

"Well, too damn bad. You get five." He gestured for me to shut the door, and I cursed a few choice words in Spanish that had Alex smirking as he closed the door.

Alex kept his smile while motioning for me to head inside. "Sorry about him," he said once we were in the elevator and I was fishing my key card from my pocket. "He's in a bad mood, as you can tell." He scratched his jaw, eyes on the mirrored doors.

He reminded me too much of my brother. Looks-wise, at least. "You understood me out there, right?"

"I did." He gave me a nod, still peering at me through the reflection of the doors. "American born and raised like you, but my parents are from Cuba."

"Still alive?"

"They are." He let go of a sigh and faced me. "I really wish you didn't take off on us Saturday."

Great, now I have you on my case, too?

"We understand why you're doing what you are. Well, maybe not the cartel part—that's a curveball. Wanting to work with Ángel Morales is insane, in my opinion. But we get why you're so upset and have done everything you've done after . . . well, what happened . . . We don't blame you." All those uncomfortable pauses. "Brave, yes." When the doors opened, he waited for me to walk ahead. "Also dangerous coming here and risking going into that club."

I wanted to argue, but he wasn't wrong. I knew what I was getting myself into. "Tell me something . . ." Once in front of my door, I swiped the key card across the small control panel to unlock it. "Is Ryder's horrible mood because—"

"Because he was terrified of you being in that club by yourself and angry you'd take a chance like that," he interrupted as we went into my room, the lights automatically turning on from the motion sensors. "And my trying to stop him from getting into that ring didn't help."

"You didn't want him to fight?"

"No, but there was no reasoning with him. Once he's made his mind up about something, he's all in." There was some double meaning in his words, and all I could do was nod and save his statement for later to digest.

"I can't believe I'm letting you guys force me to go to your place. I should put up more of a fight." Continuing on the train of *not* doing that, I went to work by throwing my stuff in my bag to pack up.

"Your gut is telling you not to. Listen to it." I looked back at him as he hung by the door, patiently waiting for me. "Why didn't you reach out to your handler Saturday night? Worried there's a traitor who betrayed you? Or did Lev roll over on you?"

That had my hand going still, stopping me in my tracks. "You know about Lev?" I hadn't even known about Lev—not until it was too late. Not until I unknowingly placed a bull's-eye on my head by telling Ezra that Lev was stealing from him. Had I not done that, where would I be now? Still working for Ezra and undercover. "That asshole sold me out, and he either made it up and lied, or someone talked." *Most likely made a lucky guess.*

"Lev definitely should never have known about you, and if he really did, that means someone at the DEA or in the FBI screwed you over, even if they only mentioned they had an insider in passing."

"FBI?" That was news to me. "What aren't you telling me?"

"Just . . . ignore me." He shook his head, and I opted not to push him for now.

My resistance to all of them was taking a beating anytime I remembered they were why I was alive. But that didn't change the fact I would put up a good fight to continue with my mission if they tried to stop me. I went back to packing, trying to shake off my emotions.

"Not trusting the agency isn't the only reason you took off without a word, though, am I right?"

Smart man. After placing my phone and laptop in my bag, I zipped it up. "I don't want to be thrown into WITSEC." *I have a backup plan, and I'm working on executing it, thank you very much.* I kept that part to myself for the time being.

Alex came over and picked up my bag for me. "Not interested in spending your life looking over your shoulder. Yeah, I get that." He met my eyes. "I suppose you also want your revenge."

"But do you plan to help me, or try and be a hindrance to my cause?"

He gave me a lopsided smile before walking to the door. "I guess we'll see what boss man has to say about that."

"What are you doing?" I asked Ryder as he checked the window in my new prison of a bedroom, seeing if it'd open.

"Making sure you can't escape again." Still growly. Those five minutes apart at my hotel and the silent three-minute ride to the condo they were renting as a safe house had done nothing to ease his tension.

Or apparently mine. "We're on the fourth floor. Do you think I'll jump?"

"I'm beginning to think being four floors up wouldn't be a deterrent if you wanted to get away." Satisfied the window was sealed shut, he turned to face me. "I'll be parking my ass in the hallway outside your door, too. Just to be sure."

"Now, that's overkill." I opened my arms wide and dramatically. "I'm here, aren't I? I came willingly." *After you picked me up and tossed me over your shoulder.*

"I'm not taking any chances, not with you defending a Morales. You clearly—"

"I wouldn't finish that sentence. We were just starting to get along so well." I faked a smile just to chip away at his control even more. Such a fantastic idea. I was full of brilliant ones tonight.

Tequila and I were like fourth cousins—distant strangers. I barely touched alcohol in general, but never while employed by Ezra. It was basically liquid truth serum for me.

When his hands settled on his hips and he bowed his head, I spied dried blood on the side of his neck. I felt a twinge of guilt, which interfered with my desire to be angry at him.

"I wish you didn't get into that ring," I admitted, softening my tone. "You had me worried." My confession was genuine, a sharp contrast to my bullishness before.

"How do you think I felt watching you go inside that club?" Hands falling to his sides, he closed the space between us, and all I could smell, think, and feel was one word: *man*. He was all man. Every inch of him. Every ridge, curve, and line, right down to his scent. "Helpless isn't a feeling I'm accustomed to, and you made me feel that way tonight."

That confession cracked through the wall I was trying to keep up between us—the wall that was there to protect all I had left. Plan B. "I'm sorry." I meant that. Honestly. Even if he drove me crazy with his overprotectiveness.

He frowned. "Don't do it again."

"Which part?"

"Any part that risks your life," he said almost somberly.

"You don't even know me." More truth, only that line didn't feel quite as honest.

"That doesn't change the fact I don't want anything happening to you." He lifted his hand between us, then curled his fingers into his palm as if fighting his compulsion to touch me. "I'm also worried I now know why you're here, and if you think I won't do everything in my power to stop you from using yourself as bait, you don't know a damn thing about me."

I walked back two steps, bumping into the bed. *Bait* was putting it mildly. Not that I planned to tell him that.

"Sleep. We'll talk in the morning, like we never had the chance to do in Miami since you took off on me." Without waiting for me to respond, he quickly left, closing the door behind him, probably worried I'd argue.

Fair enough. I would.

I bit back the emotions trying to dominate me and went over and locked the door. Like that'd do any good.

I went through the motions of getting ready for bed, telling myself everything would be okay no matter what, that I was safe with them, even if they'd basically taken me hostage.

Using the en suite bathroom, I changed, washed my face, and brushed my teeth.

Once back in the bedroom, I crawled into the bed with my phone. I opened up to my three contacts saved. I had no plans to text the first one, my former DEA handler, but I did need to talk to someone, and ASAP.

Martín Gabriel, who I'd always referred to as my uncle even though we weren't blood related, was a good friend of my father's. He lived with his wife in Tulum. He was also the one who'd been helping me as much as he could ever since . . . well, ever since my life changed. He'd provided me with an identity and safe passage to Mexico from Miami on Sunday. He was very much tied to plan B as well.

ME: There's been a slight change in plans, but you were right about Ángel, and I think he's on board. He'll get there with a little pushing, at least. I'll keep you posted.

UNCLE: By change in plans, do you mean those men found you?

The blood rushed from my face, and I nearly dropped my phone.

ME: How do you know about that? About them?

UNCLE: We have a mutual friend. I was given a heads-up they were on their way to you and to stand down. I was reassured by someone I trust very much that they're safe. Good people.

ME: So, you didn't tell this "mutual friend" where I was?

I felt bad even asking that, but this was quite the curveball. What mutual friend was he talking about? Who had connected Martín and Ryder together? This was feeling more and more fate-like that I'd ever met Ryder in the first place. That gave me too much hope, and I wasn't ready to sink into that feeling. It was bad enough I felt myself caving to the lure of safety Ryder seemed to provide just being in his mere presence.

UNCLE: Of course not.

ME: If someone connected the two of us, that means Ezra might soon.

UNCLE: You don't need to worry about me. I've told you that a dozen times.

ME: I don't want your family in danger.

UNCLE: I'll be fine. But would you like me to come to you now? Say the word.

ME: No, not yet. It's still better for you to stick to where you are. Word will get out if you move anywhere in Mexico, and you know that. Stay with your wife. Keep her safe.

ME: I'm not ready for you to come here yet. Just digesting this new information. Let's stick to the plan.

UNCLE: If anything happens to you, your father will come back to haunt me. I'd prefer that not to happen.

ME: For a man who is nicknamed THE GHOST . . . I think you can handle it. 😏

UNCLE: Not funny. So help me, niña, if you die, my wife will kill me too. Then I shall haunt YOU.

ME: I won't let that happen.

ME: And, Martín, I don't know what I'd do without you.
UNCLE: You'll never have to find out. Call me tomorrow, or I'll be on the next flight there burning down the city to find you.
ME: Roger that. Good night.

I blinked back the tears in my eyes, trying to stick to my guns. Remain on course. Not to falter. Whether I wanted to admit it or not, particularly to Ryder, I was happy to have him here. I didn't want to put him in danger, but I was also afraid he'd never approve of my plan—and who was he to decide what I did or didn't do with my life?

I set my phone on the nightstand while staring at the bedroom door, curious if Ryder was really on the other side of it. Then, against my better judgment, I picked up my phone again and went to the third contact. While I'd doubtfully ever forget his number, I'd added him anyway.

I stared at his name, my frustration with his growly alpha-ness becoming second to my gratitude for what he'd done tonight. *You saved me last weekend. Wanted to protect me tonight. But also . . . you're here because you have orders, so there's that to consider.*

ME: How'd you even find me?

This was probably supposed to be part of our conversation for tomorrow, but there was zero chance I'd be able to sleep anytime soon.

RYDER: I see you didn't forget my number. Too bad you didn't use it sooner.
ME: I didn't text, because I didn't need your help.
RYDER: From where I'm sitting you did (and still do).
ME: And where exactly are you sitting? Don't tell me you're really outside my room.
RYDER: Right where I told you.

The man was possibly more stubborn than I was, and I shouldn't have been smiling at that, or going to him . . . but I did both.

I swung open the door, and my chest tightened at the sight of him. He was sitting on the floor, back to the wall opposite me, one knee bent and the other lazily stretched out. His forearm rested across his knee, phone in hand, and he pulled his eyes up to my face.

"Told you I wasn't leaving your door. Unlike you, I keep my promises."

"Low blow." *Even if fair.* "You were a stranger in Miami." *Still kind of are.* "Lies to strangers don't count."

"Stranger or not, a lie is a lie. Plan on telling me any more while I'm stuck here with you?"

"You're not stuck with me. You can, and should, go." I kept my voice low so Alex and the other guy with us wouldn't hear.

"You've yet to answer me."

"Well, it depends. Do you plan on following your orders and turning me over to whichever agency tasked you to find me?" I still needed to drill him about who he worked for, but since I had no choice other than to stay here regardless, I'd hold off on that conversation until tomorrow. Same with asking him about the mutual friend he shared with Martín.

"I told you I'll do what's in the best interest of your safety."

"That's a nonanswer, and maybe I know what's best for me. Ever think of that?"

"Nope. You have no damn idea, clearly, or you wouldn't be here on your own, playing around with the cartel."

"I wasn't, and I'm not . . ." *I have people.* Well, I had Martín, and he had people. Loyal, loyal people who'd do anything for him.

Ryder took me by surprise, abruptly standing in one fast movement, causing me to walk back into my room. I didn't stop him from joining me. I even let him shut and *lock* the door. He shoved his phone in his pocket and faced me.

"Did I invite you back in?"

"The moment you opened your bedroom door, you did."

I gulped, worried that little show of alarm was obvious to him and he'd be able to read me. Read the fact that no matter how stubborn and fight-sy I was trying to be, I was losing the battle with him. Those eyes as weapons and all gave him an unfair advantage. He was able to peel my layers back and expose me as the woman I hadn't been in so long. The woman I'd left behind in California.

You fought for me. You're nuts. I fisted the sides of my nightshirt. *And sweet.* No one had ever done something like that for me before.

Forget going to war with him; I was at war with myself. Hot and cold. Angry and aroused. All the yins to all the yangs existing inside me and between us.

"Well, now that you're in my new prison chambers, what are you planning to do? Park a chair in front of my door and sleep in that?"

"Some prison." He scoffed, looking around the beautifully decorated room as if he'd pre-selected this condo with me in mind. A woman with excellent taste no doubt lived here when we weren't occupying her home.

"Better than the one I've been living in for the last nine months."

He narrowed his eyes, a flash of darkness crossing his face. Not angry with me, but at a much more likely suspect: Ezra, the warden to my past prison.

Standing before Ryder now, I realized it was possible he was a much bigger threat than all the Ezras in the world combined.

Because I was here in Mexico for a reason, and that reason wasn't to fall all over myself for a man. A man who was staring at me like he couldn't make up his mind what to do with me: yell at me, or fuck some sense into me. And here I was, hoping for option two, which was why it was risky to be around him. I couldn't think straight in his presence, and I hadn't since the moment we met.

Ryder's gaze flew over my body, as if only now realizing I was in a thin pale-blue nightshirt that went to my midthighs, without a bra. Were my nipples the only thing hard right now?

"You're going to be the death of me, aren't you?" His husky voice stretched out between us.

"That's what I'm trying to prevent," I whispered.

"Not"—he closed his eyes, expelling a deep breath—"what I was talking about," he said steadily, nostrils flaring.

Ohhh. Turning to the side, I tossed my phone on the bed and demanded, "Look at me." Probably a bad idea, since it was clear now more than ever that those blue-green eyes of his unlocked some deep parts of me I'd thought were gone forever.

"If I do, I won't be responsible for what happens next." The heat in his tone stoked the flames and had me padding even closer to him.

"Are you standing in my room because you have to be, or because you want to be?" *Why'd you really take the case to find me?* That answer would determine what happened next.

When he didn't respond, I cut the space between us to nearly nothing and set a hand on his chest.

God, his heart was flying, matching mine beat for beat.

"You said you're an honest man, so prove it to me. Tell me the truth."

His eyes slowly opened, and his chin dipped as he studied my hand. "You know the answer to that."

I wet my lips, waiting for him to look at me once again. "Maybe I need to hear it anyway."

He gently secured a grip on my wrist and finally met my eyes. "I'm here because I haven't been able to stop thinking about you for one damn minute since you climbed out that window."

CHAPTER THIRTEEN

Ryder

Walk away. Walk the fuck away.

The command in my head did absolutely nothing to get me to move or for me to get a grip. Not with this woman smelling like clean soap and fresh linen, with those pouty lips and big brown eyes pointed at me.

"You want to kiss me?" The question was soft and sweet, like nectar of the gods.

Fuck yes I do. I didn't give her my truth, though. I didn't give her anything. Just kept hold of her wrist, willing myself to walk away but being completely unable to do so.

She was now my assignment. I'd vowed never to mix business with pleasure again after what happened with Lainey. Yet there I was, contemplating all the different ways I'd break that new rule, as well as the law, if it meant kissing this woman. Even just once.

That was what scared me. I needed to pull myself together. Control-override. Focus up.

"Are you going to answer me?" she whispered.

I dropped my gaze to where I held her wrist, and when I didn't speak—because I was still fighting the good fight to resist these odd feelings—she went ahead and did it for me.

"Look at you, being responsible and not taking what you want." She lifted her brows twice, calling my bluff like I'd dared her to do in the Tahoe.

I brought her hand up to my mouth and dragged my lips along her knuckles. "I don't take; I give." My lips hovered an inch from her skin. "As much as I want to . . . I won't. Free will applies here."

"But it doesn't when it comes to my safety?" Despite the sass embedded in her tone, she shuddered. She couldn't hide her body's response to me any better than I could around her.

I straightened and let go of her, needing to stand my ground on this important point. "Correct." I gestured to the bed with my head. "Try the sleep thing again before I forget I'm a gentleman and kiss that smart mouth of yours."

Her eyes narrowed on my lips, taunting me to do exactly that. "What about my free will?"

I smiled, probably some smug, asshole-like grin. But fucking A. "That'd still apply, because you'd be the one begging me for it."

"Oh, is that so?" She crossed her arms, and thank God for that, because if I had to see those perfect tits of hers straining against the fabric of that nightshirt any longer, I was going to be the one pleading on my hands and knees. I'd beg for whatever she'd give my poor, pathetic soul.

This woman was trouble. Far too much. And that made her dangerous.

"Yes," I breathed out.

"Cocky much?"

"Honest. As already established."

Now I had to back away from her. Go into the hallway. Maybe choose a different door to stand in front of, like the main exit. Space between us was needed. Hell, it was required if I planned to think clearly and find a path forward that made sense. I just didn't believe turning her over to DHS was the right decision.

"How much tequila did you have tonight?" I asked at the memory of that important detail, grateful my mind had thought of it before I made a mistake I couldn't take back.

She lifted her gaze to the ceiling, stretching out the slender neck that I now wanted to kiss, too. "Enough to be a bit of a brat. Not enough that any decision I make with my body isn't of my own making. So, somewhere in between a little and a lot."

So, hands to myself no matter what. Understood. I was the first to break in our game of chicken and cut away from her. I started to turn, to retreat, but froze at the sight on her dresser.

I went over and picked up my dress shirt on top of a stack of her clothes. "You kept my shirt." Holding it out, I faced her, shocked she hadn't tossed it back at the storage center in Miami. "Why?"

She lowered her hands to her sides, giving me another view of her nipples piercing the fine material of her shirt. So much for being a legs man. Consider me obsessed with every part of this woman. Head to fucking toe.

Deciding to kill me even more, she lifted her hand up into her hair, which made her shirt go up to show more of her golden-tan thighs.

Tangling her fingers up in her wavy, brown hair should've been my job, right before making her come.

"It's just a shirt. Don't make a big deal of it." Her defense was weaker than my self-control.

Realizing we were both hanging on the edge, that fine and very breakable line on the verge of snapping in half, I returned the shirt to her stack. Even folded it up. No point in talking more about it.

"Keep it." The idea of her wearing my shirt and nothing else would live rent-free in my head for all of fucking eternity. "Get some rest. Maybe we'll both feel better in the morning."

"Maybe ice your face instead of sleeping outside my room? Or your right hand. Shoulder. Whatever hurts. You were in a fight."

"Your concern for my well-being is confusing but appreciated." I shook my head. "Also, not needed. I'm fine." The only thing in need of icing was my erection.

"It shouldn't be confusing." Her cheeks puffed up with air before the breath softly whistled free. "Maybe I'm more like you than you realize and I don't have to know you to care about your safety. That's part of the reason I walked away from you in Miami. I didn't want anything to happen to you because of me."

"And the other part of why you left?" I went to the door and waited there for her answer. I refused to do something I'd regret, especially with her under the influence.

"I had a feeling you'd try and stop me from going after Ezra and his wife."

"Wife, huh? I must've missed the memo his wife is—"

"Probably just as bad," she finished for me. "Story for tomorrow." She waved a hand between us. "The point is, I couldn't let you stop me from getting my vengeance." Her tone deepened as she added, "Just like I won't let you stop me now."

CHAPTER FOURTEEN

Seraphina

The smell of bacon and eggs and heaven had me walking barefoot down the hall, following the delicious aroma. I'd nearly forgotten where I was and why I was there until I found the quiet stranger who'd yet to speak a word to me, not even back in Miami, cooking in the kitchen.

"Good morning." I hung back in the living room on the other side of the breakfast bar in the open-concept space. Bright light spilled in through the floor-to-ceiling window, offering new-day vibes I wanted to latch on to. They were certainly needed.

The guy cooking looked over at me and nodded his hello, and my greedy stomach growled at the smell and sight of the food.

"Don't mind him. He doesn't like people." That was a voice I recognized.

I turned to see Alex joining us, a mug in hand, which I hoped meant there was coffee for me. I lifted my nose, searching for my favorite smell, but it must've been smothered by the scent of bacon and eggs cooking.

"That's Reed, by the way. A ray of fucking sunshine, isn't he?" Alex walked past me and went into the kitchen.

"Fuck you," Reed countered in a semi-amused tone without looking up at him.

"See? He speaks. He's just not people-y." Alex set aside his cup and wasted no time in pouring one for me.

"I could fall in love with you for this," I teased, grateful that the sleep I'd somehow managed to get had helped my mood.

"Please don't." Alex's brows pinched, and he didn't let go of the handle even though I'd parked my palms on either side of the hot-to-the-touch mug.

"Oh yeah? Why not?"

He looked over my shoulder somewhere, and then it clicked. *Ah, because of the grump.* "Gotcha. You're safe, don't worry."

"Appreciated. I like my head as it is: attached." Alex winked, then finally let go of the mug and stole a piece of cooked bacon set aside on a paper towel.

"Where's Ryder?" I asked after taking that first incredible sip.

"In his room. First door on the left." Alex crossed one ankle over the other and rested a palm on the counter at his side. "I sent him there a few hours ago when I found him sleeping in a chair in front of the door here. Took over for him."

"Doesn't trust I won't run, huh?" I gave a little teasing bow. "Still here, as you can see." After a few more indulgent sips of the java, I turned toward the direction of Ryder's bedroom. "Give me a minute alone with him?"

"Take all the minutes you need," he said as I mindlessly held out my mug his way, assuming he'd take it from me, and he did.

I went to Ryder's door, and from the corner of my eye, I could still see Alex and Reed in the kitchen, bickering now like a married couple about the appropriate crispiness of bacon.

Two knocks later, Ryder wrested my attention his way.

Door open, he was standing there with a pale-green towel hung low around his hips. Water droplets rolled down his naked chest. Wet eyelashes framed those ridiculously beautiful eyes. Hair slicked back from the shower. There were a few noticeable welts on his body from the fight last night.

"Sore?"

"I'm fine." That was a lie. It had to be.

"I thought you were supposed to be honest?"

"I've dealt with much worse; that was me being honest." His bladed jawline tightened, and I decided to leave it at that.

He propped his hand up on the doorframe, blocking entry to his room. Maybe that was for the best. Hallway conversations were safer, especially with him in a towel, with his hard body and those sexy V-lines on display.

"You're still here, I see. You didn't leave."

"Not that you'd have let me escape if I'd tried." I planned to make a valiant effort to look away from his body and up to his face. But God help me, a toned, strong body like this needed to be studied. Appreciated. Maybe I was objectifying him, though? And at that thought, I finally spoke again. "From what I heard, you didn't sleep much."

"Alex gave me no choice, forcing me to rest." He raised his voice and added, "Thinks he's my father even though he's younger than me."

"By only a year," Alex shouted back. "And if I don't look out for you, who will?"

Ryder shook his head, then removed himself as an obstacle to his room. "If you'd like to talk, let's do it without him listening."

I wasn't sure it was the best idea to be alone with him in only a towel, but I couldn't say no. His muscles lured me in, and I quietly obeyed without another thought.

"I take it you're here to apologize?" His stiff arms flew swiftly over his chest as he eyed me, placing his back against the bedroom door.

"Is that your way of starting the morning off with a joke?"

"It was worth a shot." He shrugged, still sporting a grumpy expression that he managed to pull off as sexy. "So, did you come to your senses?"

The jabs kept on coming. Maybe he wasn't a morning person like I was.

"Clearly not, or I wouldn't be alone with you in your bedroom." Zero excuses this time. Totally sober and rested just enough to make my own choices. Candy wouldn't bait me to be alone with a stranger, but a happy trail beneath a handsome man's navel leading to happier places certainly could.

"Would you like to go?" He motioned to the door.

"Like *go* go? As in leave this condo?" I smirked, and he hit me back with a little growly frown that I couldn't help but find adorable and endearing. Doubtful that'd been his intention. "I'm where I currently need to be." I extended my arm, offering my hand. "I thought we could start over. New day, new start. I'm Seraphina Torres."

He stared at my hand as if there were a grenade in it. So, you know, off to a great start.

"Ryder Lawson." The hesitancy in his tone was unmistakable, but the moment he accepted my palm, a current of electricity thrummed from his warm skin up into my fingertips, shooting straight into my arm, becoming an arrow to my heart.

Still holding his hand, I lifted my eyes to register his reaction. Had he felt that, too? Based on the quickening of his breaths and nostrils flaring, albeit subtly, he had.

"Before I spill my guts about everything—like I assume you all plan to ask me to do—I thought maybe you could convince me why I should." Message delivered. Mission accomplished.

"Would you like me to get dressed first before we have this chat?"

I finally found the strength to remove my hand from his grip. "Something about sharing your truths while naked has me believing you'll be even more honest." I blinked a few times. "Or maybe I'm mixing that up with the picture-your-audience-naked-when-public-speaking thing."

He granted me the smallest of smiles, then decided to tease me back. His hand went to where the towel was tied at his hip. "So, *naked* naked, that's what you want?"

Yes. *But* I shot my hand out to stop him, and he grinned and lowered his hand to his side. "Good to know you have a sense of humor and other sides to you. Gentleman hero one minute, cocky fighter the next. And, well"—I waved my hand between us—"whatever this side of you is."

"We're only just getting started," he said huskily. "I have a feeling you'll be seeing a lot more of me."

Did he realize how that sounded, especially with how he'd said it? Because damn.

His shoulders relaxed, and so did the muscles in his face. "What would you like to know that'll have you feeling more compelled to become an open book for me?"

"Well, I assume you have a file on me, yes?" At his nod, I announced, "Then it's only fair I know more about you."

"Why do you need to know my background?" He angled his head, eyes tight on me.

"You want me to trust you, then prove to me I can. Stop being a stranger."

He looked down at the floor, possibly contemplating his options. Weighing the decision of what to do and how to best handle me.

While I waited for him to make up his mind, I went over to his bed and sat.

"Thank you for wearing clothes, by the way," he grumbled.

"As opposed to a towel like you?" I sighed, fighting a smile, knowing the effect I had on him was the same he was having on me. He wanted me to be an open book, and here we were, already on the same page.

His lips twitched, and if I were looking south of his navel, maybe his dick did, too, but I'd never know, because I was locked on to his face. That angular jawline covered in scruff. The sinful mouth I imagined against mine.

"Bullet points," he said instead of entertaining my teasing towel comment. "I'll give you a few."

"Any context with them?" I set my hands on either side of me as he approached the bed.

"No context was given in my file about you. So, fair is fair." His hands flexed and unflexed at his sides, drawing my eyes to the one vein shooting down his forearm. "I'm thirty-eight. Raised by my mom. Went to Princeton on a scholarship because I'd never be able to afford school otherwise. Spoke to some military recruiters my senior year and signed up for the army after graduating. Became a Tier One guy. Delta Force. Two years ago, I got out. Joined a PMC firm that only hires Delta. Small unit. Only three of us now."

Ah, right, there were four Saturday. Now I was wondering what happened to the other guy, but not enough to ask.

"We take cases for the government when their hands are tied by red tape," he added. "And also, I speak four languages, but I'm now wishing it was five."

I'd been about to press him on which government agencies, but he caught me off guard with his last line. "Which language?"

"Español." A smile came and went with his answer.

"Oh." I wet my lips, and he redirected his focus to my mouth.

Moth. Flame. No chance to resist. Same for me.

"And, um, where were you born and raised?" I asked.

"Born in Chicago. Moved to North Dakota when I was seven and lived there until college." Short, quick, and to the point, which told me he didn't want to go in-depth.

"Any siblings?"

He shook his head. "Just me."

"Well, um, I'm going out on a limb here and assuming you're single?"

His facial muscles tensed, the same as his arms did at that question. "Single, yes."

There was more to that *yes*, something he hadn't revealed in those bullet points. Like context. *Someone hurt you, didn't they?*

His gaze journeyed down my body, and my skin tingled beneath the heat of his stare.

I had a mission to complete, and so did he. His mission was in direct conflict with mine, since I was his mission. So I needed to stop feeling whatever this thing was. Put the brakes on, and fast.

"I still feel like we're strangers," I admitted, standing.

"So I wasted those bullet points on you, is that what you're saying?" He backed away from me as if realizing he was too close with me on my feet.

There was no obstacle between us like last night. No alcohol or post-fight adrenaline.

Just a towel in our way.

"Maybe it'd help to ask you a few more questions to get to know you?" Okay, I was stalling, but I didn't want to go into that kitchen and share my past. It was messy and ugly but the reason we were there.

"Like my horoscope?" he asked sarcastically. "I'm a Leo, like you."

Fire sign. Sounds about right. "Never mind," I said after an exasperated sigh, turning away from him.

He encircled my wrist, stopping my escape. "How about you tell me something?" There was a gravelly plea in his tone as he unhanded me.

I kept my back to him, resisting the urge to lean against him and allow his naked chest to hold me up. I'd been standing alone for so long, it'd feel good to let my posture wane, even for a second.

"Like what?" I closed my eyes, shocked to find myself doing it. Letting go. Leaning against him, letting him catch my weight.

He slipped his hand around my waist, parking it on my abdomen, keeping me steady. With his chest flush to my back, he quietly held me like that. Quite the pivot from me trying to leave.

He whispered, "Tell me something not in that file. Something no one would know."

Like how you're making me feel right now? Aroused, hot, and flustered. "I haven't been touched in a very long time. I haven't wanted to be."

"When?" His free hand skimmed my silhouette all the way up to where my hair rested over my shoulder. He shifted it around, giving himself access to my neck, and I angled my head, breathing softly through my nose. "When was the last time?" he murmured in my ear.

"Over thirteen months ago. I broke up with my boyfriend because he refused to support me in what I planned to do. What I *needed* to do."

He was quiet for a few moments; then he took me by surprise with the words he laid between us next. "I'm jealous. God help me, I am. I'm jealous of every hand that's ever touched you, which makes no sense."

This man and his honesty. It just might be my undoing. Or maybe, with any luck, possibly my salvation.

"Because you're a stranger—is that why it makes no sense?"

"No." He sighed, his breath tickling the side of my neck. "Because I've never felt like this before, not even when . . ." He let his words trail off as he let go of me.

I turned to face him as he adjusted his towel, preventing it from falling, which was too bad. There was an unmistakable bulge, front and center, he couldn't hide.

He cleared his throat and, without looking at me, asked, "What if I try and stop you from doing what you feel you need to do, same as he did?"

"You know what will happen," I admitted, wasting my downturned lips on him since his eyes weren't on me.

"I promise you I'll take Ezra and every one of these assholes down for you. You'll get justice, but I won't let you become a casualty in the process." And he skipped right to it. To the ultimatum I could hear loud and clear. His way or the highway—and in his case, the highway was probably him actually locking me up in a room for safekeeping.

Not happening. "I refuse to go into hiding. That's one reason I didn't reach out to the DEA Saturday night." I waited for his attention, then declared in the firmest voice I had, "I'm deep in this, and I have no plans to walk away."

He quietly tore his hand through his hair, and when he didn't fight back, I decided to stand my ground further.

"You don't even know why I'm really here. You haven't heard my plan. Maybe you'll be on board with it."

"I know enough. I know you're willing to die for vengeance. Be a martyr to your cause. You wouldn't have done everything you did if you weren't—"

"And what would you have done if you were me?" I cut him off, closing the space between us, angry that tears were now burning my eyes, threatening to break free. "What would you have done if someone murdered your entire family and you weren't there with them like you should've been? Would you let those responsible get away with it?"

"No, I'd kill them," he said in a low, growly voice. "I'd kill them all."

"Good," I bit back right away, chills slipping down my spine as a result of the intensity of his stare. "So we're on the same page. Glad we cleared that up." I quickly spun away from him before the tears spilled free. He needed to see me as tough and hard, not someone weak and soft. He'd never go with my plan B otherwise.

"Seraphina, look at me." His voice was hoarse as he said my name like he owned it, like I'd already submitted, giving him total power and authority over me.

The fact I almost wanted to scared me. I'd so easily walked away from my ex without a second thought, and here I was, struggling to even leave a stranger's room.

"No," I sputtered as my eyes betrayed me, allowing tears to fall.

Nine months working for Ezra hadn't broken me, but I was about to fall to my knees and sob.

"Look at me," he demanded again, but I knew the second I did, the dam would officially break.

"No," I cried, my voice cracking that time.

Ryder circled me, and I kept my eyes on the floor. "You're allowed to cry." His tone was softer that time. "You're the bravest woman I've ever met in my life, and crying doesn't change that fact."

I sniffled, trying to abstain. To return to being numb. Why'd it feel like since he'd come into my life there was no going back to that? To being detached.

"Stop being so stubborn for one damn minute and just give it to me." His gritty order pulled my eyes up to him.

"Give you what?" I licked the tears from my lips.

"Your pain." He reached for my side and hauled me against him, and then he did something I desperately needed but hadn't known it until now.

He hugged me. Brought my cheek to his chest, cradled my head, and held me like that.

And there it was.

Dam broken.

An ugly sob followed.

Goodbye to numbness and detachment; hello, sadness and pain.

Memories of my parents, the best people on the planet, filled my mind. From the first time Dad taught me to ride a bike to my mom helping me through my first heartbreak.

And then there was my brother. Younger but always there for me. He'd just graduated from the US Air Force Academy, only to have his future stolen from him.

"The tattoo on my arm . . ." I found myself whispering. **You are your only limit.**

"You got it after they died?"

"Yes," I said around a hiccup, not ready to pull away from the comfort of his embrace. "A reminder to myself every time I wanted to run and hide, not to. Anytime I looked at Ezra, I'd look at my arm and remember to be strong."

"I hate that. Hate all of it. That you have to go through any of this," he hissed, his voice low and painfully intense, like he'd absorbed some of my suffering and taken it as his own burden to carry.

"You know . . . you're making me feel things I don't want to feel," I said through my mess of tears. "I think I don't like you very much." I buried my fingertips into the hard, sinewy flesh of his back.

"I know you don't," he lied right back. "Almost as much as I dislike you."

CHAPTER FIFTEEN

Ryder

"You were in there for a long time." Alex wasted no time in giving me shit when I joined him in the kitchen after Seraphina had finished crying.

She'd decided she needed a shower to pull herself together before facing the three of us and our questions, and I had hesitantly let go of her when all I wanted to do was never stop holding her.

"Breakfast is cold." Reed offered me a plate of bacon and eggs, and I declined, shaking my head while slipping my solid-black ball cap on backward.

"I'm not hungry." I ignored Alex's side-eye and went over to the Nespresso machine to make myself coffee instead.

"You good?" Alex and his constant concern for me, dammit.

I secretly appreciated it but would never admit it. "Nope."

"Want to talk about it?" Of course he'd press.

"Also no." *Because I lost control.* I didn't trust myself. I thought last night was a one-off. I'd been wound up from the fight, so I'd been out of my head.

But being alone with her in my bedroom proved this thing between us wasn't an isolated incident. It was going to be something I had to navigate and work around if I wanted to keep her safe.

I ignored the fact my cup was now full and planted my hands on the counter, hanging my head.

"Lainey's resorted to blowing up our phones since you've clearly been snubbing her," Alex said when I remained quiet, stewing in my confusing thoughts about this woman I barely knew yet felt like I'd known forever.

"You answer her?"

"No, so Director Hernandez called." Reed laid the bad news on me. "He knows we're in Mexico. Tracked our flight. We didn't tell him we found her yet."

"No escaping Big Brother, you know that," Alex commented, his tone joking even if his remark was true.

"So I take it you've decided our mission is to help her, not to turn her over to DHS?" Reed asked.

"I'm not turning her over. But that doesn't mean you have to come along for the ride." I stared down at my hands on the white marble, remembering where they were minutes ago. On her. Holding her. Craving to touch more of her, and had I not switched back to mission talk, that may have happened. My tongue would've wound up in her mouth, too. "Up to you both if you want to stay or not."

"We'll follow your lead on this. We've got your back." At Alex's words, I looked up to see Reed nodding in agreement.

I pushed away from the counter and snatched my coffee. "Yeah, well, if you change your minds, you can say so."

"Do you think Martín Gabriel will also be a problem for us?" Reed asked as I finally drank my coffee. "Do we need to add him to our list of people to keep an eye on?"

"No, I spoke with Carter before my shower. He gave Martín the heads-up that we were in town and not a threat."

Carter had managed to track Seraphina to a family friend in Mexico, discovering he was the one who'd hooked her up with an alias and transport out of the United States. It was by sheer luck (or an act of God) that Martín happened to be a friend of Carter's, too.

While Martín wouldn't tell Carter where she was in Mexico, it didn't take him long to track her down for us, finding her a day or two faster than we would've been able to. He had a lot more money, contacts, and resources than I did.

"Martín's probably part of Seraphina's plan, which means she's not as reckless with her safety as I first thought. But I still think she wants to use herself as bait to draw Ezra to Mexico, and I refuse to let her do that."

"She doesn't seem like a woman who will take no for an answer," Alex said, pointing out what was already fairly obvious, given everything she'd accomplished since her family was murdered.

"Well, she won't have a choice in the matter if I think her plan could get her harmed or killed." And she'd have to deal with it. I wouldn't bend when it came to my stance on that.

Alex's smirk had me rolling my eyes.

He was going to accuse me of being obsessed again—and he was right. But it was more than that. It was something I couldn't quite put my finger on. Something I didn't yet understand.

"You have a chance to look into the club owner yet? Confirm if she was right about him?" I asked Reed since I'd tasked him with researching Ángel Morales last night after I'd become a bit unhinged, nearly sleeping in a chair in front of her bedroom door to ensure she didn't escape.

"From what I can tell, he left the family business, but that doesn't mean they still don't have their claws in him, you know?" Reed shared. "I'm guessing it was Martín who gave her the lead, since he's made quite the name for himself down here for going after the cartels."

"And he wouldn't risk her life by sending her into that club unless he was certain she'd be safe with Ángel." That was my hope, at least. But my leash of trust was short when it came to almost everyone.

"I guess we hear her out and see what she has to say, then we go from there on what to do next," Alex proposed, dropping his empty plate into the sink. "Your buddy reach out again? The one you have watching Ezra?"

"No movement yet. Ezra's still in Miami. Sent my contact a text to locate his wife, though." I explained why I had concerns about Nina Sokolov, then let them know, "She's not in Miami. So he's looking into it. I take it there still haven't been any hits placed on Seraphina, or you'd have told me that." I set aside my mug, eyeing Reed as I waited for confirmation.

"Not yet," he answered. "If Ezra does work for someone else like we suspect, it's possible he doesn't want them to know there's a woman out there with knowledge of their operation. He'd be blamed for allowing that to happen."

"She's probably counting on that, and she's going to dangle herself as the carrot, hoping he'll come himself, especially if Ezra learns she's hanging out with one of their main competitors." The idea made me physically sick, but I shouldn't have been surprised she'd purposefully go to the cartel to place a bull's-eye on her head, not after she'd been beyond gutsy to work for a man like Ezra in the first place. "Hell, Ángel could even stab her in the back and offer her up to Ezra for the right price if he finds out she worked for him, and she'd be okay with that, as long as she draws Ezra down here."

"Right. Lovely fucking idea," Alex said both bitterly and sarcastically. "So, is the plan now for us to grab Ezra since we're here? Question him ourselves?"

I picked up my coffee and parked myself at the kitchen table in front of my laptop. "Let's first see what Seraphina has to say before we talk next steps."

After a few minutes of staring at my screen, I looked up to see her in the doorway.

Her hair was wet and wavy, framing her face. She had on a white tee and short gray shorts that showed off her long legs.

It'd taken all my willpower not to get hard as steel in that bedroom with her while wearing only a towel, and I had a feeling each passing hour around her would become increasingly more difficult to keep my thoughts in check.

"Your food is cold." Reed spoke first, and I turned to see him already on the move, preparing to heat up her breakfast.

"No longer hungry. Thank you." She gave him a small smile. "I'll take a new cup of coffee, though."

"On it." Alex was going to trip over Reed trying to please this woman.

I told myself not to be jealous. They were only being polite, and they also had eyes. They could see she was the most beautiful woman on God's green earth.

While she wasn't mine and probably never could be, I also knew they'd never make a move on her, because they weren't Jeff.

"Thank you." Still barefoot, she slowly walked over. Instead of joining me at the table, she went into the living room open to the kitchen area and took a seat on the couch.

I assumed she was ready to talk, so I closed my laptop to join her. I circled the couch and sat across from her in one of the two leather armchairs.

She had one leg tucked under her with a pillow on her lap, and she was staring at it instead of me.

"You okay?" I couldn't help but ask.

"I'm fine." Giving me back the same answer I'd given her about my bruises.

And was I sore? A little. Did I care? Absolutely not. I'd have gone in that ring over and over again for her.

"Sera." Alex offered her the coffee, and she smiled and nodded her thanks.

"Sera, huh?" I side-eyed Alex, and he lifted his palms.

"What?" He frowned. "She told me to call her that." He dropped down into the other armchair, and Reed hung back at the breakfast bar with his laptop open.

Seraphina shot me a coy look, raising one shoulder while bringing the cup to her full lips.

I held on to the chair's arms as her eyes flew over my body. From my bare feet to my jeans, up to the black T-shirt, and lastly, to my face. Reading my thoughts, or more than likely the tight line of my lips, she said, "Seraphina to you."

Sarah-feen-ah. That was how it sounded when her name rolled from her lips, and I could listen to her repeat it again and again, especially when she threw in a sexy accent that time.

I buried my fingertips in the leather, wishing I was holding on to her instead. The fact she'd told me she hadn't been touched in over a year was a good reminder of why I needed to behave. She'd been through a lot and made sacrifices to get to where she was now.

I'd yet to make up my mind if "behave" meant go slow and take my time with her . . . *or* abstain from touching her at all. I knew what I needed to do, but it wasn't what I wanted to do.

Alex fake-coughed. *Real subtle, man.*

"I suppose you'd like me to explain?" She leaned forward and set her mug on the glass table in front of her before resting both hands on the pillow, wringing her fingers together.

"Maybe start from the beginning," Reed suggested. "We read your file, but I'd like to hear the full story from you."

She looked back and forth between me and Alex before once again staring at her hands.

"I'll do my best." Her strained voice killed me, and after she'd already cried in my arms, was it fair to make her relive the nightmare of what happened with us? "It's okay." She gave me a little nod, somehow reading my mind again.

"Take your time," I told her, loosening my grip on the chair's arms.

"Rather pull the Band-Aid off fast."

I understood that feeling all too well.

Coffee mug back in hand as if it anchored her to the moment instead of to the past, she shared, "My brother had just graduated from the Air Force Academy, and to celebrate, my parents wanted to take us all on vacation. As much as I wanted to join them, I was worried about all of us leaving when we had so much work at the office. My family owned an accounting firm. Just the three of us worked there. I put up a fight, telling them one of us should stay and keep up with business so we didn't fall too far behind. I promised I'd join them on the weekend, though."

Survivor's guilt because you stayed back. There it was. I fucking hated that for her.

"We weren't exactly rich. But one of my father's clients was, and he had to postpone his vacation. He told my dad to stay at the place he'd rented in Cabo since it was paid for and he couldn't get a refund. My father couldn't turn down that generous offer." She closed her eyes. "I never had a chance to meet up with them, because they were killed. An explosion. The whole house and . . ."

I'd already read those details in her file, but hearing them from her lips did a motherfucking number on me. I wanted to go to her, but we weren't alone, and I knew her well enough to know she wouldn't want me holding her in front of them. She'd been resistant to cry in my arms even alone.

"First, the authorities tried to write it off as a gas leak," she continued. "But then they discovered evidence of C-4. They blamed the cartel, saying they probably hit the wrong house, but there was nothing they could do for me."

I was surprised what happened hadn't been all over the national news. According to the file Lainey had given me, her family's death had been shared only on the local news in San Diego. That felt like a red flag in itself.

"I identified what was left of . . ." She visibly trembled—and fuck it, I stood and went over to her.

I ignored Alex's and Reed's eyes on me as I sat next to her. I didn't want to crowd her personal space. More like suffocate it. But I held back. Behaved. Just sat alongside her like an obedient Doberman ready to provide protection and comfort if she needed it.

I glued my hands to my jeans so I wouldn't touch her. "Take your time." Now I wished we were alone, also as far away from here as possible. The other side of the world from Ezra and the cartel would be preferable.

"I, um . . ." Eyes open now, she slipped a finger along the words tattooed on the inside of her forearm as if drawing the strength I wished I could give her. "It was the right house. Wrong people, though."

"They were after your father's client," Reed spoke up. "He was supposed to be in the house that week."

She slowly looked up, her hand falling to her lap, and she turned her head in his direction, catching my eyes in the process since I was now right there. "Yes, and a day later, he was found murdered in Costa Rica. He must've gone into hiding, assuming he'd been the original target, but he was clearly found anyway."

"I'm guessing this client wasn't just an attorney like the file said?" Alex asked, drawing her attention back around, and she paused on me for a brief moment, brows drawing tight, before peering at him.

"Not just an attorney, no," she whispered. "He was Ezra's brother-in-law."

CHAPTER SIXTEEN

Seraphina

Based on the surprised expressions hitting me all at once, that news was clearly not in whatever file they had.

Ryder stood and removed his hat, holding it by the brim. Eyes narrowed, he scratched his throat before driving his fingers through his thick hair.

I watched.

Waited.

Hoped for words to come back my way at some point.

If this was how they were reacting to this news, how would they handle the much bigger shoe I still needed to drop?

"Well, damn." Alex, thank you for breaking the silence. "I guess Lainey only gave us the information she felt was relevant to finding you." Something told me the bitterness in Alex's tone wasn't just the fact they hadn't been completely read in on every detail surrounding my case.

And I am your case. Your mission. I had to remember that we had different goals. Theirs was to take me home, but I was there to face my enemies head-on.

For a woman who'd placed herself in the belly of hell for nine-plus months, you'd think I'd have a spine of steel and my nerves would be better equipped to handle these types of conversations. But reliving what happened to my family, regardless of the audience, always produced the same results. Tingling sensations in my body, an anxious feeling in my stomach, and a tightness in my chest. Because my family was everything to me, and they were taken away.

I should've been with them that night. "Ryder?" I stood, wanting to be a bit more eye level with him.

He tamed his unruly hair with his ball cap, parking it backward again while he waited for me to finish the start of what he could probably tell would be a question.

"Who assigned you to find me? You said it wasn't the DEA, but who? Also, who's Lainey?"

I'd swear the man's eye twitched the moment I said her name, and I also didn't miss the fact Ryder looked over his shoulder in Alex's direction as if sending him a not-so-subtle message: *Why'd you have to bring her up?*

He kept his shoulders arched back, his posture firm. Battling the weight of the world as he stood there, which reminded me a bit of my father.

My dad never let anyone know how much he was carrying. He'd held it all himself, and I had no idea the sacrifices he'd made to ensure my brother and I wanted for nothing. Like the second mortgage on the house so I didn't have to swim in student loan debt, or working twice as much to help put my brother through school. The truth came out after he died, because the numbers told me the story he'd never told himself.

Shit, don't cry. Not now.

"We took the case from Homeland Security." Ryder finally relinquished his answer, a harsh breath floating right behind it. "The objective was to find you before Ezra got his hands on you."

He proceeded to explain more facts, laying them out even faster than the bullet points he'd provided me about himself earlier in his bedroom. Everything from the DEA-FBI task force being formed to pulling DHS in this week. Then, lastly, he covered *why* his team had specifically been chosen to find me.

"So, you were at the party to help capture terrorists?" Time for me to be shocked. How lucky had I been that they happened to be there? Also, I had no clue Ezra associated with *that* kind of evil. How'd I not know that? And what else didn't I know? "And did you stop them?"

"We provided the government with a target package, and they'll be sending an active-duty team to take them out," Ryder let me know. "I was on the balcony that night to get a better look of the property."

"And I happened to come out there." *Everything really does happen for a reason.* Had I not asked for air, I'd have never left the office while Lev threw me under the bus. "Then you were assigned to find me after that because you told Homeland what happened?"

Ryder nodded.

"And how much did the file they provided you reveal about what I did for the DEA?"

"Details were sparse." He was standing so close I could smell his cologne, and he'd be able to get a whiff of my perfume. I'd taken time to apply it to the side of my neck and the inside of my wrist. I knew why I'd done it, and I was staring into the *why*'s eyes right now.

"Are you aware I went undercover as Anna without their help, and I only reached out to them four months ago when I felt it was safe? I wanted to wait to ensure Ezra completely trusted me before I risked sharing information with a government agency."

Round two (or were we at three now?) of shocked looks from them.

I took that as no, that they'd assumed I'd been working with the DEA that whole time.

"You lone-wolfed it for five months without them?" Ryder hit me with a hard look, one that told me he was terrified to hear what else I'd done. Like his heart wouldn't be able to handle it.

He was in for one speed bump after another. *Better buckle up.*

Alex came closer, standing on the other side of the coffee table, drawing my eyes away from the man who could knock me off-balance with his. "No, it's safe to say we didn't know that. We assumed 'Anna' was the cover the DEA provided you."

"How'd you pull it off? This friend in Mexico help you?" Reed's turn to join in, but I couldn't look in his direction—not when I was too curious to check Ryder's reaction.

Was he simmering angry? Worried? Somewhere in between those two emotions at the news?

Would he call me crazy? Reckless?

And why did I care so much what this man's opinion was of me? He was a stranger. Kind of sort of still one. Despite the bullet points shared and the hugging while I cried with him in only a towel. You know, despite that.

He answered my curiosity with a strained jawline paired with narrowed eyes. His chest slowly rose and fell from shallow breaths. He had the look of a father who'd learned his kid had snuck out after curfew and was in a car wreck but somehow survived unscathed. Grateful they were alive and angry that they'd put themselves in a situation that could've killed them.

Shit, what was I supposed to be talking about again? *Right, my family friend here in Mexico.* "You already know about Martín Gabriel. You have a mutual friend. He told me last night. And yes, he's the one who's had my back in all of this since my family was murdered. So no, I wasn't quite lone-wolfing anything."

Doubt that'd alleviate Ryder's tense stance and hard look, though. Nope, pretty sure he doubled down on it. "Did he have eyes on you while undercover before you reached out to the DEA?"

You won't like my answer. "No, Martín's reach doesn't extend outside Mexico. He did as much as he could, including trying to talk me out of my plans. He was the one to provide me with my alias, as well as a backup in case my cover was ever blown. I would've been fine if I didn't expose the truth about Lev on Saturday. It's my own fault. I had no idea I was sealing my fate by sealing his."

"Explain." Ryder's clipped tone wasn't lost on me, but I wrote it off as being a worried old man. Okay, he wasn't much older than me, but he was still playing the role of a concerned dad pretty damn well right now.

No sense in wasting time, so I unveiled the information as fast as possible, not interested in reliving Saturday night. "Ezra asked me to verify whether or not Lev was stealing from him. I ran the numbers and confirmed his childhood friend turned. I just had no idea how much, being forced to work with the DEA starting a few weeks ago."

"Which was when the joint task force was formed between the FBI and DEA," Alex said. "Possibly not a coincidence, but also not enough for us to assume someone at the task force is dirty. If they were, they'd have clued Ezra in about the both of you."

I glanced at Alex, remembering our conversation last night; I wasn't sure how much he'd told Ryder about that. "It's still possible Lev had no clue about me and he lied to try and save himself. Just got lucky. He's definitely the type to do that."

Ryder lifted his eyes to the ceiling before saying, "For now, let's assume someone doesn't have your best interest at heart on the task force. Rather be overcautious than sorry."

I doubted that, but regardless, I was on board with being paranoid. Already was anyway. I waited for him to look at me again and asked, "And that means?"

"Our mission is now to keep you safe and help you get justice," he revealed in a steady voice, "not to turn you over to DHS."

Relief filled me, and I hadn't realized I was possibly as tense as he was until the moment everything in me relaxed. I'd assumed I'd have a much bigger fight ahead of me to convince Ryder to break orders.

"But"—Ryder tipped his head to the side, eyes riveted on mine—"we need more details. I need to understand how you wound up in this situation and what you plan to do down here. That plan better not involve you placing yourself in danger."

I could promise that. Mostly. Maybe not the last part. So some arguing was bound to happen. "Fair enough." I stood and stepped around the table so I could better look at the three of them without straining my neck. "Thank you."

"Hold off on that until we hear more," Ryder remarked.

Back to growly and overprotective so fast, I see. "I suppose you're curious how I connected the dots to Ezra's organization being responsible for my family's death?" I scanned the three men, landing on Ryder last, and he gave me a little *go ahead* nod. I picked up my coffee, discovering it'd gone cold, but took a sip anyway. "After my father's client Andrej was murdered, Martín began looking into his death, and from what he found out, the cartel didn't have my family or Andrej killed. Believe me, if it were true, he'd have found out. But someone wanted Andrej dead, so I had to think outside the box to figure out why."

A few more bitter gulps of coffee later, I returned the cup to the table.

"I'll get you a new one," Alex offered.

I smiled my thanks, and he went into the kitchen. "I decided to do a deep dive into Andrej's files. Looked over all my father's records on him. Everything seemed normal at first glance, but the deeper I dug, the more anomalies I found. Numbers don't lie, and there was too much that didn't add up."

"Right, you also specialize in forensic accounting," Reed noted.

I was skilled in tracing funds, identifying hidden assets, and so on. I just never thought I'd have to use it to help solve the murders of my parents and brother.

"Andrej received regular monthly payments from his sister and Ezra for legal consulting services, as well as from four other investors that have a relationship with the Sokolovs. Two on the West Coast and two in Miami. But I also found payments from an unknown source that, after a lot of research, Martín tied back to the cartel. All the dates of payments were recorded on the same day, and something felt off. I couldn't prove it, but I was sure someone planted a trail they wanted found."

"So, they wanted it to look like the cartel was responsible, which matched what the Mexican authorities claimed happened," Reed said, and I nodded. "You think Ezra or his wife set him up? Made it look like the cartel, but they hired the hit team?"

"That's where my head went, which is why I targeted Ezra as my mark to go undercover with," I explained. "But while working with him, it didn't take me long to realize someone above him is actually calling the shots. In fact, I think he's the right hand to the right hand who works for the devil."

"And who's the real right hand?" Alex asked when he returned with a new cup of coffee.

"Possibly Ezra's wife." *Also the reason Ezra never touched me.* I kept that part to myself as I accepted the coffee. "But I don't know who the Sokolovs answer to. There's got to be a devil, though. And either the Sokolovs are responsible for my family being killed, or whoever they answer to is."

Alex offered up an idea I'd floated in the past. "It's possible Nina's brother pissed her off, or Ezra, and they didn't want his death on their hands. Hence the frame job."

"Since I could never find out that answer while I worked for him, I guess now we have no choice but to ask Ezra ourselves."

Ryder's whole body seemed to frown right along with his downturned mouth. "And that's why you're here?"

"Ezra will come for me himself, I'm sure of it. I know how he thinks and operates."

"*Or* Ángel calls Ezra up after realizing you worked for him and offers you up on a silver platter instead of whatever you proposed to him," Alex suggested. "He could cut a deal with Ezra."

"That'd be a risk if I thought Ángel was a bad guy, but he's not." I had to believe that, at least. I also wanted to redirect the conversation away from why I was here for now. "I'm assuming Ezra told his wife he sent me somewhere for work to explain my absence. Wouldn't be the first time I'd been on a trip for him. He wouldn't want her to know the truth."

"Which is why there's been no hits placed on your head." Alex took my cue for a redirect and ran with it. "He wouldn't want anyone—especially her—to know you tricked him."

"Yeah." *Bad for his ego, and for keeping his head attached to his body.*

"How'd you manage to go undercover as Ezra's accountant and fool him in the first place?" Ryder asked. "Wouldn't he know who you are since your family was mistakenly killed?"

I'd been waiting for that question, and they were about to get the biggest whiplash from me since I'd started sharing my story.

"Why weren't their deaths on the national news?" Alex asked, temporarily stalling me from having to answer.

"I think someone with power had it swept under the rug. Someone with enough influence who could make a call to every major network and demand the story never wind up as part of any major news cycle," I shared before finally taking a drink.

"The head of this criminal operation the Sokolovs work for must have major power and influence in the US, then," Alex said, pointing out what I believed to be true but had yet to prove.

"Back to my question, though," Ryder prompted, and I cleared my throat, not ready for this part of the conversation, like diving back into memories of confronting Ezra for the first time. I also knew what my answer would do to this man: give him a heart attack.

Past is past, though. I can't let my past be my prologue. "I canceled my lease in San Diego. Put all my things in storage. Left my life behind as Seraphina." *Kept my parents' house, though. I couldn't part with that.* Not the time to get choked up. "I became Anna in Miami, both online and in real life. I did my best to show up at bars and clubs Ezra was known to frequent. I tried to get on his radar, get him to notice me."

Ryder palmed his jawline, eyes shooting to the floor, probably hating hearing these details.

"I knew Ezra was married, but the few times he noticed me at the club he hung out at it was obvious that he, um . . ." I paused, not for dramatic effect, but because Ryder had abruptly jerked his focus back to me at that, like he was ready to go scorched earth on the world and throttle the life from Ezra if he ever found out he touched me without consent. "One night, when his wife wasn't out with him, he cornered me. It was just the two of us, outside of the view of security cameras. The man was careful. My first clue that he really didn't want to get in trouble with her."

"'Cornered' you, how?" The deep grit to Ryder's tone slipped right under my skin and heated me up far more than the first taste of the fresh cup of coffee had.

"He asked for my name and what I wanted. Asked if I was following him. I realized in that moment, even if my background check cleared his scrutiny, he'd see right through me. The plan would never work. He'd never believe I was Anna, a woman looking for a job as an accountant."

"What are you trying to tell me?" Ryder came over, took the cup from me, and set it down, waiting for my answer.

"I told him the truth," I confessed. "I told him who I really am and that my family had been murdered."

CHAPTER SEVENTEEN
Ryder

Are you serious? Did she just drop that bomb on us and head into the kitchen?

Drop that on me like I wouldn't lose my mind and imagine all the horrible things that could've gone wrong for her that night in the club? Because what if something did happen when he'd cornered her? Or something went sideways any of the other days during those nine-plus months she worked for him?

I wasn't the kind of guy to get chills, but there they fucking were, shooting right up my spine. I was pretty sure both my shoulder and my eye twitched as a reaction.

This was not the second bolt-of-lightning feeling I'd been hoping for. This was pure, unadulterated rage striking me. Because no one, not even the president himself, would stop me from going to Miami if I so much as found out Ezra had set an unwanted hand on this woman. Ezra's blood wouldn't just be spilled—I'd fucking swim in it.

"I need a minute," Seraphina called out to us, and her words stole my attention away from the dark-red pool invading my mind and back to her. "Can I take a break?"

She didn't wait for an answer and went over to the sink and— *Is she washing dishes?*

I looked over at Alex and Reed, and Alex hiked a thumb over his shoulder toward the front door.

"Yeah, uh, do a security check," I said in agreement to his silent suggestion. "Inside and outside the building. Wait to come back until I text." *Until the both of us calm down.*

Reed grabbed the keys. "What are we doing about DHS? Lainey?"

I turned to the side so Seraphina was still in my peripheral view as she scrubbed a pan. "Buy us time. Tell them we've yet to find her exact location but we're getting close. Just make something up that they'll believe."

"Roger that." Reed nodded, then went over to the door and held it open, waiting for Alex.

"Good luck," Alex mouthed, and once they were both gone, I locked up and made my way into the kitchen.

Keeping her back to me, she flipped her hair away from her face as she continued to soap up the pan, the water running in a slow trickle. "I'm sorry."

"You don't owe me anything, certainly not an apology." I came up behind her, doing my best not to set my hands on her hips or reach for her arms, to try to stop her from cleaning the dishes. "You definitely don't need to be washing our dishes. We're grown men; we can do that ourselves."

"My mom could never focus if there were dirty dishes sitting in the sink."

I took a moment to translate what she was trying to tell me. "So, you'll feel better if the dishes are clean?" I stood alongside her, her glossy eyes meeting mine from over her shoulder.

"Yes," she breathed out before resetting her focus on her mission.

I picked up a clean towel. "Then I'll help you." I took the pan from her and went to work drying it, and we remained like that for a few quiet minutes. Washing and drying. It felt oddly normal. Like something I could do for the rest of my life. Stand beside this woman in a kitchen doing the dishes, and I'd be happy.

When the sink was empty and there was nothing left for her to clean, she turned off the faucet and bowed her head. Her hair fell forward, shielding her face from me.

I put away the last plate, tossed the towel, then did the only thing that felt right. I reached for her arm and guided her around to face me.

I lifted her up, set her on the counter, and braced my hands on either side of her so I didn't touch her bare thighs.

Gone now were thoughts of Ezra. Gone were thoughts of the murdering rampage I'd need to go on if he ever hurt her.

He wasn't here with us right now. The past was exactly where it was supposed to be: behind us. All I could see, feel, and, God help me, wanted to taste was in front of me. No one or nothing else mattered as she lifted her dark lashes to look at me.

Lightning.

Fucking lightning, all right.

There it was. In her eyes. A storm of emotions. I'd take every single painful one from her. Absorb them all so she'd only be left with the good ones.

I shifted a bit closer to her without our bodies touching, her knees between us serving as a barrier. But then she all but green-lighted me. She parted her legs and bent her knees, creating a tantalizing V shape between us that I needed to do everything in my power not to fill with my body.

"Are you okay?" Why was it when this woman asked me that, compared to Alex always badgering me, I actually wanted to answer?

I wanted to tell her I was far from okay, that I hadn't been okay in a long damn time. Probably not since my father walked out on our family when I was six, if I was really being honest.

But today wasn't about me. "I should be asking you that."

"Why, did I say something that'd indicate I wouldn't be okay?" Sarcasm, in a playful way, cut through. She was one strong woman, I'd give her that. Her eyes fell to that V I'd yet to fill. "This is probably hard to believe, but I used to be funny despite being a total nerd. I just didn't always have the best timing with humor. You know, like nervously-laughing-at-funerals kind of thing." She looked back up at me.

"You're talking to a guy who used dark humor to survive war. I get it." I smiled. "Also, it's not hard to believe you're funny. You made me laugh the first night we met."

"I did, you're right." She settled her hands on the counter to maintain her balance.

I wanted to help ease her concerns. Take away her problems and pain. Distract her with my body. *But* I behaved. I behaved because she deserved that from me.

She didn't deserve for me to be thinking about peeling down those too-thin, tiny gray shorts and getting as close to heaven as a man like me would ever get, burying my face between her thighs.

"I know you have questions, but I'd prefer to talk about something else before you get to them. I hate small talk, though. And frankly, I don't give a damn what your favorite color is."

I loved her honesty as much as I loved even the smallest of touches from her. And right now, her pinkie was brushing up against my thumb. So help me, that little touch was all it took to nearly send me over the edge, and I was two seconds away from jumping. Testing to see if I'd land on my feet or fall on my face.

"What would you like to talk about to fill the space until you're ready to get back to it, then?" It took effort and an act of God to get me to say that instead of what I really wanted to say. Start off slow. A simple command, like *Sit on my face.*

"Do you like math?" She tipped her head to the side, studying me as if this would be a make-or-break answer. *Also* not where I'd been expecting (or hoping) she'd go.

"I love it." I'd say anything to make her happy right now. She could tell me the sky was purple, and I'd be on board. Three plus three was eight. Abso-fucking-lutely.

She stopped brushing my thumb with her pinkie, and I lowered my attention to our hands as she moved hers on top of mine. "Math is straightforward. Comforting. It's always been there for me."

This woman could *math* me anytime, just as long as she kept her hand on mine.

I also wanted to tell her that I could take math's place. Comfort her and be there for her.

"Seraphina?" I lifted my head to find her eyes again. "Are you nervous right now?" Was that why she was talking about this?

Her expressive eyes softened. "You'd think after what I've done the last year I wouldn't be—but yeah, maybe."

I didn't want to remember what she'd done in the last year, because then two plus two would equal four again, and I'd have to focus back on color, and she didn't give a damn about color, but I did. One color in particular: red. The color Ezra's blood would become once I cut his throat.

"Why do I make you nervous?" I tightened my brows, remaining locked on to her face as I waited for her to share more.

The woman sitting before me wasn't the one who'd boldly gone into that club full of fighters last night.

The woman in front of me had lowered her guard, letting me get a look at who she was behind the shield.

And I was drawn to both. The badass and the angel. Both still kicked my protective instincts into gear around her, but for much different reasons.

"Because you make me feel things I didn't think were possible ever again." Her shoulders collapsed as if that'd been heavy and hard to admit. "And that scares me." Ah, there it was. Fucking same, too. "Because I don't understand it the way I understand math, and I hate not understanding something."

I didn't have an answer for her, because I was just as confused. "Maybe we should try and figure it out, then? Problem-solve together."

She squeezed the side of my hand, and I took that as her okay.

"Any theories?" I couldn't believe we were going to talk about this thing between us instead of discussing Ezra and her plans here with the cartel. But why was I surprised? I'd been incapable of thinking clearly since we met, and I didn't even give a damn. If being around her meant I'd never think clearly again, then so be it. I'd stay dazed and confused for the rest of my life.

She lifted her free hand from the counter and reached for my face, dragging her palm over the scruff I needed to shave. "We're obviously attracted to one another. I mean, you're ridiculously handsome, so it's impossible to not want you."

I was pretty sure men rarely received compliments (or hugs). So hearing this woman tell me I was handsome had me fighting a grin. "And you're . . . well, the most beautiful woman I've ever seen, so it's impossible not to want you, too, you're right."

"Am I?" Her dark brows lifted, and a sexy smile cut across her lips. She moved her hands to her legs and curled her fingers inward, resting her little fists on those tan thighs I desperately wanted to feel. "Aside from obvious attraction, though, it could be that I feel this way, at such an inappropriate time, because I haven't even touched myself in thirteen months."

Fuccck, I'm so done. The sky was officially purple, and as of now, three and three would forever equal eight. No one could ever prove me wrong.

I shoved away from the counter, my arms going dead at my sides. I replayed her admission in my head and tried to soldier forward and speak, but I was still hung up on the fact this woman just told me she hadn't had an orgasm in over a year.

She'd already told me in my bedroom she hadn't been touched, but this was another level of that. I shouldn't have been surprised, given what she'd gone through. Yet there I was, working to get a grip, to not ask her to let me be the first to get her off, to show her beauty could still exist after pain. I hoped it did, at least. I was still searching myself to see if that was possible. If there really was life after death.

"So, you know why I'm nervous." She licked her lips, because if she was going to kill me, why not make it slow and long-lasting? "Now, what's your reason for wanting me at a time like this aside from attraction? I don't take you for a guy who hooks up with the women he rescues."

"I'm definitely not," I answered immediately, a bit roughly, too. I needed her to know her assumption of me was accurate. She was the epitome of *this is different*. Special. Lightning striking the same place not twice, but over and over again.

"You were drawn to me on the balcony before you even knew the truth about me, when you still thought I worked for a criminal. Is it rebound desire, though? Is that all this is for you?" There was a timidness to her tone she'd never really exhibited before that had me wondering if it stemmed from jealousy.

Jealous of an ex? What ex? "'Rebound'?" I choked on the word, and it came out muffled. "What makes you ask that?"

She unclenched her hands, spreading her fingers out on her thighs. "Lainey and your reaction to that name. You weren't happy to hear it, especially in front of me."

Lainey. Oh, that *ex.* Fuck, I was so wrapped up in the woman in front of me, I'd forgotten other women existed.

"Is she an ex? How long ago did you split? Did you end things, or did she?" The questions struck my chest like bullets, sending me back a step.

Was she really suggesting what I was feeling for her was because I was on the rebound? And was she right? Fuck, I didn't think so. The thought hadn't crossed my mind once, not even when I'd tried to understand why I'd become so obsessed with a woman I barely knew.

"Yes. Three months ago. She broke up with me." My answers were succinct and to the point, and I hated delivering them. I hated that she'd think what I was feeling for her was because she was a rebound.

I wasn't some fuck boy. I hadn't had sex since Lainey. No one-nighters to try to get over her. Because in truth, I hadn't been all that beaten up about the split, which meant Lainey was right to end things with me. I'd returned the engagement ring I never gave her a week after we broke up.

I'd only been upset finding out she'd cheated with my friend. Learning about the betrayal had done a number on me Saturday, but not the breakup itself.

Closing the space I'd created between us, I reached for her chin. "You're the one who admitted you only want me because it's been a long time since you've been touched. What am I supposed to think?"

I let go of her, angling my head, trying to remember how we got here. What kind of U-turn did we take from her telling me how she'd wound up undercover, working for Ezra as an accountant?

"It's not just that. I haven't wanted anyone to touch me in over a year." She finally gave me her eyes. "And yet here I am, feeling like I'll die if you don't." Emotion strangled her last few words, and I hung my head.

She was vulnerable. She'd lost her family, had put herself through hell for revenge, and was currently in danger. That was the definition of *a lot*.

She may have been sober right now, but fear and stress could still do a number on the mind and body. Did I think she had Stockholm syndrome, falling for her rescuer? No, definitely not. And I didn't need to verify with the alleged psych expert on my team, either. But until I knew without a doubt her feelings were genuine and not artificial, I couldn't risk that I was taking advantage of her. So I had to sit on my hands and behave. To obsess from afar.

Unfortunately, my body missed the memo, and I didn't sit on my hands. Instead, I touched her. Went straight for her leg, skimming the soft flesh of her outer thigh. "We're here to take down these assholes so you can have your life back." That was my valiant effort to redirect us somehow.

"I told you, my life in California is gone." She closed her eyes. "All that's left there is my parents' house. I don't have it in me to sell. I only had two close friends. We were basically a triangle. My group was that small, and they already replaced me. And my ex? He's now engaged to his female best friend, the one he told me not to worry about."

"Screw them. Their loss." Jealousy fueled those words. Because fuck her ex and anyone who'd ever try to replace her. The woman was irreplaceable. "You'll start over. Somewhere better and new. But without any threats hanging over your head."

"You really think I can just do that? Let go of the past?" She opened her eyes, and they were gleaming. She was on the verge of tears, and that was all the proof I needed that she was confused, and I had to remember that. To pull my hand away from her and stop touching her.

In one more second I would.

Just one more.

My hand went still on her leg as a thought hit me. "Did you go into this assuming you'd never make it out alive?"

She was quiet for a moment, and that felt like an answer in itself.

"I went into this feeling like I had nothing to live for aside from my revenge, but I never thought about what would happen if I actually got it." Her voice broke as one tear escaped down her cheek.

I moved my hand from her leg to her face and caught her tear, as if I could take her problems away with it. "Well, you didn't have me before. You have me now." I cleared my throat, realizing how forever-like that sounded. "My team, I mean. You have us. We'll take them all down, so you better start thinking about that future you never considered. It's happening."

She reached for me, her small hand resting on my forearm. "Then I guess I better finish my story so you can get me that happily ever after sooner rather than later."

CHAPTER EIGHTEEN
Ryder

I wasn't ready to move yet. To back away. To stop breathing her in. For it to no longer just be us in the kitchen. Even if it'd been, in a way, my idea to get us back to the mission.

But it needed to be done.

I needed to back away.

Sever the connection.

I set my hands at her waist to help her down from the counter, as if she couldn't hop down herself, which was ridiculous, but I didn't care.

What I didn't expect was for her to extend her legs and hook her ankles behind my back, locking me in place instead.

I didn't exactly resist, and how could I? I went with the flow, because being close to her felt like the most natural thing in the world.

My hands went from her waist to the counter to brace myself so I wouldn't fall right into her in this position.

There went that V of space. It was gone. My crotch pressed against her, and she went so far as to scooch to the edge of the counter to ensure we were touching even more.

"Well then," I rasped, which was the best I could come up with since she'd done a one-eighty on me.

She knocked my hat off and ran her fingers through my hair.

I closed my eyes, hanging my head forward, and I was about to become her Doberman all over again. She could scratch my head, and I'd roll over and let her rub my stomach next.

So much for space, for ensuring she really wanted me and her desire wasn't misplaced because of X, Y, or Z. Because fuck the alphabet. All the letters. Right now, if she wanted me, she could have me. She owned me. In this moment, she owned all my decisions. I was no longer a Tier One operator, just a man. A man who hadn't felt this kind of connection in maybe ever.

"Have a thing against hats?" I'd meant that as a joke, but my desire had the words coming out as if they'd traveled across sandpaper to get to her.

"I'm sorry, I . . . couldn't help myself. I guess I'm still not ready to face reality," she murmured, continuing to slide her fingers through my hair. "I've been wanting to do this since we met." Her soft, sexy-husky voice had me about ready to lift her off the counter and take her to my room.

What are we supposed to be doing again? Hell if I could remember, when she rotated her hips—and was that moan from her? Or had it come from my mouth?

I opened my eyes and located where my hands were now. They were no longer on the counter but back on her waist. A tight, firm grip. I told myself it was to keep her from falling, not so I could pin her tight to my body. Plausible enough.

"I'm not normally like this with anyone. I—I don't . . . I'm sorry."

"I, for one, am glad you're not like this with anyone else." I let go of a deep breath, trying to secure hold of my control, which kept vanishing around her. "Also, another apology you don't owe me."

Her hands left my hair and found a new home on my chest.

Finally remembering why we were in Mexico and in this kitchen, I forced myself to make a polite request that part of me (a really big part) wanted her to reject. "Would you like me to call the guys back up? Is it safer for us to talk with them here?" *I want you all to myself,* is what I wanted to say.

"Safer for our control, you mean?"

I wasn't a great liar, so I conceded with a nod.

"I'd honestly rather only tell you the rest of my story, and then you can share everything with them. Is that okay?"

Another nod from me. I was doing a bang-up job of being Delta One. "Maybe not in this position?" I suggested, my voice gravelly again.

She sent her beautiful brown eyes to my chest, where her hands remained fixed in place. Then she pushed out her elbows to create space between, and I realized it was so she could look down.

I followed her line of sight, and, God, how I wished I hadn't. Because all that separated my dick from feeling her were my jeans and her thin shorts, and the image of our bodies in this position had me drumming up a new one in my head. One where we were naked, and we were fucking.

"Space," she sputtered. "Right. Good idea if we want to focus."

Did I want to focus? Yes, focus on dropping to my knees, taking her shorts with me, and licking her clit as she screamed out my name.

I closed my eyes, breathing through my nose to salvage what was left of my restraint and try to build it back up brick by brick before I looked at her again.

"You okay?" That was the voice of the angel, not the sexy little devil I wanted to come out and play with me right now.

But no, she needed to be good so I could behave. *Yes, do that. Be my good girl.* Fuck, I was still painfully hard.

"Give me another second." *Did I just growl? What the—*

I let go of my thoughts when she teased, "I'd apologize for whatever discomfort I think I've caused you, but you'll just tell me I don't owe you one."

And there you are. My bad girl. Dammit. Keeping my eyes closed, I brought my hands around to her thighs and died on the inside as I resisted my basest of impulses to fuck the ever-loving hell out of this woman. Unentangling our bodies instead, I helped her stand.

Once my hands were to myself, and so were hers, only then did I open my eyes.

Face off with the head of terrorist groups, no problem. Barely a spike in my blood pressure. But having to look this woman in the eyes and keep it together had me cooked.

It was time to control-override and switch to operator mode. A few steps back coupled with some awkward throat clears, and I focused up. "Tell me why Ezra knows your real name, and why he let you work for him as Anna even after knowing that." Those words took about as much effort as the Q course back in the army. Selection had nothing on what I was up against when it came to her.

"Right, okay." She knelt, grabbed my hat, and handed it to me like a peace offering before placing even more distance between us, reading the room well—as in the fact my dick had yet to heed my mental command to go down.

If she continued to stare at my crotch, I was going to throw that control I'd just secured out the window. "Eyes up."

The order had her gaze returning to my face. "Sorry."

I shook my head, frustrated with myself, then put my hat back on, forward-facing this time. "I didn't mean to be an asshole."

"You weren't." She stepped forward, and I extended my arm, a quiet request not to come closer.

"Please don't. I'm fighting with everything I have inside me not to fuck up right now." *Because this isn't a rebound feeling for me.* I wasn't sure *this* was even of this world.

"Define 'fuck up.'"

I wasn't so great at lifting just one brow—in my opinion, that was actually not easy to do—so I raised both as my answer. My *You know exactly what I'm talking about* look. When she didn't respond, I went ahead and said the first thing that came to mind. "No longer nervous around me, I see. That didn't last long."

She smiled. "Was it my legs wrapping around your waist that gave me away?"

Ohhh, this woman. Maybe she was confident in what she wanted after all, and I shouldn't question her. She could be vulnerable after everything that had happened but still know what she wanted. Both could exist at the same time, just like she'd shown me she could flip back and forth between sweet and naughty depending on the situation. People weren't two-dimensional caricatures, I knew that damn well.

"I'm not going to win this fight, am I?" Not in the long-term, that was for sure. But I wasn't sure how much resistance was left in me short-term-wise, either.

"I think we both lost it the moment we met, don't you?" Her dose of honesty sent me a step forward.

She stared at my arm as it fell to my side, following the path of an exposed vein down to my wrist, which made me remember to check the time. We had two hours until this former cartel pal of hers was supposed to call. I could do a lot in two hours if I made up my mind.

"Just so you know, it's clear to me now," she began, officially erasing the space between us I'd worked hard to place there, "that math is no longer the only thing I find comforting, reliable, and safe." She rested her hands on my forearms and dragged her palms up to my biceps and squeezed. "Maybe we need to release some tension so we can focus? Maybe that's the problem. Get this out of our systems. I bet we'd think clearly after that."

Not a chance I'd be getting her out of my system today or any other day. "Oh really?" I reached between us and crooked my finger under her chin, urging those beautiful eyes on me. "How do you suppose we do that?"

"I mean . . ." She looked over her shoulder in the direction of the front door. ". . . does this building have a gym?" Her lips spread into a sexy smile as she returned her attention to me.

"As much as I could use a good workout, I don't think that's the answer to our problems. *But* I can't take you to my bed. As much as I want to." I added quickly, "Not *today*, at least."

"I think I get why. It's one of the reasons I'm so drawn to you." Yet she frowned, and I hated being the cause of that reaction. "You're a good man. A sweet, honest, and kind man. And just like you wouldn't risk touching me because of tequila last night, you won't now because you're worried about my state of mind, especially after everything I shared this morning."

She still had more to share, and I didn't know if that "more" would send me on a plane to Miami to kill Ezra today. Another reason I was tense.

As for me being "good," I wasn't so sure about that. If I was, I wouldn't be having such an internal battle on what to do right now. I wouldn't be visualizing all the different ways I'd make her come in the two hours we had until that phone call.

I reached for her wrists and held on, slowly lowering her arms to her sides without letting go. "You haven't touched yourself in over a year. I think it should be by your own hand that you get off for the first time." Saying that without my dick saluting this woman was a challenge, but I somehow succeeded. "Maybe it'll help you take the control back that you had to give up because of . . ." I couldn't say that fucker's name without my rage slipping through, so I let her interpret the rest of my train of thought for herself.

She closed her eyes, her lashes fluttering. Her pouty lips beckoning me. Testing me. "What about you? Will you be doing the same in your room?"

"Do you want me to do the same?" *Stroke my cock? Say the word, ma'am, and I'll do it for you.*

"For the sake of our focus, yes, I think you should."

"For focus's sake," I said, doing my best not to smile, "I will, then." The bulge returned in my jeans. Though it probably had never really left. "Come find me when you're ready. I won't need long, and then we can do the focus thing and talk about what we've left unsaid."

There was quite a lot left unsaid, too.

She opened her eyes, then killed me by winking and tossed out a sexy, "Roger that."

CHAPTER NINETEEN

Ryder

Back to my headboard, hat at my side, shirt off but jeans on, I stared at my bedroom door, my heart thundering out of control at the soft knocking.

Did I leave the door unlocked on purpose, hoping she'd defy my orders and come to me anyway? You know, so I wouldn't be the bad guy and could remain, in her eyes, "good"? Why yes, yes the fuck I did.

"Come in," I called out, my arms falling like dead weight in anticipation of seeing her.

The door slowly opened, and my lungs filled with air, inflating my chest at the sight before me.

Seraphina wearing only my dress shirt from Saturday wasn't what I'd been expecting. It was more perfect than I could've dreamed up.

I exhaled that heavy breath as I waited for what she planned to do.

She closed and *locked* the door. Good call, just in case the guys also defied my orders.

Facing me again, she leaned against the door, fidgeting with the material of my shirt, staring at me with suggestive eyes and parted lips.

The blinds were partially open, so there was enough light to make out every detail of her.

"I think you're right. I should do this by myself for the first time." Her soft tone had me sitting a bit taller. "Well, the touching part."

Shit, why'd I ever suggest that? "But you're here?" *And now you're unbuttoning my shirt.* I watched her fingers gracefully move down the center of the material, and swallowed.

"When I close my eyes, I just see . . ." Her fingers went still. "People and things that I don't want to see or think about. It's distracting." She lifted her eyes back to mine, resuming with the buttons. "But when I'm around you, I forget it all. I feel at peace."

I make you feel at peace? That was probably the best compliment I'd ever been given. "What are you asking me?"

I needed clarity here. For her to be pretty damn specific about what she wanted from me. I didn't want to fuck this up. Say or do the wrong thing.

"Do you want to . . ." I shockingly managed to lift only one brow. ". . . in front of me?" My normally vulgar mouth was failing me. A glitch in the matrix. At least, in my head, since she was standing in my room unbuttoning *my* shirt.

"Yes. I was hoping that'd be okay?" She finished the job of killing me with those buttons but left the shirt on. Her tits were hidden, but I could see her soft, flat stomach and her pale-pink underwear.

"Take those off. Leave the shirt on." The commands ripped from my mouth of their own volition. And I was back online. Resumed normal programming of being a man in lust in front of a gorgeous, nearly naked woman.

When she went to hook her fingers at the waistband of the pink silk, the shirt opened more, allowing me to see one of her breasts. My fingers curled into my palms as I took in her golden-tan skin and her taut, hard nipple; her full, round tit that was perfect for my hand.

My gaze traveled down, tracking her movement as she followed my order and let her panties fall to her ankles. She stepped out of them, toeing them to the side.

I brought my fist to my crotch and pressed down on my erection, the pain unbearable there at the sight of her bare cunt. "Would you like me to keep telling you what to do?" Would I be able to sit here and watch her finger fuck herself and not blow my load?

"Yes, s-ss . . ." Her eyes went to the floor as she bit her lip before peering at me again. "Yes, please." I was pretty sure *sir* had almost fallen from her mouth, and I had to hold back my curiosity and not ask why she clearly disliked that word. And if Ezra had anything to do with it, I was going to see red again and forget about my blue balls.

"No going back. Just forward, okay?" Maybe I was saying that for myself, too. "Don't focus on remembering how you used to touch yourself. Do what feels good now. Here, with me. Where it's safe."

Her gaze roamed over my chest and down my abdomen before her hand slipped between her thighs.

"Come closer." I gestured with my head to the wall immediately off to my left. "Here." That'd place five feet of space between us. Safe enough for me not to reach out and touch her myself.

She did as I asked and circled the bed, and the light from the window on the other side of the room lit her up like the angel she was.

I shifted my legs around so my feet hit the floor and set my fists on either side of me. "Open my shirt wider so I can see you better." My voice was raw and scratchy, need hijacking everything.

She did as I asked, and any blood left in my head rushed all the way down to my cock. "Perfect. My God." I swallowed. "You're beautiful." I committed the image of her so I could hold on to it forever. "Are you wet?"

"Very," she mouthed.

"Show me," I grunted, trying to sequester the primal urges dying to come out and take over. "Stick your fingers inside yourself and drag your arousal over you."

She shifted one shirttail around behind her, pinning the material between her body and the wall to give me a better look at what she was about to do. Then she proceeded to do the same with the other side of the shirt.

The moment she slipped her middle finger in the place where *I* belonged, then dragged it to that tight bundle of nerves, I couldn't help but stand. A knee-jerk reaction to her touch, to her moan.

"How does it feel?" Tightening my hands at my sides to keep my desire locked inside, I forced myself to tear my eyes away from her beautiful, glistening pussy to look up.

She was staring at me, mouth hanging open as if tasting something. Like the fruit of the gods. And it was sinful and sweet. "It feels good," she whispered.

I lowered my gaze again. "Palm your breast with your other hand while you touch yourself. Pretend it's me. How would you want me to touch you? Gentle? Hard?"

My sweet girl held her breast as if it weighed as much as my hard cock did right now. Then she rolled her nipple between her fingers and thumb. "Like this. Maybe use your tongue, too."

"Oh?" Now I was the one breathing hard, and I wasn't even moving. Just a block of steel as I stood there dying on the inside, watching her touch herself without me. "That's what you want, huh?"

"Yes," she breathed out.

"And between your legs. Want my tongue there, too?"

"God, yes," she murmured, her breaths quickening.

I dropped my eyes between her silky thighs again, finding her strumming herself faster—also finding my sanity gone. My control, also MIA.

I had to do something, something different, before I snapped.

"You need to see yourself," I said, making up my mind. I'd use any excuse to get close to her. "Stop," I ordered before reaching for the wrist that was close to her breast. "Come with me." Without waiting for her to understand, I gently tugged her, guiding her to follow me to the mirror over the dresser.

I had her stand in front of me and brought the shirt back, tucking it between our bodies so she could have a better look. Her hands were at her sides, eyes closed.

"Look at yourself. Look how fucking beautiful you are. You need to watch yourself come." *Before I beg you to let me take over.*

She shifted her ass back and rotated her hips while opening her eyes to catch mine in the mirror.

"If you don't want me to fuck this ass, I'd stop doing that," I nearly snarled.

"Mmm." She bit her lip for a moment to screw with me. "That sounds painful." She brought her hand between her legs again.

"I'd make it feel good, don't worry." I leaned forward, drawing my erection tight against her. "Now, be a good girl and get off before I change my mind about behaving." I swallowed, shooting my eyes down her soft belly to her clit. The woman was soaked, and I could practically taste her arousal on my tongue. "Please," I begged. "Behave so I can behave." My voice broke that time, the need to feel her overwhelming. I shifted my hands to her waist and held her against me. "Come for me. I need you to do that for you, for me—for us."

For us. Why'd that sound so fucking good?

"Yes, s-s . . ." There it was again. The word she couldn't say, and I was going lose my mind thinking about why.

"I don't need to hear that, it's okay."

"But—"

"No. This is about you. About you making yourself feel good." And giving me a heart attack, but it'd be worth it. Every second. I tightened my hold on her hips, wishing, praying, hoping like some sick fuck I could touch more of her.

I'd sell my soul for five minutes with her if my soul had any value, but the devil already owned it. It was taken during war, so I didn't have it to give.

She ground her ass against my cock, drawing me back to the moment. "Do I need to warn you again what I'll do with that ass?"

"As long as you fuck my pussy first, you can do whatever you want with me, to me, and—" She let go of her words when her orgasm built inside her to the point she couldn't talk.

And I was here for it.

She looped her arm back and around my neck, her tits going forward, back arching, as her stomach visibly clenched with every breathy moan.

"Yes, oh yes, yes, yes, yes." She rubbed herself harder. Faster. Grinding against me with each thrust of her two fingers between her legs. "Yesssss."

Fuck, fuck, fuck. I'd never witnessed anything more beautiful in all my life than this woman coming.

I let go of her hips, moved her arm down from around my neck, and circled her. "Seraphina?"

"Yes?" she whisper-cried, still coming down from her orgasm.

"I'm going to kiss you now, okay?"

The second she began to nod, I took that as my okay and snatched her face between my palms and slanted my mouth over hers.

She moaned, and I captured the sound with my tongue and parted her lips to taste more of her.

Her hands went to my forearms, holding me like a lifeline, the same way I held her face.

I had to slow down.

Calm down.

Not fuck her mouth the way I wanted to.

But I was ravenous and spinning out, and she was matching my energy. My pace. My hunger. My *peace.*

She arched into me, drawing her bare pussy against my jeans, and fuck the material between us.

I kept kissing her with everything I never knew I had in me as she continued to rock against me as if chasing another orgasm, or maybe riding out her last one.

On the edge of exploding, I finally pulled back. Nose to nose, I stared into her eyes, my thumbs sweeping in small circles over her cheeks as she kept hold of my tense forearms.

"Let me watch you now." She slid her tongue along her swollen lips.

I smirked. "I can't. Not with you in here."

"Why not?"

"I'm always in control. Always. Except with you. I barely have any when it comes to you," I admitted. "I can't have my cock out with your pussy bare. Only two things would stop me from fucking you: you telling me no or an act of God. Maybe not even the second."

"But I—"

"You won't say no." I narrowed my eyes, knowing damn well I was right, and she knew it. She'd let me fill her. Beg me to, in fact. I'd be at her mercy, not the other way around. "Go change. I'll handle my situation and meet you in the kitchen."

I dropped my hands, and she let me go. I pulled my shirt together, unable to handle the view of her tits and not touch her right now.

"You're sure?"

"Yes." I sighed, hating myself for this, but doing the right thing didn't always feel good. I slipped my hand through her hair and slanted my mouth by her ear and promised, "The next time you get off, though, it won't be with your hand or mine. It'll be with my mouth, and then it'll be with my cock."

CHAPTER TWENTY

Seraphina

With another fresh cup of coffee in hand, I rested my shoulder against the window by the kitchen table, taking in the view down below. A statue of angels. One bowing alongside another, bathed in the soft glow of the midmorning light. I was definitely much more relaxed now than before, but still reeling from what happened.

Hearing the bedroom door open, I found myself murmuring, "Did you know Puebla is also known as City of the Angels?" *And I came here to speak to a man with that name to help me. Kind of ironic.*

I looked up to see Ryder hanging back in the doorway, fully dressed, with his ball cap hiding his hair. He should've looked a bit more relaxed, given he'd been in there to relieve his own tension after watching me relieve mine. Yet he still looked like a tense block of steel.

When he remained quiet, leaning against the doorframe, his thumb hooked in the front of his pocket, just staring at me, I had to remind myself we weren't on vacation together. We were there for a reason, and it wasn't to have copious orgasms. *Unfortunately.*

"Great library here, too. Colorful houses. Cobblestoned alleys. Beautiful churches." Okay, I wasn't sure why I was acting like a travel guide. "Would be nice to walk around. See the city."

"Too dangerous." Bossy response, of course. *So, we're back to that.* "You're stalling."

"I guess I'm still tense." More so nervous about the fact I needed to get this stubborn man on board with a plan he wouldn't like—so yeah, maybe I'd been stalling all morning.

"Still?" His forehead wrinkled as if he was surprised or offended.

"Unfortunately." *Don't try to tell me you're not, too.* "I still want you. Not out of my system."

"Good." He lifted his chin like that movement was a word in itself. "*Unfortunately*, you're not out of mine, either."

"So, what you were doing in there while I dressed and made coffee didn't help, huh?"

"I think you know the answer to that." He flashed me a small devilish smile that was irresistible, and then I couldn't erase the mental image of him jerking off in that bedroom from my mind.

"So that's why we're still . . ." *Horny?* Maybe I wasn't only stalling. My body was just too responsive to him. And why was I suddenly shy after I'd parted my legs for him and let him direct me in getting off?

I pushed away from the window and set the mug down on the table. At some point, I'd finish a full cup of coffee.

"Maybe it's because we didn't touch each other?" I proposed.

He straightened, changing from that sexy-lean pose to being upright and a sharp line of tension. "You think after I put my mouth between your legs, you'll get over me then? That'll be all it takes to move on?" That low, raspy tone of his, along with the dark look in his eyes as he stared at me, had my body coming alive in anticipation all over again, and I was only ten minutes post-orgasm.

I held on to the top of the chair at the table, maintaining eye contact with him. "I guess we'll have to wait and see?"

He cut the space between us in half, long strides bringing him my way. "I guess so." His voice was anything but flat, and instead, laden with desire.

I sighed, because what else could I do right now since I needed to keep my hands to myself?

He'd given me my first orgasm in thirteen months without even touching me. He gave me so much more than that, though. He gave me hope. Gave me pieces of myself back.

I glanced at the front door when a thought hit me. "You weren't worried I'd take off on you while you were in there."

"Why, do you want to leave?" He rounded the table, standing on the other side as if feeling the need to have an object between us. Like it was safer that way, since our willpower around one another was practically nonexistent.

"Depends."

"On?" He copied my movement, gripping the top of the chair—but, from the looks of it, much harder than I was, since his knuckles whitened.

"On whether or not you agree to my plan here." Could I actually run away from him again like I did Saturday? No, which meant I had no choice but to convince him to agree with me.

I checked the time. An hour and a half until I was due for the call. That gave me ninety minutes to get him on board.

"I think we've established I won't allow you to do anything that puts you in danger."

I smiled, unable to stop the reaction from happening. He loved bossing me around as much as I loved *not* submitting. Well, okay, I'd submit all day long in the bedroom, but that was a different story. He could fuck the attitude out of me for eternity. In fact, I'd purposefully find a reason for him to adjust my attitude in the bedroom. "We also established I have free will. I'm not your prisoner."

"Unless it's to keep you safe. I'll veto any decision you make that risks your life." He went around the table to stand before me.

I let go of my death grip on the chair to face off with him. I had to look up with him so close.

He captured my chin. "And in that case, fuck your free will."

"So it's going to be like that? Are we really back to—"

He dropped his mouth over mine, capturing whatever I'd planned to say, because hell if I remembered the moment once he kissed me.

This was why we shouldn't share the same space.

This was why it was so dangerous to our focus to even breathe in the same air.

"You drive me crazy," he rasped, moving his hand from my chin to hold the side of my face, his fingers slipping up into my messy hair. "I can't fucking think straight when you use this mouth of yours to do anything." His words vibrated against my lips before he groaned, wrapping his free arm around me to draw me tight to his body as his tongue took command of mine, invading my mouth.

And it was perfect. It was bliss. It was all the things.

Also, it was surrender. Submission. It was him letting me know that when it came to my safety, he'd win, and part of me was okay with that. Part of me forgot what it was like to give the control over to someone so I wouldn't have to worry or even think about anything if I didn't want to.

"What are you doing to me?" Another husky rasp from him before he deepened the kiss, exploring the inside of my mouth as I rotated my hips, feeling his hard length press against me.

The definition of *not over each other* was happening now. Tension back, stronger than ever. Our orgasms hadn't rid us of anything. More like spurred us both on to only want more.

"No, what are *you* doing to me?" I managed when his fingertips dug into my ass cheek over my gray shorts and squeezed.

"My turn to stall, I guess," he said between kisses.

I reached up between our bodies, searching for his wrist. One of us had to get a grip. To focus. I didn't expect it'd be me, since this was his job—Delta operator and all. But I had to remind myself I'd spent almost thirteen months with one objective in mind: justice for my family. I couldn't give that up now; I was too close.

"Ryder." His name came as a plea from my lips. "We should . . ."

He licked my lips back open, and I parted them without hesitation, giving right in. How could I not? I'd wanted this man since the moment he zipped me up on Saturday, which was only six days ago.

After a few more dizzy and intense seconds, my clean panties now drenched, he pulled back and found my eyes. "We need a barrier. I know you don't want them up here, but if we're going to talk with our clothes on, then—"

"Okay," I interrupted in understanding, even if the idea of being naked in his bed and wrapped up in his arms was much more preferable to talking about Ezra and the cartel. "Text them to come back." I released my hold of his wrist and set my hand on his chest.

"One of us should back away." Two sharp lines formed between his brows, and I took that as his request for me to be the stronger one and do it.

"You should unglue your hand from my ass and face, then." I smiled, and he returned mine with a handsome boyish grin I adored. It was the first time I'd seen this hard operator go soft on me. Well, definitely not soft beneath his jeans, or anywhere else.

"Roger that." He winked, then he closed his eyes, as if it'd be easier to let go of me that way. He slowly did so, and I removed my hand from his chest, and we both stepped back.

With his eyes still sealed from view, I knew there was something he needed to know that I'd yet to confirm, and I wanted to get that over with before the others joined us. "Ezra," I whispered. "He never touched or hurt me like that."

His eyes flashed open, obvious relief crossing his face, but his body remained tense and rigid.

I wet my lips and continued, "He wanted to, but his wife kept him in line. She *may* be responsible for my family dying"—I still wasn't sure—"but I'm fairly confident she was why I never had to endure . . ." I cleared my throat upon realizing the anger was returning to his face; he had to be thinking about what *could've* happened even though it hadn't. "To be clear, if he'd tried, I wouldn't have gone down without a fight." Shit, was my lip trembling? Or was that my whole body?

"Fuck," he said with a shake of the head, then closed the space between us, circled my wrist, and hauled me over. He crushed me against his hard body, wrapping me in his arms to hug me.

"You're going to kill him anyway, aren't you?" I asked, my cheek to his chest as he held me in a much different way. "You're not that guy, though. I—I don't want you becoming that guy for me."

He was quiet for a moment before shifting back to locate my eyes. "The thing is, I'm already that guy." In a dark voice he murmured, "You have no idea just how much."

CHAPTER TWENTY-ONE

Seraphina

I was determined to finally finish my morning cup of coffee. *Fourth cup's the charm.* I looked up from my mug and over at Reed and Alex at the breakfast bar, eyeing me as if they knew exactly how Ryder and I had spent our time apart from them.

Alex lifted his cup, eyes meeting mine as he sipped his coffee.

Yeah, he was just like my brother. Probably a lot older, but still. That knowing little smirk he hit me with after he lowered his cup to the counter was proof of that.

And now I missed Joaquin. Not that I ever stopped missing him, but he was currently at the forefront of my mind, and I had to get through the rest of my story without crying.

"Lainey give you a hard time?" Ryder's question did a bang-up job of stealing my focus. Well, more like the mention of his ex's name. I'd rather think about some faceless woman than remember the pain of my past, though.

I really had no business being jealous of this woman, or the fact they still worked together post-split. And yet there I was, wondering what she looked like. How long they were together. And why in the world would she ever break up with a man like him?

"Of course she did, but we bought ourselves time. Not too much," Alex answered as Reed opened his laptop. "So, you two didn't finish without us, then?" He shot Ryder a lopsided grin, like there was some double meaning there.

Oh, we finished all right. Was I blushing? I'd become a totally new person, or maybe a better version of my old self, ever since Ryder had walked into my life. Almost too quickly, because my brain had yet to play catch-up with my body. My heart was a confused pile of mush stuck somewhere in between the two speeds of fast and faster that my body was locked on to.

"We decided it'd be best for you to hear everything, too," Ryder said, pulling off casual better than I could.

"Ah, okay, so what were you doing all that time? Dishes?" Alex's comment earned him a less-than-discreet elbow from Reed. "See? He really isn't a people person, not even with me."

"*Especially* not with you," Reed grumbled without looking up from his screen.

"I'm not really a people person, either," I let Reed know, and he glanced at me, giving me the slightest of nods. "So, um, where did I leave off again?"

I looked over to locate Ryder. He was standing alongside me with his back to the counter, an ankle crossed over the other, and a fresh cup of coffee in hand. "You told Ezra your real name and that your parents were killed, worried he'd figure out you weren't Anna."

"How'd you pull that off?" Alex asked, drawing my eyes back to him, and my stomach tightened at the brotherly reminder all over again. Same dark hair, eyes, bronzed skin, and, from what I could tell, humor.

Stalling, I blew on my coffee as if it were too hot, which wasn't remotely the case. "Well." I lowered the mug, drumming my nails against the side. "An enemy of my enemy is my friend." There it was. My so-called battle cry. My mantra. I'd let it loose. Let them hear it the way I had said it last night in the fight club. "I told Ezra that I changed my name and moved to Miami with one mission in mind: that I wanted to destroy the people who murdered my family, and I'd do anything to make it happen. I told him I assumed we shared the same enemy, since I discovered his brother-in-law was the original target."

"Damn." Alex pushed away from the counter and stood. "That's brilliant." He repeated his words in Spanish, adding a bit more flavor to them, and I couldn't help but smile. "Hiding behind the truth. Smart."

From my peripheral view, I spied Ryder standing tall without the support of the counter. I waited for him to speak, but when he didn't, I took that as my cue to continue.

"I told Ezra what happened to my parents in Mexico and that the cartel murdered them while staying at Andrej's place on vacation. I let him know how his brother-in-law and my family were connected. That my dad had been his accountant." I relayed the facts fast, not wanting to walk down memory lane any longer than necessary. "I asked him if he planned to seek revenge, and if so, I'd like to be part of it."

"I'm in awe. No other way to put it." Alex tore a hand through his hair, pride that I appreciated in his eyes. At least one of them was impressed—because knowing Ryder, he was pissed.

Well, that was how I was gauging his quiet rigidness. He was probably having a coronary thinking about all the things that could've gone wrong with plan A. I mean, I was in plan-B territory now, so he wasn't totally off base.

When I chanced another sideways glance at him, he was in the process of rubbing his chest with his free hand, eyes cast down on his mug.

"Clearly, Ezra agreed to the plan," Alex said, sitting back down. "Risky assuming he would, though."

"'Risky' is putting it mildly." And there was my grumpy overprotector. Using the heel of his hand, he continued to push at his chest. I was doubtful the pain there was a result of heartburn from the coffee.

"I could tell Ezra would . . ." I swallowed, knowing Ryder would hate what I was about to say next, so I looked away from him. ". . . get off on the idea he knew damn well the cartel didn't kill my family, and every time he looked at me, he'd relish in the fact I was working for the true enemy and didn't know it."

Ryder abruptly turned and set down his coffee, and his hands landed on either side of his mug.

Now wasn't the time for me to go to him and ease his worries. We had to get through this conversation to proceed to the next phase, which started with receiving that call at noon.

"Ezra told me he had no plans for revenge. He said nothing could be done about the cartel, but he felt bad that my family was killed by mistake because of his brother-in-law, and so, if I wanted a job with whatever name I chose to go by, he'd give me one." *Yeah, right—felt bad. Sure.* "I figured he wasn't ready to trust me at that point, but I'd take what I could get."

"I'm assuming when you reached out to the DEA four months ago, that was when he'd started letting you in on the truth about his business?" Reed kept his voice low and matter-of-fact.

I nodded. "Every month or so of working for him, Ezra slowly trusted me more and more. Then one day, about five months ago, he told me if I was serious about wanting to take down the cartel responsible for killing my family, he had a plan. He said the only way to ruin them was to replace them. He said if I was truly willing to do anything it'd take to destroy the cartel, then I'd need to prove it. And that's when he lifted some of the curtain, showing me what he really did on the side. He tested me to see how I'd react. The more I proved to him I was committed, the more he showed me the ropes. Gave me real numbers to work with tied to the illegal drug trade he was running."

"That must've been damn hard to act like you didn't know the truth about everything." Alex frowned.

Especially when I wanted to throw up on him for the first several months. Well, that and stab him. "Yeah, and I realized I was in over my head, so I finally made the decision to reach out to the DEA. I explained to them the cartel didn't kill my family, but Ezra or someone tied to him did."

"Guessing you didn't tell them how you infil'ed his organization by using your real identity?" Alex asked me.

"I let them think my story as Anna worked. I was afraid they'd say the risk was too great."

"And it was too risky." There was unmistakable frustration and concern in Ryder's tone.

Did I need to remind him I was okay and standing there? No, because then he'd remind me if he hadn't been at the party Saturday, I'd be dead.

"Um, so the guy I talked to at the agency said they were already onto Ezra but didn't have definitive proof, but they did believe it was possible he was reporting to someone higher up, which tracked with what I'd suspected. The goal became to find out who was in charge of the whole operation, and my personal goal was to establish who actually called the shots to have my family murdered: Ezra, his wife, or someone else."

"And speaking about his wife, what else do you know about Nina?" Reed with the question that time. "You said earlier you think she may be as powerful as her husband."

I shared what little I knew. "Possibly, yes. As for her background, she doesn't have any living blood relatives. Her brother was it. Born in Russia. Their parents died when they were kids. They're only two years apart in age. They were raised by their aunt here in the US. Nina's thirty-four. Married Ezra three years ago."

"Maybe she's a Russian spy and she's working for the Kremlin." Alex shrugged. "Hey, you never know. It's possible."

"Reed's supposed to be the conspiracy theorist, not you." Ryder pushed away from the counter, aligning himself next to me.

I let my hand fall between us, and our pinkies brushed. That little touch gave me back the life I didn't realize I needed to help me get through this.

"*Theory* implies a lack of evidence to determine proof," Reed grumbled. "Anything I ever say is always based in fact."

"Sure it is." Alex's smirk came and went fast. "It's possible Nina has ties to someone over in Russia who scares Ezra into doing whatever she says, and they're why he fears his wife."

"The Russian theory isn't too far-fetched," I revealed. "Nina's made several trips to Moscow in the nine months I worked for Ezra. It's possible she's even there now." I set aside my coffee, realizing my java dreams of finishing a full cup weren't going to happen this morning. I was jittery enough from anxiety; I didn't need to add insult to injury with caffeine.

"What are you thinking?" Ryder asked, catching my eyes. "You have a theory, don't you? You know a lot more than we do."

"That's all it is, though." I placed my hands on the counter. "It's possible our person in charge is someone in Russia, and they're pulling the strings, as Alex suggested, and Nina is somehow tied to them. And that someone is why Ezra behaves."

"You mean, why Ezra never . . ." That uncomfortable pause from Ryder pained me to hear. ". . . tried anything with you?"

I nodded. "Ezra didn't want Nina—or anyone else—to know my real name or why I was working for him. He told me to keep that story between us." *For his own reasons.*

Ryder discarded his cup in the sink, a scowl marring his lips.

"Let's assume someone in Russia is actually the one in power, and they're responsible for taking over the drug-trade business in the US from the cartels," Reed began. "Would they also have the power to keep the story of what happened to your family from making it to national news? Last I checked, our media wasn't owned by any Russian conglomerates or the Kremlin."

"And, for that matter, I still don't get why Nina's brother was targeted. Not unless he planned to betray them, expose the truth about their operation, and so they made it look like the cartel took him out," Alex tacked on.

Ryder stroked his jaw, quietly contemplating everything, before saying in a firm tone, "Let's assume the worst about everyone and everything until we know who and what we're up against."

"You never admitted to Ezra on Saturday you were undercover for the DEA, right?" Reed asked. I'd forgotten I never told them exactly what happened that night.

"No, Ezra was questioning me in his office, but then a call came in. I assumed it was Nina. He had me taken away. He'd planned to meet us on the yacht afterward, but he never had a chance, thanks to you all."

"If Ezra doesn't know for sure you're DEA, then I think it's safe to say Lev got lucky when he tried to throw you under the bus. It's looking more and more like no one from the task force told him there was someone else on the inside," Alex pointed out.

He was probably right. There were too many holes in the theory that Ezra had a contact at the DEA. The biggest one of all: I'd already be dead. Long, long ago. A mole at the DEA would never withhold the information from Ezra that I was undercover. That thought had gone through my head after leaving Miami, but I couldn't take the chance I was wrong. Nor did I want my handler at the agency to stop me and throw me in witness protection, either.

"I have no plans to turn myself over to the task force. I'm finishing this my way." I looked at Ryder, expecting him to fight me on that, but he kept eerily quiet, which was almost more nerve-racking.

"Ezra will assume you're guilty no matter what, since two of his men were killed the night you took off," Reed said. "He'll think the DEA had people watching over you and it was them who rescued you."

"Not necessarily." Ryder studied me for a quiet moment before continuing, "When Ezra learns Seraphina's in Mexico hanging out with a main competitor of his, he'll wonder if it was the cartel who planted her undercover with him and they were the ones who saved her Saturday night."

"An enemy of my enemy is my friend," I murmured under my breath as Ryder put two and two together, understanding yet another reason why I'd specifically chosen this cartel to target. "Ezra will more than likely realize I knew from the very beginning the cartel was framed for my family's murders and his organization was responsible."

"Once Ezra confirms you're really here and have been talking to a Morales, Ezra may reach out to the cartel and try to negotiate—if Ángel didn't make contact with him first, for all you know." Ryder's jaw tightened. "Hell, Ezra may have already started the conversation with the cartel, too."

"Ryder," I whispered, worried he was about to fall down a rabbit hole of worry where the only outcome he'd decide was acceptable was to reject my plan.

"Don't 'Ryder' me," he grunted, shaking his head. "Ezra will offer Ángel or the cartel whatever either one wants if you're turned over to him, including coming himself." The man's eyes were going to bulge from his sockets as stress lines bracketed his mouth. "This has been your backup plan all along, am I right? This is what you were afraid to tell us. It's why you've been stalling. You're not just drawing Ezra here; you're planning to put them all together, with you right in the fucking middle." He stepped closer to me, crowding my space, and I forgot we weren't alone. "Are you out of your mind?"

Maybe a little. But what choice did I have? Plan B was all I had left. "It's possible they wind up turning on each other. That Ezra and the cartel won't hold up their end of whatever deal they make. Can't trust criminals, right? Ezra will never actually give them anything, and the cartel has to know that. But they can't pass up a chance to go after the organization who's been ruining their business." I was growing lightheaded as I tried to stand my ground and pretend I wasn't actually terrified of my own plan. "And I'm not going to be alone in all this," I reminded him. "I do trust Ángel not to turn on me, and I also have someone—"

"Martín," Ryder said, cutting me off.

"Martín can't operate outside of Mexico without risking arrest, but here, he's both revered and feared. A local hero to the people. An enemy of the cartel. And he's why the plan needs to take place in Mexico," I explained. "Best-case scenario, we take all these assholes out in one swoop. Ezra's organization right along with the top members of the cartel." Then Ángel would also be free of his family's hold once and for all.

Surely Ángel would understand those risks and would probably even be on board with taking them all out. *An enemy of my enemy and all*—and, well, his own family was also his enemy.

"A win-win," I added before Ryder tried to shut me down.

"Not a win." Ryder stabbed the air in the direction of the ground. "It's a suicide mission for you, and if I . . . if I wasn't here, then I can't imagine . . ." He snarled and turned away as if unable to handle looking at me right now.

"Martín will have my six. He'll never let anything happen to me."

"And where's Martín now? Why'd he let you come here alone?" Ryder snapped, turning back around to face me.

I supposed that was a fair question, one that deserved answering. "Any time Martín moves around Mexico, word gets out. He's too well-known here. I couldn't risk anyone connecting him to what I'm trying to do and screwing up my plan before it even starts. I need to get the cartel to agree to a meeting with me first without them thinking I'm setting up a trap for Martín to take them down."

"This is insane. All of it." Ryder removed his hat, slapping it on the side of his leg as he dragged a hand through his messy hair.

"Martín and his team will protect me when it's go-time." I reached for his arm, but he pulled away, and I had to lie to myself and pretend that didn't hurt. "I now have you here, too. If you still want to be, at least. You'll keep me safe." My body shuddered as a worst-case scenario unfolded in my mind of its own accord. "But if something does go wrong, then it is what it is. I told you already that all I have left is my revenge. I have no family. No friends. I have nothing. So if I die, I die. As long as we take down the bastards who killed my parents and brother, too."

From the corner of my eye, I spied Reed and Alex standing. Leaving us alone. Sensing this wasn't their fight.

Shit. Tears broke through my defenses, unleashing holy hell on my system, free-falling to the point that my vision became blurry.

"Nothing to live for?" Ryder rasped, returning his hat to his head. "How can you say that? You're young. You have your whole life ahead of you. I never want to hear the words *if I die, I die* from you ever again."

I swiped at my tears, hating them. Where were numbness and detachment when I needed them? "Did that stop you from putting your own life on the line for the military? Even now, with what you do? No, you do what you think is right every day, even if it means you may not survive to see another." My lip quivered as I did my best to not become a complete blubbery mess. "How is what I'm doing different?"

He dragged both palms down his face. "I knew you were going to be a stubborn pain in my ass, but I had no idea just how much," he gritted out, then reached for my waist and pulled me against him.

I wanted to resist. To fight him. To push back.

But instead, I allowed him to take control, becoming dead weight in his strong arms.

"Let me make one thing crystal clear." Without releasing me, he reached between us with his free hand, taking hold of my chin. He urged my eyes up and to his face, and I found his blue greens glossy and narrowed. "I'm allowed to risk my life, and now that I'm in yours, you need to accept the fact that under no circumstances are you ever allowed to risk yours."

"You can't just decide—"

"Oh, I can, and I will." His nostrils flared as he stared at me without blinking, waiting for my submission. "Yes, you're brave and smart, and ridiculously strong-willed and also . . . well, amazing." He dropped his face closer to mine, our mouths nearly brushing. "But you've done things your way for long enough. You got this far; now it's time you let me help you finish things." He brought his hand from my chin to his heart. "And that means it's time we do things my way."

"And your way means what, exactly?"

"That I'm the only one who will ever have an *if I die, I die* moment for the sake of a mission. Got it?"

CHAPTER TWENTY-TWO

Ryder

"And what's *your* way?" This woman, dammit, she really was going to give me an ulcer or a heart attack. It wouldn't be the Sokolovs or the cartel who killed me—it'd be her. "Let me guess," she went on before I could answer. "The safe way. The way that doesn't use me as bait."

"Finally on board with my plan," I tossed out with extra sarcasm. "Thank you." I was only now aware we were alone. Never a good idea when it came to us. "If you want to question Ezra, then so be it. I'll head to Miami today and snatch and grab him. We'll have answers from him by tonight."

"Sure. Go kidnap a businessman on American soil. Solid approach. If his guards don't kill you, you'll wind up in a prison cell."

She gave me a dose of my own sarcasm. I offered her some of my arrogance and revealed, "I don't get caught. It's on the list of things that have never and *will* never happen. Right along with the fact I'd never use a woman as bait. And also, did I not take someone from Ezra's house Saturday night in your presence without a problem?"

She attempted to chase away the goose bumps I could visibly see on her arms, rubbing and rubbing. "Hmm . . . yeah, well, I vaguely remember you did encounter a problem."

"Yeah, the problem is standing in front of me now." That was an asshole comment I didn't actually mean.

"I wasn't your problem. I didn't have to be. Still don't have to be." She tipped her head in the direction of the door.

The sass kept on sassing from her, and I hated that it turned me on. I wanted to give it to her as good as she gave me.

We're a pair. I positioned my arms over my chest so I wouldn't take her over my shoulder, then spank that ass of hers en route to my bedroom. That wasn't how to solve this. Wrong head to think my way through this. And yet it was also the only one that seemed to be working right now.

"Have your Homeland Security friends given you the green light to go after Ezra?" She shook her head. "Nope, didn't think so. I won't have you doing something illegal on my behalf."

"Fine. I'll do it for me. Not for you. Case closed." I circled my finger like a blade of a helo, giving her my signal. Time to spin up and head out to Miami.

"Not so fast. I'm putting my foot down. Telling you no. You're not going to lone-wolf it to Miami." Lips parted, teeth clenched, she—

"Did you just snarl at me?"

"Ugh, because you make me crazy," she shot back, flustered.

And she also distracted me from what I'd been seconds away from doing and still needed to do with her adorable display of growliness.

Growly was supposed to be my thing. "Do I need to remind you that *you* lone-wolfed it?"

"That was different and you know it." She rolled her eyes. Of course she did.

So I rolled mine. Fucking hell.

I didn't know what to do with this woman. Never had anyone make me so frustrated and aroused at the same time. I was in over my head—not that I'd admit that out loud.

I'd been surrounded by smart and strong women my whole life. My mom, for one. Every one of my exes. Women I worked with in the military.

But so help me, this fireball in front of me . . .

She was everything I never knew I wanted but now had no clue how I'd live without.

Grit, strength, and bravery. I could go on and on with a list of adjectives that described her, and I also knew those descriptors were why I wouldn't be able to easily get my way, mission-wise. I couldn't control-override her into submission.

Settling my hands at my hips, I hung my head forward, trying to map out a plan to get me through this conversation first before we both snapped.

"There is no plan that works without placing me at the center of it, and you have to know that. The house of cards falls without me."

She did come this far on her own, some dark part of my mind said, playing devil's advocate. I didn't like it. *But she would've died Saturday if we weren't there.* That was the part of my brain I needed to listen to.

"I have intel and notes on my laptop about the Sokolovs' operation. Maybe your team can offer a fresh perspective." She dialed down her tone, probably realizing that aggravating an already agitated control freak wasn't the best idea. "We can come up with a plan that—"

"Doesn't put you in the middle?" I looked up at her. "Because that's the only way we can work together."

She lifted her eyes to the ceiling, hopefully taking a moment to consider my offer instead of coming up with a retaliation or rejection. "I have to meet with the cartel myself, or there is no plan. I'm not trying to be a stubborn pain in the ass like you think I am."

She set her back to the counter. Not the best position to be in, because I just might box her in and never let her leave that spot—not until she came to her senses.

"I don't have a death wish. Not really. I was scared of dying Saturday." She wet her lips, slightly shaking her head, calming down even more, which I needed to do as well. *"Y no soy un tonto imprudente."*

"Translate, please." The words grated out low and deep as I worked to resist my desire to cage her in.

"I'm not some reckless fool, like you also seem to think I am." She pursed her lips and frowned.

Standing this close and not touching her was like being told not to squint while looking up at the sun. An impossibility. I reached for her arm and slid my hand up to her biceps and gently held her. She tracked the movement, her dark lashes sweeping down to take in the sight. "I've never once thought you were a fool."

"And reckless?"

"Nothing you've done has been reckless, either. Just brave." I hated to admit that, but it was true. "That doesn't change the fact that the longer you stay in my life, the more I'm going to need heart pills."

She scrunched her nose, and I had to fight the good fight yet again not to lean forward, not to kiss the tip of that cute nose. "I better not stay in it long, then. I don't want to be bad for your heart."

Those words were much worse for my heart, but I kept my mouth shut, because I couldn't ask for a shot at forever after less than a week.

"We have to figure this out," she said softly.

"We will. The plan will—"

"No." She closed her eyes, set her hand on my wrist, guiding mine off her body.

Well, that stung. I let my arm fall back to my side and shook off the rejection.

"We can't think clearly around each other. You're not making the best decisions as team leader, are you?"

She had me there. All the way fucking there, in fact.

She kept her eyes sealed tight, as if she wouldn't get through what she needed to say if she had to look at me. "I've been committed to my mission for justice for thirteen months; then you came into my life, and I'm so incredibly grateful you saved me and want to help, but I . . ."

I backed up a few steps, waiting for her to finish. To kill me with what I felt coming. *More* rejection. Been there, done that. Over and over again. Starting at the age of six, when my dad left and never looked back.

I was used to it.

I could handle it.

It was fine. *I'm fine.*

"Just say it." I tossed my hat on the other counter and tore my hands through my hair, turning away from her.

"Aren't you worried, too? That this thing between us is interfering with the mission?" Her trembling voice compelled me to turn. Her eyes were open and on me now. "It's like someone voodooed us or something."

Now I was the one closing my eyes, unable to look at her. Unable to see her quivering lip and the chills coating her skin in the form of little ridges. "I know."

"Maybe we commit to not touching each other until after the mission is over so we can focus?" Her words reinvigorated me. They gave me life.

"What are you saying?" I kept my distance but opened my eyes as I waited for her to continue.

"After it's over, maybe we can explore this thing between us. Once we can think clearly without Ezra and the cartel between us, we can see if there's something here." She curled her fingers into her palms at her sides, quietly staring at me.

That wasn't rejection; it was being reasonable.

"Does that mean you'll at least consider a plan that doesn't center around you being bait to take down these assholes?" I was trying to meet her in the middle here, which was the best I could do when it came to her safety.

"As long as you'll agree to go with a plan that does involve me if it's a better one," she countered.

"Fine." That hurt me to say, but I didn't want her trying to take off and run again.

"Good." She tossed her thumb over her shoulder. "Should I get my laptop? We can get started on going over everything while we wait for the call to come in."

I picked up my hat and parked it backward. My eyes fell to her toned thighs. Memories of her on the counter this morning, with those gorgeous legs wrapped around my waist, hit my mind. *This is not going to be easy.* "We can't be alone together. If this is going to work, we need a barrier. Always."

"I agree." Her gaze flicked to the tattoo inside her forearm as if needing to recite the words to help her get through this.

Maybe I did, too. *You are your only limit.* I was about to say something else, probably nothing all that enlightening, but my phone began ringing in my pocket.

I removed it, and Seraphina looked at my screen, eyeing the name that appeared there. *Lainey.*

"Oh." There was jealousy in that little sound, and I was about to send the call to voicemail, but she stopped me. "You should talk to her. She might have something important to tell you." She met my eyes, giving me a nod. "I'm gonna grab my laptop and phone. Get the guys back in here, and we'll meet up in a few minutes in the living room, okay?"

"Yeah, sure." I waited for her to leave, and on Lainey's second attempt to get ahold of me, I finally answered. "Hey, what's up?" I set my hand on the counter for support as I waited for her to give me more orders I wouldn't want to hear.

She cut right to it, her voice dry. "There's been a change in plans. Director Hernandez will reach out soon, but he's in a meeting with the DNI, Director Johnson."

Johnson was the director of National Intelligence, which meant he sat at the top of every one of the nation's spy agencies. That news, and this call, felt ominous as fuck.

"What's going on?" My patience was already worn down from my confrontation with Seraphina, and I had a feeling my head was about to really spin now.

"The task force has been shut down. The plug has been pulled. Orders came from up the chain of command." She leveled me with the shocking news.

I shoved away from the counter, my heart racing all over again as I noticed Alex and Reed making their way back into the room. "I don't understand."

"Your mission is over. You're being ordered to return to the States without the asset."

The asset? Seraphina was far more than an asset. "Spell this out for me: Why's the task force being disbanded, and why's my mission being called off?"

Alex caught my attention, his eyes widening in surprise.

A long sigh from Lainey crackled over the line. "We're not being told anything other than to close up shop, stop looking into the Sokolovs, and Director Johnson said another agency will be taking over. We're forbidden to be involved from this point on."

Another agency? Like the Company? "Just tell me the CIA isn't coming here for her." I did not need that problem. I already had enough to deal with.

"I know you won't actually come home," she said in a low voice. "You won't leave a woman in danger out there on her own. It's not who you are."

She was right about that.

"I know you're not ready to trust or forgive me, but I'm going to do my best to earn it."

"And that means?" I gritted out, my stomach banding tight.

"It means I'm going to try and buy you some time with Director Hernandez, and I won't keep you in the dark. If I find out something, you'll be the first to know." She ended the call after that, and I lowered the phone as Seraphina reappeared, coming up behind the guys.

She looked at Reed and Alex, then back at me, her eyes narrowing as she read the room, the what-the-fuck energy passing through it. "Shit, what'd I miss?"

CHAPTER TWENTY-THREE

Ryder

"Lainey, she said . . ." I lost my train of thought with Seraphina's curious eyes on me the moment I said my ex's name.

She was as jealous of my ex as I was of hers. And I was jealous of all of them, not just her last one, because surely there'd been more than one ex who'd ever been lucky enough to date her.

One day you'll walk away. Everyone always leaves. I shook my head, angry those words had infil'ed my head.

And now I was thinking back to the Iraq War. Quite the transition, but a pastor who used to visit base always told us how to tell the difference between evil and good thoughts: *The devil gives you problems, and God gives you solutions.*

"Ryder?" Reed calling my name jarred me from my head and away from the thoughts planted there by the devil—trying to ruin something with this woman before we even had a chance to start.

"You okay?" Seraphina remained on the other side of the breakfast bar, her laptop and phone in front of her, eyes on me.

We definitely needed more than my friends as barriers. We needed counters and furniture. All the fucking things. With how I was feeling,

I still might mount and climb every obstacle to get to her. Then toss any remaining barriers, like my teammates, out the window.

"Bro?" Alex was before me now, clapping in front of my face. "We lost you, man." He cupped the back of my neck, drawing me closer, trying to bring me back to the room. To the issue. To the mission. "You see a ghost or something?"

"Not funny." I'd probably prefer that, though. An apparition was easier to explain than what was happening to me now.

"Well . . ." Alex let go of me but didn't move. "You look like you've snapped, crackled, and motherfucking popped."

"Also not funny." And he *also* needed to stop blocking my view of Seraphina.

"What's going on? Why's the mission being called off?" he asked, turning to the side so I could see everyone now.

I quickly sped through the facts before I lost my head again, sharing what Lainey had told me.

"What the hell does this all mean?" Alex asked while rounding the breakfast bar, returning to his seat.

"It means the CIA is probably gunning for the Sokolovs themselves, and as soon as they got wind of the task force, they made a call and had it killed," Reed said, opening his laptop. "They don't play well with others, and they don't want the task force getting in their way. So they took them—and by association, *us*—out of the game."

"They must have a reason to do this to warrant the director of National Intelligence executing those orders." I filled up a glass of cold water and guzzled it.

"You really trust Lainey will come through for us?" Reed asked.

"She wants to make amends." I refilled my glass, deciding I was dehydrated, not crazy. Not obsessed.

Okay, that was bullshit, and I couldn't lie to myself. I was hooked and ready to go all in with Seraphina.

"Yeah, well, after what she did, screw that," Alex bit out.

"What'd she do?" Her gaze flew my way, and it took me a moment to rewind what Alex had said to understand why she was giving me some serious puppy-dog eyes.

I set my hands on the counter next to my glass. There was so much tension in my upper back that it was pushing up my spine and all the way to my temples.

"I have a few contacts at the Agency that owe me some favors." Reed with the redirect, saving me from butchering my way through answering her.

If I told her Lainey was pregnant with Jeff's baby, she'd think I still had feelings for her, and that wasn't close to being true. I didn't want her getting in her head again, believing I was in rebound territory.

"My only concern is if I make calls, that I might also make waves," Reed went on. "We need someone who has connections that won't draw attention to the fact we're not leaving Mexico as ordered."

Someone like Carter? Because now that we were being pulled off the mission, we'd no longer have help from Uncle Sam. No QRF to save our necks since we were here of our own accord.

The drawback of being a three-man team without US support meant we wouldn't have enough bodies to go up against our enemies, and we were more than likely looking at a few enemies.

"It's a good thing I have a plan to fall back on, then, right?" Seraphina's words had me looking at her.

Back to wanting to be bait? Not that she'd ever relinquished that idea.

"Are you two going to fight again? If so, I'll come back when you're done. Giving me flashbacks of my parents going at it as a kid, and I—" Reed immediately dropped his words when we all turned his way.

"No fighting—and please stay." Seraphina dialed in on Reed, and he gave her a small nod, then reset his focus to his screen as if he hadn't just shared something about himself that none of us knew. The man was Fort Knox about his past. "Ángel should be calling soon, and maybe while we wait on, um, Lainey to reach back out with news, I could use that time to fill you in on what I've learned since working for Ezra."

Stalling on that bait plan of yours. Nicely played. She was right, though. The more I knew about Ezra and his operation, the better I could craft a plan that wouldn't involve her winding up in the middle of danger. "Thank you."

"You have the floor, ma'am." Alex smiled at her, and she remained standing but opened her laptop. Once it was powered on, she swiveled it to the side so we could all see the screen.

She gave us an introduction to drug trafficking as if we weren't aware, but I wasn't about to stop her. She was talking animatedly with her hands, and I loved it. She could lecture me all day, every day about anything she wanted to, and I'd ace the fucking test with her as my instructor.

"So, you're saying Ezra was able to slowly take over for the cartel because he's a better dealmaker?" Alex asked her once she was done with her speech. "That he negotiated better deals with the suppliers for the chemical precursors they sold to produce fentanyl? He made them more competitive offers, and in doing so, he undercut the Moraleses."

"Right. He could take out the Moraleses without having to lift an actual finger against them." She turned the laptop around, typed something in, then showed us a map of the Eastern Seaboard of the United States. "Ezra's main goal has always been to interrupt the current drug trade and take over, cutting Mexico out altogether. Basically, remove anyone he saw as a middleman to a billion-dollar business."

"How so?" I asked her.

"Instead of using the trade routes the cartels had a monopoly on, Ezra—or whoever he works for—devised a way to bring the chemicals into the US directly and bypass Mexico." She clicked on the city of Wilmington, North Carolina. "Smaller ports have much less scrutiny and police than the big ones. So Ezra tested his theory, and it worked."

"What do you mean?" I followed up again.

"Ezra has smaller fishing boats meet up with the larger ships that are owned by the suppliers before they reach the ports. They transfer everything from the ships to the small boats. No one stops a fisherman docking at the pier and checks what they're carrying. Ezra is able to move twice the product this way and remains totally undetected and independent of the cartel's trafficking routes. All without a single bust. Now *he* has the monopoly on trade."

Maybe it's fate I ran into Hudson Ashford in DC the other day? Given the new project he was working on, it was possible he could help us out. "If Ezra's established a safe way to move drugs here without having to go through Mexico, then my guess is, he's moving more than just drugs. Or at least plans to."

"He did have a guy connected to a terrorist cell at his party Saturday," Reed reminded me, "which was why we were there in the first place. He could be getting into the arms business next."

"And that might be why the CIA is involved and is taking over. Director Johnson would prioritize terrorism and possible WMDs getting on US soil over drugs." That made sense, but that also meant the CIA would be interested in talking to Seraphina. And if they called us off the mission, it was because they wanted to intercept her themselves.

"China's clearly a main supplier," Reed said. "But are we assuming Russia might also be connected to this, given Ezra's wife's been making trips to Moscow?"

"The Russians could be behind this, and the Sokolovs are the middleman making it happen," Seraphina continued with his line of thought. "Nina's the one with the established relationship in Russia." She clicked open a file and slid her laptop over to Reed. "Everything I have on her and her brother, Andrej, is there. It's mostly theories, though, as well as why I think her brother was killed."

"We need to divide and conquer. Split up the research," I said as her phone began vibrating from a text. "I thought he was supposed to call."

"It's an unknown number, but it's him," she confirmed, opening the text to read it out loud. *"I'll help you, but it can't be here."* She read the next message from him: *"Head to San José. When you arrive, text me, and we'll discuss next steps."*

"San José?" I dragged my hand down my throat at yet another curveball.

"Ezra must've made contact with the Moraleses; then Ángel told his family he had someone who wanted to meet them, and they obviously knew about me because of Ezra. And either Ezra or the cartel connected me to Martín, and they're drawing me outside of Mexico so he can't help."

"And the fact they picked Costa Rica of all places?" I shook my head, thankful all over again I'd bumped into this woman that night in Miami and she wasn't here alone.

"Right," she whispered. "It can't be a coincidence I'm being asked to go to the place where Ezra's brother-in-law was hiding out before he was murdered, after my family was . . ." She swallowed. ". . . killed."

CHAPTER TWENTY-FOUR

Seraphina

"Ángel may turn on us—or already has for the right price." Reed said what I refused to believe. "He could've told his family we're with you as well. He saw Ryder and Alex at the club."

"No." I walked away from the breakfast bar, facing away from everyone. "I don't believe that. If he was turning on me, he'd have told me I had to come alone." Plus, Martín trusted he was safe, and I trusted Martín.

"All possibilities have to be on the table, including assuming he double-crossed you or that he will." Ryder's deep voice had me turning around, and I acknowledged his remark in the only way I could think of for now.

I conceded with a nod of surrender. As much as I wanted to believe there was no way Martín's judgment about someone could be wrong, it was better to be safe than sorry. "So what do we do now? We're going to Costa Rica, right?" Why'd I phrase that as a question? I should have been firm and put my foot down.

Ryder looked over at Reed. "Talk to me about Costa Rica. Bullet points," he requested.

Is that a yes? I did my best not to run over and throw my arms around the growly man, thanking him for not making me fight him on it. He hadn't technically agreed or answered me, so I'd wait. I was also the one who'd just said we shouldn't get physical. *So hands to myself it is.* Not my favorite idea, but it was probably needed.

Reed twisted on his barstool to look back and forth between everyone, then took point on answering Ryder. "Limited extradition treaties there. Makes it a safe haven for fugitives. High number of tourists, so it's easy to blend in. Law enforcement has limited resources there. Dense rainforests and remote areas make it easy to hide evidence. Then you have coastal access to both the Pacific and the Caribbean to smuggle goods." He didn't even need to pause for a breath as he sped through more details. "Plenty of jungle hideaways. Underwater stashes near the Nicoya Peninsula are known dumping grounds for evidence. And as for San José, you could easily bribe a local official to look the other way."

"Also, neutral territory for the Sokolovs and Moraleses to meet. Martín can't go there, either," I let them know. "He'd be arrested the second the plane landed."

"Why?" Ryder asked.

"He may or may not . . ." Cue awkward pause. ". . . have killed their police commissioner a few years ago." I lifted my hand and patted the air. "In his defense, the commissioner worked for an arms dealer, so he was just taking out the trash. I don't know if Ezra or the cartel has even connected me to Martín, but regardless, it'd make sense Ezra wouldn't want to come to hostile Morales-controlled territory here in Mexico."

Ryder stroked his jawline, smoothing his fingertips along the scruff, eyes on the floor. Thinking-mode activated?

"Who do we know in Costa Rica?" Alex asked. "We're going to need a safe house, access to a helo, an armory."

"Same man who helped us locate Seraphina is probably our best bet in helping set us up in San José," Ryder said.

Who was this mystery person who was a mutual friend of Martín's?

Also, I really needed to take a moment and text Martín, let him know what was going on. Had Ryder and his teammates not come to my rescue down here, what would I have done? Plan B wouldn't have worked if it meant I had to go to Costa Rica alone. I'd have zero chance of survival.

"Carter's in Switzerland right now at a hotel he acquired last year, but I'll see if he can help again. He might be able to arrange safe transport for us as well, so we don't need to fly commercial," Ryder responded, and this was sounding more and more like a definite yes. "I also have a SEAL friend I bumped into the other day who specializes in hunting drug traffickers. I'm going to reach out and see what he knows and if he can help."

I looked out the window at the view of the city. So much for exploring the town. Not that Ryder had planned to let me, anyway. "We're leaving today, right?"

Ryder retrieved his phone, keeping his eyes on it instead of me. "I don't know if you should come with us."

I probably skipped about three steps in my rush to get to him, also banging my knee into the furniture on my way, so that was great. I concealed a wince from the pain, waiting for him to acknowledge that I was standing in front of him.

"If Ezra and the cartel are in Costa Rica, it's safer for you to stay in Mexico." Ryder's intense eyes breezed up to mine. "We'll take you to Martín's before we head there. He can protect you."

"Like hell you're doing that," I rasped. "I'm coming. Ezra won't show up unless I'm there, and you know it."

"I'll find them without you. All of them. It's what I do. I find people." His tone wasn't authoritative or harsh—it was worse. It was numb and detached.

Two emotions I knew well, so I recognized them in others immediately. He was trying to do exactly what I asked him to do so we could focus on the mission: build a wall between us. "I'm not staying behind. You know I'll never agree to that plan. You have to know that."

He pinched the bridge of his nose and closed his eyes. Yeah, numb and detached weren't easy to maintain if they weren't coming from a place of pain. He was already failing.

"What if they did connect me to Martín and they send a hit team to his place when they realize I'm not in Costa Rica? How will you feel if innocent people are killed so they can get to me? How will you feel if I die?" I swallowed the moment his hand fell and eye contact was made.

"Don't do this to me." His voice was rough and a little broken. Like shards of glass had scraped across both our bodies and we'd bleed out together. Right on this floor.

"Who do you trust the most to keep me safe?" I couldn't back down—and in truth, as much as I loved Martín like family, I hadn't felt as safe as I did being with Ryder since my father was alive to watch over me.

He quietly stared at me before saying in a low, deep voice, "You know the answer to that."

"I hate to say this, because I don't want to piss you off, but I think she should come with us." Alex corralled Ryder's attention right along with mine, and his words also helped break the staring contest we'd been engaged in. A battle of wills and stubbornness.

"I agree," Reed tossed out without looking away from the screen. "She started this whole thing, and she should be part of it when it finishes. It's not our place to take her revenge away from her. She knew the risks thirteen months ago, and she knows them now."

For not being a people person, he just became my favorite one. "Thank you."

"But for the record," Reed continued, slowly shifting on his stool to look over at us, "the odds anything bad will happen to you have drastically decreased now that you have that man in your corner."

"Reed's right," Alex said to Ryder. "You know he is. You're a control freak for a reason, and it's kept us all alive so far. Now, control freak your way through this new problem and find a solution that involves her coming with us."

And I love you, too. Thank you. I couldn't believe it, but I had his teammates on my side. Now I just needed this stubborn man to get over here, too.

Ryder's jaw visibly clenched as he lifted his eyes to the ceiling, his arms remaining rigid blocks of muscles at his sides. "So help me . . ."

"I'll take that as a yes, that I'm coming with you." Not waiting for him to acknowledge me, I spun around toward my two unlikely heroes and smiled my gratitude.

"Not so fast, miss." Ryder banded an arm around my stomach and swiftly, but somehow still gentlemanly, had me about-facing his way.

"Yes?" I breathed, meeting his eyes.

He lightly shook his head. "*If* you come with us, then consider yourself part of the team. Delta Four."

"And that means?" I whispered, because I knew he wasn't asking me to hold a rifle and engage in direct battle. Hell would have to freeze over, then the sky would have to rain puppies, before he'd allow me into a gunfight.

"It means you have to take orders from the team leader and do what he says without objection," Reed interpreted for me in a matter-of-fact voice.

This was truly our meet-in-the-middle moment. I supposed I could place my trust in this Delta operator if he was willing to let me join his team. "Fine, you have my word."

"You broke your word before," he was quick to remind me.

"That was different. I'll keep it this time." This next part took effort, but I managed to get it out. "I'll behave and follow orders."

I wasn't sure if he was ready to believe me, but instead of protesting, he took things in an unexpected route. "Alex, you're now Delta One for this mission." He straightened his posture, stepping away from me, putting eyes on him. "Consider yourself in charge."

"What? Why?" Alex came over, looking back and forth between us.

"Because I . . ." Ryder shook his head. "I'm not in control of . . ." He cleared his throat. This wasn't easy for him to say or do. "I don't trust myself to make the right decisions, got it?" He leveled his friend with a hard look, one that said *Don't make me tell you twice or explain more.*

"Yeah, okay." Alex blinked a few times. "Well, then, my first order as your boss is to go call Carter so we can exfil out of here and get to Costa Rica A-S-A-fucking-P."

"You're going to enjoy this, aren't you?" Ryder asked, a gruff tone to his voice.

Alex smirked, winked at me, then focused back on Ryder. "Absolutely."

CHAPTER TWENTY-FIVE

Seraphina

In the air

I closed my eyes and prayed. *Because damn.* As of ten minutes ago, I'd unlocked a new fear: flying in small planes on a cloudy, windy day.

This was my first time in a plane where I could see our pilot, too. I didn't find that comforting at all. Way too many buttons and switches in my line of sight.

"Don't worry, we have enough chutes if we need to jump." I had no clue if Alex was making a joke, but I couldn't open my eyes to get a read on him.

We hit another air pocket—or whatever the technical term was for them—on our way up, and my stomach dropped yet again as we were jostled around in this toylike plane. Was this thing actually meant for jumping out of, not landing? *Hell, maybe it is?*

Working up the nerve, I pried open my eyes to check the window to see if we'd yet to puncture through the cloudy sky.

Nope. Since my favorite distraction wasn't sitting next to me, I shut my eyes and tried to think about something else.

Of course my thoughts landed back on the flying death trap in the sky. The ride was courtesy of this Carter guy, but maybe flying commercial would've been safer, even if we ran the risk of Ezra tracking the flight.

I'd been in the middle of texting Martín about the change in plans when Ryder had returned to the living room after making his call to Carter in private. He'd let us know Carter would secure safe passage for us. But if this was Carter's definition of *safe*, then what was unsafe in his eyes?

Ryder had also shared the news that Carter would set us up with transport, weapons, and a place to stay upon arrival. Who was this guy? Batman?

And it didn't stop there.

The gifts kept on gifting.

Our mystery man—well, not a mystery to Ryder or Martín—would also work on finding a crew to send us for backup should we need an assist once in San José. Apparently, Batman was busy doing other hero-things and couldn't come himself. It was almost too bad; I'd love to meet the man who could whip up Black Hawks out of thin air. (Did I mention he'd have one of those for us, too? Because, yup, apparently).

I'd been in a rush to change and pack, worried Ryder would switch to his default setting of overprotective and refuse to let me come, so I forgot to finish my texting conversation I'd been in the middle of with Martín. He'd called me on my way to the airport, so I filled him in then.

Martín promised I was in good hands if Carter was arranging everything for us in Costa Rica, and he agreed it was better for me to go with Ryder than stay behind, but he hated not being able to come and help. I'd keep in touch with him, updating him once we were there.

I was still in awe of how fast everything had been thrown together, not even two hours after the text from Ángel. Plan C was now in action, which was kind of perfect, given Batman's help and his real name began with a C.

Fate. Everything is happening as ordained. I had a feeling my parents and brother were looking out for me. Sending whoever and whatever I needed my way, especially Ryder. I chose to believe that, at least. *And that means we'll survive this flight. I didn't make it this far to die in a plane crash.*

A former Navy SEAL held our lives in his hands right now. Owen York happened to be on vacation with his family not far from us in Mexico, so Carter called him for the favor. Carter had even wrangled this not-so-lovely private plane for us to use.

Just like that. Done deal. All good to go.

Owen's family stayed back at their resort, so I didn't have a chance to meet them, but maybe one day I could thank his wife for lending us her husband on short notice.

I kept telling myself, though, that we were safe with a SEAL in the pilot's seat. But also, since when did Navy SEALs fly planes?

At another hard bump that knocked us around, I squeezed my chair's arms even tighter, gritting down on my back teeth.

Alex patted the top of my hand, which did nothing to ease my nerves.

Ryder had asked him to sit next to me when we'd boarded, continuing to honor the request I was currently regretting—to keep some distance between us.

I should've asked for a pause in that plan, postponing the start time until after I felt the ground beneath my shoes again. Because I really needed Ryder next to me.

"We're good," Alex promised. "No sweat."

"Allll the sweat," I cried out, my voice embarrassingly squeaking. "Can someone distract me?"

"You should open your eyes. You're missing the view." Alex nudged me in the side. "There's a volcano out the window."

"Just tell me about it instead," I whispered, barely opening my mouth to speak. Seriously, how had I survived working for Ezra all that time, and now a small plane was what put my heart into overdrive the most? Well, second to Ryder. That man seemed to have rewired my entire existence altogether, especially my heart's rhythm.

"Reed probably knows something about volcanoes," Alex prompted, while I worked to steady my breathing.

"A thing or two," Reed mumbled.

I gulped. "Anything about the ones down there?"

"There's a legend about them, yeah. An Aztec story." Reed was sitting next to Ryder behind us in the four-seater plane, so his voice was close.

Alex laughed. "I swear, the man knows more about the dead than the living."

"You want a story or not?" Reed shot back.

"Yes, please," I said before Alex could piss him off.

"Fine." Reed was quiet for a moment, and I hoped that meant he hadn't changed his mind. A few seconds later, he finally shared, "The story is about a princess who fell in love with a warrior, but she died from grief when she was told he was killed in battle. When Popocatépetl returned home and discovered the woman he loved was dead, he carried her to a mountain, lit a torch, and stayed with her there to watch over her forever. Whenever the volcano erupts, legend says it's Popocatépetl remembering the woman he loves."

"Fucking A, man. Don't ever do story hour for kids or something. That was depressing as fuck," Alex said with a laugh. "And how the hell do you know that? I was expecting some scientific bullshit from you." I could feel him twisting around, probably looking back at Reed. "But a princess?" He chuckled again. "You need to get laid, I swear."

Reed didn't respond, but these two had managed to accomplish one thing with their joking: calming me down. "Thank you. I do feel better now."

"So you going to open your eyes?" Alex asked me, but I kept them squeezed shut and shook my head.

"I don't feel *that* much better."

"Let the bumps put you to sleep instead of make you nervous," he suggested. "I have a feeling we've got a long day ahead of us, so rest while you can."

"Is that an order?" I teased.

Alex didn't answer, and when a hand gently gripped my arm, I went still at the prickle of awareness that it was Ryder, reaching between the seats to touch me.

He had to be leaning forward, because I felt his breath by my ear, and my body responded, erupting in chills.

"Do what he says." He kept hold of me and, in a much huskier voice, murmured into my ear, "And that's an order from *me*."

CHAPTER TWENTY-SIX

Ryder

San José, Costa Rica

Why the hell did I never learn Spanish? Am I too old to learn now? I was eavesdropping on Seraphina talking to our host as if I could actually understand instead of focusing on the conversation happening in front of me in English.

Owen was talking to Carter over the phone, so I took a moment to see if Ángel had texted Seraphina back.

Upon landing, she'd let him know we'd arrived; then I quietly opened my palm, a silent request to hang on to her phone. I also had Reed check it before we'd even left Mexico, ensuring she wasn't being tracked by anyone.

Still nothing. It'd only been thirty minutes since the plane touched down, so I wouldn't jump to worst-case scenarios as to why there was a delay.

I pocketed the phone, training my attention on the Balinese-style villa, Casa Paraíso, where my team would be staying for however long it took to complete our mission here. The place sat on top of a hill, with a view of Santa Ana, a province of San José, in the distance.

While Owen wrapped up his call, I stole another look at Seraphina. A goddess standing beneath the sunlight, talking enthusiastically with her hands to the hostess, someone Carter had promised we could trust.

This whole op was starting to feel like one giant trust mission, and it was taking all my effort to do exactly that—trust people, the process. Also, trust myself in making the right decisions, like handing over my team leader role, for one.

"Yeah, yeah, of course. Will do. Later." Owen ended the call with Carter and turned toward me, which meant I had to stop staring at Seraphina. "Carter's team, Falcon Falls Security, is already on another op on the other side of the world. But if anyone can pull off a miracle and help out, you know it's him. He's trying to move things around so he can come himself."

I wasn't about to ask Carter to fly from Switzerland and stop his own work for the sake of our mission, even if I wanted him to join in. "I'll figure something out. This may not even be our final destination." I had no idea what Ángel had cooked up for us here or whose side he really was on, and that didn't sit well with me. "You didn't need to drive out here with us. You did enough leaving your family to fly us here."

"Yeah, well, I wanted to make sure you arrived safe."

"Didn't you tell me you also promised your wife you wouldn't get into any gunfights on your quick trip away?" I smiled.

Owen hooked his aviator sunglasses to the front of his shirt. The sun was no longer in our eyes from where we were standing on the driveway. "And I did keep my word."

"We could've run into shit on the way out here."

"Which is why I joined you," he said with a laugh. "But we both know if Carter said we'd be good, we'd—"

"Be good." And he was right. Carter even had power over the skies, as in he'd made sure we didn't have drones overhead watching us leave the airport to get here. Carter, on the other hand, did. He'd had eyes up there tracking our movement to be certain no one was tracking ours. Regardless of that fact, I'd still wanted Seraphina in the SUV with me, instead of in the other with Reed and Alex, en route here. She'd sat in the back while I drove, and Owen rode shotgun.

She'd spent the ride asking Owen questions, filling in the awkward gaps of silence, and I'd listened to every word as I drove. The sounds she made between pauses. The way she'd roll her *R*'s a bit more even though she didn't have an accent when talking, which I'd found sexy as fuck.

"A helo pad and Black Hawk at a villa. A beautiful sight." Owen's comment reset my focus back to where we were, and I followed his gaze.

"Yeah, no pilot, though. Maybe you should stay after all. Forget what I said."

"Well, I'm in Mexico for a few more days, so if you can't find yourself another pilot and you wind up needing one, you have my cell now; just call me."

"I don't know your wife, but I'd prefer not to piss her off." I tipped my head in the direction of the helo. "On that note, you should get back to sipping mai tais on the beach."

"Roger that." He set two fingers to his head, giving me a quick salute as his goodbye. "I mean it, though—call me if you need me. My wife is forgiving, I promise."

"Let's hope I don't have to find out, but thanks." I waved him off, and he headed over to the other SUV to leave.

When I turned around, Seraphina and our hostess were walking my way.

"Señor Dominick had me arrange everything you'd need," the woman told me. "Clothes and food." She removed her sunglasses and smiled. "An armory."

"Thank you, we appreciate that." I returned her smile and nodded, catching sight of Reed off in the distance wrapping up a perimeter sweep with Alex, clearing the property and home before we'd enter. "Does Dominick normally stay here when he's in town?"

"Yes, and I can assure you of my discretion. Señor Dominick's also footed the bill. Stay as long as you need."

Seraphina sidestepped me, and at the realization she was planning to go for her bag sitting by our other SUV, I quickly beat her to it. Distance between us needed or not, chivalry wasn't about to be dead on my watch.

She gave me a gracious little nod instead of trying to take the bag from me.

"The living room and kitchen windows are made of bulletproof glass. Same with the primary bedroom. Can never be too cautious, right?" Yeah, this woman knew a thing or two about Carter and the company he kept. "Well, you have my number. Don't hesitate if you need anything."

That was the general theme of the evening, and I appreciated all the offers. *Anything to keep Seraphina safe.* Even if it meant pissing off Owen's wife, I'd do it.

The hostess said goodbye and gave Seraphina a hug. Then she patted my shoulder and went to her Mercedes.

And now we're alone together. Great. I cleared my throat, rocking back on the heels of my boots while looking up at the sky, feigning interest in the bird flying overhead.

"Beautiful day, despite the skies being so angry on our flight over," she murmured. "Bumpiest ride of my life. I guess I should be thankful we didn't have to jump from it, though. I bet you've jumped from quite a few planes in your life."

I lowered my chin to find her eyes and smiled. "Always on purpose."

She parted her lips, her tongue flipping up to cover her teeth. God, that was too sexy. She stared over at the villa as if in a daze, running her hands up and down her arms over her lightweight jean jacket. It was late October but still fairly warm out, so I doubted her shivering was from the temperature. "This place was on my bucket list to visit before . . . well, you know."

Yeah, before Andrej was murdered here. "What else is on that list of yours?"

She looked over at me, her hands diving to her sides. "Nothing now. Wiped it clean. Blank slate. Hoping to start over and make a new list once this whole mess is done."

I wanted that for her more than I could express. I gulped, working to hide the unexpected emotion crowding me, moving up from my chest into my throat.

"So, um, I take it nothing from Ángel yet, or you'd have led with that?"

"Nada."

She playfully lifted her brows a few times. "So you do speak Spanish, huh?"

"I know about ten other phrases, none of which are good."

"Let me guess: Alex taught you a bunch of naughty ones."

"A few dirty jokes and curses, yeah."

"Mm-hmm. Just like I thought. He really reminds me of . . ." She closed her eyes and her lower lip quivered—and shit, her emotions weren't hiding like mine were; they were now on display for me to see.

And on that note, there it went: my heart. I was ready to give it to her if she wanted it.

Unable to stop myself, because she was clearly drawing some type of parallel between her brother and Alex, I dropped her bag and reached for her.

I secured a hold of her wrist and drew her into my arms the way I wished I could've done on the plane when she'd been shaking and nervous.

She wrapped her arms around me, smashing her cheek to my chest as I rested my chin on top of her head. She was the perfect height for me to hold her like this. Perfect in every way, actually.

"I know we're supposed to keep our distance, but I'm going to override that decision for a minute," I said, keeping her tight in my embrace.

"Such a control freak," she said while sniffling, her words vibrating into my chest. "Don't ever change."

CHAPTER TWENTY-SEVEN

Ryder

While in our new command center, which was the office, I reread Ángel's response that had just come in.

Seraphina was off exploring the villa, so I'd have to find her and fill her in.

I'd demanded she sleep in the only bedroom with bulletproof windows. I did my best not to go as far as offering my body next to hers as an additional shield.

"Five hours until he wants to meet," I let Alex and Reed know. "He'll text the location thirty minutes beforehand, but he didn't say she had to come alone." Not that I was sure any of us would be going at all.

Alex checked his watch. "So he wants this to be a zero dark thirty meeting?"

Yeah, timing-wise, that placed us just a half hour after midnight. Not that it'd be ideal to send Seraphina to a meeting with a former cartel member at any time of day. The fact she'd gone solo to that club the other night would forever haunt me.

"Is this a meeting or mission?" Reed raised a valid point. We had no clue what we were actually getting ourselves into if we did go, because what if tonight was a trap?

"Yeah, that question doesn't do wonders for my mood." *Or my heart rate.*

"Thirty minutes won't give us enough time to scout out the place to ensure it's safe," Alex said, voicing what the three of us were all well aware of, and that fact made my skin itch, right along with my trigger finger.

"No movement from Ezra. He's still in Miami. He could make it in time if he were to board a plane now. We'll have a heads-up if he goes to the airport, though," I shared. "No location for Nina yet. Something doesn't add up. We should've found her by now."

"We've been a bit preoccupied here. She was less of a priority," Reed reminded me. "I'll switch gears and work on tracking her down if you want?"

"You're the boss right now," I said to Alex. "You decide what to do."

He settled his hands on his hips, staring at the tiled floor. "Where are we at with that other friend of yours you reached out to before we flew here?"

"If Hudson can help, he will." I'd had Reed encrypt Seraphina's files and send them over to him earlier today, and he promised he'd assist. Between him and Carter, I felt good about our odds of getting to the bottom of this situation much faster than we could solo.

"So what's your take on this, and what we should do?" Reed asked Alex since I'd deferred to him.

"I don't know." Alex bowed his head. It was never easy being the one in charge with lives on the line. "Part of me thinks we should focus on figuring out if Nina's brother was in Costa Rica for a reason other than hiding out. And if he was, maybe that reason will help us understand why we're here now."

"So, focus on Nina's brother," Reed said with a nod, and I did my best to bite my tongue and get settled into the position of Delta Two and accept orders instead of give them.

"You take Nina's brother, and I'll keep looking into Ángel. I still have concerns he may be playing both sides and he'll ultimately swing whichever way he decides works in his favor," Alex concluded, and I was on the same page.

"I'll take point on Nina, then," I suggested. "Even if I have to reach out to Carter for another favor, which I hate doing, but—"

"Doesn't he have one of the world's best cyber experts on his team? Gwen someone-or-other?"

How'd Reed know about her? I didn't remember ever mentioning Gwen to him.

At my confused look, Reed smiled and shrugged. "What? I'm an admirer of her work."

"Yeah, well, have you heard about her dad?" I laughed. "Wyatt Pierson?"

"You're serious? Wyatt's Gwen's father?" Reed swiped a hand through his hair. "The man's a legend."

"Leave it to one of the world's best snipers to have one of the world's best hackers as a kid," I remarked. "But yeah, we may need Gwen to help us with this. She's already juggling two cases for him, but I have a feeling she can handle three."

"Is Carter still trying to scratch together more bodies to send us for help?" Alex asked.

"He's working on it, yeah. But no one will get here in time tonight. So we need to ensure this meeting is just a fucking meeting and not an op."

"That sounded awfully order-like." Alex smirked. "You sure you don't want the job back?"

I tossed Seraphina's burner on the table alongside the leather couch. "No, I'm good." I turned toward the door, curious what Seraphina was currently doing. "She doesn't join this meeting tonight unless we can assure it's not a trap."

"Also, order-like." Alex winked, and I rolled my eyes.

"Fuck off." I lifted my chin his way. "And that is an order." I motioned to the door. "I'm going to check on her and make some calls." I extracted myself from the office, eager to go see what she was up to.

I found her in the kitchen before a cutting board, chopping a pepper. She had hockey on the TV, of all fucking things, but it was muted. Music played from the corner speakers, and she was swaying her hips to it while slicing and dicing.

I remained stuck in the entranceway, mesmerized by the scene, *almost forgetting that the sport I despised with a passion was on the screen.*

The music was in Spanish, and the way this woman moved her body . . . God help me and the mission. Help save me from drawing her around into my arms. For her, I'd even embarrass myself and attempt to dance.

She set down the knife, no longer moving to the beat, then looked over her shoulder at me.

"Don't stop on my behalf." I folded my arms and leaned against the wall, crossing my ankle over my other boot.

"I, um . . ." She locked eyes with me. "Dancing makes as much sense to me as math. It's comforting. The beats turn into numbers in my head." She lightly chuckled, then faced the counter again and moved on from a pepper to a yellow onion. "I thought I'd cook us dinner. It's getting late, and none of us have eaten. I'm not going to be of much use on the research end."

"The guys have the research covered, don't worry." *And I should be making calls.* "Dinner isn't necessary, but it's appreciated."

"Nothing too fancy. Just *arroz y frijoles*. Rice and beans. Side of roasted peppers and some veggies."

"Sounds perfect. Thank you." My gaze casually drifted over to the TV on the other counter. It was wild how memories could create physical pain even so many years later, but now my chest hurt and my stomach turned.

Hockey. Fuck that sport.

"The season just started," she said, somehow realizing my eyes weren't on her but the game, despite the fact she wasn't looking at me. "My brother liked to watch it, so it reminds me of him, and I tune in on occasion."

I closed my eyes, needing to let go of the hurt inside me because her pain was much worse than mine.

"I know nothing about it. Sticks and pucks. And the players seem to do some erotic-looking stretches on the ice as a warm-up. That's about it."

Her last words made my lips slip into something shocking: a smile. I never smiled when it came to anything hockey related.

"Hip and groin stretch, I think," she said while swiping away a tear. I wasn't sure if it was an onion-related tear or from remembering her brother.

"Onions always make my mom cry."

"Same." Still holding the knife, she pivoted around to look at me. "Are you okay?"

"You're the one with tears in your eyes, not me." I set my other boot back to the floor and straightened my posture.

"Yeah, well, you look a little grouchy."

Way to call me out on the truth. "I'm fine," I lied, because hockey made her remember her brother, and her brother was dead when he should've been alive and thriving, so I had no plans to tell her I was grouchy because of a sport on TV.

So yeah, I'd be good. Fine. For her, I'd be anything and everything she needed me to be. I'd even help her cut onions and find out if they made me cry, too.

"Need a hand?" I deflected, even though I was supposed to be making calls.

"As much as I'd love to have an assist, I should probably brave these onions alone because you have more pressing things to do."

Right, I should also tell you about that text. I shook off my thoughts, tucked away my hate for hockey, and pressed forward. I let her know everything discussed in the office with Alex and Reed.

Knife down again, she turned to the side, resting her hip against the counter. She pointed her beautiful brown eyes on me, quietly waiting for me to get to what she assumed I'd soon say: the ultimatum that hell would have to freeze over before I let her meet with Ángel, unless I was convinced it was safe for her.

"I need you to trust me," she said, breaking the silence. "Ángel will have our backs. He's not like his family, okay? He won't set us up."

"But will he be okay with them dying? His uncle? Brother? Cousin?" From what I'd learned, his parents were long since gone, and his dad's brother had taken over the business along with Ángel's older brother.

"Yes. Maybe." She wrung her hands together. "Probably."

Mm-hmm. Very confident. "Why does he want to meet so late, and why's he waiting until the last minute to give us a heads-up as to where we're going to chat?"

She opened her mouth as if ready to challenge me, but she must've changed her mind, because she resumed cutting the onion.

"Well, I need to go make some calls. We'll talk about this later."

I started to leave, but she called out, "Ryder?"

"Yeah?"

"Why do you hate hockey?" she whispered.

Not what I'd been expecting. I'd rather she press me about using herself as bait. An argument would be preferable to that topic.

"Who said I hated hockey?" I glanced back at her from over my shoulder.

"You looked like you couldn't decide whether you wanted to cry or throw the TV out the window."

To the point. I admired it. Even if I wouldn't be telling her the truth.

I tore a hand through my hair, not exactly selling myself on being fine, but at least she couldn't see my eyes. "I don't cry," was all I said; then I took the fuck off.

CHAPTER TWENTY-EIGHT

Seraphina

We didn't sit together like a family at a dinner table eating. Instead, the guys devoured their food while working in the office, barely taking time to breathe between bites.

Ryder had been in a shit mood ever since he hauled ass from the kitchen after I'd pressed him on hockey. Aside from a few *thank you*s for the food, he hadn't said a word to me. I did my best not to take it personally, and once everyone had finished up seconds, I took away their empty plates, refilled their glasses to keep them hydrated, then busied myself by cleaning the kitchen.

Without anything else to do after that, I went back into the office and let them know, "I'm going to explore the house. Find something to do." I waited for Ryder's attention, surprised to find all three of them giving it to me. "Unless you want my help?"

"Stay in the house," was all Ryder said, in a low, detached voice that I bet he had to work hard to use.

Alex gave me a one-shoulder shrug next, letting me know he was unsure why there was a new stick up Ryder's ass. Alex probably blamed me for placing it there. Maybe I unintentionally had.

"Okay." I gave a little nod to the allegedly antisocial one, who ironically was the only one to smile at me.

I took my phone from where Ryder had left it, sent a quick text to Martín to check in, then hightailed it from the office, searching for a distraction.

A tour of the villa wasn't needed, since I'd done that before dinner, but I did it anyway. The place was beautiful, with Bali vibes. I made a mental note to add *Visit Bali* on my new bucket list, were I to ever make one again.

After meandering around the place, I wound up back at the center of the home at the indoor rectangular lap pool.

Remembering the closet in my room and the dresser full of clothes, I made a beeline there, deciding I'd swim. I wasn't sure how our hostess had known my size, but she'd nailed it. She'd even thought to buy a swimsuit, so I quickly changed into the *Baywatch*-red one-piece and went to the pool. It was heated, the perfect temperature.

After completing twelve laps, I broke the surface, my breath catching in surprise at the pair of black boots in my direct line of sight.

With one hand, I held the side of the pool to keep myself afloat in the deep end and pushed my hair away from my face. I dragged my eyes up his jeaned legs right to the scowl waiting for me.

"What are you doing?" He crouched, becoming a statue of hard muscles at eye level.

His gaze briefly dipped to the swell of my breasts as I answered, "I'm doing exactly what it looks like. I'm trying to kill time." *And tension.* "You hate swimming as much as hockey?"

He grimaced, shook his head, then stood tall and backed away from the pool, bumping into the lounger, which had my towel on it. "Ezra's on the move and in the air."

Oh, shit. That news required me to get out of the pool. I hoisted myself up and out, and Ryder had my towel waiting for me, dangling from his hand.

His eyes weren't on me but on the tile pavers as I wrapped myself up in the plush towel. "Is he coming here? Did the plan work?"

"By 'plan,' if you mean dangling yourself as bait, then yeah, looks like it worked. He's not set to arrive until zero two hundred."

I blinked. "Wait, what? That's good, right?"

He worked his jaw left, then right. "Yeah, he gets in ninety minutes after we're supposed to meet with Ángel. Decent window of time for a clean exfil before his arrival. We were also able to confirm Ángel's family is still in Mexico, but Ángel's at a resort in Santa Ana fifteen minutes from here."

"How do you know that?" This was all good, and I was desperate for good news.

"Carter's cyber expert, Gwen, hacked the CCTV footage in and around San José, then used facial-recognition software to get a hit. She was also able to confirm the whereabouts of Ángel's family the same way. Unfortunately, no sign of Nina, but that could mean she hasn't been anywhere in public in a couple days."

"So, have you decided it's safe to meet with him?"

"I don't know about 'safe,' but based on what we could determine, he's only traveling with two guys. I recognized them from the club the other night. Nothing we can't handle." He added, "That doesn't mean Ezra, or the Moraleses, didn't send other people we can't identify here ahead of time and we'll get ambushed."

Shit. That last line poked a hole in my hope that he was ready to agree to the meeting. "But we're going anyway, right?" I tightened my hold of the towel, starting to shiver from the contrast of the cooler air and being out of the water.

"For now, shower and change. Once you're back in the office, I have more news to share with you as well."

I'd take his lack of an answer as an optimistic *maybe*. "Can't tell me the news here?"

He zeroed in on where I clutched the towel at my chest. "Office." He scrubbed a hand along his jawline as if in a daze. "And I'll give you an answer about the meeting after Ángel reaches out."

"Alex, you mean? He'll decide, not you." I raised my brows. "Or are you back to calling the shots?" *Who am I kidding, when were you ever truly not calling them?* Title of Delta One or not, this man was in charge. Clearly of me, too, and part of me hated how much I was okay with that. The other part of me wanted to argue. Talk about a tug-of-war of emotions.

"The decision will be made once we know the location of the meeting," was all he said before gesturing in the direction of the bedroom. "Now, please change out of that red bathing suit."

"Does red have you feeling like a bull wanting to charge?" I was playing with fire. Starting to wonder if I was born to do exactly that.

He rotated his neck, taking a moment to pause, then murmured, "If you want me to follow your orders, then you need to go change. You need to walk away from me."

My orders? Right. The decision for us to keep our hands off each other had originally been meant to help us focus on the mission. But he wasn't team leader now, and he did take me to Costa Rica like I wanted, so there was that to consider.

"You're not currently Delta One." What was I doing? Saying? He had news to share with me, and there I was . . . provoking him? *Not walking away like he asked me to do?*

And yet I couldn't seem to stop myself from engaging. I wasn't ready to face reality or the news he had to share, so when he shook his head no in response, I dropped the towel.

He'd get the message loud and clear what I wanted. Right or wrong, shitty timing or not, I didn't care. He slowly allowed his eyes to roam over my body, taking all of me in this time.

"Since neither of us are in charge of what happens now, well . . ." I moved my wet hair to my back just to be crystal clear that I wanted him to look at me. ". . . that changes things, then, doesn't it?"

CHAPTER TWENTY-NINE

Ryder

The bedroom door had been left unlocked, and when I tested the handle of her en suite bathroom door, it turned as well.

At that realization, I let go, set my palms on either side of the doorframe, and bowed my head.

After she'd dropped her towel and laid that comment on me, then quietly strutted away in that sexy red bathing suit, I'd remained stuck in place for a few minutes, contemplating my options. The only one I kept landing on was *Go to her.*

I continued staring at the door, unblinking. I wasn't technically the team leader right now, and I had nothing to do but wait on calls, texts, and more intel. The news I had for her could wait.

So we weren't really doing something wrong by stealing a moment or two, especially if she'd had a change of heart about wanting us to keep our hands to ourselves until after the mission.

Ah, fuck it. Who am I kidding? I was going to rationalize my way into that bathroom one way or another. I'd cross, skip, and hop over any fucking lines to be with her, if she wanted me. I'd been screwed the second she'd lifted those long eyelashes to look at me while standing by the pool dripping wet.

I shoved away from the door and went to work removing my boots and socks. I peeled off my shirt and tossed it next. Jeans and boxers after that; then I finally went for the handle, relieved to hear she hadn't lost patience waiting for me and the shower was still going.

Door open now, I filled the frame as my metaphorical walls fell at the sight of her beneath the shower. Every last one of them, in fact. Because heaven was real. It was on Earth. In Costa Rica. It was Seraphina standing with her back to me as water rolled down her body.

The shower was open to the room. No partition or walls, which meant I could see her in vivid, perfect detail as she washed the shampoo from her hair.

I stood there slack-jawed watching the soap slip down her spine. Her bronzed skin glistened, and I followed the trail of water and soap as it continued to make its path over her body, from her narrow waist to her full hips, and to an ass that couldn't have been made only in the gym, but was God-given.

Mine. All. Fucking. Mine. That was all I could think, feel, and know to be true.

I slowly walked up behind her and set my hands on her wet skin. Parked them at her hips while drawing my chest to her back.

It was as if her entire body sighed as she relaxed against me. She reached for my wrists, guiding my hands around her frame, resting them on her stomach. Our fingers interlaced, and we quietly stood beneath the water like that. I no longer needed to chase the elusive feeling of peace, and instead, it was being given to me just by being this close to her.

She angled her face, chin up, brown eyes pointed at me. "You came."

Jealous of the beads of water on her lips and the way her tongue caught the drops, I found myself leaning in, whispering, "Of course I did," before I kissed her.

She laid to rest every last negative thought in my head with our mouths fused.

But I needed even more of her.

We needed to be closer.

I spun her around. Crushed her against me while capturing her face between my palms. Finding serenity.

"Ryder." I felt the tremble in her lips against mine as she spoke my name.

Breathing hard, I choked out in understanding, "I know." She didn't need to explain. I understood it. Got it. Felt it deep in my bones.

The connection. Forged in fire or in heaven.

I moved my hands to her back. Wandered even farther. Explored more of her. Desperate and needy to touch as much of her as possible. Roaming over every curve, every soft inch as I kissed her lips. Her cheek. The side of her neck.

She held on to my shoulders. Then my back. My waist. When she fisted my cock, I went still. Dead fucking still.

"I want to taste you." Her words silenced my brain for a moment. Shut off the sounds of the water, too.

It didn't function again until she started to go to her knees, and then my mind played catch-up, and I freed myself of her touch to snatch a towel.

I should have said no, but I . . .

Well, I was still a man. A man hungry for this woman. An insatiable need for her ran deep through me that I knew could easily be eternal.

I folded the towel and set it on the tile as a cushion. I rested my hand on top of her head and gently guided her down.

On her knees, and with both hands, she took hold of me.

"For a minute, then it's my turn. Got it?" My leg muscles tightened as she gripped me harder and lowered her mouth to the crown of my cock without actually touching me.

"Yes, sir." She blinked as if surprised at what she'd said, but then she returned her attention to her mission of torturing me and licked the circumference of my head, and I forgot all about her dislike of that word, a word I was sure Ezra had ruined at some point.

Holding my balls with one hand, she stroked me from root to tip before dropping her mouth over me. The woman took as much of me as she could. Hell, she even choked and gagged.

And I died.

Right then.

My soul left my body, and I was gone. Because fuck my life—this woman could kill me with her lips wrapped around my cock.

I threaded my fingers through her hair, unable to stop myself from assisting her in the slow death she was delivering.

I wasn't some sixty-second fuck, but God help me, I was about to be a thirty-second one, because this woman—

"Stop," I hissed and gently pulled at her hair. "I don't get off before you do. Not happening. Not ever," I gritted out. "Now, be good and stop." I didn't want to toss a clichéd *good girl* at her, but fuck if I didn't love calling her my bad one. I probably had issues, but oh-fucking-well. Such was life. No one was perfect. "So naughty, I swear."

She licked my entire length. Swirled her tongue around my head before doing what I'd asked. She sat back on her heels beneath the water, looking up at me. I took a moment to stare at her, mesmerized, then bent forward, hooking her arms to help her back to her feet.

I needed her mouth on mine again. I needed to kiss her. Touch her. Feel every part of her again. Hold her breasts in my hands. Rake my fingers along her skin and her ass cheeks.

Most of all, I just needed the fire in her that reignited mine in a way only she seemed to be able to do.

"Seraphina." Now I was the one saying her name like it was three gruff sounds strung together. "I'll die if I don't taste *you*."

She smiled and nodded, so I stepped back, catching sight of a wooden bench off to the side. I brought it over and had her sit on it beneath the stream of water to stay warm.

"Spread open your legs for me."

With her foot, she shifted the soaked towel over, offering me the same padding for my knees. But I didn't give a damn about any part of my body except for my mouth and where it belonged: between her legs.

I waited for her to part her knees and show herself to me before dropping before her. "Hold on to something; you're going to need it," I warned before I inched my face closer to paradise.

I scooted her ass to the edge of the bench and guided her legs over my shoulders. She rested one forearm on the bench for balance and sent her other hand into my hair.

"Ready for me?" I raised my brows, waiting.

"I have been since last Saturday."

That was all I needed to hear.

I leaned forward, forgetting all about Ezra and the mission, all about hockey and war, as I sank my mouth over her and dragged my tongue along her sex.

She immediately clenched her thighs around my head as her arousal hit my tongue. I licked and sucked. Went slowly at first like a gentle tease, nudging her closer and closer in the direction I wanted her to go.

Here. Now. With her. Nothing else mattered.

"You taste so good," I hissed while adding my fingers inside her.

Her response was to rock against my face. To moan. To cry for God.

"Don't . . . don't . . . stop," she panted. "Yes, yes . . . yesssss."

Fuck. I'd wanted it to take longer, spend all night here.

Her body went lax, and I kissed her swollen sex before lowering her legs so she'd be in a more comfortable position to ride the wave of tranquility that followed her orgasm.

But my girl didn't seem to care about anything but getting me off now. She urged me to my feet while standing as well, then shifted the bench out of her way. "I have to . . ."

I wasn't about to gentleman my way out of this and say no.

She kneeled on the wet towel and gently took me in her mouth. She deep-throated me, taking as much of me as she could into that slick, warm heaven, and I swore I saw God that time. The entire universe and all the galaxies beyond that.

I was going to last about as long as she did.

I lost my thoughts and my sanity as I came hard, hanging my head forward.

She sucked me bone-dry, swallowing every last drop after I'd exploded into her mouth.

After I helped her stand, I seized her face again, unable to stop myself. I had to kiss this woman. I had to let her know how I felt even if it was without words.

I stepped back a minute later and tore my hands through my wet hair. "What was that?"

"It was . . . well, it just made sense."

"Made sense like math does?" I asked, moving us out from under the water while reaching for her chin, needing to look her in the eyes and gauge where her head was at.

"I'd say math has nothing on what happened between us, don't you think?"

That's what I want to hear.

"I honestly don't know what's happening between us, but . . ."

"Lightning," I began, feeling groggy and dazed, "striking the same place twice."

CHAPTER THIRTY

Seraphina

The city lights off in the distance blinked a few times, like the buildings were signaling good night in morse code. It was after eleven, but it felt like we were already borrowing hours from tomorrow. It'd been a long, long day.

I waited for Ryder to realize I was now in the bedroom with him. For him to turn around and give me his attention. He had to have heard the bathroom door open, and yet he kept his back to me, his focus out the expansive window. His jeans were all that he'd taken the time to put on since leaving the bathroom.

He set his hand on the window, stretching his fingers open as I strode up behind him, searching for his gaze in the reflection.

"You're going to get the window dirty." I tied the belt of my robe, cinching it tight, and he tracked the movement of my hands in the glass before sweeping his eyes up to find mine.

"If only dirty windows and zippers were our greatest problems," he said as somberly as I had last weekend. Well, minus the window part.

"If only . . ." I let my voice trail off with a sigh, leaving it there like a beacon of hope maybe we could both follow.

I shifted directly behind him and trailed my hand over his back, sweeping my finger along the hard ridge of an old scar.

"Shrapnel from an IED in Iraq," he answered without me having to ask.

I moved on to another wound. "And this one?"

"Afghanistan. From a sniper. Not sure how I survived. Somehow missed every vital organ and made a clean exit." There was a gruff texture to his voice, as if he had to fight off demons to get those words out, and that hurt my heart.

"You were in both wars?" I followed the line of another jagged scar that ran adjacent to his right shoulder blade.

"I was in both, yeah." Those words came out even breathier.

"How long were you in the army?" I circled his waist and hugged him, drawing my cheek to his back.

He lowered his hand from the window and covered mine with his. "Fourteen years. My goal was twenty, but I couldn't do it."

"Why not?"

His hand slid under the sleeve of my robe, and he gently stroked my skin in calming motions. "Are you sure you want to hear this?" The dark undertone to his words reverberated from deep within his chest, cut straight through his back, and hit me as I clung to him like the lifeline he'd become since we first met.

"Sounds like you don't want to tell me." I closed my eyes and held him even tighter.

"I'm worried you won't like the man you see anymore if I do. Because if I really think about everything I've seen and done, then I probably wouldn't be able to look at myself either, so . . ."

I untangled myself from his touch and pulled away. Not as rejection, but to face him and prove I had every intention of looking him in the eyes and not changing how I saw him no matter what he said.

When I urged him to turn around, he set his back to the window and anchored his feet to the hardwood while leaning against the glass.

He took hold of my hips, walking me closer to him. I slipped my hands up his chest.

"How'd we go from oral sex to why I assume I'm going to hell?" One side of his lip lifted as if undecided whether he wanted to smile or frown.

"Why would you ever think you're going to hell?" My palms climbed higher on his bare chest, landing at the sides of his neck before I let one hand wander up into his hair.

He relaxed a bit, allowing me to run my fingers through his wet locks.

"I killed a lot of people."

I continued to massage the side of his scalp. "Not your fault. You were in the military."

"But is that an excuse for killing fathers, sons, and brothers?" He hung his head, closing his eyes.

I waited for him to continue, knowing he would when he was ready and didn't need prompting.

"One night, my unit had breached a house in Iraq. Zero three hundred in the morning, the guy drew his weapon, and I took him down without a second thought. And then it dawned on me . . . what would I have done if someone broke into my home in the middle of the night? I'd have defended myself, my family, and my property. Maybe that's all he was trying to do. Maybe I was the bad guy?"

We'd gone from one intimate moment in the shower to a much different one now, and I wanted to be here for him in the same way. Hold him. Touch him. *Heal* parts of him the way he was already helping me heal.

"So, that's why I decided not to re-up, and I got out once my contract was up. I had a feeling the next house I breached, I'd hesitate and question whether to shoot to kill, and that could endanger my unit. But civilian life didn't agree with me. The work I do is different now at least, but maybe I just didn't know who the hell I was without a gun in my hand, so I—"

"No." I let go of his hair to hold his face, needing him to look at me. "You didn't know who you were unless you were helping people, which is why you're still helping people now. People like me. Nothing to do with a gun."

He opened his eyes but remained quiet.

"I need you to forgive yourself for whatever you think you've done and move forward, because you're not going to hell. Not on my watch."

A shaky exhalation fell from my lips as I stared at him, as I waited for him to heed *my* orders.

"You don't know anything about me." His forehead pinched, resistance tight between his brows. "Not really."

I expected his stubbornness, but he'd get mine back, and by now he had to know that. "You're right. You've given me bullet points without context. So give me more, and then problem solved—I'll know you. What you've told me so far hasn't changed how I see you." I whispered, "To be very clear, I want you even more now than I did five minutes ago. You took my pain from me this morning, so let me take yours from you."

"It doesn't work that way. You need to accept that I will never let you hurt if I can help it."

"But someone or something, not just being in the military, hurt you. You're in pain beyond that, and I want to help you. It's only fair. I want context so I can do that."

"You don't need—"

"I do need to know."

I'd been the one to suggest we keep our hands to ourselves until the mission was over, and now there we were, doing the opposite of that. Opening up on so many levels. Physically and emotionally. I had no plans to backpedal or flip-flop on that decision; instead, I was prepared to charge ahead even more.

He moved my hands down to my sides and straightened his posture, as if towering over me would prevent him from giving in the way I was asking him to do.

When he leaned in and kissed my forehead, I reacted on instinct, whispering, "Forehead kisses should be illegal without a commitment."

He stood tall, threading his fingers through my hair before he dipped in to kiss my forehead again.

"Is that you conceding? Are you letting me know you're going to let me help you the way you helped me?"

A small but still kind of sad smile crossed his lips. "I don't need help."

"Yes, you do." *Stubborn, stubborn man.*

He momentarily distracted me by unfastening my belt with one hand, allowing the silk to fall open. He wordlessly palmed my hip, drawing me closer, smashing my tits to his hard chest.

His other hand left my face, going to my bare back, traversing up and down my spine. "Tomorrow is only a week since we met."

"And that means, what? That it's too soon for you to drop your baggage at my feet? Meanwhile, you've had me doing that since day one." I did my best to stand my ground and not fall victim to those gorgeous eyes of his and the way he was touching me, like he was trying to coax me into forgetting about his problems.

"I don't know what it means." His voice was strained and tight, yet his touch was anything but. It was sweet and soft. Imbued with kindness and warmth. Grace that he didn't seem to want for himself.

"Well." I parted my lips, hiding my teeth behind my tongue as I considered the best route to take with a man hell-bent on carrying both his burdens and mine squarely on his shoulders. "For some context from me, my parents met while on vacation. They never spent more than two days apart after that. Insta-lust, or love—whatever you want to call it—turned into thirty years of marriage. My dad claimed it was love at first sight." I couldn't help but smile, despite wanting to cry at the memory of how he used to tell the story. "Love at *third* sight for her, though. Three days for her to reciprocate his feelings."

His mouth tightened as he continued to stroke my back. "I wish I could've met them. Maybe your father could give me advice on how to handle his stubborn daughter. Tell me what to do next with her." Soft breaths left his nostrils as he took a moment to pause. "He could tell me how to navigate these feelings I've never experienced before, since I didn't have a father to teach me."

A shiver fell down my spine that he had to feel with his hand at the arch of my back. I unpacked his words and their meaning. "Your father's who hurt you."

He tipped his head, eyes narrowing on my mouth to escape looking straight into mine. "Maybe," was all he said, and I had a feeling that was all he'd give me right now.

"Well, I wish you could have met my parents. Talked to my dad." I blinked a few times, freeing tears in the process. "My father would've loved you." There was something else I had to tell him, something he needed to hear since his own dad hadn't been around to tell him. "My parents may not have been born in the US, but my dad had been so proud that his son was going to serve in our military. And I know he'd be so damn proud of you and your service, too, and—"

"Ah, fucccck," he interrupted, emotion choking up his words. With his eyes finally back on mine, I could see him fighting like hell not to give in to his feelings. "You're going to make me cry, and I told you I don't cry." He opened his mouth, searching for air without ever losing hold of me. Still rubbing my back, soothing me in the way I wished he'd let me do for him.

"You're allowed to cry. It doesn't make you less manly—you know that, right?" I chewed on the side of my lip, reaching between us to anchor my palms on his cheeks, tethering us together in this moment.

"Did your dad ever cry?" The man was still holding back. Tapping into all his strength not to let me witness the emotion I'd expressed in his arms only this morning.

"He did. Mostly during movies, though. I think he used watching them as an excuse to let go."

"I guess I need to watch a movie, then? Got any recommendations where a dog dies? Those will undoubtedly do a number on me."

"One or two," I whispered, my voice breaking. "Ryder, I—" I dropped my words at the knock on the bedroom door.

"Yeah?" Ryder stepped away from me, shaking his head as if trying to regroup and remember where we were and why.

"There's something we need to show you both," Alex called out.

"Yeah, uh, okay," Ryder answered quickly. "Give us a minute."

Alex didn't bother to respond, and I had to assume he'd already taken off to offer us privacy.

"You okay?" I asked him as he went over to his shirt on the floor and quietly began stretching it over his head.

"Of course." He picked up his boots and sat on the bed. "Why wouldn't I be?"

I pulled the red silk together and tied the belt. "Ryder." I stamped out his name hard into the air.

"Would you like my middle name so you can three-name me for more effect?" Boots on but unlaced, he looked up at me, smirking. A switch had been flipped. He'd zipped up his emotions and his pain and hidden them in some distant land or universe, where I had a feeling he hoped they'd never be found again. "It's David. You know, for future reference."

I hoped there would be a future with us and that he wouldn't push me away once I got too close. I had a habit of doing the pushing thing myself, so I recognized a fellow "pusher" when I saw one. This was one time I wanted to do the opposite. Pull. And pull hard.

"I was wrong this morning. About waiting until the mission is over."

He discarded a deep exhalation. "I got the feeling you felt that way, since you let me put my tongue between your legs." A lazy smile that distracted me moved across his mouth.

"You're deflecting." I lifted a hand. "I know, I know. Pot calling the kettle black, here. I'm a hypocrite." This morning, not to mention what had just happened in the shower, and our conversation here was the definition of stalling.

He stood there for a few moments, simply observing me, then strode over, held on to the sides of my arms, and kissed my forehead. "Just so there's no mistake in what I want," he rasped. "Meet you in the office when you're dressed." He let me go, went to the door, then shot me a backward glance and tossed out, "Technically, this is day three. Just so you know."

He opened the door, then walked out and closed it behind him, leaving me alone to process that kiss and what he was trying to say to me.

Saturday, we first met. Thursday was the fight club. Today is Friday. Those were the days we'd spent time together in the last week. I peered at the door, feeling a bit lightheaded. *Are you asking me if I'm like my mom and I've fallen for you? Or are you telling me I already have?*

CHAPTER THIRTY-ONE

Ryder

I closed the bedroom door and turned, preparing myself to face the team, to get back to the mission, but fucking hell, the pressure in my chest was unbearable, and I couldn't budge.

She was doing a number on me in so many ways, and something inside me actually hoped she'd keep at it. Never stop. Never give up on me. For the first time in my life, I could see beyond six feet in front of me. Beyond war, the missions.

But I also knew how easily the future could collapse out from under me and be taken away, so I had to keep that in mind.

"Hey, you good?" Alex, of course, sensing there was an issue since I'd yet to haul ass to the office and join him after his cryptic message through the door.

At the sight of him standing at the other end of the hall, I finally got my ass moving. "I'm fine."

He gave me his signature look, one that read *The fuck you are.*

"Just tell me you found something." I motioned for him to start walking, and I'd continue on mission and do the same.

Another sideways glance from him, coupled with a shake of his head and a low hiss before he began walking. "Reed pulled Andrej's images from a few security cameras the week he was killed, but there was nothing suspect about anything he found. So he called for an assist."

We stopped outside the office door. "Let me guess . . ." I smiled, but at least the achy pain in my chest was starting to let up and I could breathe again. "To the hacker on Carter's team? Gwen?"

He nodded. "We really need to get better funding. The tech we're working with feels like we're stuck in the Stone Age compared to the software Carter has."

"Yeah, well, he's a billionaire. Tough to compete with."

"And Homeland's discretionary funds are well into the billions, and yet they expect us to MacGyver our way through our problems."

He wasn't wrong, but we were also not answering to anyone but ourselves right now, which meant we had even less to work with.

"So I take it Gwen pulled off a miracle and that's why you interrupted me?" I checked my watch. It was going on 23:30, which meant Ángel would be reaching out with a location soon.

"And what, exactly, was I interrupting?" he asked while we went into the office.

"A heart attack," I deadpanned.

In part, that was true. A metaphorical attack on my heart, at least. Because I'd opened up to Seraphina about my service time, spilled a drop of truth about my old man, then nearly broken down when she told me her dad would have been proud of me.

"Just tell me what you have." I went over to where Reed was working at one of the two desks in the room.

He looked up, but instead of focusing on me, his gaze cut to the doorway. I turned to clock who was there, assuming it'd be my girl.

And she was mine.

Fuck, was she ever.

Seraphina hung back in the doorway in jeans and a white button-up blouse, which was partially tucked in. Her wet hair was in a braid at her back, and she gave me a nervous little smile. "What'd you all find out?"

Alex motioned for her to head over to the desk, and I worked the lump down my throat and faced the laptop again.

"We found something out about the brother-in-law," Alex told her, which was also news to me since he'd yet to fill in the blanks about what Gwen had helped them find. "Something that we think is relevant to our meeting with Ángel."

Seraphina came up next to me, and I caught a whiff of her coconut-scented shampoo. "And, um, what are we looking at?" She began massaging her arms as if cold, and I had to curb the impulse to tug her to my side and warm her up myself.

Alex explained to her what he'd already told me, then added, "Andrej met with someone while he was here two days before . . ." He cleared his throat, circling Reed's desk to face us. ". . . well, before your family was killed in Cabo."

"They were careful never to be seen on any security footage together, *but* there was one camera that caught them. It took a lot of work to clean up the image and the angle was shit," Reed began while typing, "but—"

"Wait," she blurted once Reed had the image on screen. "Andrej was with *Ángel?*" She set a hand on the desk, leaning forward for a closer look. "You're saying Ángel met with Andrej the same week he died?"

"Yes," Reed answered. "Looks like Ángel took Andrej for a ride, and they used the privacy of his rental Suburban for their meeting." He zoomed in on the open door of the SUV and to Ángel sitting there, facing the street with Andrej outside on the sidewalk.

"No real-time footage, just a static image?" I asked him.

"This photo wasn't taken from CCTV footage. It's from a selfie a tourist posted online," Reed explained. "Thanks to Carter's software, Gwen was able to do a more advanced search than I was and find this."

"I need to sit." Seraphina went over to the leather couch in the middle of the office. "Why would Ángel meet with Ezra's brother-in-law?" She clutched a pillow to her chest, looking my way, and I wished I had answers for her.

I rested my fist on the desk, trying to come up with a plausible explanation for their meeting—particularly the timing of it—and I landed on only one. "What if Andrej was going behind his sister and Ezra's backs, helping the cartel? He could've been using Ángel as an intermediary and this wasn't their first time meeting."

"But it was his last," Alex muttered. "And maybe Ezra and his sister found out and had him killed. They just didn't know about this meeting, or they wouldn't have sent a hit team to Cabo first."

"The payments from the cartel to Andrej's account were a frame job, though," she reminded us, sitting taller. "Is it possible Ezra didn't know Andrej was meeting with Ángel, just assumed for some reason he was betraying them and helping the cartel?" She grimaced, shaking her head. "I know Ezra, and he'd have sent a team after Ángel if he knew about him. He'd never let him live. He'd tie up loose ends."

Like he's trying to tie up with you now. That thought had me pushing away from the desk. "Ezra may have believed Andrej was betraying them, but maybe he didn't have proof, so he had someone hack Andrej's accounts to add those wire transfers from the cartel to set him up; that way his wife didn't question the decision to have her brother killed. But why would Ángel work with Andrej?"

"Because Ezra's operation was interfering with the cartel's business, and . . ." Her eyes widened. "Ohhh."

I quickly rounded the desk and went over to sit next to her. "What is it?"

"What if working with Andrej was how Ángel bought himself extra protection from his own family bothering him? I offered him a similar deal last night. The cartel is Ángel's enemy, and Andrej must've viewed his sister and Ezra as his enemy. They may have made some type of deal to help one another out."

Alex pitched an idea. "We're assuming Andrej betrayed the Sokolovs, since he was murdered, but are we certain it wasn't the other way around and it was Ángel selling out his family to Andrej to help the Sokolovs? And the Moraleses didn't know it was their own blood helping Andrej, or Ángel would have been killed." He turned his attention to Seraphina. "You're sure those payments to Andrej from the cartel weren't legit?"

"I am," she said with confidence, and I trusted both her gut and her numbers.

"Our government stages hits like this all the time. They frame others for their handiwork so they're not culpable," Reed said, sitting back in the desk chair, eyes on me.

"He's right. It's not like we weren't part of CIA ops like that overseas doing the same damn thing," Alex responded.

"I think there's a third possibility," Reed said. "Andrej was a CIA asset and Ezra found out and had him killed. Someone made his death look like a cartel hit to cover their tracks."

"And who's powerful enough to make a story like that never make it into national news?" Alex crossed his arms. "The same group who doesn't play well with others and would never let DHS, the FBI, or DEA know they already turned someone inside the Sokolovs' operation," he went on, answering his question himself.

"This is why we were pulled off the op and the task force was killed. The CIA found out we were tangled up in something they already have an inside track on, and they wanted us off the case." That realization had me standing, tracking a hand through my hair as I put it together. "The CIA probably turned someone else after they lost Andrej, and they're worried we'll screw up their op."

"If only they shared intel with other agencies, this never would have happened," Alex grumbled as Seraphina set aside the pillow to stand.

"We need to talk to Ángel and have him confirm this." I just had no clue if the man would put his own interests, like self-preservation, above what was morally right.

"That means when Ángel texts the location, you're going to let me come, too, right?" She stared at me expectantly, and it killed me more than anything to do this, but I deferred to Alex for an answer.

"I'm not sure what the best call is, to be honest. Any number of things could go wrong. It could be a trap, for starters." Alex tightened his lips, shaking his head.

"We have a narrow window of time to meet with Ángel. It's a now-or-never kind of thing." Seraphina bounced her gaze back and forth between the two of us, waiting. "Without him and without me, this whole thing falls apart."

"I'm aware." I went over to the Nespresso machine at the bar on the other side of the office. It was going to be a late night. "It doesn't change the fact your safety trumps everything else."

"We didn't come to Costa Rica for nothing." She was right on my ass, tugging at my shirt. Of course she wouldn't back down. Did I really expect her to, just because Alex was now coming around to my side on this? "We have to make this work."

"And we will," Alex told her. "We'll figure out the best course of action," he added, and she let go of my shirt. "Still nothing from Lainey yet?" His redirect was appreciated.

"Lainey's kept the director off our ass, and she's still chasing down leads for us." I started the Nespresso machine, then faced the room. "And as for that other contact of mine," I began, about to share the update I'd yet to tell Seraphina but had already told the guys, "he sent three of his guys to Moscow. They'll arrive in the morning."

"Wait, what? Why?" she asked.

"Sorry, I meant to tell you this before"—*but got distracted by our shower together and conversation after*—"but that friend of mine I mentioned earlier, Hudson, spent the day poring over the files you gave us with his team."

She narrowed her eyes at me. "And that conversation led Hudson's people to Russia?"

"Your numbers did," I revealed. "Hudson and I were able to follow the trail you gave us to a bank in Moscow, which then led us to what we believe is a shell company for the Sokolovs' operation there. As in, a front for whoever is really in charge."

"Okay, that's good news." Her eyes lit up. "That's a huge find."

"Never would've found it without your math." I semi-smiled, impressed by everything she'd accomplished while working for Ezra. It still hurt my chest to think about, but I had to focus on the fact she was standing before me and had survived.

"Well, thanks to you as well. You find people, right? It's what you do." She returned my smile. "Guess we make a good team."

Fuck yeah, we do. I cleared my throat, remembering we weren't alone, so I couldn't haul her into my arms and kiss her. "Anyway, this, uh, squares up with Nina's visits there, too."

"So we might find out who the Sokolovs are actually working for?" Her lips parted, and she flipped her tongue up, covering her teeth, like she had a habit of doing.

"And if we find out who's in charge, we—"

"We don't need to question Ezra," she finished for me, her shoulders falling. I wasn't sure how to read that. Disappointment, or relief?

I can just go ahead and kill the fucker instead. "So, you see, if that's the case, there's no need to place you in any unnecessary danger."

She closed her eyes, and *fuck*, I knew what was going to come from that gorgeous mouth of hers next.

"But we don't know for sure if they'll be successful or how long it'll take them to hunt down the lead in Russia." She confirmed what I thought she'd say. "We can't afford to lose this opportunity to get our hands on Ezra while he's here."

"She's right." Not what I wanted to hear from Alex. "We need to cover our bases, have multiple plans in place—and if Sera wasn't in the middle of this, you'd be saying the same thing, and you know that. Which is why you—"

"I know," I cut him off, hanging my head. "It's why I asked you to be in charge."

CHAPTER THIRTY-TWO

Seraphina

"Pull over." Ryder was sitting next to me in the back of the Tahoe, and when Alex didn't do as he asked, he leaned forward and tapped his shoulder. *"Pull. Over."*

Alex swore in Spanish but did as he was told, easing the SUV off to the side of the back road. Once in park, he undid his belt and swiveled around. "We agreed to the meeting, to the plan."

"Something doesn't feel right about this," Ryder said in a low voice. He had his 9mm in one hand, resting it on his jeaned thigh. "This whole thing is too fucking perfect. Too neat. I don't like it."

"Would you prefer it be sloppy?" I countered, unbuckling to twist around in the captain's chair and face him. "Ezra's still airborne, and the Moraleses should still be in Mexico. We're heading to a car-repair center, which is part of a chain that Ángel owns, and only Ángel and two other guys are inside with him waiting for us."

"Which is why it feels too perfect," he growled. "Like a trap."

My eyes had adjusted to the dim lighting, but it was still too dark to make out his facial expressions. I reached for his free hand and squeezed.

The man became a human wrecking ball when it came to my safety, determined to knock down anything and anyone that might endanger me—including his own teammates right now, from the sounds of it.

"Ángel has a SCIF in the back of the shop, which is why he chose this place, and I'm good with ensuring no one can record us as well," Alex said. I'd had to google that word after he mentioned that at the villa. SCIF, which was pronounced *skiff*, was a secure room meant to protect against electronic surveillance and data leakage.

After Ángel had texted the location, it'd taken quite a bit of convincing on my part to get even Alex to agree to the meeting, but at least he had. Ryder, though, *whooa*, that man. More stubborn than me. The three of us had to pull our collective energy together to get Ryder to commit. And now there we were, probably three miles away from the meeting with Ángel, and he was on the verge of putting a stop to it anyway.

"We can't go in on comms. You'll be sitting in the parking lot while the two of us are inside, and we'll have no way to communicate with you if something goes wrong," Ryder pointed out. It was an issue I couldn't argue with, because he was right. "You won't be able to give us a heads-up if we have incoming, either."

I pointed to the laptop on Reed's lap. "That view is in real time, right?"

The satellite feed on the screen was courtesy of Carter; he'd helped us access an overhead shot of the repair center via "hacking" for the meeting. Without that, I knew I'd never have been able to get anyone on board with the plan.

"Yeah," Reed confirmed. "Thermal-heat imaging still suggests there's three bodies currently inside the building, one SUV in the parking lot."

Ryder pulled his hand away from mine. "There could be other armed tangos waiting to move that we can't detect. Ready to infil once we're inside."

"How far out can you see? If there are people waiting somewhere, wouldn't you notice using the thermal thing? Or have enough time to come inside the shop and warn us if you spot people moving our direction over the satellite?" I asked Reed.

"I can position the view anywhere I want and see what's happening. It's like having one giant camera in the sky," Reed said, which was what Ryder needed to hear. I hoped Reed could do a better job at getting through to him than I could. "Which means we should have time to personally alert you both if there's incoming, yes."

"And you're allowed to go in armed," I reminded the grump. "Just not armed with a phone or comms. You can protect me in there if need be." Not that I believed that would be necessary. When Ryder refused to even look at me, I continued, "I need you to believe me when I say we can trust Ángel. Martín knows the cartels inside and out, and he's promised me that Ángel is safe." I reached for his hand again, and at least he didn't reject my touch. "We're so close to the truth, I can feel it. I need you to trust me now."

"And I need you to trust *me*," he shot back, finally turning his head. "I'm not bulletproof. So even if I throw myself in front of you if shots are fired, you could still catch a round."

"Are you suggesting we reschedule?" *This isn't a dentist appointment.* I kept that thought to myself. No sense in pissing him off even more. Can't fight fire with fire.

"Yes," he said without hesitation. "We'll pick the place and the conditions. And that gives us time to pull in additional backup."

"Ezra will be local by then," I reminded him. "The rest of the Moraleses could also be here soon. Ángel wants to meet with us before they get here to keep us safe."

"Why are you so trusting of a man you barely know? Just because Martín thinks Ángel will come through isn't a good enough reason for me." Ryder let go of my hand, shooting his gaze out the side window.

"I sat across from Ángel at the club and looked him in the eyes," I said softly, speaking my truth, hoping he'd hear it and believe me. "I know evil when I see it. I had to work with evil for over nine months. And he's not that."

Ryder spun his finger in the air like a directive to move. "I'm sorry, but it's not happening. I've changed my mind. We shouldn't have ever left the villa."

"But you're not in charge right now." I hated pulling that card, but I hadn't worked my ass off for this long and come so far to turn around now.

"You mentioned trust," Alex began, drawing my attention his way, "and I trust Ryder's gut. He's never been wrong before." He faced forward and shifted the SUV into drive but didn't pull back onto the road yet. "Ryder's saved my ass more times than I can count. I have a habit of placing the mission above my own life, and he doesn't let us do that."

Well, that was . . . *Shit*. "I, um . . ." It was one thing to endanger myself, but was I seriously placing my desire for revenge over the lives in this vehicle?

Had I become *that* person? I had a man next to me ready to fight the whole world to keep me safe, and there I was, prepared to risk his life and . . . I cupped my mouth and closed my eyes as guilt punched through me.

"Who have I become? What has working with Ezra done to me?" I hadn't meant to verbalize my thoughts, but out they came. "I'm so sorry. Revenge would be meaningless if anything happened to any of you." Tears slipped down my cheeks. "I'm so freaking sorry."

"Hey. No, don't talk like that." I could feel Ryder leaning closer; then he reached behind my head, gently urging me to face him. "We do this every day. We're good, so don't go there. You hear me?"

I resisted looking at him, not ready to face the truth, to face the facts. "I was selfish and not thinking about—"

"I never want to hear you call yourself that again," Ryder remarked in a steady voice, still holding on to me. "That's not the case, so don't start with me on that nonsense."

Reed spoke up. "Hate to interrupt, but I have to. Lainey's calling your phone."

Ryder let me go, and I opened my eyes as he took his phone from Reed. "Yeah?" he answered. "Tell me you have something." He was quiet for a moment, listening to whatever his ex had to say. "Thanks for letting me know. If you hear more . . . Yeah, yeah, okay." He ended the call and gestured for me to buckle up and pointed forward, signaling to Alex to drive. "We need to head to the villa now. Make sure we don't have a tail."

"Why? What'd she say?" I fastened my seat belt, and Alex turned us around, heading in the direction we'd come from.

"Lainey's still at the office, and she overheard chatter. She learned Beth's in Costa Rica," he shared in a hesitant voice.

Who was Beth?

Alex cursed in both English and Spanish, hitting the heel of his hand against the steering wheel. "This is a trap."

"Someone going to enlighten me on why?" I asked them.

"It means the CIA's in town," Reed answered blankly. "We have incoming. Satellite is picking up three SUVs hot on our asses," he added a moment later. "Thermal-heat imaging shows eight bodies total."

"They had to have been tracking Ángel, and they're also using thermal-heat imaging and marked our position," Ryder hissed.

"And now she's calling me. Fuck," Alex swore again, probably glowering at the phone mounted to the dashboard that had the name *Beth* flashing on the screen.

"So, who's Beth? CIA?" That was the only thing that made sense.

"Yes," Alex gritted out while taking a sharp turn down a side road, not answering the call. "And she's also my ex-wife."

CHAPTER THIRTY-THREE

Seraphina

"I'm sure she's giving us a heads-up it's them so we don't shoot." Alex sent the call to voicemail again, continuing to drive away from the meeting site. "And is that a helo I hear?" He cursed, switching back and forth between English and Spanish.

"The Agency's using the same satellite as us. We're the ones who hacked into the government's feeds," Reed pointed out. "We're not going to be able to outrun them."

"And as much as I hate your ex, I'm not getting into a gunfight with her or any GRS operators." Ryder leaned forward and patted Alex on the shoulder. "We have no choice but to pull over and talk to them."

"What's GRS?" *So many acronyms to get straight ever since we met.*

"Global Response Team, also known as SOG, the Special Operations Group," Reed answered as Alex did as Ryder instructed and pulled off the back road onto the dirt. "They're a paramilitary unit that works for the Agency. They protect officers and agents. Most are former Tier One operators like we are. Hell, some in those SUVs may even be our friends."

Alex canceled another call from Beth while parking the SUV. "Clearly, this is why she was at our hotel in DC. She somehow got wind of what happened in Miami, and she planned to try and tag me like an animal to follow us to Sera, but she didn't have a chance to."

"Because we called you away from her to my room," Ryder finished for him. What in the world were they talking about? "DHS knew we were in Mexico. The Agency probably followed us down there, then told Lainey to have us back off."

"Knowing damn well we wouldn't. They used us as bait to get to Sera. Those motherfuc—" Alex cut himself off when his phone started up again. "So help me." He began talking under his breath in Spanish, probably forgetting I could understand him.

"They're on our six," Reed alerted us, focused intently on the satellite feed. "About to box us in, more than likely."

"You mean, trap us so we can't drive away and escape?" I asked, and Reed looked back at me and nodded.

"You've gotta be Delta One again. I'm sorry." Alex grumbled more curses, facing Ryder. "I won't be able to think clearly with Beth involved. You know how she mindfucks me. The fact I didn't see this coming with her pisses me off."

"I get it," Ryder was quick to say, somehow remaining calm in the face of this new chaos. "We'll figure this out."

Honestly, his tone was much more relaxed than I'd anticipated, considering three SUVs did exactly as Reed had predicted. They closed in on us. One in the front, one in the back, and one parallel to our Tahoe. The only place we could drive would be into the woods, which wouldn't be happening.

For whatever reason, my heart wasn't beating wildly. I remained calm and collected. I had to be mirroring Ryder's behavior.

"I'm not letting them take you. Got it?" Ryder kept hold of his 9mm and, with his free hand, reached for mine, probably worried I was going to spin out.

"I don't want you going up against your allies. I mean, that's what they are, right? Or should I say frenemies in this case?"

Ryder pulled his hand away so he could use his phone, and he quickly began typing. "I need to get word out to Carter about this. I gave him a heads-up earlier that the CIA might be coming down here, but now we've got confirmation of that. He has connections at the Agency. He might be able to pull—" He stopped talking only to swear under his breath. "She's jamming the signals."

"So you can't send the text?" I asked as two guys slapped their hands against the sides of the SUV.

"No, it won't go through." Ryder lifted off the seat to shove his phone in his pocket. "Carter will figure out something's wrong when I don't make contact."

"Get out. Hands up," one of the two armed men shouted.

Alex was the first to open his door. He didn't waste time and began facing off with the only woman out there.

You must be Beth. With them standing in between our SUV and hers in front of us, and with our headlights on, I could easily make out Alex's ex. Her no-nonsense, boring black pantsuit didn't hide how obviously pretty she was.

"Come out my side. Stay right next to me." Ryder set down his weapon and opened his door, then offered me his hand.

I hesitated. Stared at him as delayed fear caught up with me. The inside lights were on, so I could make out his pinched brows and concerned eyes.

"It'll be okay. I won't let them hurt you." I wanted to latch on to his promise, but my dad used to say the same thing, and now he was dead.

It took someone coming up behind Ryder to snap me out of my shocked state. Seeing a rifle could do that.

Reed had already set aside the laptop and was now exiting, so I finally worked up the nerve to do the same.

Ryder's big hand swallowed mine, and I bent my head and ducked out.

"We're unarmed," Ryder let the guy behind him know, and he gave us both a subtle nod and remained quiet, backing off to allow us to walk around the vehicle to join the others gathered on the road. Thermal imaging had shown eight bodies, but there were only five in present company. The other three must've remained behind the wheels of their SUVs.

When I turned, I had to squint from the harsh high beams coming from an SUV. I shielded my eyes with one hand, searching out Reed and Alex.

From the sounds of it, the helo was taking off, which meant the CIA didn't plan to open fire on us. Well, not from above, at least.

When a second guy came around to face us, I stumbled forward in recognition. *I know you, don't I?*

Ryder hauled me behind him in one swift movement. "You son of a bitch."

I kept hold of Ryder's waist, then stole a look behind me, realizing there was another armed operator a few feet back. How would Ryder shield me from so many?

"What the hell are you doing here?" Ryder asked him, then clocked the fact we had company coming up from behind, so he switched me over to his side. He slung his arm possessively around me, burying his fingertips into my hip.

"Please, give Beth an excuse to let me Taser your ass," the guy said while resting his hand on an object strapped to his outer thigh.

"I knew I couldn't trust you." Ryder's calm state turned to boiling hot real fast. "Was pulling Leo into this your idea? Is the ink even dry on the GRS contract you had him sign before flying him down here?"

"Leo's here?" Alex abruptly spun in our direction and away from his ex.

The fourth guy on your team that night—so that's how I know you.

"We heard things didn't work out and offered him a position with us." Beth kept her tone as cold as her Icelandic-blue eyes.

"How convenient," Ryder muttered, no longer walking us forward.

When Leo held up his rifle, pointing it at me, Ryder immediately stretched his arm out, fearlessly wrapping a hand over the barrel, nudging it away from me.

"Whatever you're thinking, pause and rethink it," Ryder warned.

Beth waved her hand in the air. "I don't need a pissing contest between the two of you." She turned to Leo. "If he gets squirrelly, I'll let you handle him. Right now, just stand down. Got it?" She pointed to Alex and Reed next. "Same goes for you two. If you don't want to be put down and you want to stay at Miss Torres's side, then I suggest you behave."

The idea the CIA would try to snatch me away from Ryder wasn't one I wanted to consider. I also knew Ryder wouldn't go down easily. He'd put up a fight if they tried to take me from him. Outgunned, though. Outmanned. Out-everythinged.

"Are you running your own team now?" Alex asked her as Ryder let go of the rifle.

"I'm in charge of a special team and operation, yes," she said, like she was answering an interview question for a job she didn't want.

"Talk," Ryder demanded.

"You need to continue on mission." Beth faced me. "I need you to head to the meeting with Ángel Morales as you intended to do before you changed your mind. We'll meet you right after. We have a safe house, so you'll no longer need the place you're staying at now."

"What?" I blurted out. "You're not trying to stop us?"

"On the contrary, I want you to go through with it. The whole plan, in fact. I'm here to make sure you do. With a few adjustments, of course."

"What does that mean?" I asked.

"It means they're using us as bait," Ryder explained, his tone softer since he was speaking to me. "And that's not fucking happening." And *that* was for her.

Beth gestured to her armed men. "Please explain to me how you're in a position to tell me what can or can't happen."

Point taken yet again. We were currently at her mercy.

"So help me, Beth . . ." Alex circled her, lining himself up on my other side. "Do not do this."

She lowered her hand, casually glancing in his direction. "Alejandro—"

"Don't 'Alejandro' me."

"I'm doing what needs to be done. My job," she responded almost casually. "It's nothing personal."

"Yeah, well, it's personal to me." Ryder broke forward, taking me with him, and Leo didn't waste time training his rifle on him.

I lifted my free hand, my silent request to not point a weapon at the man I was falling for.

"Tell us what's going on." Alex held both hands up, stepping forward as well. "We're in this together now, so clue us in. What's this special team and operation you're running? You owe us that much since you're trying to hijack control of our mission."

She directed Leo to lower his weapon, and my body relaxed when he did. "We recently learned the DEA had assets embedded with the Sokolovs' organization, and the Feds lost those assets. The director had the task force disbanded—not that it should've ever been formed in the first place."

"Director Johnson? Not your immediate boss at the CIA?" Ryder asked her. "Why's the director of National Intelligence—"

"Need to know," she interrupted him.

"How'd you find out about the DEA assets?" I asked as I clocked Reed exchanging a look with another operator. Did they know each other?

Beth smoothed a hand over her blonde ponytail. "You were told by Homeland to stand down and abort mission." That was an asshole nonanswer from her.

"You knew we wouldn't back off—and let me guess: That's what you wanted." Alex folded his arms. "You were at my hotel for a reason on Tuesday. Don't lie and pretend it was a coincidence. Director Johnson probably realized DHS planned to assign us the mission to track Sera down, so you came up with a plan after that."

"And you pulled a Houdini on me at the hotel and disappeared. Some things never change," she said bitterly.

Alex rolled his eyes at her jab. "Then you found out we had a disgruntled former associate you could pull in to help track us." He tipped his head in Leo's direction. "How'd you track us to Mexico? Leo sure as hell didn't do it."

That was a good point. How *did* they find us?

Alex *tsk*ed, not waiting for her to oblige him with a response. "You've been monitoring Ángel ever since Andrej was killed."

That had Beth's attention. *Yup, we know about Andrej being your asset.* Reed's theory was right.

Eyes on me, Beth shared, "I read the DEA's file on you this week." She about-faced the hell out of that topic, giving me whiplash. "Brave. A little reckless, too." She let those adjectives sit between us for a moment, and I allowed them to roll right off my shoulders. "My associates somehow missed the connection that you were Anna Cruz, but you'd have made an excellent asset for *us*. You chose the wrong agency to go to for help."

Yeah, thanks to Ezra not wanting anyone to know my real name. I had to believe he wanted to keep me around for his own despicable reasons, ones he'd never gotten around to trying to commit.

"I suppose everything happens for a reason. Even I can't argue with fate." Her tone was as bland as her pantsuit. "The way the dominoes fell, not even I could've planned it that perfectly."

"What cryptic BS are you talking about?" I asked, not interested in having her mindfuck me the way Alex had claimed she did to him.

"I'd really prefer not to get into this now." Her dull, casual voice grated on my nerves. "But it appears your stubborn curiosity is going to slow me down if I don't give you something."

"You boxed us in with rifles and a helo, but that's all it is," Alex gritted out. "Stubborn curiosity on our part."

"Fine." She'd probably always planned to offer up a little something to try to get us to bite, to move forward with her plan. She quickly began listing facts as though she'd rehearsed. "A former member of my team provided Homeland with the tip about the money launderer for the terrorist cell you went after. He was told not to act on it, but he passed that intel over to a friend at DHS anyway. The mission then landed in the lap of your security firm. That's domino one." She held up a finger. "Your team winding up at Ezra's party to capture your mark is domino two. Saving Miss Torres from death, domino three." She showed us three fingers as if we couldn't count.

I really, really hate you.

"Then DHS was pulled into the FBI-DEA task force this week because the DEA lost their only assets and needed help. Director Johnson was alerted to the situation when the DEA let Homeland know they had one dead and one missing asset."

She'd confirmed Alex's theory with that remark.

"Well, you get the picture, don't you? Domino after domino, and now here we are." She looked at Ryder next, a devious smile crossing her lips. "Who do you think nudged Lainey's boss, Director Hernandez, to give you the mission to go find Miss Torres on Tuesday? Well, Director Johnson did, but at my suggestion."

A blur of dominoes falling one by one flashed through my mind as I put everything she'd said together. I still didn't understand what she was getting out of all this. What was her team's endgame?

Beth stepped forward, and Ryder protectively pulled me back. "Maybe everything really does happen for a reason," she droned on. "Including my colleague defying orders and tipping off Homeland." She pierced me with those blue eyes of hers again before they took a slow journey over my body as if doing a quality check, and the tight draw of her lips told me she didn't think I'd make the cut. "If you died Saturday night, then this opportunity wouldn't have presented itself to my team."

"What opportunity?" My patience was long, long gone when it came to her.

"To set a trap for the Moraleses," Reed said, offering his own theory. "Using you as bait to draw out Ezra—and in doing so, draw out the highest-ranking Moraleses in the cartel. Something the Agency never had a chance to do, not even when working with Andrej and Ángel before Andrej was killed."

"Or, more likely, never thought to do until this week, when they got smacked right in the face with your bold plan," Alex tossed out flippantly.

"So it's never been about going after the Sokolovs for the CIA?" Ryder joined in on what felt like a cross-examination, and I was here for it—anything to get to the truth. "Otherwise, you'd intercept his flight when he lands and interrogate him. You could throw him in some black site and ask him who he works for, but you don't want to know. Or maybe you already know but you don't care."

"You're *only* after the Moraleses? Both myself and Ezra are bait in this?"

"Is that such a bad thing?" Beth looked directly at me. "Think about this: You have a chance to help take down one of the worst cartels we've ever faced. Imagine all the lives you'll save."

"What about Ezra? What about what he's doing? Why not also take him out?" *That part makes absolutely no freaking sense.* "And don't you dare tell me that's need to know."

"He's their fall guy." Reed was quick to offer his theory, and he seemed to be doing a decent job at reading her mind. "The Agency doesn't want to take credit for the hit."

She didn't answer, which I took as confirmation that Reed had nailed it.

"Ezra needs to survive," Beth said flatly, her gaze roaming over me yet again, which was starting to make me even more uncomfortable than I already was.

"Something tells me it's not so you can ask him who he reports to," Ryder said, calling her out on that. I was on the same page.

Reed leaned against our SUV, casually staring her down. When she kept quiet, he asked, "Since when does the CIA get involved in the drug trade?"

"Since the Chinese did, and they started using the Moraleses' trafficking routes to funnel not only drugs, but terrorists and weapons across the border." Beth spun her finger in the air, signaling to her operators to get a move on. "As you correctly called it, we need the attack against the Moraleses to look like a rival hit. It can't fall back on the CIA. The Chinese will retaliate if they know we're involved."

Alex grimaced. "Yeah, right. There's a hell of a lot more to the story than that."

"Think whatever you want," she answered in an unbothered tone. "Whether you believe me or not doesn't change the plan."

"You're using us, too, right?" Ryder interjected, probably worried about a new argument between Alex and Beth starting up. "You need us here so Ezra doesn't know his guardian angels are the CIA coming in for a surprise assist."

"What about justice for my family?" They were why I was there in the first place. A much-earlier domino she failed to mention—and had she, I would have found something tangible to shove down her throat instead of a metaphorical something. "They were killed because you turned Andrej—"

"Your family was a casualty of war." Blunt and heartless from her. I hated her more and more each passing second.

"What the *hell* is wrong with you?" Alex's tone was as pained as his expression. "You didn't used to be like this. But let me be very clear: After this ends, don't ever come to me for anything ever again. Don't even breathe my name. Got it?"

"You always say that, and you never mean it." She shoved her jacket sleeve up to check the time. "You have a meeting to attend. You need to go now. You'll have backup." She switched gears and slipped back into her suit of numbness and detachment, wearing it far better than I ever did. "Air support as well. We don't anticipate any problems, but in case things go sideways, we won't let you die."

Not yet, you mean. Not before you get what you want.

Still holding my hand, Ryder squared up with her, and Beth motioned to Leo to point his weapon, and he didn't hesitate.

"We have a problem, Lawson?" Beth angled her head and leaned in closer to him, then whispered loud enough for the two of us to hear, "I never liked you, and considering your ex is four months pregnant with your friend's kid and you only broke up three months ago, looks like she didn't like you, either."

What. The. Actual. Hell? I stumbled, but Ryder kept me upright.

"So please, please fuck around and find out. We can do this without you if we have to," she hissed, but I was still hung up on the fact that it sounded as though Lainey had cheated on Ryder.

When Ryder didn't step away, continuing to engage in a staring contest with her, I could tell he was channeling everything he had inside himself to remain in stand-down mode.

I squeezed his hand, reminding him I was still there, and as long as we were together, we'd be okay.

And screw Beth. Fuck Lainey, too.

Beth focused on me next. "Maybe you're the only one here with some sense. So if you don't want to see the man holding your hand Tasered, convulsing on the ground in two seconds, then get in the *fucking* SUV and go to that meeting."

CHAPTER THIRTY-FOUR

Seraphina

"I should have known Leo would find a way to create a problem for us," Alex said from behind the wheel while driving. We had chaperones this time, as in the CIA's eyes in the sky watching over us to ensure we reached our final destination like Beth wanted.

Since Beth had taken our phones, the laptop, and every weapon the guys had had on them, we had no way of letting Ángel know we were running late. I had to assume he hadn't taken off, though.

"Beth's plan for you is not happening. I couldn't open my mouth back there, or I'd risk—"

"I know," I interrupted Ryder, not wanting him to beat himself up over anything. He'd been in an impossible situation. "This is my fault. Beth basically hijacked my plan and turned it into a real-life game of Jumanji against drug lords." I hated calling another woman a bitch, but damn . . . if anyone qualified, it'd be her.

Ryder reached over and set his hand on my leg. "Not your fault."

Reed broke his silence for the first time since we'd parted ways with the she-devil, swerving the conversation away from my guilt. "In six hours we're in daylight territory. That means the meeting between Ezra and the Moraleses won't happen until much later. After sunset. That gives us a chance to pull in the support we need."

Take the plan back from Beth? I was still skeptical that was possible with the CIA involved, even with Batman's help.

"We have to part ways with Beth and her team without anyone becoming collateral damage," Ryder said. "Can't kill her or Leo, either."

"Not that I'd shed a tear if either of them got caught up in the cross fire." Reed and I were on the same page there. "No offense."

"Trust me, none taken." Alex turned us down a side road. "After this, I'm done. So help me, you have permission to kill me if I try to change my mind."

"I'll remember that, but I better not have to remind you," Ryder said gruffly.

And speaking of exes . . . Lainey cheated. She's pregnant with your friend's child. Now I knew why Ryder's teammates hated her. The poor guy. *And I probably shouldn't be thinking about this right now. One problem at a time.*

"How do we get extra support if Beth takes us to her safe house?" I asked, speaking my thoughts out loud.

"I'll get ahold of a phone somehow so we can contact Carter and Hudson once we're there. I'm pretty good at the whole sleight-of-hand thing."

"Like a magic trick?" Was he serious?

"Something like that." Alex's voice was calmer now than it had been going up against his ex. Hopefully, that meant he'd managed to lower his blood pressure.

I couldn't help but wonder how long their marriage had lasted, because the man seemed night-and-day different from her. You know, as in he was a good person.

Reed gave us some good news. "Also, I think there was a friendly back there on the GRS team. Our paths crossed a few times when I was still active duty. Garrison was Special Forces before becoming a paramilitary contractor. I can talk to him, get him on our side."

Right, I saw that exchange between you two. "And, um, how will you snatch a phone if they lock us all up once we're at their safe house, even if you have someone on the inside to help?"

"His dad was . . . well, a pretty big deal in Vegas," Ryder explained, more than likely reading my thoughts since he couldn't read my confused expression in the dark.

She called Alex Houdini back there. Now it's all making sense.

"I'll convince Beth to give us an inch if she wants that mile she's after," Alex explained.

"And by mile, you mean us willingly cooperating with her plan to use me as bait to take down the Moraleses?"

"Yeah, but we won't let that happen," Ryder said before Alex could answer. "I'm going to do everything in my power to stop her."

I rested my hand on top of his, which was still parked on my leg. "I don't want you doing something you'll regret, like hurting any of those GRS people. Or Alex killing his ex."

"Don't tempt me," Alex said under his breath, and then an eerie silence filled the air before I decided to break it with some awkward questions.

"Not to piss anyone off—and by 'anyone,' I really mean you," I rushed out, dialing in on my overprotective hero, "but what if we let Beth think we're going along with her plan, but we amend it? Tweak it with the help of Carter and Hudson? Would it be so bad if we helped take down the Moraleses? They're the people who disembowel their enemies and hang innocent people in the streets who refuse to work for them." Talk about a horrible image. "We could keep Ezra alive in case Hudson's lead in Russia is wrong and we need to question him. Screw what Beth wants."

"I agree with you about Beth because I don't give a damn about her." Ryder pulled his hand out from under mine, resting it on his own leg, curling his fingers inward. "But your plan requires you being bait. I'm not taking that chance, and you know it. For the record, the idea *does* piss me off."

The grumbly growliness at the end there was expected. I'd seen it coming, but I had to try. And also, speaking of "chances," well... "What are the odds I wound up reaching out to the same person the CIA already had working for them? I don't believe Martín set me up."

"Ángel left the cartel a few years ago and lived to tell about it. That's not exactly common, and that places a bull's-eye on him. A target for rival cartels or three-letter agencies to try and use him to get to their enemies. It's a name Martín would know, and he'd decided was a viable option for your backup plan." Reed, always with a plausible explanation. "Ángel would probably say no to anyone who approached him for help, but clearly, he wasn't given a choice or a chance to decline Andrej's request."

A.k.a. Beth's plan. "So you don't think Ángel continued working with the CIA after Andrej died? Do you think he called the Agency after I made contact with him at the club, and Beth wasn't having him watched?" I didn't want to think that, because I really wanted to trust Ángel.

I waited for an *I told you so* comment about trusting Ángel, but it never came. I supposed I hadn't been *wrong* wrong about him. Ángel hated the cartel, but maybe not as much as I hated Ezra. Beth may also have had him by the balls. You know, in the literal sense. I wouldn't put it past her.

I had a running list of names to call that woman in my head now. It was growing by the second.

"Hopefully, we'll know more after we talk to Ángel," Ryder said in a steady voice. "But given what you told us in Mexico about the change in Ezra's trade route tactics a few months ago, it sounds to me like Ezra began thinking outside the box to eliminate his competition."

"He cut out the Moraleses by making better trade deals with the overseas suppliers, no longer needing additional help from an insider like Ángel. I suppose Ángel was kept alive as a back burner contingency plan." *And that time is now.*

"That'd be a Beth thing to do," Alex grumbled.

"Well, Beth's team at the Agency wants the cartels taken out for good, not just to outbid them with the suppliers," Reed said. "Beth likes the idea of using Seraphina and Ángel to do that." He shifted gears, targeting his next question at me. "Did you give Ángel the name Anna when you met last night?"

I nodded. "Yeah, I did."

"Ángel had to have realized you were Ezra's accountant, and he assumed you were double-crossing him. He decided a better plan would be to go behind your back and reach out to a contact he had on speed dial with the CIA," Reed continued. "At that point, Beth already knew your real name and that you were on the run."

"Another domino falling in place for her." I hated using that woman's analogy.

"She was in the process of trying to track us down. I bet she was halfway to Mexico when Ángel made contact with the Agency." Alex parked and turned off the engine, shifting around to look at me. "Beth had to prevent us from ruining her undercover operation with the Sokolovs that the Feds accidentally stepped in, and either Ángel called her, or she had people watching him when you arrived . . . and she turned lemons into motherfucking lemonade."

I considered his words, trying to wrap my head around everything. "Do you think the Agency is allowing Ezra's organization to remain active because, in a way, Ezra's helping clean house with the cartels by taking over?"

"I mean, fuck, it's kind of smart. I hate to say it. Allow a monopoly in the drug-trade business to happen so then there's only one enemy to go up against, and if they have people on the inside, they can pull their strings without them even knowing it," Reed said, shaking his head. "Her team can keep a better eye on the Chinese suppliers and how the drugs—or any contraband, for that matter—come into the country."

"That's why Beth's colleague was in trouble for tipping off DHS about the terrorist cell." Ryder leaned back in his seat. "Director Johnson didn't want to risk drawing attention to the Sokolovs or their overall organization with that tip. He'd rather protect their operation than throw the Sokolovs into the spotlight."

"But Beth had no idea the DEA was already onto the Sokolovs," I said, adding on another point. "And what happened Saturday led to Beth finding out about the task force and that her operation may be compromised if they don't stop me." *And use me.* All I could see now were lined-up dominoes falling.

"That's what happens when government agencies keep secrets from each other," Reed grumbled. "Step on each other's toes without knowing it."

"Beth's team isn't going to let you walk away from this alive." Ryder pivoted in his seat, facing me. "You know too much. She'll make sure you become—"

"A casualty of war," I finished for him, a feeling of dread filling me. "We're all a threat to exposing her operation."

He reached for my hand and bent forward, kissing my forehead. "I won't let her hurt you, or any of us." In a deep voice, he added, "Even if I have to go to prison for murdering a CIA officer, then so-fucking-be-it."

CHAPTER THIRTY-FIVE

Ryder

Ángel was parked behind a cheap folding table in a plastic chair, one booted foot hooked around the leg as he stared over at the two of us. "Get held up in traffic?"

"Took a wrong turn." *Right into CIA hell.*

"I bet you did." He gestured to the two armed guys off to my side to give us space.

With my hand at Seraphina's lower back, I guided her over to the table. We were inside what I assumed was the break room. A few tables, a coffee maker, and fridge. Nothing else.

Reed and Alex were told to wait out front, which didn't do wonders for my trust or patience.

"Miss Torres." Ángel motioned for her to sit when she remained a statue next to me, and it took all my energy not to wrap my arms around her as though that'd shield her.

"They told you my real name?" The question came out pillow soft, which had to be quite the contrast to how she'd boldly confronted him Thursday night.

Now I knew that "her" was just an act. She'd been Anna in that club. Standing next to me now, she felt safe enough to be herself.

"By 'they,' I assume you mean the ice queen?" His dark brows lifted before he revealed, "No, I already knew who you were before I spoke to her."

Ice queen was too nice for the demon spawn from hell that was my best friend's ex.

"Please, sit." He verbalized his request this time. "Nice fight, by the way. You should consider stepping back in the ring again."

Once Seraphina was seated, I circled the table to stand off to the side. No plans to have my back to the door or to the two armed guards standing by it. "I think I'll pass."

His gaze briefly flicked to the light fixture overhead. I took that as a signal this wasn't really a SCIF and we had eyes on us now.

"I thought we had a deal." Seraphina's words lured my focus back to her, her hands slipping to her lap, probably fighting a compulsion to fidget.

"No, we had an agreement to talk and see if we could make a deal. You, though, weren't forthcoming at our first meeting. Only one of us lied, and it was you, Anna Cruz."

"I deserve that." She allowed a moment of silence to pass. "Did you know I worked for Ezra Sokolov before or after we met?"

"I looked you up before we met and discovered you worked for him, but that's not why I said yes to meeting with you. I'd have never agreed to see you if that were the case." That wasn't what I was expecting him to say. "It was when I saw your photo that changed everything."

"I don't understand," she murmured, her hands shifting to the table.

"I recognized you. I knew about the family that was killed in Cabo by mistake. A daughter left behind. The cartel, *mi familia*, blamed for their deaths. I saw your photo online. This, of course, was back when you weren't yet Anna." He pointed to the floor next to him, the tiles fractured there. "The cartel was accused of murdering Andrej here in

Costa Rica as well, but we all know if *mi familia* wanted that man dead, his death would have been much more painful and overt."

My gaze volleyed back and forth between the two of them while I kept careful watch from the corner of my eye of the two men by the door.

"So why'd you meet with me, knowing that? I'm not understanding. It's been a long day. Please spell it out for me."

"I figured out what you did and why. You wanted justice for your family, so you went undercover as Ezra's accountant, realizing the cartel didn't kill your parents and brother. You believed he did."

"And did he?"

No way would he give her an answer while we were on candid-fucking-camera.

"Perhaps the better question to ask yourself is why Andrej was killed, which led to the deaths of your family members; then you might find the answer you're looking for."

She slumped in her seat, then followed his gaze to the light, and I caught a flicker of understanding in her eyes.

Yeah, we're being watched.

"You said you have information I could pass over to the cartel, and I assume that intel is a result of your undercover work with the Sokolovs. *Sí?*" Before she could respond, he added, "Some of that information may be traced back to its source."

That rules out the cartel's watching us. Beth. Of-fucking-course.

"Your family will find out it was you who helped the Sokolovs, and they'll discover Andrej passed that information over to Ezra back when he was alive." She interpreted what he said in a more matter-of-fact way.

"The only thing of value I have to give *mi familia* now is you, the accountant to the man who's destroying their business."

"And that's the deal you worked out with the ice queen?" she asked.

He lowered his eyes to the table, remaining quiet.

"You stopped working with *them* after Andrej died, or . . . ?" When he didn't respond, she pushed forward. "Then I showed up, and you found a new opportunity to pursue. Ezra's never been your enemy—only your family, right?"

From where I was standing, I was damn certain there was another person he couldn't stand.

"Did they no longer need you after Andrej died because Ezra came up with a new plan to undermine the cartel?" I had no clue if he would or even could answer her, but I patiently waited, letting her take the lead. "She kept you on the back burner just in case, though, am I right?" And like that, the bold and brave woman was front and center. Not necessarily as Anna, but as a woman who was done taking shit from anyone, and I loved that.

"Big Brother is always watching, are they not?" He opened his palms to the ceiling, maintaining eye contact with her.

"The ice queen found out I came to see you and forced you to work for her," Seraphina said decisively; then her shoulders relaxed as if she was relieved by something. "You didn't call them."

"Not everything is always as it seems. If anyone knows that, it is you, *sí*?" He stood and shifted up his sleeve, checking the time. "The cartel will arrive later today. The meeting will take place at ten p.m. as long as they agree upon a location."

"I take it the cartel is waiting until the last minute to pick it out?" I asked him.

"Paranoid, *sí*. I'm required to have you in my custody to join *mi familia* thirty minutes before they intend to meet with the Sokolovs. Your new *friends* will ensure you know where to go once I provide them the location."

His time frame gave us plenty of room to pull together a team for backup. Not that I intended to allow Beth to hand Seraphina over to him, but I wouldn't miss a chance to go after both the cartel and Ezra.

"Why here in Costa Rica? Why'd you bring us to where Andrej died?" she asked him. "Can you answer that?"

He rounded the table but didn't try to bypass me to get to her as she stood. "To bring Ezra back to the place where Andrej was killed."

To let this also be where it ends for Ezra, is what he said with his eyes. That's how I interpreted his look, at least. He'd never be able to say that out loud, because he knew Beth was watching us and must also have known she wanted Ezra surviving the showdown with the Moraleses.

"I am sorry about your family." Ángel sounded sincere that time. He nodded his goodbye and started for the door.

She faced him, asking, "Did you ever save him? The no-show fighter, I mean. Did you get him back from the cartel?"

"No. The cartel won that round," he said somberly, then glanced at us from over his shoulder. "But we'll win the war."

CHAPTER THIRTY-SIX

Ryder

"You good?" Alex asked as he and Reed surrounded us out in the parking lot.

"I don't know about Ryder," she began as I opened the side door of the Tahoe for her, "but I'm slightly more confused now than I was before we spoke to him."

"They had cameras on us, so we couldn't talk too much about what we knew," I explained once we were all inside and the doors were shut. "But I don't think he has a choice in any of this. He wants the cartel taken out, but Beth's pulling his strings, same as she's pulling the Sokolovs'. Only difference, Ezra doesn't know about it."

"So I take it we were right and Beth has had her claws in Ángel, even after Andrej died, in case she needed him again?" Alex asked us, and we explained as much as we knew, which wasn't a whole hell of a lot.

"Beth must've flipped someone else within the Sokolovs' organization after Andrej died," Reed said, reminding me of our earlier conversation. "I mean, she has to have, right?"

"His wife," she blurted. "Nina's Beth's other asset. Beth turned her, too. And if we're right, and Nina's the one with ties to the Russians in charge, that gives Beth a direct line to what's happening at the top of the organization."

Beth was making my head spin with her fuckery in all this.

"Nina's Ezra's link to his boss in Russia, so he has to do whatever she says," she went on. "We were right, we were just missing the link to Beth."

Also right about why Ezra never set a hand on you. I was ready to kill that man all over again. Use his blood as paint, Stephen King's *The Shining*-style. RED-FUCKING-RUM. Murder the son of a bitch.

"So, are we really suggesting the CIA created a brother-and-sister team of assets?" Her question pulled me back to the present, reminding me we had a few hurdles to deal with before I could prove to Seraphina exactly what I'd told her—that I really was "that guy," the one who'd take the life of a man like Ezra without a second thought.

"It could be why we can't find Nina anywhere," Alex answered her, and what was the question again? I needed to focus the fuck up. "The Agency may have Nina stashed away for safekeeping until the cartel is handled. Backup plan in case things go south with Ezra. Move the queen into position if the king dies."

"Ezra must've stumbled upon the fact someone was betraying him, and it was actually Beth who decided to throw Andrej under the bus to protect her most valuable asset. To protect Nina." Seraphina concluded what made the most sense to me as well.

"Beth—or, well, her team—would rather let Ezra believe Andrej was double-crossing him than pull him out of the field." *Is Beth really that ice cold? Apparently so.* Well, assuming it was her call to make and not Director Johnson's. Something told me Johnson had a *don't ask, don't tell* policy with her.

"How could his sister be okay with that?" Her voice became fragile as pain from her own loss had to be catching up with her.

"Maybe Nina didn't have a choice?" *Seems to be going around when it comes to Beth's manipulation tactics.* Her whatever-it-takes-to-get-the-job-done mentality front and center.

"Or Nina's enjoying the power and lifestyle she has a little too much courtesy of Beth, and she'd rather her brother died than give that up." Alex was probably thinking about Beth with that comment. The man was going to need to see a therapist after the hell his ex put him through. One thing at a time.

"This would confirm our theory the CIA buried the story from the national news when Seraphina's family was murdered." Reed pivoted us in a new direction, and he was right about that. The pieces were all adding up.

"So," she began, "are we thinking Beth's team turned Nina and Andrej before or *after* Nina married Ezra? What if . . ." She gripped my leg and said something in Spanish that I assumed she'd translate. "You and Hudson traced the information in my files to a shell company in Russia, to the same place where Nina's been visiting, right?"

"Yeah." I rested my hand on top of hers, taking a moment to process where she was going with this. Then it hit me as I remembered what Ángel had told us back there. "Not everything is always as it seems. The shell company is a front for—"

"Beth's dark money team," Alex cut me off, and he must've taken his foot off the gas pedal, because we were abruptly slowing down. "Ezra doesn't work for the Russians at all. He works for Beth's team."

"And Ezra most likely doesn't even know it, but clearly his wife does as Beth's asset," I said in agreement. "Nina's trips to Russia are to sell the idea the organization is run by someone over there. Not just to throw off Ezra, but the suppliers and cartels. Hell, to throw off everyone."

"Knowing Beth, she preselected Ezra as the mark for this whole damn thing," Alex gritted out. "She knew his background. He was probably a shady motherfucker to start with, and she helped him up his game and take it all the way home. Set Nina up with him to marry."

Talk about a case of entrapment. "Beth's team is the real devil at the top. Beth would prefer to keep Ezra in power, but she has Nina off the grid as a backup plan to take over if need be."

"At that rate, I'm shocked she doesn't just let Ezra die and have Nina take over. No more playing games," Alex grunted. He made a valid point. "Unless my ex-wife has something else up her sleeve."

"Are we really saying what I think we are?" Seraphina whispered.

The doom-and-gloom guy on my team was about to lay it all out for us, I could feel it. "Director Johnson devised a way to take as much power from the cartels as possible by creating a fictitious enterprise that no one—especially the cartels—could compete with."

"Not so much fiction anymore," I tossed out.

"People will get drugs anyway, why not be the ones controlling the market and selling them? The US loves their monopolies," Reed continued with the ugly truth. "Hell, I bet they'd have a better quality check on the drugs, too."

"But, I mean, is this *really* what we're suggesting?" she asked, shock hedging her tone.

I had a hard time believing the president had signed off on this.

"I think so. It's speculation right now, but Reed's rarely wrong." Alex increased our speed as if we could actually outrun his ex. No, we'd be boxed in anytime now. "When did Nina marry Ezra, again?"

I deferred to Seraphina on that since I couldn't remember. "Three years ago."

"That tracks. I got divorced, what, sixteen or seventeen months ago? She started changing before that, though. Became a different person."

"This can't be just about drugs. That's not CIA territory." *Doesn't add up.*

"Beth brought up the Chinese, remember?" she reminded us. "She said something about them being too close to our borders and working with the cartels."

"Right, right." Alex stepped on it even more, so I reached over and buckled her in. "Beth doesn't want the Chinese finding out they're not really working with the Russians. Her whole house of cards collapses, her illusionist act over."

"The Chinese suppliers would switch back to working with the cartels and start flooding the market through Mexico again, and the CIA loses their new monopoly. Not to mention, the Chinese may retaliate in more ways than one." That point wasn't to side with the she-devil, but it was still a fact I couldn't ignore, and a shitty one at that.

Looks like there will be an even greater need for Hudson's new project after we take everyone down here in Costa Rica. I really had run into that man for a reason.

"The more cartels Beth's team can wipe out, the better their odds are at keeping our main enemies off the borders and out of the US." It would have been a solid fucking plan *if* people weren't dying by her hand. *If* her team destroyed the drugs instead of selling them. But the real world rarely operated in *ifs*, more like in dollars.

"So, this is about a cold war with China." I hung my head. *And that's CIA territory, for damn sure.* "Not to mention funding that very war with the drug money Beth's team is bringing in from taking over for the cartels."

"And this all means," Seraphina whispered, "that Ezra may have put out the hit on Andrej that led to my family dying, but in reality—"

"Their murders are my ex-wife's fault."

CHAPTER THIRTY-SEVEN

Ryder

"Was that really necessary?" Alex asked after Leo, of all fucking people, removed the black bags from our heads. We'd just made it to the CIA's safe house after they'd forced us off the road ten minutes ago.

Beth had Leo cut Alex's zip ties, allowing him to stand. She nudged a cup of coffee his way like a peace offering. "If you know our location, you'll get a signal out somehow to someone to try and save you."

Alex shoved the mug back at her, liquid sloshing onto his hand, but he didn't react. The coffee was probably cold, like Beth's heart. "Not interested in ingesting arsenic, thanks."

Beth wasn't the eye-rolling type, so her response was to drink the coffee as her answer to him. Prove it wasn't poison. You couldn't kill what was already dead, and she was that. On the inside, at least.

Alex targeted Leo next. "You wouldn't help us in Miami when Sera was in danger, but you're okay with working for Beth?"

Leo stepped forward in between the two other operators standing there. I took them to be more of the silent, just-doing-what-they're-told types. "She pays enough that I forget to care." A sly smile crossed his lips; then he stole a look at Seraphina and winked.

Well, that was the wrong move. He was lucky my hands were currently zip-tied behind my back. More importantly, he was lucky I couldn't act out of anger right now. I had to keep my head on straight so Beth wouldn't Taser me or God-knows-what-else she might do.

"I also pay you not to have an opinion," Beth said in her typical no-fucks-given tone.

They say opposites attract, but that woman was on the other side of the world from Alex.

"Go ahead and untie the others," she ordered.

Seraphina, Reed, and I were all on our knees like hostages inside the living room of their safe house. Once we were cut free by one of the quiet operators who'd yet to piss me off, I helped Seraphina to her feet.

I took a moment to scan the room, count the armed operators we'd be up against if need be, along with what kind of heat they were packing. Ten tangos in total, which included the she-beast, a new name Seraphina had said under her breath while we'd been bagged earlier. Thermal had picked up only the eight, but we hadn't accounted for their pilot and another passenger in the helo.

"What's next in the playbook, boss lady?" Alex offered up a heavy dose of sarcasm at the end there.

"No conversations are happening in here. Not in front of everyone." Her answer was revealing.

I had to assume most of the GRS operators weren't actually part of her special team and it was possible we could pull a few over to our side. Not Leo, of course.

Beth set down the coffee and removed her suit jacket, tossing it on the couch. "There's nothing you all need to do right now. We can't come up with an infil and exfil plan without a location. So for now, why don't you sleep?"

"Sleep?" Alex fake-laughed. "You gotta be kidding me."

"Did you get everything you wanted from the meeting?" Seraphina squared off with her. Brave and bold. Ready to throw down. "You were watching us, right?"

Beth methodically rolled up her sleeve before moving on to the next one.

It took all my energy to stand there and bite my tongue, to not engage. We could probably handle the numbers presently in the room, because the rest were patrolling the property, but I didn't want to kill them. Injure Leo, though? Yeah, he deserved an ass whooping. But unless these guys were in on Beth's plans, they didn't deserve to die.

"Nothing to say?" Seraphina took a step forward, provoking her. So I took one right along with her.

"Life is all about choices, Miss Torres. Some sacrifices have to be made for the greater good. To preserve American values and protect our country." What a scripted DC answer.

Seraphina didn't respond like I knew she wanted to. She was probably reminding herself of the same thing I was. We all agreed not to expose how much we knew about Beth's dark money team.

"You'll be escorted to your bedrooms now." Beth waved her hand toward the hallway off to our left. "Don't think of this as a prison, but more so a time-out."

Alex opened his mouth, then snapped it shut. He smartly kept that *fuck you* he wanted to say to himself.

"Alex, you'll be coming with me to my room." Beth tipped her head toward the hall at our right.

"Ah, you're looking to get lucky, are you?" Alex leaned in, fucking with her. "Not on your life, Bethany."

Beth maintained her composure and simply pointed to the hall. "Now."

He closed his eyes and let go of a deep breath, and I knew it pained him to do what she said, but he had no choice.

"Before you leave, though," she said to Seraphina, "I need you to do something." She produced a phone from her pocket. "You have a message to send. I know about your friend in Mexico. I assume if you don't check in, he'll get worried. I'd prefer to avoid any conflict with a man who's an enemy of the cartel. An enemy of—"

"Please don't finish your sentence," Seraphina cut her off, reluctantly accepting the phone. "I'm so sick of those words." She went ahead and typed in the six-digit passcode and scrolled to Martín's name as I looked on. Hell, with everything that'd happened, I'd forgotten about him. "What am I telling him?"

Beth raised her brows. "Not even putting up a fight?"

"I don't want him getting hurt, and he'll fly here if he doesn't hear from me. So yeah, you win right now."

"Just make sure he doesn't suspect anything and buy yourself time."

Seraphina quickly did what she asked before Beth took the phone back.

"I'll hang on to that." Beth flicked her wrist, motioning for Leo to walk over. "Take the three of them to their rooms."

"I'm not leaving her alone." That was a hill I'd die on. Game, set, and match if Beth wanted to go there. "Unless you want to spill blood—which *will* happen—don't try to split us up."

"She's not just a mark to you?"

I let her words pass over me, refusing to allow her to get under my skin.

"Fine. I know when to pick and choose my battles," she said almost casually.

Seraphina's back relaxed against my palm.

One of the quiet GRS operators abruptly stepped forward, blocking Leo's path to us. "Maybe not the best idea to have him be their escort? Why don't I show these two to their room?"

I discreetly checked Reed, gauging his reaction to see if he was our possible ally coming to our rescue. Reed gave me an answer of no with a subtle shake of the head.

"Fine. You've got them." Beth waved someone else over next, and Reed signaled to me yes, letting me know Garrison was accompanying him.

That's something. I started for the hall, keeping hold of Seraphina, then shot one last look at Alex, worried about him having to be alone with Beth.

She was going to sink her claws into him. Draw blood. Inflict as much pain as possible, and that big-ass heart of his would be powerless to hurt her back.

Alex narrowed his eyes and lightly nodded. I hoped that meant what I needed it to mean. He really was done with that vindictive woman for good.

Because after this, if it were up to me, I wouldn't stop Seraphina from killing her like I knew she wanted to. Hell, I might even give her a gun to do it.

CHAPTER THIRTY-EIGHT

Ryder

"There aren't cameras in here," Body Four said as I stood on the bed, checking the light in the ceiling fan.

Aside from Garrison, I'd assigned every operator a number. I had to separate emotion from the equation just in case they wound up on the other side of my rifle at some point.

"I'm going to sweep the room anyway, and you know it," I finally answered after confirming the light was clear.

Once I hopped off the bed, Seraphina took a seat on it, the cheap mattress sinking down. "Are you part of her special team? Do you really know what's going on here?" she asked him as I proceeded to check the only window in the room, testing whether it'd open. I doubted it but had to try.

"You'll need something heavy duty to crack it." Body Four remained in front of the closed door with his booted foot propped up against it, arms folded. "I just go where I'm told, ma'am. I'm here for protection." He acknowledged her question when I moved on to another object in the sparsely decorated room.

"Protection for . . . ?"

"The OIC," he told her as I took a knee, checking the vent near the baseboards.

"You guys with your acronyms. Officer in charge, right? And that'd be Beth?" When he didn't confirm, she continued with her mission for answers. "Are you okay with using me as bait to bring together two ruthless criminal groups? Are you good with letting one of those bad guys walk away alive even if I don't?"

"I'm not paid to have an opinion, either. I just follow orders." Based on his tone, he wasn't buying what he was selling, which could work in our favor.

I pushed up off the floor and stood to face him. "You're going to wind up a casualty yourself if you don't formulate an opinion real fast." I cut across the room, and he lowered his boot to the floor and rested his hand at the sidearm strapped to his hip.

"I take it you plan to tell me what opinion to have?" Despite the sarcasm, he didn't offer up the same kind of attitude Leo would've.

"What branch were you in?" I took a U-turn from my original plan to dehumanize him.

He couldn't be but a few years younger than me, but he looked far more jaded. *That's what working for the Agency will do to you.* Goodbye black and white. All gray, all the time. Not morally gray, as my book-loving mom would call it, either. This was CIA gray. Dark money gray.

"That's none of your concern." He removed his hand from his Glock and turned, preparing to exfil from a conversation he clearly didn't want to have.

I was 90 percent sure he wasn't in the know about Beth's team or her plans, just an operator pulled in for a quick op. Beth would be fine sacrificing him for the sake of her mission.

So it was possible I could get through to him before he walked out. At least plant a seed of doubt in his mind about this mission and why he was there. "Hold up."

He shifted around, catching my eye.

"No, don't look at me." I pointed to Seraphina. "Look at her. Think about why you ever put on the uniform in the first place. Was it to answer to DC bureaucrats and a bunch of spies playing war games as if real lives aren't on the line? You know better than they do that we don't have three lives. Just the one. If we die, it's game over for good. We're just replaced by another body. Easily replaceable to people like Beth."

His Adam's apple moved as he swallowed, a touch of humanity breaking through when he set his eyes on her. He became a soldier again. Or sailor. Whatever he'd once been while in the military, and not Body Four.

"Beth won't hesitate to let you fall on the sword for her crusade, and my guess is you don't have a clue about why she's really here."

He folded his arms and zeroed in on me. "Enlighten me, then."

Could we trust him not to betray us and tell Beth the truth?

"How much do you already know?" If he was candid with me, then two things were more than likely true: There really weren't cameras in here and he was someone who'd help us.

Hesitation passed over his face as I waited for him to answer, and now I remembered he'd been in the helo, not on the ground, when Beth had pulled us over both times earlier.

"We're mostly here to point and shoot when and where directed. Only two operators here know all the details. And in case you're wondering, I'm not one of those men." He lifted his eyes to the ceiling, clearly at war with this decision and what to do. "All I know is that a criminal enterprise run by the Russians will be meeting with the Morales cartel in approximately twenty hours. My mission is to protect the OIC and my team, and to ensure your people take out the Morales cartel. That's it."

"What about me?" Seraphina stood, coming up next to me.

He mindlessly reached for his ring finger as if searching for a wedding band that was normally there, but he'd more than likely removed it for the mission.

Tell me you have a spouse at home. A family. Someone you love and wouldn't want in this position.

"I was told you were a Russian asset working for that criminal in Miami, and you betrayed him. You're planning on selling him out to the cartel." He looked over at me next. "But I'm familiar with you, Lawson—at least, with your reputation. And if you're protecting her like this, then . . ."

"That means you know you should be helping her, too," I finished for him. "Do you have a phone?"

"Not on me, no. She made sure we were only carrying weapons and no tech of any kind when entering the house. Only Beth and those two operators from her DC team have access to phones and laptops."

I figured as much.

"And no, that asshole Leo's not one of the two operators," he added, letting me know he was perceptive, picking up on the fact Leo was a dick. "I'm Nate. I was SF before working for the Agency."

Army Special Forces. Good. "So was Garrison," I said at the memory of what Reed had shared with us. "You close with him? He's also not one of the two operators in the know, correct?"

"We're friends, yes. And no, he's not one of the two." He went ahead and gave me the names of the operators, along with their descriptions. Body Three and Six. "So, why am I really here?"

I reached for her hand and squeezed, then went ahead with the reveal, hoping we could truly trust him. "We believe Director Johnson devised a plan to stop the flow of fentanyl coming into the country from Mexico. And sure, take down the cartels and stop drugs from hitting our streets? Great, that's needed—and the cartel? Well, they're fucking horrible people, I can get behind that. The problem is, their team didn't stop the drugs from hitting our streets, and instead, they took over. And that Russian organization in Miami, that's actually Beth's team. We don't think Ezra Sokolov knows he works for the CIA, and the Chinese suppliers are unaware they're selling to Uncle Sam."

He blinked his eyes up to my face in shock. "I'm sorry, but what?"

So I spelled it out for him. Word for fucking word. Including what happened with Andrej and our belief that Nina was Beth's other asset.

Nate looked back and forth between us. "How could Beth get away with this?"

"I don't think POTUS is aware of all the details of their project, and the other agencies sure as hell didn't know the CIA had ties to the Sokolovs, or they wouldn't have been investigating them," I explained.

"I was also an informant for the DEA." Seraphina kept her voice soft as she shared that fact. "*Not* a Russian asset."

"So, the Russians are really Beth's team in disguise." He tore a hand through his hair. "This is wild. And Beth's team is using you to draw out the Moraleses." At her nod, he asked, "But she wants to keep Ezra alive, because he unknowingly works for her."

"That about sums it up," she said.

I gave him a few seconds to process before speaking. "So, you see why we're all here now, and Beth has a lot at stake if things don't end the way she wants them to. I don't think the CIA director even knows the truth about her team, which is fucked up. But yeah, Beth's managed to create a monopoly on the drug trade, and she's using that money to fund a cold war with China."

Nate held up his hand, shaking his head again. "Does she think if the Agency doesn't sell the drugs, that'll somehow give the cartels back their power? Assuming people will find drugs another way if they want them bad enough?"

"Presumably," I said. "If fentanyl isn't hitting the streets because of the monopoly the CIA's shell company has, then the cartels will start pumping the drug in. But does that make what Beth's team is doing right? Hell no."

"They took the *if you can't beat them, join them* approach to a whole new gross fucking level." He closed his eyes, hanging his head while pinching the bridge of his nose.

"So now that we're on the same page, are we going to be outside this room, too?" I asked him.

He slowly looked up at me, then over to Seraphina. "How can I help?"

CHAPTER THIRTY-NINE

Ryder

After Nate left—locking us in the room, as he'd been ordered to do—I pulled Seraphina into my arms.

"He's on our side." Her face was smashed against my chest, so her words came out muffled.

"And if Reed hasn't already done so, he'll make sure Garrison is, too. Everything is going to be okay."

"Still can't imagine what would've happened had you not gone up on that balcony last week."

I let go of her so I could look her in the eyes. "I'm glad we'll never have to find out."

She gave me a small smile, but I knew she was in knots about everything. Not that I could blame her. We were hostages, so there was that obstacle we had to navigate before we could move forward.

"Guess we still need to find a way to get word out to someone for backup, though, or Beth's going to lead the operation tonight."

"Just like Martín would've come here if he didn't hear from you, Carter will realize something is wrong, too," I reminded her. "Carter will get word to POTUS, and if we're lucky, he'll pull the plug on Beth's op, but I don't think the president will want to miss out on the opportunity to take out the Moraleses while we're here."

She swept her fingers across her mouth, and I lost her eyes to the floor. "And what will the president want to do with Ezra? He's essentially a pawn in Beth's spy games. Not a good guy by any stretch of the imagination, but he may want to have him questioned, right?"

"Maybe." *Doubtfully.*

"And the only way to draw out the Moraleses is with Ezra, and to do that, I'm still needed." She went over to the bed and sat, resting her hands on her thighs. "And that's why you're still in broody central despite turning Nate on our side and being optimistic Batman will still come through for us, phone or not."

Batman? I smiled. She wasn't wrong. Not that the guy had a Batsuit, but he certainly had the tools. Knowing him, probably also a cave. "Let me just check the rest of the room for cameras and listening devices," I deflected. "I highly doubt Nate was playing good cop and he's secretly on Beth's side."

"But you're not one to take chances. Not in your control-freak nature."

"Not when it comes to the safety of my team. You're still Delta Four. Not my mark or my asset." I quickly went over to the lamp by the bed to check it.

"Not a mark or an asset. But not bait, either, not even if that means we could save so many lives by putting an end to the Morales cartel?"

My back muscles pinched at what she was getting at, steering us to the conversation I was working to avoid.

I set down the lamp after determining it was clear. "Seraphina," I said on a defeated sigh while facing her, finding her unlacing her sneakers. "I, uh . . . Let me finish clearing the room first. Bathroom too. Just give me a minute." *Give me a minute to pull myself together. Think clearly.*

She nodded, then kicked off her shoes and removed her lightweight jacket.

I went to work on ensuring the room was clean of listening devices and cameras, and once I was satisfied that we were good, I returned to the bed and offered her my hand to stand.

"Let me truly be Delta Four." She wasted no time killing me with that. "I want to be part of your team for this, and if one of you had to go undercover to put two evil enemies together to take them both out, you'd do it. Pretend I'm not the woman you fell for after only three days."

It's first sight for me. I kept that to myself for now, my chest tightening.

"Remember, I was undercover with Ezra for over nine months and managed to avoid winding up on Beth's radar. I've got skills aside from acting and math. I can shoot. Fight."

I took a moment to absorb what she'd said, and her eyes lit up, probably assuming I was coming around to her idea.

But no, I was picturing the fact she'd unknowingly been working for Beth all that time. It had my head going ten different directions of *what the fuck* with all that could've gone wrong. Ezra, not telling his wife, or anyone for that matter, that his "accountant" was really Seraphina wound up saving her life. Not that I'd credit that man with protecting her. But fate swung in her direction with that one, and thank God, didn't miss.

"Okay, since you're still processing . . ." She rested her hand on my chest, looking up at me. "The only way we'll ever have a chance to date and see what this thing is between us is if we take down the Moraleses."

Date? God help me, that word felt so small and insignificant for what I wanted to do.

"The Moraleses know about me now." She continued with that heart attack she was determined to give me. "Even if the president handles Beth's team and Ezra, too, if we don't stop the cartel, there will always be a target on me. At least, on Anna Cruz, and by extension of my alter ego, on me."

I hung my head while securing hold of her wrist but didn't remove her hand from my chest.

"I trust you and your team to keep me safe. I need you to trust me not to die on you. I have something to live for now. Not my revenge. But a future I'd like to explore with you." Her voice broke from emotion.

There was so much I wanted to say, so much I wanted to give her of myself, but I . . . had issues. Quite a few, in fact.

"If you can come up with a way to protect me that also takes down the bad guys, then promise me you'll consider it?"

I wasn't sure if I could make that promise. One thing at a time, though. First, we needed to relieve Beth of control, then go from there.

"Let's talk about this once we know more, okay?" That was the best I could give her right now.

"Yeah, okay." She glanced at the bed, and where was her mind going? "What do we do while we wait?"

I had a few ideas, none of them appropriate. "You could try closing your eyes and resting. I'll sit next to you. Hold you, if you'd like?"

"I'm not tired," she said as I let go of her, and she lowered her hand to her side, away from that organ in my chest rapidly coming back to life, thanks to her. "Can I ask you something? And I swear, it's not about being bait."

I gave her a hesitant smile. "Okay, then. Go for it."

"How'd Alex ever end up with a woman like Beth? And what about Lainey?"

What about her? My smile immediately vanished. Could I take back the *go for it*? I'd forgotten all about the fact Seraphina overheard Beth mention Lainey's cheating earlier.

"Sorry. If that's not my business, I understand."

"No, uh, that's okay." *Maybe it was easier to argue about being bait?* "Our jobs aren't easy for most people to handle. Makes it hard to date. Or to marry. We're always operating. Spinning up without notice. Dating someone in a similar line of work helps, I guess. They understand our lives, because the same goes for them," I explained quickly, unsure if I really got to the point of her question. "Lainey's not like Beth. I mean, she works for the government, and she fucked me over," I admitted, "but she's not evil."

"But she cheated and is pregnant? I mean, that has to hurt."

How do I answer that? "I didn't know she cheated, not until last weekend."

She blinked in surprise. Yeah, talk about timing.

"I'm good, though." I lifted my hand between us, a plea not to worry about Lainey, and I truly meant that. "I promise." My arm fell to my side. "It happening with a good friend, well . . . that part sucks." I dropped onto the bed, feeling the full weight of my words hitting me. "But, uh, about Beth—maybe she was never a good person and Alex missed the signs. I don't know."

"Oh." I wasn't sure how to interpret that little sound.

"That doesn't mean I *have* to date someone I work with, just to be clear," I hurried up and added so there was no mistake about my intentions with her. Then I fucked that up by admitting, "My relationships are usually pretty short-lived, regardless."

I'd expected her to turn her back on me at that. Instead, she sat next to me and threaded our fingers together, resting our palms on top of her leg. "Do you think your relationships aren't long-lasting because of *him*?"

She really was good at math, putting two and two together. "Are you asking if my father not being in my life fucked me up?" Probably not the same words she'd have used, but I was generally more of a direct and to-the-point kind of guy.

"Sorry, if this is the wrong conversation to have right now, we could kill time and discuss something else, like your favorite color." She filled the quiet and went on, "Although, I'm thinking I already know the answer, and it's red."

"I thought you don't care about that." I teasingly nudged her in the side, then glanced at her from over my shoulder. "But also, you're right. As long as it's a red something you're wearing." I kissed the tip of her nose. "And to answer your other question, yes. My dad may be tied to my relationship issues." I cleared my throat, let go of her hand, and stood. *First time admitting that out loud.* I waited for the weight on my chest to lift, hoping it would now that those words were out in the wild, but it didn't. Not yet, at least.

When I faced her, she was in the process of standing as well. Her long lashes fluttered, and she closed her eyes.

"Ask whatever you'd like." I was already in uncharted territory in so many ways, why not open up even more?

She would need to know about my baggage eventually to decide if she wanted to stick around. Until Carter pulled off the miracle we needed, I could go ahead and have a heart attack. You know, why not?

"You're sure?" She opened her eyes, and I nodded my surrender. "Well, um . . ." Tongue over her teeth for a momentary sexy distraction before she asked, "Will you tell me about him? Like, what happened? Why'd he leave?"

Could I do that and remain standing? *I'm about to find out.* "My father was a hockey player."

Her mouth rounded into a little O shape, recognition dawning fast at my attitude in the kitchen.

An awkward throat clear later, I continued, "Minor league stuff when I was a kid, but then he landed a contract with the pros." *Bullet points or real context?* I went for option two for the first time in my life. "I probably learned to skate before I could walk. I thought hockey was in my blood. A future star like him."

The little "oh" from her that time was much different from how she'd said it before. It was concern and worry and all the things a woman with a big heart would have for a child.

I wasn't a kid anymore, and I had to remind myself of that for a minute before I continued.

"Well, uh, not even a year into his contract, he packed up his shit and left. He decided being a pro and having a family wasn't in the cards for him. He signed over full custody of me, cut her a check, and never looked back. My mom gave him another six months to change his mind and come back, and when he didn't, she moved us out of Chicago to where her sister lived." Maybe I sped through that a bit too fast, but it wasn't exactly easy to talk about.

When she slid her arms around my body and hugged me, I stared blankly at an empty spot on the wall. "I'm so, so sorry." Her strangled voice had me finally remembering to hug her back.

"It's fine. I'm fine." The lies didn't leave my mouth quite as easily that time, and I skated a hand up and down her back, preferring to soothe her than seek comfort myself. "I kept playing hockey," I went on, working hard to keep my voice flat, to not let the past trip me up. "I convinced myself if I became really good at it, he'd come back. Like that'd somehow fix things." I shook my head, remembering my young, ridiculous self.

"Did you ever talk to or see him again?"

No one, not even my mom knew what I was about to tell her. "I saw him one time. My senior year at Princeton. He wasn't playing anymore, but he was an assistant coach for a minor league team. I'd secretly followed his career, still stupidly hanging on to the hope that one day he'd give a damn. Fuck, even the scholarship to Princeton was for hockey." I pulled away from her, tapping the side of my head. "Not because of brains. Sorry to disappoint."

She blinked a few times, freeing tears I didn't want her shedding on my behalf. The woman had lost her entire family, and my dad had only walked out on me. "You're smart. Don't start with that shit, I mean it." She was somehow scolding me without actually scolding me.

I even managed a smile, forgetting the pain for a moment. "Maybe a little." I winked, doubling down on taking a much-needed pause to live anywhere but in the past.

After a few quiet seconds passed, I realized I'd left my story unfinished.

"Anyway." *Shake it off.* "My father showed up to one of my games. He was scouting for his team, and my coach didn't give us the heads-up. To say I was blindsided by seeing him out in the stands watching me skate, well . . ." Damn the lump in my throat. Also, damn the fact my eyes kept trying to violate the oath I'd made to myself to never cry about him.

"I can't even imagine what you must've been feeling when you saw him there."

"The fucked-up thing . . ." I shook my head, working damn hard to not shed a tear. "I thought he was there for me." Eyes closed, I let the memories stab me in the chest all over again. "He didn't even recognize me. No connection made with our shared last name on the back of my jersey. He was there for someone else, which is probably why he knew nothing about me. He pulled another player aside to talk to him about a position, then he left. I considered chasing after him, but I had too much pride." I opened my eyes, finding my vision blurry. "After that, I went to the army's recruiting office and signed up for the military. Traded my hockey stick in for a rifle, and *I* never looked back."

Her tears were starting to wear me down, but it was her next words that broke me. "I feel so bad I brought up my dad at the villa and how proud he'd be of you without knowing all this."

Maybe only a few tears fell, but fuck, that was more than I'd wanted to happen over that man.

"Come here, you." I framed her face with my hands, chasing the only feeling I wanted right now: the peace this woman could give me.

I kissed her softly. Slowly. She was hesitant, worried about me after what I'd shared, but then she finally surrendered and let go of my pain the way I wanted her to.

The kiss deepened as I pushed the memories not to the past but out of my mind altogether.

"I hate him. I hate Lainey. I hate anyone who ever hurt you," she whispered.

I felt the same about her past, but we found our way to one another now, and I'd do everything in my power to have a future with her, which meant the Moraleses had to die. She was right about that.

"Lainey didn't hurt me, I promise," I reassured her. "I'd need to have truly loved her for her to do that."

"Are you sure, because—"

"I am." My fingers dove into her hair, tangling it up as I stared into her soulful eyes. "Everything happens for a reason." I grimaced. "Well, maybe not *everything* everything." Her family shouldn't have been a casualty of war. "Just kiss me, okay?" I swallowed. "That's all I need. Just you."

She was breathing hard, blinking back more tears. "And if I want more from you right now than only a kiss?"

My heart skipped three fucking beats. "'More' how?" *Here? Now?*

"I think you know what I mean and what I want." She clutched hold of my forearms like she had to tether herself to the moment so she wouldn't get taken away.

There was also another pressing issue aside from our current location and circumstances. "I don't have anything on me." *No protection.*

"Are you safe?" she asked as if it pained her, but I respected her for it.

But also . . . ? Was she asking me to take her bare? I untangled our bodies so I could lose my mind a bit and track my hands through my hair.

Turning this woman down wouldn't be happening. I lost total control somewhere in between her getting out of that pool and when she wrapped her mouth around my cock hours ago.

"I'm safe, yes."

"Same. You know, in both ways." She stepped forward, and maybe I should've stepped back, but I couldn't bring myself to do it. "IUD. I got it just in case Ezra or anyone ever managed to, well . . . assault me. I—I didn't want to get pregnant." She held her hand out between us. "Forget I said that. Absolute mood killer. Ugh, I'm so sorry. That's the equivalent to nervous laughter at a funeral, isn't it?"

"Seraphina?" I lifted my brows, and she wet her lips.

"Yeah?"

"Am I making you nervous again?" *Because you're making me that way.*

"You want to three-name me, don't you?" she asked. "Tell me I'm insane because of where we are and what we just talked about. But that's kind of been our thing since the moment we met, right? Unable to focus because we're so desperate to be in each other's arms? Lightning strikes during storms. And we seem to create the perfect conditions for a storm together."

When she slowly lifted her eyes to meet mine, that was all it took for me to finally snap.

I swallowed the space between us in one fast movement and lifted her from the floor, guiding her legs around my waist. I brought my mouth to her ear and rasped, "Fuck it. Let's make it rain."

CHAPTER FORTY

Seraphina

Ryder had me against the wall, and I kept my ankles locked at his back as he made love to me with his mouth.

The way this man kissed . . . it was like nothing I'd ever experienced before. Slow and sensual. Never sloppy or rushed. The perfect amount of tongue. The perfect everything altogether that I didn't know existed before him.

"Are you sure you want this?" he asked a few heated moments later, arching back to meet my eyes, still holding me up against the wall. One hand braced over my shoulder, and the other comfortably at my ass. "Here? Tonight?" He rotated his hips, letting me feel how hard he was.

"Technically, it's the morning," I teased. "Also, now our one-week anniversary."

"What if I missed a camera?" He grimaced and relaxed his hold of me, and I slipped my legs down, my feet finding the floor.

"You didn't." I set my hand on his chest and leaned in, wrapping my other behind his neck before shifting my fingers up into his hair.

I kissed him softly, trying to pull him out of his head. Being stuck in our thoughts was the opposite of what either of us wanted or needed.

"And I mean, if you did miss a camera, it's totally a bucket list item of mine to be a porn star."

He laughed, and the husky sound vibrated into my chest, which meant my joke had the desired outcome. "You got rid of your list, missy."

I kept my hand casually toying with the strands of his hair while my other coasted over the hard ridge of muscles in the arm he had propped up. "Right, right." I lazily trailed my finger along the prominent vein there.

His facial muscles went taut again. I could see the wheels of indecision turning. "What if someone unlocks and opens the door?"

The man was an alpha to the core, but in a way I loved, and I knew it'd make him crazy to have someone else see me butt-ass naked and having sex. I wouldn't be a fan of a woman seeing him, either, so I couldn't argue there.

"I'm guessing *they'll get a free show* isn't the answer you'll want to hear from me."

"You'd be correct," he said in a semi-amused tone while he pushed away from the wall, drawing his palm to my waist. "I want you. More than you can possibly know."

I was well aware of that truth based on the bulge in his jeans. "You're going to back out? Take some type of moral high ground instead of being crazy like I want? Offer a *rain* check, right?"

His brows tightened. "More like a weather delay," he said with a quick wink, continuing with our analogy, and God did I love an intelligent man.

Strong, protective, handsome, funny, *and* smart. I was done. Cooked. Ready to go all in. We just had the minor inconvenience of the CIA and cartel in our way. You know, no big deal.

"I have plans for us. Like taking you up against this wall," he said, while drawing his fingers along my waist and beneath my shirt. He shifted my bra to the side, and his big hand engulfed my breast. "Maybe on the bed for our first time, then a good hard fuck against the wall."

"Well . . ." I swallowed at the delicious imagery he'd painted. "When you put it that way . . ." I held my breath for a few seconds, not looking forward to him telling me we needed to wait for so-called clearer skies before being together. "But not now?" I asked when he'd yet to continue.

Was there something wrong with me that I wanted to have sex minutes after he'd opened up about his father? In my defense, I wanted to show this man love and affection. Help ease his pain in the only way I could right now since it was too soon to share my feelings with words.

"You're pouting." He lightly squeezed my breast, then played with my nipple. Such a tease. "Don't be sad. I'm just thinking we wait an hour or two. Not until after the op, just until Beth gets her ass handed to her by POTUS. I'm assuming Batman will make that happen sooner rather than later." He kissed the tip of my nose. "Trust me, I can't wrap my head around waiting any longer than that."

Oh, thank God. My whole body relaxed. "Neither can I. Crazy or not, I don't care. I have to feel you or I won't be able to focus. It's probably the only way I can get my head on straight, feeling you come inside me."

He blinked not once but twice. Recalibrating? Replaying what I'd said? "Beautiful?"

"Yes?" Also, he could call me that every day of the week.

He removed his hand from beneath my shirt and smoothed the pad of his thumb along the line of my lips. "If you mention me coming inside you again, I won't be able to wait. I will give zero fucks about the mission or any possible interruptions." His other hand went to the waistband of my jeans, and he hooked his thumb at the side. "I *will* take you right now, and it'll be hard. Dirty. And not soft and slow like you deserve for our first time."

"Who said I want it soft and slow?" I caught his thumb with my teeth and licked. "Maybe I want you balls-deep inside me up against this wall right here and right now. Maybe I want to see you fall apart in under a minute, knowing I'm the reason."

His hooded eyes flew over my face to where I licked his thumb again. "What am I going to do with this mouth of yours?" He shifted his hand to my cheek, angling his head while studying my lips.

"Take me now. Save the soft and slow way for later. For when we have time to explore each other's bodies without interruption." I fisted his shirt, drawing myself closer to him in desperate, achy need. "Please, Ryder." My voice cracked that time, the desperation hijacking my normal tone and taking over.

His jaw strained as his eyes darkened, and then he stood back, freeing me of my caged position, and unzipped his jeans. "I'm going to taste you first. Get you close. Then fill you, okay?"

Can't argue with that.

"In the bathroom, against the wall. Need a layer of protection in case someone walks in." Keeping his jeans up but unzipped, he took my hand and guided me to what felt like would be the promised land.

He shut the door behind us, cursed at the lack of a lock there, then whipped out a towel in preparation for the cum that'd be spilling down my legs after he did what I wanted.

After hanging the towel on the hook next to us, he stepped in front of me and demanded, "Tell me again. Tell me this is really what you want. Like this?"

"More than anything," I told him without hesitation, and at that, he helped me out of my jeans but opted to leave on my panties.

With my back to the door, he lowered before me and hooked my panties to the side. "So wet." Eyes up on me, he dragged his tongue along my sex, and I had to bite down on my molars not to cry.

"Fuuuuck," I whispered when he stroked me with his tongue, returning his eyes to my clit. I grabbed hold of his hair, relishing in every delicious, wonderful second of this man's mouth on me. *Beth who? CIA what?* Not even a minute later, I patted his shoulder, begging, "Now. You need to fill me now. Right—right . . ." I panted. "Now."

"Yes, ma'am." The confirmation vibrated against my sex, then he returned my panties in place and stood. He shoved down his jeans and boxers to his thighs and wasted no time, hoisting me into his arms, wrapping my legs around him.

Fatigue from lack of sleep didn't impact his ability to hold me. He had to have insane strength and energy to keep me upright like this.

I reached between us to move my panties to the side, feeling his hard length nudging against me.

"Are you ready?" I asked him, breathing hard, on the verge of coming already.

"More than you know," he grated out, barely parting his teeth as he stared deep into my eyes.

One week since he zipped up my dress, and here he was unzipped and about to drive his cock inside me. *Whatever will be, will be.* I thought just as I guided him to my center, and he placed both hands beneath my ass and shifted me up against the wall, only to use the force of gravity to allow me to take him. And I meant *all* of him.

One hard and fast thrust had joined our bodies. Was this what being whole felt like?

I cradled the back of his head with one hand, burying my fingertips in his back with the other. I rocked against him in this position. Moved right along with him as he held me there. Giving me the hard fuck he promised while somehow managing to make it sweet and intimate.

He held on to my ass, using the wall for support to help us move, to help me ride him like this, hitting the bundle of nerves in the most pleasurable and erotic way.

He leaned back, his body going still as he found my mouth. "You feel . . ." He brought his mouth near mine. "I don't know what to say."

Tears filled my eyes, not because I was on the cusp of an orgasm—which I was—but from the emotions passing between us.

He set his forehead against mine. "First sight for me. Not day three, just so you know," he said before he began moving again. Thrusting. *Fucking.* Killing me in the best possible way.

I let his words wash over me like the rain he promised. Let their meaning latch on to my heart. I dropped my mouth to his shoulder and lightly bit him without sinking my teeth into his flesh. I had to stop myself from screaming as I shuddered. As I came.

He waited until I was done, and then I felt the tremor of his release shoot through him and into me.

Breathing hard. Panting. The both of us.

He slowly let my legs down while kissing me.

The sticky wetness of his ejaculation slipped down my thighs, and I hooked my arm behind his neck to keep us together, not giving a damn where we were. I just needed another minute with him as we held each other.

I opened my mouth, prepared to share my truth back with him, but someone was knocking. Someone was outside our door. *Ah, shit.* Reality slapped me in the face hard and fast.

"It's Nate. The president wants to talk to you."

CHAPTER FORTY-ONE

Ryder

"Does this mean what I hope it means?" Seraphina asked after cleaning up and dressing so we could head into the bedroom.

I zipped up my jeans and smiled. "Batman." Relief was still cycling through me as my mind played catch-up that Carter had come through for us even though we hadn't been able to call him. "He probably tapped into the same satellite feeds we were using and saw Beth and the others box us in." I reached for her hand, lacing our fingers together. "Looks like he got ahold of POTUS."

"Doubt Beth went down easily after that call and simply passed off her phone to Alex."

Yeah, I was with her on that. I opened the bathroom door, assuming Nate would be there with answers.

Nate had a peace offering in his hand in the form of my Glock. "Here."

The comfortable weight of it felt damn good. I nodded my appreciation, tucking it at the back of my jeans, then took hold of her hand again.

So, what went down while we were having sex up against the wall? Sex I didn't regret, not for a fucking second.

He cut to it. "The president should be calling back on a secure line in a few minutes."

Good. There was time to fill us in first.

He tipped his head toward the door, and I noticed Alex hanging back, out in the hallway.

"My ex-wife is now the one in time-out," Alex said with a shit-eating grin. "Along with two other operators who are part of her special team."

About time we had things turn around.

"Courtesy of orders that came from the Commander in Chief himself. You should've seen her face when the CIA director called and he handed the phone over to POTUS. Probably shit her pants." The man was smiling like the Cheshire cat. Hell, at the news, I probably was, too. "Relieved of duty."

"And she really surrendered?" Seraphina beat me to the question burning through my mind.

"Definitely not, so I had to restrain her when she gave me no choice but to do so." He lifted one shoulder. "I'd never hurt a woman, but tie *that* one up? Without question."

"Beth called out for help from the two operators on her team, but we handled them before they could get to her," Nate added.

"What about Leo? The other operators? Whose side are they on?" I asked as we left the bedroom, following Alex to the main living area.

Alex glanced back at us. "The other guys are solid, on our side, but I don't trust Leo, so he's in time-out as well."

"He give you hell, too?" I scanned the living room, counting the operators, who I hoped would become our temporary teammates while down here.

"Leo wasn't a happy fucker," Alex said. "Any excuse to deck him, though."

"You Tasered the guy." Nate laughed, and I'd swear his eyes already looked less jaded without Beth in charge.

"He had it coming," Reed chimed in, joining us alongside Garrison.

I slung my arm behind Seraphina's back, drawing her close to me, worried we still weren't 100 percent in the clear even if Beth was behind a locked door.

"Apparently, it's a small world." Garrison shook my free hand. "We have a mutual friend outside of Reed."

"Oh yeah? Who?" I asked as Alex offered me Seraphina's phone, and I passed it over to her to hang on to.

"Wyatt Pierson's wife, Natasha. Well, you've made the acquaintance of her stepdaughter, so I heard. While you were, uh, in the bedroom . . ." Garrison cleared his throat. Did everyone know what had gone down five minutes ago? "I learned you received an assist from Gwen. I used to protect Natasha back in the day."

"Does that mean Natasha's CIA?" Seraphina asked, her tone lowering.

"That's classified." Garrison smiled. "But not everyone at the Agency is a douche, I swear."

"I'll have to trust you on that one." She gave him a hesitant smile, and I had a feeling she was still trying to wrap her head around the quick change of events. Going from hostages to back in charge thanks to Carter.

Before I had a chance to speak my mind, Garrison let me know the president was on the line. "He's in the Situation Room." He accepted the call, and I let go of Seraphina to take the phone, my mind reeling a bit at talking to the Commander in Chief himself.

"Mr. President." My heartbeat doubled its rate as I turned from the others, grabbing hold of the back of my neck, working at the tension there.

"Lawson," he greeted. "I was woken up in the middle of the night and alerted to your situation by a very persistent man."

"Carter." Because of Seraphina, a bat signal in the sky popped into my mind, and I couldn't help but smile. "Sorry about that, Mr. President."

"I should be apologizing to you, son. This should never have happened. I've regretted a few appointments I've made in my time in office, but Director Johnson's deception stings the most." He let his words sit for a minute, and I had no plans to speak until I was told to.

I wasn't someone to idolize another person. My dad did a bang-up job fucking up the father role and all, but President Bennett was certainly a man I looked up to and admired.

"While I understand what Johnson set out to do in the beginning, which was to thwart Chinese influence and power over the US, the means and methods he used to go about it I don't approve of." The man shared an uncanny resemblance to Denzel Washington, and I realized on the phone with him now, he even had the same soulful and deep voice. "And it's why Johnson's special unit has been disbanded, and their operation will be shut down indefinitely."

Thank fuck. I'd keep the swearing to myself, given who I was speaking to. "How can I help, Mr. President?" I slowly faced the room, finding everyone's attention set on me.

"Nina Sokolov is in CIA custody. I'm not sure if you're yet aware of this, but she and her brother were recruited by the Agency over three years ago to help launch the operation . . ." The president continued speaking, sharing what my team had already figured out, and I listened to him as he verified and validated everything we'd assumed to be true, nodding along with every detail he shared.

"Yes, sir. We came to that conclusion ourselves," I let him know after he finished his explanation.

"The woman you were charged to find by Homeland seems to be critical in helping us take out the Morales cartel while we have the chance, though, am I correct?" That was what I didn't want to hear from him, but I knew it was coming.

I met Seraphina's eyes, and the hand massaging the back of my neck dropped to my side. "Yes, Mr. President. We're under the assumption Ezra Sokolov isn't aware he's a pawn in all of this, and we believe he's after Seraphina to protect himself, and the original plan was to draw out the Moraleses and—"

He went ahead and cut to the point. "I need this mess cleaned up, son. All of it. Do you understand? No ties to our government or military."

Son? I missed being called son by a father figure. I'd happily be POTUS's "son," but not if he was asking me to use Seraphina to clean up the mess Director Johnson and Beth's team had created.

"This is going to be an off-the-books operation." He sounded as tired as I felt. "I have access to three elite special operations teams that don't require Congress to . . ." He let his words go, allowing me to catch the drift of what he couldn't seem to say.

Yup, classified.

"I believe you already met the pilot for Bravo."

Owen York works for you? Well, fuck.

"My son happens to be on his team. They're presently on leave, but I'm pulling them in. They'll be the ones to meet you in Costa Rica and spin up with you. I anticipate we can have them to you in eight hours."

I let that news sink in. Floor me, actually. *Your son, huh?*

"My other two teams will be tasked with handling the suppliers and the trafficking routes. The intel we pulled from the files relating to this rogue special project has helped us put together one giant target package on everyone. We can wipe out this whole damn thing that never should've been started in the first place."

"And you want to hit everyone and everything at once? Does that mean you don't want Ezra walking away from this alive, Mr. President?" *Please say yes.*

"That's an affirmative."

I immediately looked up at Seraphina, and she rested her hand over her heart at the nod I gave her, letting her know the president's answer.

"We're not giving up on the war on drugs, or from trying to keep our country safe from threats both foreign and domestic," POTUS began. "But this was never the moral or right way to go about it."

"I agree, Mr. President." *But I can't use Seraphina as bait.* How the hell did I tell POTUS to fuck off on that part?

"What are we doing with Beth?" Alex asked, catching my eye, so I repeated his question.

"Assign someone from the GRS team to stay back with her while you go out tonight, and my guys will bring her back to DC with them after the mission is complete."

We could also use Hudson's help as well. He could target what was left of Ezra's operation in Miami, so I went ahead and gave that suggestion. After POTUS agreed, I couldn't help but ask, "And Carter? Where does he fit in?" I had to believe he'd juggled his plans around to help out.

"Since he's on the other side of the globe, it makes more sense he lends a hand to my two teams that'll be operating in Asia."

"What about the rest of the cartel?" Seraphina asked. "Not all the Moraleses will be here. What if we also have them handled, too? So no new head of the snake can grow back."

Good idea. I held the phone away from my ear for a moment. "Martín?"

She nodded. "Martín and his team can take down the rest of the cartel there while the others are here."

That was a plan I could get on board with, and I had a feeling the president wouldn't pass up that offer, either. I presented her idea to him, grateful that'd been a quick yes from him as well.

There were still a lot of moving pieces and unknowns, but if we were back in charge with the president in our corner, I was confident we'd make it work. Minus the one part. Minus Seraphina being placed in danger.

"It falls apart without me," she whispered, reading my thoughts.

I closed my eyes, not able to look at her, or anyone, for that matter. I had to think.

To find a way out of this that didn't involve her.

But at the familiar sounds coming from outside, my eyes flashed open. We had company.

"Is that a helicopter?" she asked, beating me to it.

Alex was already on the move. Reed and the others as well.

"Sir, I'm going to have to call you back." *And I just hung up on POTUS. Fuck.* I chucked the phone at Garrison and, on instinct, pulled Seraphina behind me.

I made eye contact with the GRS team's pilot, confirming he was in there with us, so it wasn't him flying the helo.

He went over to the window and parted the blinds as I accepted a rifle from Nate. "Not our bird, and they're fast-roping down. Prepare for a breach."

"Beth. It has to be her. She must've had a backup plan in case her op was canked." Alex immediately started for the second hallway, accepting a 9mm from Garrison on the way. "She had to have secretly texted someone," was all I heard from him before he disappeared from view.

"We have them outnumbered," Reed said, at the window now. "But it looks like they're about to hit us with smoke or gas. They're wearing masks."

"What do we do?" Seraphina stepped around me, somehow managing to keep calm.

"We get the fuck out of here, is what," Nate said for me. "Come on, there's another way out."

"They're after Beth. We'll go after her later." First priority, get Seraphina to safety. I yelled out to Alex to get his ass back here and exfil with us.

"I've got him." Reed waved me off. "Go. Get her out of here."

I hesitated.

And I never hesitated.

But fuck.

I peered back and forth between Seraphina and Reed, becoming acutely aware of gunshots outside. The GRS operators patrolling the property were engaging, but I doubted they'd be able to hold off a helo overhead for long.

"Go, dammit," Reed ordered, then went after Alex.

"I'll go with him," Garrison offered. "Nate and the others will get you two to safety. I'll hold off as many as I can to buy you time."

The last thing in the world I wanted was to leave without my teammates, but I couldn't help anyone if we were knocked out by a gas agent.

"Yeah, okay." With my free hand, I took the Glock at my back and offered it to her as we followed Nate and the others in the opposite direction from Beth's room. "You said you know how to use one of these, right?"

She quickly accepted it. "Point and shoot," she said as I patted her lower back, urging her to move faster. "I've got this."

I hated this. That she was in danger. That my teammates were. And that I was leaving them behind. I hated this whole damn situation, but I soldiered the fuck on and focused up.

"And I've got you," I promised.

CHAPTER FORTY-TWO

Ryder

"Motherfucking son of a . . ." Alex snarled, baring his teeth, and I had to push him back down on the ground.

"Hold still, dammit." My hands were soaked in his blood, and if he didn't stop moving, he'd bleed out on me. "Can you keep the flashlight right there?" I directed to Seraphina, who was kneeling next to me alongside our patient.

She smoothed the back of her hand across Alex's forehead as she held the light up so I could see outside in the dark. "You'll be okay." The fact he reminded her of her brother had to make this situation twice as hard on her.

"He's not swearing up a storm because he's in pain; he has morphine in him," I explained while zeroing in on the main problem, and thank God these GRS operators had a decent medkit on hand. "He's mad because—"

"The bitch shot me," Alex barked out, trying to sit again, and Reed had to help me pin him back down. He was ready to go after his ex-wife, who'd successfully been extracted less than ten minutes ago.

"She's gone off the rails." Reed kept hold of Alex's arm, trying to prevent him from moving around too much so I could deal with his wound.

"The smoke... I couldn't..." Alex finally stopped resisting, which worried me even more that he was fading.

"One more second. Hang on, brother." I continued to manage his wound, working to stabilize him. I was using the innovative device Nate had provided after we'd made it out of the safe house and were no longer under enemy fire.

"She got away." Alex started cursing, which was a good sign the device I was using was doing its thing and helping.

"What's that do?" Seraphina asked as I used the syringe-like applicator at his side where his flesh had been ripped apart and he still had a round embedded beneath his skin.

Reed spoke for me, explaining, "He's injecting these small sponge-type things into the wound cavity. They expand and exert hemostatic pressure. Think of it like temporarily sealing a flat tire so no air can leak out. Or in this case, blood."

I opened my hand palm up, a silent request for gauze, and someone handed it to me so I could finish patching him up.

"Better?" Seraphina asked him.

"No," Alex grunted, clearly still in pissed-off territory. *Yeah, you and me both.* "My ex tried to kill me, and she got away." He tried to sit, and I set a hand to his chest to encourage him back down on the grass. Not the best operating table, but we had no choice.

"I'm done with the light," I let her know. "Not sure if the bullet hit any major organs. There was a lot of blood. We need to get him to a hospital ASAP."

"No, don't you dare medevac me to an ER." Alex, dammit, with the protest. Always putting himself second to a mission. "We need our helo and pilot to chase after her." The stubborn man tried to sit again. "Beth had her people blow up the bird here."

"Do you have a death wish, brother?" Reed gritted out. "We'll get her, but we need you alive."

We had to first get our Black Hawk back at the villa. I had no clue where the hell we were, but we couldn't be too far given the time it'd taken to leave the meeting with Ángel to arrive at this safe house.

I pivoted around, searching out the GRS pilot who was now on our side, and he gave me an okay nod he'd have our backs on this. Thankfully, he hadn't been a Beth loyalist.

After the windows to her bedroom had been blown out so her team could breach, smoke had filled the room just as Alex walked in. I assumed he'd been caught off guard, and knowing him, couldn't shoot her. However, *she* hadn't hesitated. She grabbed a 9mm from one of her rescuers and shot Alex in the torso before her team extracted her, taking her out the window.

She'd only exfil'ed with her two loyal operators that Nate had already warned us about. She'd left Leo behind after rendering him unconscious.

Two more tangos had fast-roped down to the other side of the property where I'd been exiting with Seraphina, and they were after her, not us.

Nate and I took them down. Headshots. No hesitation. Zero fucks given at that point. Thankfully, Seraphina never had to shoot anyone with the 9mm I'd given her. I never wanted her to experience what it was like to take a life.

A door gunner inside Beth's escape vehicle, a modified Boeing Apache that had no business being anywhere in Costa Rica, had opened fire on us once she was safely on board. He'd forced us to take cover while he blew to high hell the helo parked there, along with the three SUVs.

Only when we were in the clear could we safely move Alex to handle his wound. Hopefully, we hadn't lost too much time. The fact he was still conscious and could swear were good signs. The morphine I'd shot him up with may have helped the pain but not his anger.

"So, not to state the obvious, but how are we getting to our villa?" Seraphina asked.

"We can't carry him for miles, and we have to be at least a good ten mikes out from our place, if not more," I said, trying to work the problem. To think.

"We could call for an ambulance, but then we have to explain what happened, and I don't think we want to deal with the police. We're not technically here, remember?" Reed reminded me of my conversation with POTUS.

"We have no choice. We have to get him there somehow." I finally stood, helping Seraphina up as well. I set my hands on my hips, assessing the scene, along with our options. I did a three-sixty, checking out the chaos around us.

While there were no other houses around that I could see, the explosions and "fireworks" would have drawn attention. The authorities were more than likely en route now. We'd all get thrown behind bars until POTUS could negotiate our way out. That was a problem second to our first one: Alex's GSW.

"Ángel," she announced, and I turned to see her holding her phone. "He's calling." I'd forgotten I'd given her cell back before I spoke to the president. "Maybe he can help us?"

Great. Get help from a former cartel member. What choice did we have at this point? "Okay," I agreed after exchanging a look with Reed, who nodded as well.

Ángel cut straight to it once she had him on speakerphone. "I saw what happened. I didn't trust her, so I had you all followed after you left my shop. We had a drone up."

My hands fell to my sides at the news. "Tell me you still have eyes on her."

"I do. They've already landed about six miles due north of that safe house you're at. I'm not letting them out of my sight. I also have a team on their way to you. Looks like you need a lift."

That we do. We'd be leaving Leo behind here, though. He could find his own ride home.

"Thank you," I finally managed, hanging my head in relief. I'd never have thought this man would become a guardian angel for us.

"I need to go after her." At Alex's words, I spun back to find him trying to sit, and Reed was at his six, easing him down yet again before he hurt himself.

"We will," I promised. "The team sent to help her, do you know anything about them? Are they CIA? GRS?"

"This was a surprise even to me," Ángel began. "But the house she was taken to, well—"

"Don't tell me," I cut him off. "I already know." I swallowed, then lifted my eyes to the dark, starless sky.

"Who?" Seraphina asked.

"Ezra Sokolov," Ángel answered for me.

"Wait, no, that doesn't make any sense," she whispered. "He can't be in the know, because then . . ."

"I don't think Ezra's a CIA asset like Nina is. But Beth is the one he's afraid to piss off, not his wife." My shoulders slumped as the pieces came together. "He knows he's not working for the Russians, because he's working *with* her."

CHAPTER FORTY-THREE

Ryder

"I hate you for making me—"

"At least you'll be alive to hate me." I slid the door shut and spun my finger in the air, signaling to head out. "Make sure no one gets near him at the hospital," I told the other GRS operator who'd be accompanying Alex as an escort on the helo.

Ángel's men had delivered us to our villa, as Ángel had promised they would. Ángel would be joining us soon, bringing with him the coordinates for Beth and Ezra's location. He assured us he wouldn't let them out of his sight, and God help me, I couldn't believe it, but I trusted him.

I waited for the pilot to take off, a foreboding, sinking feeling in the deep pit of my stomach. Not going along with Alex was killing me. Once they were out of sight, I started for our villa, grateful all over again for this place Carter had provided us.

I nodded at the two GRS operators who were keeping post outside on my way in. I needed to call the president, but first, I had to remove the blood from my hands and talk to Carter and Hudson.

Seraphina was hanging back by the front door, quietly waiting for my return. The only reason I was keeping my shit together, to control-freak my way forward through this, was because of her.

I was seconds away from reaching for her hand, but then spied the blood staining mine, so I signaled with my head to come with me.

Once we were in the bathroom en suite, I cut straight to the sink to wash my hands.

I stared at the blood circling the drain, trying to wrap my head around the turn of events and the fact I nearly lost one of my best friends tonight. I could've lost her, too. I closed my eyes, clenching my teeth as I continued to scrub and scrub. I couldn't stop, not until she set a hand on my forearm.

A heavy breath sailed from deep within my lungs as she whispered, "What are you thinking?"

It was the first time we'd actually spoken since we realized Beth had more than likely double-crossed her own team by going behind their back to have a side thing with Ezra Fucking Sokolov.

"A lot." I opened my eyes, turned off the water, then dried my hands before facing her, resting my hip against the vanity counter. "Ezra's how Beth found out you were undercover for the DEA. Same with Lev. Now it all makes sense."

"Oh shit." She blinked her way up from where she'd been staring at my hands and to my face. "The phone call he had to take in his office that night, which bought me time before he'd have started torturing me . . . it was from Beth, not Nina." She visibly cringed. "Makes sense why she was staring at me like she was, like . . . well, like she was jealous."

I wasn't sure how to interpret that. Beth was ten times the control freak I was, which was saying a lot. So maybe she was pissed she didn't have total power over Ezra, hating he'd kept Seraphina's real identity from her.

"So, he kept you a secret because . . ." I didn't want to finish that sentence, dammit, but I had to. "Because of his attraction to you. He probably hoped one day he'd be able to have you for himself." *Fucking asshole.*

"He'd know Beth would've never let me work for him if she knew the truth about my background." She fidgeted with the hem of her shirt. "Beth clearly didn't recognize my face from any surveillance she must've had on him, which means my family's deaths weren't a significant detail to her." Those words punched out hard, and I was right there with her in hating Beth for so many reasons now.

"What are you thinking? I can tell there's something in that beautiful mind of yours."

"What if they were lovers? I don't take her for the jealous type, but the possessive one? Yeah." Her lashes fluttered, and she finally met my eyes as her brows pinched. "It was never Nina keeping me safe by demanding her husband remain faithful, but Beth."

I didn't know what to say. I refused to believe Beth had a heart and was capable of love. No, it had to still be about power and control for her.

"But why is Andrej dead, then? His death, not to mention knowing who I really am, was why we thought Ezra was just an asshole figurehead in all of this. Just a bad-guy pawn."

I folded my arms, working through everything we already knew. At this point we'd been right about so many things, and wrong only about a few, but I was starting to forget what was still based in fact and what was speculation on our part.

"What if Andrej found out Beth and Ezra were secretly working together on the side?" I proposed. "He threatened to expose them."

"So she had him killed. They set him up. Made it look like a cartel hit." Her gaze flew between us to the tiled floor. "That frame job was to cover her ass and hide the truth from her team. From Director Johnson, too. Beth killed my family. They weren't a casualty of war. They died so she could try and save her own ass and keep whatever money I bet she's been pocketing on the side from all of this."

"And had Ezra ever told her your real name," I said after letting go of a deep breath, "she'd have killed you, too."

The woman needed to die. Slowly. Painfully. For everything she'd put everyone through, including shooting Alex.

"Dominoes. She actually set most of them up. This whole thing down here has clearly never been about drawing out Ezra. She let her team think that. Us too. She wanted Ezra to take credit for finishing off the Moraleses, and they'd effectively have the monopoly they were working to create."

I shook my head. "You were the curveball she didn't expect."

"And she lucked out because of me." She huffed out a deep, exhausted breath. I was on the same page of fatigue, too. "She turned Ezra's lie to her about my real identity, and the fact I escaped, into an opportunity. The bitch knows how to play chess, that's for sure." She rested her hand on my chest above my folded arms. "Nina doesn't know about them. She'd have narc'd or done the same as I bet Andrej tried to do. Blackmail them. The fact Nina's still alive, unlike her brother, means she was ignorant. A true pawn. Then, at some point, Beth came up with her own plan. At least a side hustle."

What a fucking hustle.

She swept her hand from my chest up to my shoulder. "Beth's plan is a bust now. I was truly only bait for the Moraleses. Beth just wanted the Moraleses to leave Mexico so they could be taken out, and with the US government's assistance."

Like we're doing. Only now, it's not because she wants it done.

She closed her eyes, and I relaxed my arms and brought my chin to the top of her head.

"What do we do now? How will we draw out the Moraleses without Ezra?" she asked, turning her cheek to my chest to talk. "The Moraleses won't be coming here."

"If the president wants them dead, then he'll have to deal with them on his own." I pulled away so I could frame her face between my palms. "You'll be staying here while I go and kill Ezra and Beth."

"Beth? You'll really take her out?"

"I've never killed a woman, but . . ." I couldn't finish what I'd planned to say because Reed filled the doorway.

"Hudson reached out. His guys in Moscow managed to pull a clip from surveillance footage there that confirms our theory," he shared. "Beth and Ezra were there together before."

We walked out of the bathroom and into the bedroom. "Anything else? You talk to Carter, too? POTUS?"

The pained expression on Reed's face had me diving a hand through my hair as I waited for him to lay news on me I didn't want to hear. "The president wants us to continue on mission."

"Of course he does." *Fuck.* My hand plummeted to my side. "How? The Moraleses won't show up tonight without Ezra. I plan to kill him within the hour." I may have been running on fumes and coffee, but I was also running on anger and hate on behalf of Seraphina and Alex, so I had that going for me. "We can't send Nina down here to take his place. They'll never buy that."

"So we keep Ezra alive and force him to go through with the call. Not being killed is usually a decent motivator." Reed shrugged. He was right, but there was another glaring problem to deal with, and that was the Moraleses would want their hands on Seraphina before heading to the agreed-upon meeting point.

"The meeting doesn't actually need to take place, right?" She used those big brown eyes of hers as ammo against me. "We don't even need Ezra to show up. So, I mean, after the neutral location is arranged over the phone, we could technically kill him. He'll no longer be needed. We have Ángel on our side to help us with the cartel from that point on."

"They're reaching out to Ángel to have him deliver Seraphina to them thirty minutes before the meeting is supposed to take place." I reminded them both of that tight window of time.

"So we follow Ángel to where they're staying, and we take them down," Seraphina suggested.

I highly doubted the cartel would text Ángel an address. It'd never be that easy. No, we'd need proof Ángel had what the cartel wanted first.

"Hell, we can even leave Ezra's dead body behind after we kill them," Reed proposed. "Along with a few of his men to make it look like a meeting that went sideways between two criminals."

"And Ángel gets what he wants, too. The cartel gone. Martín can still handle business at the same time in Mexico, too." She used those brown-eyed weapons again.

A deep exhalation fell from my mouth as I worked through the roadblock still preventing me from getting on board with this plan. "I'm not allowing Ángel to bring you anywhere near his family. Are we clear?"

"How are we supposed to—"

"Beth," I cut her off, looking over at Reed. "Find out from Ángel if his family knows what Anna Cruz looks like. If not, let the plan she wanted to happen play out." I snarled in anger, "Let her see what it's like to be used as bait her-motherfucking-self."

CHAPTER FORTY-FOUR

Seraphina

The last thirty minutes had been a blur of calls and conversations. So when I made it to the office to talk to Ryder, I felt like I'd sleepwalked my way there.

Ryder had his back to me, a laptop balanced on his hand as he, Reed, and Ángel looked at something.

I quietly hung back in the doorway. It was my first time seeing Ryder dressed like an operator. Military fatigues and a light-green long-sleeved shirt beneath a khaki vest that I hoped was also of the bullet-stopping variety. He had a firearm holstered at his hip and a blade sheathed and strapped to his outer thigh. The black backward ball cap was the only familiar look.

While propping myself up against the doorframe so I wouldn't pass out from fatigue, I subtly cleared my throat, alerting them to my presence.

Ryder passed the laptop off to Reed and turned. "How'd the phone call go?" he asked as Ángel and Reed gave me their attention.

"I'll tell you if you tell me." My teasing tone had to be a result of exhaustion now whooping my ass at hyperspeed.

That full mouth of his twitched, a handsome smile that had no business being there at four in the morning.

"According to Director Johnson, the plan was never to bring Ezra into the know. Only Nina and Andrej were their assets, and he claims he was unaware Beth framed Andrej and had him killed." A few long strides brought Ryder over to me. He offered me his hand as if knowing I was running on empty and needed an assist.

That had to be the laziest push away from a doorframe in history, but I managed to do it and keep myself upright. *Slow and steady wins the race, right? I'm definitely sliding into a sleepy delusional state, aren't I?* "Was it the plan to replace Ezra with Nina if things went sideways down here? Does Nina know Ezra's been working with Beth?" The questions popped from my mouth of their own accord since my brain was still sluggish.

"The CIA Director monitored Johnson's conversation with Nina since POTUS no longer trusts his *former* DNI, and according to him, Nina said she suspected Ezra knew the truth about everything long before Andrej was killed, but she had no evidence and also had a gut feeling that was why her brother died. So she kept her mouth shut to save her own neck."

"CIA. POTUS. DNI. A few more letters, and we'll complete the alphabet." I lifted a shoulder. "Told you my humor is always off base."

"It's perfect any time." He smiled, squeezing my hand as we faced the others in the office.

"So, what'd Martín say?" Ángel asked, reminding me of the call I'd just made.

Ryder let go of my hand as if sensing I needed more help to stay on my feet, like an emotional-support forearm at my back, which he provided.

I rested my head against his shoulder. They all had places to be and people to kill, and there I was acting drugged from a lack of sleep and shock. "Martín's in, but are you sure you're good with the plan? It's one thing to buy yourself protection from the cartel as we discussed at the club, quite another to have them all killed." No sense in sugarcoating the truth.

"Only my uncle and his son are en route here for the meeting with Ezra." He said what he'd already told us when he first arrived at our villa. He swiped a hand over his bald head, eyes shooting to the floor. "This works better." He looked up at me. "I can handle assisting in killing them, but I'd rather it be Martín who handles my brother. I'm glad he stayed back in Mexico."

I couldn't imagine having a hand in the killing of a sibling. What was going through his mind right now couldn't be pretty or easy. "Are you sure, though?"

"Do you know how many people my brother has murdered?" Ángel opened his palms. "Somewhere north of fifty and south of a hundred. Give or take. That number doesn't even include animals."

Well, when you put it like that . . . My stomach turned. More like somersaulted in disgust.

"After we proceed with phase one of the plan, I'll touch base with your friend and let him know exactly where he'll be able to find my brother and his associates."

Phase one: "Snatch and grab" Beth and Ezra. Those were Reed's words before I'd left to call Martín. I was looking forward to the unspoken phase in between one and two: interrogating them.

"Will someone try to replace the cartel after they're taken out?" I managed to "snatch and grab" that thought from somewhere in my foggy brain, which was almost shocking.

"It would be best if I can take responsibility for killing Ezra as retribution for murdering my uncle and his people. I'll be both revered and feared." He side-eyed Ryder as if assuming where Ryder's head went with that statement. "And no, this isn't a ploy so I can take over for the cartel."

"We believe you, or you wouldn't be in this room with us right now," Ryder said steadily, then deferred to Reed with a lift of the chin.

"This is the aerial view we'll be watching while they're gone." Reed came over to us, turning the laptop for me to see. "Courtesy of the CIA. The, uh, good guys at the Agency, I should say. The director is on our side. The president vouches for him."

That's something. But wait. "You're staying?" That had me awake, bolstering me upright and no longer leaning against Ryder. "Shouldn't you have his back?" Reed and Ryder swapped a quick look, and sleepy or not, I easily read it. "You won't be able to focus on the mission if you're worried about me back here?" *Reed's the only one you trust to keep an eye on me with Beth and Ezra still out there.*

"I have plenty of support out in the field," Ryder said like a promise. "The GRS operators." He tipped his head in Ángel's direction. "His men."

"What about the helicopter? Will the pilot make it back here in time from the hospital?" A fresh wave of nerves hit me as I thought about Alex in surgery right now, knowing it pained both Ryder and Reed not to be there with him.

"He'll be here soon, but we're going to be infil'ing on foot. We need to keep Beth and Ezra alive. Once they're in our custody, Nate will be on the door gun in the helo, and he'll clear a path for a clean exfil," Ryder explained. We were lucky that GRS pilot guy was on our side.

"We sure we have to keep that witch alive?" The comment from Ángel earned him a surprising smile of approval from Reed.

"Just for now. Once you prove to the cartel you have her, and we get a fix on their location, we only need them to clock her with you. After that"—Ryder raised one shoulder—"if something were to happen to her . . ."

"*Whatever will be, will be,*" I couldn't help but murmur. The woman was responsible for my family being murdered, Alex being in the hospital. Probably many more lives were stolen because she'd turned her special assignment into a power and money grab for her and Ezra. So yeah, whatever was meant to be, would be, when it came to her.

"She's been an even bigger thorn in my side than the cartel," Ángel said after letting go of a deep breath. "I'm ready to be rid of her."

"So, she never gave you an option to work with Andrej?" My curiosity got the best of me, despite me being exhausted.

"No, she set me up. I found out the hard way. Never trust a spy." He shook his head. "She had photos taken of my first meeting with Andrej when I rejected his offer. She used the images to blackmail me. She said she'd send them to the cartel and allege I was working with their competitor and that's why I really left the family business."

"The woman's playbook is thicker than the Bible," Reed grunted in disgust while setting aside the laptop.

"Beth always talked to me through Andrej, never in person. She's manipulative, though. She convinced me that helping the Agency would help my people. We'd take down the cartel together."

Manipulative *is an understatement*. "Well, we'll be done with her and the cartel soon." I hoped that was a promise that'd come true, at least. *First things first. Snatch and grab two assholes.* "You don't think Beth will have Ezra reach out to the Moraleses to warn them, right? Try and spoil the mission since their plan failed?"

"No." Ryder was quick to shoot down my concern. "Beth won't ever believe I'll use you as bait to get to the Moraleses now that she's not calling the shots, trying to force our hand." And that was an excellent point.

"So, I'll be able to see your operation the whole time?"

"If it doesn't stress you out to watch, then yeah, you can keep an eye on us," Ryder said as Garrison filled the doorway.

"Jayden's here. It's go-time." Garrison let us know their pilot had returned.

"Tell everyone to get ready. We leave in five," Ryder ordered, then Reed and Ángel followed Garrison out, presumably to give us a minute alone.

Once it was just us, he looped my arms up over his shoulders, and I linked my wrists behind his neck. He had magazines loaded into his vest that pressed against me, but I didn't give a damn. I'd also forgotten all about sleep and everything else in that moment, knowing he was about to ride off into battle.

This was the hard part. The part of him that women he'd dated may have struggled to deal with. *This* was what he was worried might scare me off. The leaving me to fight, knowing this goodbye could be his last.

I'd never known my goodbye to my parents and brother was the final one.

Not going to cry, dammit.

Not now.

"You okay?" He let go of my arms and held my face between his hands, then he threaded his fingers up into my hair and tipped my head, urging my eyes on his. "Tell me you're okay."

"*You* tell me that." He was worried about Alex, worried about leaving me, worried about a lot of things. I didn't want that clouding his judgment and ruining his focus out there.

"As long as you promise me you'll be here when I get back, I'm good." His somber tone and the pained expression crossing his face about did me in.

Damn his father for leaving him. Damn every woman who hurt this man.

"Of course I'll be here. You don't walk away from a man you fell for on night *one*, now do you?" I pressed up on my toes, and he bent his head as I drew my mouth to his ear. "Some loves are meant to be, even when the odds are against them."

CHAPTER FORTY-FIVE

Seraphina

I wasn't an adrenaline junky, so watching the man I had not an insta-lust situation but a souls-finding-one-another kind of connection with fight in real time was doing a number on me. And, ohhh, you better believe I was awake now. The fog of sleep had been lifted like a curtain.

I was fully aware I was a nervous mess, but I couldn't zip up my feelings and hide them behind numbness or detachment anymore. The emotional cat was out of the bag for good. No more Anna Cruz and playing pretend.

Sitting on the couch in the office next to Reed, who was a hundred times calmer than I was, I banded an arm across my stomach to try to quell the nauseated feeling.

It was too bad we didn't have a better picture to watch. Or maybe that wasn't a bad thing. If I saw too much, I might really lose it.

I'd already become a disaster after we lost radio communication with the guys two minutes ago. Beth must have used her jammer-thing after they'd breached her place, cutting off the signal and our contact with them.

Now all we had to go on was the thermal-image satellite view, which had me feeling a bit like a radiologist studying an X-ray or MRI. I did math, not science.

I had to keep telling myself if I could survive working for Ezra as long as I did, I could get through the next ten or so minutes of high-octane intensity while my guy—and he was absolutely my guy—stormed a house with Ezra and Beth inside.

"Is that normal?" My legs were crossed with a pillow on my lap, and I rocked myself too much and fell forward.

Reed swiftly caught my arm, saving me from face-planting with his laptop.

"It's normal," he said in a steady voice, accompanied by what felt like some serious side-eye. I looked over my shoulder to discover it was just worry. "You good?" he asked.

"I know, I know. This 'me' doesn't jibe with the 'me' who worked for Ezra or went into that fight club," I said, translating his raised eyebrows and narrowed eyes.

"That's because there's someone on the other side of the screen you care about. You were only worried about your own life before. It's a whole other level when the stakes are raised with someone you love." He reset his eyes on the screen and let me go. "*Annnd* I think Alex just used me as a mouthpiece. Must be some illusionist trick he pulled off while he's under anesthesia. He's the advice giver on our team, not me."

If he could make a joke at a time like this, then maybe I didn't need to panic, especially since I didn't take Reed for the type. "Let me guess: Alex doesn't take his own advice?" At least he'd distracted me from having a heart attack.

"Was it having a she-devil as an ex that gave you that impression?" Another joke, wow. Well, not really, I supposed, because his name for her was spot on, one of the many I'd already called her.

Before I could answer, a flash of something on the screen caught my eye, and I leaned forward, which prompted Reed to seize hold of my arm again. "Was that . . . ? Is he . . . ?" Time to melt down and lose it. "Tell me I'm wrong."

Reed punched at the keys with his free hand, shifting the view around like we had access to a GoPro camera instead of a satellite in outer space. "Yeah, Ryder took a round to the chest."

My legs dropped, feet hitting the floor. Time to stand. To sound the alarm.

"He's fine." He zoomed in as much as he could without making everything totally blurry. "Chest plate caught the round. He's shaking it off. He'll have a bruise that he'll act like doesn't hurt, but that's it."

At the sight of Ryder standing, readying his rifle, I fell back onto the couch. After this mission and phase two against the Moraleses, I'd be done watching Ryder in action ever again. I couldn't handle it. I wasn't *that* cool.

"He's heading inside now. We're going to lose sight of him," he warned.

I picked up the pillow that'd fallen after my abrupt departure from the couch and rested it on my lap to hold.

"Try and relax."

I glared at him, offering him the mother of all eye rolls. "That's like asking someone with anxiety have they ever tried not being anxious."

"Well, hell, when you put it like that . . ." A hint of a drawl came out that time.

"Distract me instead?" At the memory of how he'd distracted me on the plane ride, I felt the need to clarify. "Not about volcanoes and warriors losing their loved ones, either." God no, anything but *that* kind of story. "I need a happy ending."

He switched the settings on our view so we weren't so zeroed in and expanded the picture, then sat back on the couch and looked over at me. He opened his mouth, then closed it as his phone rang, and his brows immediately tightened.

"What's wrong?" Cue worry again.

"Hopefully it's just an update on Alex's surgery," he said before answering, and I had to assume it was the GRS operator Ryder had sent with Alex.

"Speakerphone," I ordered, and he did as I asked and held the phone out between us.

"There was a complication," the operator said, which was the opposite of what we needed to hear. "Something to do with scar tissue he had from old wounds, and I—I don't know. Something ruptured. He lost a lot of blood, and he was coding. Had no pulse for a bit." Before I broke down and lost it, he added, "They revived him, but they don't know if he was without oxygen for too long. We won't know how he is until he's awake . . . well, *if* he wakes up."

If . . . ? No, no, no.

Reed dropped the phone, and it fell onto the table by the laptop as he stood and turned.

I barely noticed the fact Ryder was back outside and was dragging someone with him, and that someone . . . Was that Ezra?

Not even a minute later, the Black Hawk appeared, and bullets hit the house, then tore up the ground, paving the path for their escape.

I lost sight of Ryder. Lost sight of everyone on-screen from the dust and smoke.

"You there?" a voice called out from the phone, and I shifted the pillow aside in a daze to grab it.

"Yeah, we're here," I whispered as Reed slowly faced me, his eyes glossy. "Call us back when you have good news, okay?" I swallowed, pain punching me in the gut. "Only good news, got it?"

◆ ◆ ◆

Ryder tossed his helmet the second he saw me outside the villa, and I met him halfway and jumped up into his arms, hooking my legs around him. I squeezed him tight. Crying in relief that he was okay, but also on the verge of sobbing at the fact I had to tell him his best friend may not be.

"Told you I'd be good," he said in my ear, stroking my back.

He'd been shot in the chest, so he was probably achy, and I shouldn't press up against him like this. I unhooked my ankles and slid along his tall, masculine frame to find the ground.

"Everything go as planned?" I swiped at the tears I'd soon have to explain.

He removed and tossed his gloves to hold my face with his bare hands. "We have Ezra and Beth, yeah. Managed to keep them alive. No one on our side died."

"That's great," I sputtered.

It was still dark out, but there were enough lights outside he'd be able to read my face and my worry.

"Tell me those are tears of relief." He frowned, then lifted his head and pointed his focus elsewhere. He kept hold of my cheeks, so I couldn't follow his gaze, but I had a feeling Reed was out there. "What's wrong?" he asked in a grave voice, and it felt like my soul whooshed free from my body at his question.

That empty-vessel feeling after my family died . . .

No, I couldn't let him experience that about his best friend.

"It's Alex . . ." I cried, and he let go of me, stumbling backward.

Eyes narrowed on me, he begged, "Tell me."

"He met God on the surgeon's table for a minute," Reed said in a low, somber voice, coming up next to us, sensing I couldn't speak. "He came back to us, but we don't know if he's, well . . . *back* back."

Or if he'll wake up.

Ryder held the sides of his head—and there they were: tears he had no problem shedding for Alex, unlike his undeserving father.

I reached for his arm, but then he set his sights on a new target. I turned to see who was there. Beth. Enemy number one right now.

"I may have never killed a woman before," he rasped, blinking back more tears before looking at me after Ángel joined the three of us, "but God help me, there's a first time for everything."

"What's going on?" Ángel removed his rifle that was slung across his chest as Reed filled him in.

Ángel set a hand on Ryder's shoulder and leaned in, saying something into his ear, then quietly went inside the house.

"What was that about?" I reached for Ryder's hand, stepping directly in front of him.

A gruff breath fell between us as he shared, "He told me not to kill her. He said it'd be bad for my soul to have her blood on my hands." He looked at me, shaking his head. "But he's more than happy to spill hers for us."

CHAPTER FORTY-SIX

Seraphina

Beth and Ezra were currently tied to chairs and facing each other inside one of the guest rooms. Garrison had left them alone a minute ago, and Ryder and I were in the office, watching them on camera, waiting for them to talk. To breach the quiet and hopefully further narc on themselves. Beth was probably too smart for that, but Ezra's cockiness and his need to start a pissing match with her might come in handy in luring information from the two of them.

Ryder grimaced, shooting me a pained expression. "I should be at the hospital."

"He's going to be okay." I rubbed his arm. "The second he wakes up, we'll go over and see him. There's plenty of time before tonight's mission with the Moraleses." And our main threats were now locked up in a room, so it'd be safe to move about Costa Rica.

Reed was en route to the hospital to wait for Alex to come out of surgery, and as much as it killed Ryder to stay behind, Reed reminded him that Alex would kick his ass for coming right now.

"Sitting in the hospital won't make Alex wake up any faster," Reed had said before leaving, *"but one of the two of us still needs to."* Then Reed volun*told* him he'd be going himself.

"I know he'll be fine, because he has to be. I'm not giving him a choice but to be," he said gruffly, and if anyone could control-freak their way into making someone be A okay, it was this man.

"I feel it in my bones. In my heart." I leaned against him, resting my head on his shoulder.

"I should've never listened to this ridiculous plan." Ezra's voice dragged my focus to the screen. Finally, someone was talking. "I should've taken off last weekend for the Maldives like I wanted to and never looked back. Definitely not come down here and help you." The chair legs screeched on the tiled floor as he moved around in his chair.

"Watch what you say," Beth hissed, signaling with her head to the camera in the corner of the room.

Ezra stopped shuffling around. "I shouldn't have told you about Lev and Seraphina."

"No, you should've told me about Anna being Seraphina nine fucking months ago." Beth shockingly forgot herself there. Maybe a little more stress and time in the pressure cooker would do her some good. "You wanted to save her for yourself, am I right?" No sense keeping her mouth shut there. This was nothing new she was spilling. "You were going to take her for a spin on your yacht, fuck her, then kill her." She scoffed. Wow, was that jealousy from the ice queen?

"Maybe I wanted someone who wasn't such an icy bitch, ever thought of that?" Ah, so Ezra and I agreed on one thing.

Ryder was less than enthusiastic about the exchange. Not the kind of thing he wanted to hear, and not in the mood he was in.

"But no, you threatened to have me killed like you did Andrej if I even touched another woman. Couldn't even fuck my own wife, who you forced me to marry once you decided you wanted me last year." He grunted as if repulsed, and I was right there with him. "Not that I ever wanted there to be an *us* in that way when I proposed the idea—"

"Shut. Up," Beth barked out, and that order probably had less to do with her being insulted than not wanting him to keep exposing more information.

Not that she'd be able to save herself at this point. Facts were facts. She'd dug her grave. Soon, she'd sleep for all eternity in it. For my parents. My brother. For Alex. For everyone this woman had hurt—and for what? Why? Greed? Power? *But wait.* "Did he just admit he's known about everything from the beginning?"

"Sounds like it. And looks like Beth's the one who became obsessed with him somewhere along the lines. Well, in her own cold-blooded way."

How'd she go from a CIA officer and a woman Alex would marry to *this*? That was still the question I couldn't make sense of, and maybe I never would. Or maybe I'd ask her myself. "I want to go in there."

His brows shot up in surprise, a *hell no* on the tip of his tongue. His shoulders fell when he remembered that once my mind was made up, it was all the way up.

"Just need one thing." I patted his shoulder. "Give me a minute. Okay?"

He sighed, lightly shaking his head. He set a hand on his chest where he had a Texas-size welt from being shot. Using the heel of his hand he made circular motions, eyes on the floor.

"I wish you'd take something for the pain." Thank God the plate took the round, not his flesh.

"Mm-hmmm," he said under his breath before looking up at me. "Go." He leaned in and gave me a forehead kiss.

Not wanting to give him time to change his mind, I thanked him, kissed him back on the lips, then hurried from the office.

I breezed by the operators in the house, secured what I needed from the kitchen, then asked Garrison to unlock the door and let me in.

Ezra's pale-blue eyes slipped straight to me, and his lips twitched into a semi-smile as if oddly admiring what I'd pulled off and how I bested the witch.

I kept my hand behind my back and slowly made my way over to Beth, my actual target right now.

"What the hell do you want?" she rasped, her dead eyes sharp on me.

I stood off to her side and drew my weapon to her throat. I met Ezra's eyes as I held the steak knife tight to where her pulse visibly fluttered, and recognition dawned on him. I was about to steal a page from his playbook.

"You know," I offered in a low, dark voice, "it's amazing what people confess with a knife to their throat."

CHAPTER FORTY-SEVEN

Ryder

Seraphina was asleep next to me in Alex's private ICU room. It wasn't my first time sitting next to a friend in a hospital bed like this, and it never got easier.

But this was one of the first times it felt like my fault. I should never have let him go to her room. I could've prevented this.

I stretched out my legs, slouching in the cheap chair, a tight fit for me. The only thing that gave me comfort was Seraphina sitting next to me, her head resting on my shoulder as she slept.

I'd bulldozed my way through the ICU's one-visitor-only policy so she could join me.

After fighting the urge to pass out like she had, I finally decided to close my eyes. There was nothing we could do right now but wait.

Wait for Alex to wake up.

Wait on Bravo Team to arrive.

Wait to have Ezra talk to the Moraleses to agree upon a location.

Wait on the Moraleses to tell Ángel where and when he needed to bring "the bait," which was when we'd actually strike (no need to wait for the meet time).

I tipped my head, resting it against hers, thinking back to what went down before we'd left for the hospital, when Seraphina had interrogated Beth and Ezra.

While I'd hated her being alone with them, I'd controlled myself and stayed behind the screen to watch, letting her do her thing. And she'd done it damn well.

The blade to Beth's throat hadn't encouraged her to talk; Beth's CIA training held up there. But what Beth didn't account for was how good Seraphina was with math. She truly could make anything add up to whatever she wanted it to with enough pushing, and my girl had done a hell of a job at peeling back the layers. She'd taken advantage of Ezra's arrogance, getting him to spill his guts without even realizing it, and she'd lit Beth's fuse with that.

Seraphina turned the two against each other in under an hour. A genius move, and we'd recorded everything. We even knew where they kept their money. Not too original—the Caymans.

All we had left to do now was dismantle the rest of their operation. Well, first, I needed Alex to wake up and be A-the-fuck-okay.

At some point, I finally tucked away my thoughts and drifted off. I wasn't sure how long I'd been asleep, but when I opened my eyes, the sun was more awake than I was, splashing a bit too harshly in the room.

My head must've fallen forward, because my neck was stiff. Doing my best not to wake Seraphina, I sat up without shifting her head from my shoulder.

I was in the process of moving my free arm around to deal with the pain at the back of my neck, but my hand dropped to my lap in shock.

Alex's eyes were open and on me.

Unable to stop myself, I startled, my quick, jerky movements waking up Seraphina as a result.

"I didn't want to disturb you." Alex's voice was rough and raspy, but . . . he was talking.

Fuck. "You're okay?" I rubbed the sleep from my eyes, worried I was still dreaming.

"I am." His brows drew together. "Tell me you got her." Of course his mind went there. Straight to that demon of a woman.

Holding each other's hand, Seraphina and I both stood and went to his bedside. Relief nailed me harder than the round that'd struck me in the plate earlier. "Yeah. She's back at the villa tied up. Ezra too."

He rested his head back and closed his eyes.

"Can you go get Reed? He's somewhere in the building." I turned to her, my heart still racing. "He needs to know he's awake." I checked the hallway, catching eyes with the GRS operator I'd assigned there as protection. "Go with him. Don't be alone, got it?"

"Of course." She rested her other hand on top of our clasped ones, and I lifted her knuckles to my lips and kissed her before she gave me a small smile of *Thank God*, then took off.

"You want to know what the other side looks like?" Alex lazily lolled his head to the side, opening his eyes. "It was nice."

"You fuckin' with me, or . . . ?" I crossed my arms, trying to keep it together. Alex was a brother to me. Closer than that, because he was family I'd chosen.

His lips twitched. I had to assume the doctors had already come in and checked on him after he'd woken up. Seraphina and I had to have been knocked the fuck out to sleep through that.

"There was a light. A bright one." I still had no clue if he was serious or doped up, but as long as he was okay and good, he could tell me he had a conversation with Elvis on the other side, and I'd be on board. "Not my time, apparently. I got kicked back."

"I shouldn't have let you—"

He cut me off. "Don't start with that shit. Catch me up instead. Tell me what I missed. Is the op still on later? I, uh, don't know what time it is."

I checked my watch, unsure about that myself, then brought him up to speed.

"Wait, you're saying Ezra corrupted her?" he asked after I'd finished my bullet-point monologue. "She admitted that?" He tried to sit upright, but I overrode his decision, urging him down with a hand on his shoulder.

"Not in those words, but yeah. Beth decided to turn Ezra, not just Nina and Andrej. But she didn't get approval for that and went behind everyone's back. He was her dirty secret." One of many, apparently. Along with that bank account in the Caymans.

"She say why she did it?"

"Nina was failing in trying to seduce him, or something like that. If she couldn't get him to fall for Nina and marry her, then she decided she had to force his hand and convince him it'd be in his best interest to get married. Director Johnson had a fallback alternative if Ezra didn't marry Nina."

"Of course he did. Probably had three," he grumbled.

I pulled my hand away from his shoulder and hooked my thumbs at the front of my jeans. "Somewhere along the line, Ezra got into her head. Changed the plans. Then she fell for him. Not that he wanted her like that, from what I remember him saying." Didn't blame him there.

"Someone managed to manipulate a master manipulator? Damn." The fact he could get out that mouthful was a good sign he wasn't suffering any major side effects from "seeing the other side."

"You can't corrupt someone who doesn't have it in them to be corrupted, if you get what I'm saying." *Beth was never really a good person.*

"Maybe I need my head examined, but not because of what happened here. The fact I ever married her . . ." He closed his eyes. "I have fucking shit taste in women, don't I?"

"I mean, yeah." No point in not being blunt. The man had been given another chance at life, and I wanted him to have what I'd found this week.

"Wow. So, Beth's been going behind everyone's back and colluding with Ezra." His voice was getting better. Words more fluid. All good signs, which prompted more relief to roll down my spine.

"Yeah, and Ezra went behind hers by keeping Anna's real identity a secret from her. That had Beth jealous." *So fucking weird.* That remark had him reopening his eyes. "Andrej found out about the two of them. Discovered Ezra was actually her partner, not even an asset. He threatened to expose them."

"So she had Andrej killed and framed him." He looked up at the ceiling, his jaw visibly tensing, a different kind of hurt hitting him. The kind morphine wouldn't dull. "I have to believe she started this operation with the right intentions, but hell, maybe without me in her life as her husband to keep her balanced and in check, she spun out. Lost her way."

I stumbled forward at his remark, at what sounded like blame in his voice. "What's your point?"

"Just rationalizing how she turned into this person. Not forgiving her."

In my opinion, the woman had always been evil, and Ezra saw it in her and brought it out front and center. But I could understand Alex not wanting to believe he hadn't recognized that in her. My mind was made up in having this woman become collateral damage tonight, but . . .

"Do you want me to keep her alive tonight?" I hated asking him that, but if Beth dying would be too hard for him to handle, even after everything she'd put him through, I didn't want to hurt him more than he already was.

"You're Delta One. That's your call to make."

"But if it was yours?" I pressed him, my pulse flying.

He closed his eyes and gave me the only answer I needed to make up my mind. "Well, one thing I know to be true is, she'd rather die than spend her life powerless, wearing orange behind bars."

CHAPTER FORTY-EIGHT

Ryder

Time had blurred that day, but knowing Alex was okay certainly helped me focus on what needed to be done tonight.

"Sorry to pull you away from your family again." I removed my shades, standing out in front of the villa with Owen. It felt like yesterday since he'd dropped us off, and—wait, *was* it yesterday? I was losing track of time.

"I mean, technically, POTUS did, so you're in the clear with her." Owen patted my shoulder twice, then tipped his head toward four other operators exiting two black Suburbans.

"I'm relieved to know that tiny, little toy plane you flew us here in survived your trip back over," Seraphina said as I wrapped my arm around her.

Owen laughed. "Yeah, yeah. I can fly anything, don't you worry, ma'am." He shifted his aviator sunglasses down his nose to wink before returning them to their place. "I heard you have another pilot now. I guess that means I'll be infil'ing on the ground. Unless Carter pulled another Black Hawk out of thin air for me to use?"

Reed joined us in the driveway. "At this rate, I wouldn't be surprised." He said hello before we all turned our attention to the rest of the president's special team unloading their SUVs.

I'd always heard rumors POTUS had a few off-the-books SEALs working for him, and from the looks of it, that rumor was based in fact.

Carter had given me a few details about them over a call, but he hadn't been allowed to reveal too much. He promised we were in good hands with Bravo. Plus, we had Nate, Garrison, and the other GRS operators for support. Ángel's team, too. Our numbers were looking good.

"Our secret teams aren't such a secret anymore," one of the operators, who I recognized as the president's son, said on approach.

"At least they are to the bad guys—and, you know, Congress," Owen commented, shifting to the side as more of the guys filtered over our way.

"Ain't that the same fuckin' thing?" one of the SEALs joked.

"I take it you're the reason we're here?" the dead ringer for Thor, with the Aussie accent to go with it, asked Seraphina next.

She smiled. "Guilty."

"Wait up." Reed removed his sunglasses. "Are you telling me POTUS has both you and Wyatt Pierson working directly for him?" So, he recognized the Aussie. "Sniper legends," he told me. "Two of the best in the world."

Carter had let us know that Gwen's dad, Wyatt, was the team leader for Echo. Gwen would be joining Carter and her father's team in Asia, too. So yeah, the numbers were looking really fucking good. Odds in our favor, for sure. It was about damn time.

The Aussie closed one eye and shrugged. "Don't tell Wyatt that. The bloke's ego is big enough." He introduced himself to those of us who didn't know his name already, unlike the apparent fanboy at my side.

"Mister Doom and Gloom here is clearly an admirer of snipers, and apparently hackers, too." I wasn't sure if they'd pick up on the connection to Gwen I'd alluded to or not. "I learn something new about my teammates every day."

Reed shook his head. "I like her for—"

Owen cut him off. "If by 'her' you mean Gwen, I hope you're about to say 'her skills.' Word travels fast. Big brother—or in this case, *father*—is always watching. And you'll learn why her old man's really"—his smirk was targeted for the Aussie—"tied as the world's best sniper."

The guys on his team cracked smiles and laughed as Reed muttered, "Brains. I admire her brains, you assholes." The grump at least grinned while shaking his head.

Seraphina casually leaned against me. "Small world, though, right?" she mused, reading my thoughts.

"You have no fuckin' idea just how much," POTUS's son said—and damn, I had to admit, it was surreal to have the opportunity to be operating with him.

Seraphina straightened at the sight of a woman exiting the front passenger seat of one of their SUVs while ending a call. "Another woman. Thank God."

"That's my sister. She co-runs the team with me." Bravo One set his sights on a guy with Jason Momoa vibes off to his right. "And my best friend's wife."

"Best friend's sister, huh?" Seraphina's smile was contagious. "And how does that work with you all out in the field together?"

I couldn't imagine one of my best friends marrying a sibling. Not that I had a sister, but damn.

"We manage to survive," the woman said as she pocketed her phone, closing in on us.

"By the skin of our teeth," Owen teased as he playfully elbowed her in the side before she made the rounds, introducing herself as Jessica Scott-Hayes.

"Any other family members I need to know about to . . . well, not piss off?" Reed had me laughing with that one. He wasn't usually funny, but he was stepping up to the plate lately with some humor here and there.

"It's a family affair when it comes to us." Owen shrugged. "Just always be on your best behavior, and you avoid an angry father, brother . . . or, you know, president."

POTUS's son, Knox, rolled his eyes.

After a few more minutes of shooting the shit with everyone, Seraphina pulled me off to the side of the group. "I need to find something to keep myself busy. You know, so I'm not nervously in your way with the mission-prep stuff."

I leaned in, dropping my mouth to her ear. "By 'busy,' do you mean wearing that red bathing suit and swimming?"

"No, I can't have you distracted right now or having a heart attack." She eased back, smiling, then turned toward everyone, asking, "So, who's hungry?"

◆ ◆ ◆

Later that night

After Ezra arranged the meeting spot with the Moraleses, like we'd forced him to do an hour ago, Ángel's uncle then reached out to Ángel. Thankfully, everything was falling into place.

The majority of us were currently huddled in the office, prepping the infil plan, and I had the real-time satellite view of our *expected* target location broadcasted on the TV screen.

The property in question was just outside San José in Escazú, secluded and set in the jungle. A perfect spot for the cartel to lay low.

"This has to be the place where he plans to take us." Ángel stood alongside me, observing the screen. "Well, if we gave him the chance to, at least."

And we aren't. "It's not shocking your uncle doesn't trust you enough to hand over his address so you can GPS your way there." We'd hoped, but we'd had a contingency plan for that if not.

"But if we're wrong about this location," Seraphina said, drawing my eyes to where she was hanging out in the doorway now, "that's why Ángel needs to head to the meeting spot where his uncle is supposed to pick him up with Beth as bait?"

I did my best to smile and nod and act A-the-fuck-okay for her. When in reality, the idea of how quickly we'd had to pull this plan together didn't sit well with me. "I don't think we're wrong on the location, though," I added when it was clear she wasn't buying my smile.

Ángel must've read her worried look and slouched posture, too, because he went over to the TV and explained, "My uncle wants me to park on this back road here and wait for his guys to pick me up, and that puts us three miles out from where we believe he's set up."

"Considering that mansion is abandoned and we're picking up twenty-four heat signatures inside, definitely has me believing they're in there," Bravo One chimed in, hopefully boosting her confidence with that fact as well. "Thankfully, his uncle has no clue he'd have access to satellites and thermal imaging of this kind. We're blindsiding him."

"And I'll be monitoring the feeds the whole time and in their ears. Any sudden changes, and I can alert all teams." Jessica's reassuring words had to be for Seraphina, and I gave her an appreciative nod.

"Too bad you couldn't drone strike the place instead," Seraphina murmured before her shoulders fell from a deep sigh. Yup, nerves were still active. "But, uh, your father," she continued, eyes on Bravo Five, "doesn't want his fingerprint on this."

Bravo Five gave her a small smile and nod as his answer.

"The mansion used to be owned by an arms trafficker back in the nineties," Reed said, redirecting our attention. "So it makes sense he'd pick a spot like this. Lots of obstacles out there to get in our way."

With my back to Seraphina, I discreetly swiped my hand beneath my chin, letting him know to save those details for when she wasn't in the room. I was trying to de-stress her, not elevate her anxiety.

"There's a river we could use as one point of entry to sneak up around the back of the property and bypass security. *Río Virilla*," Bravo

One said, hopefully distracting her from Reed's warning. "My guys can infil there."

I zeroed in on a possible infil route for my team, which consisted of Reed and the other GRS operators who'd be Delta Team tonight. "We can breach from the east side. Handle their men on overwatch first before Bravo moves in."

"I'll head to the meetup spot, let my uncle's men put eyes on me so they don't know the ambush is about to happen, then you all move on target. I'll take out my uncle's men sent to pick Beth and myself up, and join you at his place after."

"I'd like to run one or two more contingency plans before we head out," Jessica said as she checked her watch, "but we're short on time."

"And you have something to do first before we spin up, right?" Reed asked me, and yeah, I did.

I had to go kill Ezra so we could drop his body, along with the rest of his crew, on the scene to blame for the cartel deaths.

I'd never killed a man in cold blood like that. I'd been looking forward to this moment, so the fact I was feeling oddly sick about it was unsettling.

"Isn't there another way?" At Seraphina's soft voice, I turned to face her.

"We'll give you two a minute." Jessica shooed everyone from the room, spinning her finger in the air.

The moment I was alone with her, Seraphina cut across the room, and I took hold of her hips. We didn't have much time to spare, but I needed her to talk me through this. To give me the okay to take the life of an unarmed man. It was much easier to talk about, but now . . .

"He killed your family. So did she. They're monsters." That was my attempt to rationalize my way through this. "He'd have assaulted you before killing you, too." The desire to commit murder, which was exactly what it would be, was front and center again.

She lifted her arms and draped them over my shoulders, linking her wrists behind my neck. "Yes and yes. But there's something more important than revenge to me now."

"And that is?" I swallowed, staring into her beautiful eyes. The pain in my chest from being shot had nothing on this uncertain feeling inside me right now.

"You. Your soul."

"Don't tell me Alex got in your head with all that seeing-the-bright-light stuff."

"I promised you that you're not going to hell. The only way I can keep that promise is if you don't kill anyone that's unarmed."

I shrugged. "Easy remedy. I give the fucker some cutlery, then take his life."

"Don't you dark-humor your way out of this on me."

I rested my forehead against hers. "Tell me what to do, then. Take the decision away from me. Because if it were up to me, I'd offer him up to the Moraleses and let them disembowel him so he had a slow, painful death. A shot to the head is too easy."

She eased back, finding my eyes. "So do that."

"What?" I raised my brows.

"Bring Ezra alive with you tonight and throw him into the lion's den. Let the Moraleses do what they do best. Evil against evil. They'll handle him so you don't have to." She brought my hands around to my face and held my cheeks. "You're a good man."

I tried to look away from her, but she wasn't having it. "Maybe I don't want to be good right now?"

"You can be bad with me later," she taunted, momentarily distracting me from anything and everything dark. "Your heart's too big to do something you'll regret," she said, shifting back to seriousness. "You left the army because . . ." She frowned. "Revenge will never be worth the price of your soul. But I still want him dead, just not because you slit his throat or shot him in the head."

Oh, how I wanted to do so much more to him than that.

But.
Fucking but.
She was right.
"Okay," I agreed. "I won't be stubborn and fight you on this." Not enough time to, anyway. "I'm not going to forget your idea to be bad later with you, though."

"I'm counting on it." She pressed up onto her toes to kiss me, and I lost myself to her the moment our lips touched.

Someone needed to bottle up whatever she made me feel and sell that instead. Fuck fentanyl. Drugs had nothing on this.

"You need to get going," I murmured against her mouth a moment later. "Don't leave Alex's hospital room for a minute until I let you know it's safe."

Our pilot and Nate would be dropping her off at the hospital while we drove to the mansion; then they'd meet up with us precisely when we needed them.

"Roger that." She smiled against my lips before breaking away to look at me. "I'd rather force Alex to watch a telenovela than the aerial footage of your mission. My heart can't handle round two of that."

"Much better plan, I agree." I hated leaving her. Hated this part. The goodbye. The I-need-to-survive kiss before I left.

"So, run this by me one more time so my stomach is less knotty."

"Hudson and his team are going to hit the Sokolovs' operation in Miami when we target the Moraleses. Martín's taking out Ángel's brother and the rest of the cartel the second we advance on the mansion. POTUS's other two SEAL teams, with the help of Carter, are dealing with the suppliers simultaneously."

"No chance of escape that way for anyone."

I nodded. "That's the hope."

"It's really almost over, then?"

"I'm sure other criminals will step in and try to fill the void, but . . ." *It's never-ending.* "Hudson will keep up the fight. But for us, for Ángel, yeah, it's over." I pulled her into my arms. "Well, or I should say, for us, it's just beginning." I slanted my mouth over hers, and we kept in that position until a throat being cleared interrupted us.

"You ready?" Reed asked. He was standing alongside Bravo One.

"He was born ready for this." Seraphina set her hand on my chest, and her words about broke some kind of emotional dam inside me. She was supporting who I was and what I did with that comment, and it meant more to me than she'd ever know.

"Let's do this, then." Bravo One signaled for us to head out; then I focused back on Seraphina as she cradled the back of my neck, drawing her mouth to my ear.

"My dad's watching over you. I can feel it," she whispered, and fuck, she was going to choke me up all over again. "He's got your six because he knows you have mine."

CHAPTER FORTY-NINE

Ryder

The humid air clung to my skin as sweat beaded down my spine. The jungle was alive, creatures all around us well aware they had guests who didn't belong there. The dense canopy diffused the moonlight, creating shadows in my green-tinted world.

My team quietly weaved in and out of the undergrowth. Moving in on our target in preparation for the strike, slipping between the trees like ghosts. Invisible to everyone but the animals. We were just other beasts in the night to them. Predators hunting prey.

Each step was calculated and controlled, propelled forward by adrenaline and the desire to make it home alive to those we loved.

I slowed my pace as my world broadened outside the jungle, expanding far beyond my current field of view and back to the villa. To Seraphina. To my feelings for a woman I barely knew but felt like I'd known my whole damn life.

"You good, boss?" Reed was at my side. Was he trying to make me feel as though Alex was with us with that *boss* shit?

"Just Charlie Mike," I ordered, then patted his shoulder twice.

With my head back in the game now, I broke off from the team as planned to cross over the fence. "TOC, this is Delta One," I said to Jessica, our eyes in the sky tonight. "I'm advancing on target." I pivoted around and used an infrared light to mark my position for her.

"This is TOC; I've got you. You have a hundred meters of open space sitting between you and four hostiles, one of which is in the back of a truck bed having a cigarette."

A hundred meters of open space without coverage might as well be a mile. "This is Delta One, that's a good copy." I turned to the side, signaling to Reed with my fist to stop.

He was blending in with the foliage. Just another shadow out there.

"This is TOC, Delta One, be advised, you also have two rooftop snipers."

I confirmed I heard her before Bravo One came over our comms, asking Ángel, "What's your status, Foxtrot One?"

Ángel had Beth and Ezra tied up in his SUV. Ezra was in the back, and Beth was in the passenger seat. I didn't trust either of them not to try and pull some shit even with their hands and ankles bound.

"This is Foxtrot One, I have eyes on the target. Headlights are approaching. His guys are almost here. About twenty seconds," he let us know, and that was now our countdown.

As soon as he alerted us the SUV had stopped, that was our cue to move in.

"Delta Team, you're up," I ordered, slinging my rifle out of my way to climb up over the fence. We needed to clear the overwatch positions before Bravo and Foxtrot Teams could safely engage.

The moment I landed on the other side, my boots hitting the damp soil, my rifle became part of me. My HK416, a short-barreled configuration, was just an extension of my body. With the compact and lightweight weapon in hand, I positioned myself next to Reed to take out the four tangos in the distance.

We had the advantage of surprise and NODs, but the element of surprise would end once the cartel learned Ángel had set them up, which would be happening within the next sixty seconds.

"Delta Two," I said to Reed, since he was taking Alex's place tonight, "you handle the snipers."

"Roger that," he answered, and I focused back on my targets.

The cat was about to be let out of the motherfucking bag that we were here, even with suppressed fire.

"This is Delta One. Engaging now," I let TOC and the other teams know. Thankfully, we could transmit up to four mikes out, and Ángel was only three away.

I zeroed in on my mark, angling my body slightly forward in preparation for the recoil, and I fired. The energy of the shot pushed into my shoulder, and I felt it vibrate into my hand and up into my chest. The suppressor turned the sound into more of a cough than a boom, and nothing else in the world existed other than my need to square up with the universe. Offer a life for a life. In my mind, for every cartel member I took out, a life on my team was protected and spared.

Muscle memory took over with the trigger as I fired again and again. The vibrations rippled through me, my movements controlled even with the recoil. Spent casings flew out the side, small flashes just outside my peripheral view with the night-vision goggles in my way.

I took a moment and scanned the setting. All four tangos immobilized, but more would soon be coming.

We were holding off on calling up our Black Hawk with Nate on the door gun for as long as possible, doing our best to make this look like a hit by the Sokolovs before they died in the ambush themselves. But it was good to know we had air support on standby if more hostiles flooded the grounds.

"This is Delta Two, snipers are down. Bravo and Foxtrot, you're clear to advance."

"This is TOC, Delta Team, you have more tangos exiting on your side of the property. Three hostiles in pursuit."

"Delta Three and Four, move in now," I ordered before taking down another target.

"This is Bravo Three. I'm setting up a breaching charge now."

"Delta One here, roger that."

Reed kept pace with me, and we advanced to the side of the mansion, watching each other's backs with the help of Jessica overhead.

"This is Foxtrot One. My team is heading your way now."

Reed tapped my shoulder twice, and I focused up, and my team flowed inside with precision.

"This is Bravo Five. Our two HVTs are making a run for it. Using tunnels we uncovered. I'm in pursuit."

The two main targets were Ángel's uncle and cousin, and the plan was a bust if we didn't take them out.

"This is Bravo Two," Owen said, "I've got your six. I'm on it."

I trusted their team to handle the marks, and my guys continued to clear the house.

I took another man down, watching the impact. A center-mass hit. I squeezed off a second round. Headshot. Controlled bursts. Casings repeatedly ejected as we flowed in. The *clack-clack* of the bolt cycling and distant noise of the cartel scrambling for cover filled my ears as I lived in a world of grainy and pixelated green. The smell of burned powder with the jungle air crept up into my nose.

"This is Delta One, first floor clear," I let everyone know before we went upstairs.

We were looking for active shooters, ready to be met with gunfire not pressure plates. But not even the best of the best and the most well-trained operators on the planet could go up against a room rigged to blow.

So the last thing I expected was for Reed to warn me about explosives, and then to yell, "Get down!"

CHAPTER FIFTY
Seraphina

"Ever heard of the whole a-watched-pot-never-boils thing?"

At Alex's question, I stopped pacing and looked up from my watch and over at him. He was sitting upright in his bed, and the color had returned to his face since we'd last visited him.

"Shouldn't they have made contact by now?" My insides weren't twisted up; they were obliterated into a mangled mess with every passing minute we waited to hear from Ryder.

I'd muted the soap opera I had on about five minutes ago because the actors' voices were grating on my nerves. My own was, too, though. The only words I wanted to hear were from Ryder letting me know everyone was fine and they had mission success.

"Something probably came up."

I morphed into my mom right then, unsure if I could pull off the "look" as well as her, but I gave it my best shot. At Alex's twitch of the lips and hand in the air, I assumed I'd mastered her *Are you kidding?* expression. "You make it sound like they got held up in traffic on their way, or the battery died in their phone and they don't have a charger."

"Distract yourself. Eat my Jell-O. God knows I'm not." He lifted the bowl, and the red cube wobbled. Realizing I wasn't backing down from acting like a nervous mother, he set aside the food, which needed to be outlawed in every country. "Trust me, sitting in this bed instead of being on that op with them is hell. I'm anxious as fuck myself."

I frowned. "You don't look it."

He rubbed his chest. "They've got me doped up. Just not enough. Heart still hurts."

Shit. I started for the door.

"Where are you going?"

I spun around. "To get the doctor."

"No, no. I didn't mean that literally." He flicked his wrist to come back over. "Thanks for caring, though."

My shoulders fell, and now my heart was hurting, too. For him. "I can't imagine what you must be going through."

He flicked the bowl of Jell-O farther away, keeping his eyes on the little red block. "I'm just upset with myself for . . ." He cleared his throat, smoothing the heel of his hand in small circles over his heart. "She was with Ezra, and still, uh, showing up at my door from time to time in the last year, so I'd like to use this spork here"—he lifted the plastic utensil—"and cut out my eyes so I can unsee the past and make it go away."

Ohhh. My stomach dropped, and I scooched a chair closer to the bed and sat. Memories of the time my brother had struggled to get over his high school sweetheart, who was neither sweet nor had the best heart, flooded my mind. What'd I say to him during that situation?

I guess Ezra wasn't enough for Beth, even though she was insanely jealous (which wound up saving me).

"Your problem—which isn't actually a problem at all—is you clearly have a huge heart. You see the best in people," I finally said all that came to mind. "Maybe too forgiving?"

"I heard the question mark there at the end." He set down the spork. "I'm not forgiving of criminals. Zero tolerance for bad guys. That's what she is now. It's who she became. There's no saving or forgiving."

Amen to that.

"I'll be fine. Just need to beat myself up about my poor decisions for a few more days." He closed one eye. "Or weeks. I'll soldier on"—he gave me a lopsided smile—"and never date again. Too late to become a priest? You think they'll hold my kill count against me?"

"Oh my God." The man had me laughing, but it was a welcome distraction from—

Ryder. Ryder's here. I jumped from the seat at the sight of him leaning in the doorway.

"What's so funny?" A slow, lazy smile cut across his lips, nearly nailing me to the floor in my pursuit of getting to him. Because, you know, smiles were positive. Optimistic. No one died on missions if you came back smiling.

"You're here. Even took time to change." I threw my arms over his shoulders and crushed myself against him.

"I figured showing up looking like an operator and strapped might turn a few heads with the staff. Prefer to blend in." That raspy, deep voice was silk to my skin and music to my ears. The only sounds I'd wanted to hear were happening now and in real time.

When I lifted my head, still hanging on to this man like a lifeline, I spied Reed in the hallway also appearing as intact as the man I was clutching.

"Sorry I didn't call. I was so anxious to get to you—"

"That I had to see him in his skivvies on the ride over here as he changed." Reed's drawl, coupled with his smile, had me over-the-moon relieved.

If the quiet, broody one was grinning, then yeah, we were better than good.

"I had to see you half naked, too, ya asshole," Ryder joked, letting go of me so we could all head into Alex's room.

Reed quickly dismissed a nurse complaining about the visiting rules, and he offered her a few broken Spanish phrases that were almost comical coming from his mouth.

"Tell me everything," Alex said the second we were together.

Reed rounded the bed, and Ryder pushed the chair away so we could stand next to Alex.

"Is everyone okay?" I blurted before anyone could answer Alex.

"The good guys, yes. I'm bruised as fuck, but that's because of Reed here shoving me to the ground and throwing himself on top of me." Ryder scowled at Reed. "Don't do that shit again. Trying to sacrifice yourself for me."

Reed rolled his eyes as his response.

"Wait, what happened?" I wrapped my arm around Ryder's, trying not to be too panicky or alarmed since he was clearly okay and not bleeding.

"There was a pressure plate. A room was rigged to blow." Ryder motioned to Reed. "This asshole tackled me, used himself as a human shield—but crazy enough, the thing didn't go off. Faulty wiring."

I covered my mouth with my free hand, trying to wrap my head around the *what ifs* that could've gone wrong. "Told you my dad had your six," I whispered, my arm diving to my side as pressure built up into my chest, threatening to come out in the form of tears.

Ryder kissed the top of my head. "You're right about that, beautiful."

"So, everyone's really okay? Mission success?" There was definitely something else Alex wanted to know besides that.

Same. So much same. Were Beth and Ezra alive and kicking? The Moraleses?

"Everyone on our side is good. *But* you know the saying about the witch being dead, well . . ." Reed immediately lifted his hand at Alex's wide eyes flying his way. "Kidding on that second part. Unfortunately."

"Beth's alive?" Alex's forehead scrunched, and to be honest, I wasn't sure I wanted to hear the answer to this myself. "Also, since when is this guy funny? You're supposed to be the know-it-all without a sense of humor." He pointed at Reed, eyes on Ryder to answer him.

"She's alive, yes," Ryder said in a low, uncomfortable voice as if displeased by that reality. "And you need to hurry up and get better, because Reed attempting to take your place as the comedian on the team is *not* funny."

Alex shifted back to the main issue at hand. "Tell me what happened."

"When Ezra was cut loose so the Moraleses could take him out, he went after Beth. Managed to pull a knife off one of Ángel's men," Reed explained. "Karma's a motherfucking bitch, I swear. He stabbed her in the side, and Ángel had no choice but to put the man down to, you know, save her. He, uh, probably could've taken him out before he managed to cut her, but I think he was okay with letting Ezra get one swipe at her first."

"Talk about a twist I didn't see coming." I gulped. "So Ezra's dead?" Relief swelled heavy, hard, and deep. "Where's Beth now?"

Ryder untangled our arms so he could draw his behind my back and haul me tight to his side. "We left his corpse there to keep with the plan we were never there. Then we did a quick patch-up job of Beth's wound and handed her over to Bravo to let them deal with her. They'll be taking her to DC for her punishment." He faced Alex next. "To spend the rest of her life powerless and in a jumpsuit."

"You okay?" I asked Alex. Maybe that's what Alex had wanted to happen, and Ryder kept her alive knowing that. Easier for Alex to truly move on if he had zero guilt about the death of that woman, even if, in my opinion, she deserved it.

"Beth didn't deserve a star on the wall at the Agency commemorating her service, which would've happened if she died, because POTUS can't tell anyone the truth," Alex said plainly, no emotion there. "So I'm good," he added, eyes on me. "Are you?"

She and Ezra were responsible for stealing my family from me, so yeah, I was okay with the outcome. Death would be too easy for that woman. "I'm great because you're all safe." And that was what truly mattered.

"The Moraleses are done, too." With his free hand, Ryder reached into his pocket and showed me a text from Martín, letting me know he was successful as well. "They're all gone. He came through for us in Mexico, and there's a surveillance clip we pulled from the op tonight that we'll ensure makes the rounds showing Ángel killing Ezra. That jibes with the story we planned on selling that he sought retribution for the Moraleses, so he has protection in that regard."

"How is he?" I asked. "I mean, they were still his family."

"I'm good." At Ángel's voice, I turned to see him in the doorway, resting his hand against the frame. "I came to say goodbye, and I truly hope I never see you again."

"Same," Ryder said with a smile.

"Thank you for everything." I pulled myself away from Ryder to hug Ángel goodbye, and he reluctantly hugged me back, probably careful under my overprotector's watchful gaze. "Good luck back home."

"Luck is no longer needed." Ángel let me go, then tipped his chin toward Ryder. "I'll send you everything I have to help your friends."

Ryder shook his hand and thanked him. "Be in touch."

Ángel gave me one last look, smiled, then took off.

"What stuff is he sending you?" I asked him.

"Everything he's ever collected on the cartels over the years. I'm going to pass the intel over to Hudson so he can ensure no one can start up shit again—but if they do, he'll be waiting to stop them."

"Does that mean Hudson and his friends were successful in Miami? And what about Carter and the other teams?" I looked over at Reed, then back at Ryder.

"Hudson had mission success, and Carter and the president's other teams are still at work taking down the suppliers, but I'm confident they'll be done within a few hours." More good news from my guy, thank God.

I faced him as if we were alone, setting my hand on his chest, finding his heart racing beneath my palm. I was still struggling to absorb the truth that my hell had come to an end. That I had my life back. A new, better one. It'd probably take some getting used to. I had to let the shock wear off. "So, what do we do now?"

"I take you home." He held on to my hips, pulling me closer while leaning in.

"Your home?" I arched my brow.

"I don't have one."

"Neither do I." Well, my parents had a home I'd yet to sell, but I hadn't lived there since I was eighteen, and too many memories crowded that place for me to comfortably move forward if I were to live there. "So where do we go?"

"You could start with a hotel room," Reed said, and we both turned and looked at him. "Or just do it here. I mean, I've already seen more of one of you than I ever wanted to."

"You've been holding out on us, brother." Alex threw his bowl of Jell-O at him, laughing. "You are a funny fucker. All this time, we never knew."

Reed flicked the block of Jello-O that'd clung to his shirt to the floor. "Don't get too excited. The second you're back operating again, I promise you I'll morph—"

"Into a Power Ranger?" Alex tipped his head back, his laugh deepening.

"How much morphine did they give you?" Reed shook his head. "You see what I have to put up with?"

"Typical of families, and you all are clearly one." My shoulders relaxed, taking it all in yet again that everyone was okay, and also, well . . . "Mind if I join?"

"Like as in, operating with us?" Ryder asked in alarm.

"No, silly." I lifted one shoulder. "As *your* girl. And by extension, their family. Like a sister."

"I can live with that." He brought his nose against mine, a soft breath floating from his mouth that touched my lips. "Hell, I can't live *without* that."

CHAPTER FIFTY-ONE

Ryder

Washington, DC; four days later

"Looks like quite a lot has changed since we bumped into each other last." Hudson parked his focus on Seraphina. She was standing by the front door of the bar, chatting with his brother-in-law, Enzo. "No longer single, huh?"

While we hadn't made anything official, yeah, in my head and heart I wasn't single. I was very much taken.

After two and a half days of nonstop lovemaking—before leaving Costa Rica post-mission, up until an hour ago—we'd only been out of bed for two reasons, other than our flight stateside and dinner with Hudson tonight.

The first time was to attend a meeting at the Pentagon to handle the aftermath of the op, and the second was this morning. A surprising call had come from the president, inviting us to the White House for brunch. Alex wasn't about to let a GSW and nearly dying stop him from that meal.

Talk about things I'd never expected to happen in my lifetime. Brunch with POTUS. Bucket list item, for sure. Not that I'd ever had a list, but I'd happily make one with Seraphina.

"You good, man?" Hudson asked in an amused tone, hauling me back to the present.

I dragged a palm across my eyes, trying to focus. He'd asked me something, right? "Not single, no. Also, I'm fantastic," I finally answered, allowing my hand to fall to my side, my gaze shooting straight to the woman of my dreams.

"Seems like there's something else you'd rather be doing than be here with me. I won't hold you up any longer."

He was right about that. But I really was thankful to have him as an ally in all this. Grateful he'd keep up the good fight securing our borders from traffickers and protecting our cities from drugs.

"Thank you again. For everything." I shook his hand. "Keep me posted. Hopefully, something in that file helps."

"Ángel gave us quite a bit to sort through. With Carter and the others handling those supply routes in Asia," he said as we started walking to the door, "it'll take a while for anyone to regroup and start shit up again. Unfortunately, I'm sure they'll try, though."

Yeah, he was right about that. "Wild you've worked with Carter and those, uh, other teams before." I kept my voice down since we weren't supposed to know those SEAL teams existed and worked for POTUS.

Hell, I was still reeling from the fact the president had asked my team to work directly for him instead of with DHS from now on. I was game. Alex and Reed happily were, too. We'd decided we'd stick to a three-man team, though.

"Yeah, looks like all of us kind of run in the same circles," he commented while we joined Seraphina and Enzo.

We said our goodbyes, and I went for Seraphina's jacket on the coatrack and helped her into it. I pulled her long hair free, then stepped around to open the door for her.

The cold air hit me in the face, but it was seeing Lainey and Jeff standing in front of an SUV that slapped me even harder. *You tracked my phone again? I have to get a new number.*

Per my request, Lainey hadn't been at the meeting I'd had with DHS when going over the AAR, the after-action report. So of course she'd sought me out against my wishes.

"What's wrong?" Seraphina picked up on my change in energy, then dialed in on the problem standing there before us. Lainey and my former ride-or-die boot camp friend.

Talk about an ambush. Fuck.

She didn't need to fill me in on the aftermath of my operation. I'd been there myself for it, along with the cleanup. Like ensuring the director, Nina, Beth, and her team were met with the appropriate consequences for their actions. Also, Beth and Ezra's $47 million rainy-day funds were now being donated to a nonprofit that helped those suffering with addiction get the help they needed.

"Why are you here? What do you want?" I swiftly pulled Seraphina to my side, protectively drawing my arm behind her back.

Lainey zeroed in on the detail of my hand placement before clearing her throat and saying, "Who would've thought everything would turn out like this?" She wasn't just talking about the op, that was for damn sure. No, she was looking right at Seraphina. And she was jealous. *Now you want me, huh? Of course.* "I'm Lainey." She offered her hand, and Seraphina left her hanging.

That's my girl. As protective of me as I was of her.

Lainey lowered her arm, then tipped her head toward the SUV and away from pedestrian traffic. "I thought you'd want to know"—she directed her words to Seraphina—"that there was no insider who betrayed you from the DEA or the task force. No one sold you out. Lev made a lucky guess."

Seraphina didn't say anything, but from my peripheral view, I caught her nodding her okay.

"Beth was the only one who truly..." A flash of unexpected emotion cut across Lainey's face. That had to be the baby inside her taking over, warming up her heart a bit. She was nowhere near as cold as Beth, but still. "You could say that I'm kicking myself for not seeing the signs about Beth. I still can't believe what happened. She'll be spending her days in a black site prison, not a regular penitentiary." She kept her voice low to avoid broadcasting to eavesdroppers walking by.

A CIA black site was much worse. *Good-fucking-riddance.* The woman deserved to rot in hell (on Earth, for now).

"I was her friend, and I missed this. Talk about feeling blindsided," Lainey went on since we both kept quiet.

"Yeah, nothing like being blindsided by someone you thought was a friend." And that was for Jeff.

He pinched the bridge of his nose, eyes falling to the sidewalk. *Yeah, don't look me in the eyes. Don't man up.* Not a shocker.

"I just wanted to say—"

"Nope," I cut her off, waving my free hand in the air. "I won't be working cases for Homeland anymore, so you and I have nothing to say to one another ever again, in fact." Feeling like a douche, even if they deserved it, I went ahead and tossed out the best I could offer them: "For what it's worth, I hope you two have a great life together. I just have no plans to be in it." I looked over at Seraphina, and a feeling of calm settled over me at the mere sight of her. "Ready?"

"More than ever," she whispered.

We left the two of them behind—in the past, where they belonged—and we walked the three blocks to our hotel.

The second we were in our room, she tossed her coat and turned to face me. "Give me one second, okay?" She pointed to the bed. "Get comfortable while you wait."

She sauntered into the bathroom, wearing a fitted red dress that made it damn difficult to not bend her over and take her with that on, but I gruffly responded, "Roger that, ma'am."

Once she was in the en suite bathroom, I stripped down to my boxers and checked my phone to see if Alex had responded to my last message.

ALEX: I'm fine. (A legitimate fine, not like when a woman tells you she's fine.)
ALEX: I also feel decent despite being shot and briefly seeing what the other side looks like.

I wasn't ready to believe him, so I sent a follow-up while I waited on Seraphina.

ME: It's okay not to be okay.
The bubbles came and went. Then he finally answered.
ALEX: You trying to Freud me? My job, remember?
ALEX: And I'm F.I.N.E. (Better than okay.) Once I can operate again, at least.
ALEX: And even if I'm not (fine) . . . I will be.
ME: Fine. (See, that word sucks even when a guy uses it.)
ALEX: LOL
ALEX: So . . . you tell her yet? (That you're obsessed and in love?) Although, I think she already knows. You're not the best actor. Told you, being obsessed is a good look on you, brother. Now, go be happy.
ME: Yeah, yeah, yeah. 😎

At the door opening, I set aside my phone, and my breath hitched at the sight of the goddess before me wearing my dress shirt. *The* shirt. The one from the night we met.

Her eyes skated to the bruises on my chest, the ones that were there thanks to what went down in Costa Rica.

"No puppy-dog eyes allowed." I lifted my brows a few times. "Just your fuck-me ones."

"Ohhh, is that so?" she teased in a sultry voice, her hand flying to the buttons as she began to kill me just as she had that morning after I'd Edward Norton'd my way through a real-life *Fight Club*.

"That shirt. On you. Damn."

"I love how you growl words like that." She licked her lips. "Feels so primitive."

"Trust me," I said, shoving down my boxers and stepping free of them, "the things I want to do to you are very much raw, dirty, and all kinds of fucking primitive and naughty."

"Mmmm." She freed the last button, allowing the shirt to part to show me her tits along with her red silk panties. "So do them to me."

I stood like a statue by the bed, taking one long look at her as every moment we'd spent together rolled through my mind in 4D. From the first time I'd set my mouth between her legs in the shower to the first time we'd made love missionary-style in the bed in the villa before packing up to fly to the United States a few days ago. And all the other times since then up until now. All perfect. All otherworldly.

I finally erased the space between us and parked my hand at her side and the other beneath her chin. "There's something I want to tell you first."

A gorgeous smile touched her mouth. "Me too." She flipped her tongue up, covering her teeth as my mind played catch-up to what she was saying.

"Is it too soon?"

"Not for two people destined to be together." She drew her arms between us and held the sides of my neck. "Remember, lightning doesn't just strike the same place twice for everyone, now, does it?"

"No, it doesn't." I kissed her forehead. "But just so I'm crystal clear here, it did for me. Love at first sight." I slowly lifted my head, parking my eyes on hers. "I love you, Seraphina Torres."

Her bottom lip caught between her teeth for a brief moment. "I love you, too, Ryder David Lawson."

EPILOGUE

Seraphina

Bali, Indonesia

"A girl could get used to this. Staring up at the stars next to the man I'm going to marry." I held up my left hand, wiggling my fingers, eyeing the marquise diamond that winked back at me.

"Good. Get used to it." He laced our fingers together, brought our hands to his mouth, and brushed his lips over my knuckles. "At least, the being-in-bed-next-to-me part. I don't know how often I can afford to whisk you away like this, but I'll—"

"As long as we're together, I don't care where we are." I rolled onto my side, and he did the same, our clasped palms becoming the only wedge between us.

"And what about when I'm operating? This time off we have right now is only temporary. Once Alex is cleared, I'll be spinning up again."

"While I've loved spending these last several weeks together nonstop so we can really get to know each other, I'm ready for the next stage of our relationship."

Planting roots. Buying a house. Making babies.

"You are?" The doubt cutting through his tone cut me, too.

Damn his father for abandoning him.

"Of course." I pulled my hand free from his to remind him I'd said yes to his proposal last night. "This wasn't a gift. And my answer was my promise back to you that I'm in this until death do us part."

"No dying on your part."

"Or yours, mister." I fisted his shirt. "That's a direct order."

"I love when you tell me what to do." He playfully lifted his brows.

"Not as much as you love telling me." I licked my lips, and before I knew it, he had me pinned beneath his hard frame, and he braced himself over me, holding himself up with those strong arms of his.

He rolled his hips forward, letting me feel the heavy weight of his cock and that he was ready to go again.

I dragged my fingers along the ridges of his muscles as he slanted his mouth over mine, kissing me softly.

A blur of wonderful memories in the last three weeks flipped through my mind.

From DC to our visit with Owen and his family in Charleston to express our gratitude once again for his help. Off to Switzerland next, in style on one of Carter's private jets. We stayed in a suite at his hotel, all expenses paid by him.

Ryder had asked me one morning while having breakfast in bed at the hotel, *"Give me your bucket list place to visit. You know, if you were to start a new list."*

I jotted down the first place that came to mind, and after a quick trip to California, he brought me here, to my bucket list spot. Dropped to one knee last night.

That'd been the easiest yes to ever leave my mouth. Not stubborn for a second on that one. He'd been ridiculously romantic and even shed a few happy tears.

Talk about the proposal of all proposals.

"You asked my dad for permission, didn't you?" I whispered, breaking our kiss when the realization hit me. He'd asked to see where I grew up. Then we visited my parents and brother at the cemetery, and he requested to have a moment alone with my father.

Ryder lifted his head and stared down at me.

"I'm taking it that Dad said yes?" The man was so freaking thoughtful.

"Both him and Martín did."

Now I'm melting. I reached around and linked my wrists behind his neck, urging his mouth to mine. "And now I need you to truly believe me when I say I'm all in. Not because of the ring. But because of you. Our connection." Tears pricked my eyes as I stared at the man my family had sent to me to save me in so many ways. "Not going anywhere, got it?"

His brows drew tight; then he shifted to his forearms, bringing himself closer, and I thought it was to thrust inside me, but instead he whispered in my ear, *"Te amo, hermosa. Por siempre y para siempre."*

My hands went around to his back as I held on to him, linking my ankles together in preparation for what I hoped would come soon—him filling me. "I love you, too. Forever and always," I repeated, meaning every word. "Learning Spanish, are you?"

He kissed my forehead before his mouth hovered over mine. "I'd like our kids to be bilingual." He smiled against my mouth, and with that statement, he officially had me in a puddle. "I need to know what they're saying, you know?"

"Sooo, you want kids with me, do you?"

"Just with you, yes." He teased my lips open with his tongue, arching against me. "Maybe take some time for ourselves first. I'm obsessed with my future wife, and I'm not ready to share her with anyone."

I laughed, rotating my hips to taunt him back. *"Yo también estoy obsesionada contigo."*

"And that means?"

"Guess you better hurry with your Spanish lessons and figure it out."

He flipped me around in one fast movement so I was now straddling him. "I'm highly motivated to become fluent real fast."

He positioned himself at my center, then held on to my hips, waiting for me to lift up and push down, taking all of him.

Resting my hands on his chest, I did exactly as we both wanted, gasping at the connection once our bodies joined as one.

He buried his fingertips deeper into the flesh at my sides while I rode him. Grinding hard and fast. Chasing the sweet surrender that only this man could ever give me.

"*Sí, sí . . . sí,*" I cried out, coming hard.

A sexy smile crossed his face. "That one I know."

◆ ◆ ◆

Ryder

Fargo, North Dakota

"You're going to get us in trouble, silly. We have to behave." My beautiful fiancée fisted my shirt, arching into me despite her mild reprimand.

I brought my mouth to the side of her neck and kissed her there before moving my hands up into her hair. I had her pinned to the wall in the hallway upstairs in my mother's home. "Just stealing a minute with you. It's Christmas Eve, and I need an early gift. I promise to give you one, too." I thrust my hips forward, letting her feel how hard I was.

She chuckled, holding the back of my head while her other hand rested at my side as I continued to nuzzle her neck, on the verge of giving my girl a hickey. "Your mom is old-school, so . . ."

My mother wouldn't let us share a room until a wedding band was on my finger. Seraphina, of course, was polite and wanted to be respectful of my mother's wishes. I, on the other hand, wanted to "fuck around and find out."

I'd stolen every moment I could with her in the forty-eight hours since we'd arrived, and I was currently using Alex and Reed to distract my mom in the kitchen. I'd assigned them both the task to keep my mom busy for at least fifteen minutes.

From the sounds of it, the plan was working. Reed was trying to help prepare dinner, and my mom wasn't having it.

"We have to stay on the nice list." Then why was she rubbing up against me?

"Oh, but naughty is so much more fun," I teased.

She was quick to surrender. "Mmm. True."

That's my girl.

"I barely survived Thanksgiving here not sharing a bed with you, and that was only two days."

"Exactly. We'll never make it five." I sure as hell wouldn't. "Just give me a few minutes. Please?" I wasn't above begging.

"What if she catches us?" She bucked her hips forward, as horny as I was.

Unable to stop myself, I hooked the waistband of her leggings to the side. I had to check if I was right. The moment my hand made contact with her clit, she buried her face at the side of my neck and nipped me right back as I'd done to her.

She wasn't wet; she was soaked.

"Come on. Be bad with me." I dragged her arousal over her sex before freeing my hand from her pants.

"Ughhh, you better not get me in trouble, I swear." She pulled away, slapping my chest, but I'd take that as a yes.

I stepped away, lifted her in the air, and spanked her ass on the way to my old bedroom.

I ignored the shrine my mom had set up of my hockey trophies, along with photos of my games from back in the day, not needing to collide with those memories right now.

"Quick and against the wall," I decided, loving that position with her since it was a reminder of our first time together.

I set Seraphina down and grabbed a towel from my bathroom so I could return to my mission of getting my woman off before we joined everyone to watch *National Lampoon's Christmas Vacation.*

I unbuckled and unzipped my jeans as she removed her leggings and panties.

"Feel like a teenager," she said with a laugh as I hoisted her up against the wall by my door, guiding her ankles around my back.

"Nothing wrong with feeling young." I licked her lips open and positioned my head at her center, waiting for her to take control of my cock from there.

Reaching between us with her free hand as my fingertips dug deep into the flesh of her ass cheeks while I held her up against the wall, she gave us exactly what we both needed, and I groaned in relief the second I was inside her, my balls already tightening and ready for release.

She brought her mouth to my shoulder, stifling her moans as I took her hard. My thighs and ass muscles, and just about everything else, clenched as we made love.

From the corner of my eye, I spied my trophies on the dresser, shaking—and fuck, if they fell, my mom would hear.

I tried to slow my movements, but when it came to her, that was impossible. I only knew one speed: All. The. Fucking. Way.

Feeling her climax and tighten around my cock was my cue to allow myself to explode inside her. We could've made triplets with that had she not been on birth control. Because fuck me . . .

Panting, I rested my forehead against hers as the relief I needed chased down my spine. Also, we had mission success with nothing falling to the floor.

"Mmm. I have a feeling you're going to convince me to do this again while we're here."

"You know it." I kissed her softly before offering her the towel.

"Give me a second to clean up." She went into my bathroom, and once I was zipped up and buckled, I went over to the dresser.

My stomach knotted at the memories in front of me. I hadn't touched a hockey stick in seventeen years. Would it be like riding a bike? Would I even know what to do with a puck anymore?

She came up behind me a minute later. "I'm glad Reed and Alex could join us."

I turned away from the blast from the past to face her. "Yeah, I usually drag Reed to most holiday things since he hates being under the same roof with his family. Alex usually spends his time with his parents, but they're on a world cruise until January." I wanted to keep an eye on him anyway, so I was relieved to have him there.

She slung her arms over my shoulders, and I brought my hands to her hips. "I can't believe next week I'm selling my parents' house. Kind of surreal," she said a few quiet moments later.

"You having second thoughts?" I didn't blame her if she was.

"No." She shook her head. "It's time to say goodbye. Time to live my own life, too." She'd told me last week that as much as she loved math, she was pretty sure she'd only become an accountant for her parents. "I'm looking forward to this next chapter. Once we move to Charleston, I'll figure out what I want to do."

"Take all the time you want. And if you don't want to work, that's fine by me, too." I kissed her, then gently set my mouth to her forehead. "Whatever makes you happy makes me happy."

"Buying a house with you in Charleston makes me extremely happy." She smiled. "Who'd have thought the pilot who'd scared the hell out of me would convince us to move to where he lives?" She held up a finger between us. "As long as he understands I'm not up for any rides in toy planes."

"Only real ones, I swear."

Honestly, I didn't care where we lived as long as we were together. But it made me feel better that when I was off operating, Owen's wife was in town to keep Seraphina company. They'd immediately bonded, which was probably why we were really moving there. She needed to find new friends, ones who wouldn't replace her like her old ones had. She deserved ride-or-die friends like I now had with Alex and Reed.

"Well, I . . ." My words trailed off when the doorbell rang. "Mom didn't say she was inviting guests."

We untangled ourselves, did a quick check to ensure we didn't look like we'd just had sex, then went downstairs. The door was already open, with my mom standing there, blocking my view of the front porch.

"I think I'm at the right place. I couldn't find a current address for Ryder Lawson, but with the holidays, I was thinking maybe he'd be here." The woman's words had the hairs on the back of my neck standing up.

Who's that?

Seraphina shot me a nervous look from over her shoulder before my mother stepped to the side, giving me a clear view of the blonde on the front porch.

The woman's blue-green eyes narrowed on me, but I didn't recognize her. So why was she looking at me like she knew me?

I kept hold of Seraphina's hand, walking her with me to the door. I barely registered the fact that Alex and Reed were now hovering behind us in the foyer.

"Do I know you?" I asked her.

She fidgeted with the zipper of her white puffy jacket. "I'm so sorry to drop in on you like this, especially the night before Christmas, but we . . . Well, this is a long shot, but I just thought . . ."

The woman was damn nervous. Why? Who the hell was she?

"I went to see him first. I thought he'd want to know he has a grandson. Showed him proof I was his daughter. Turns out, that wasn't the best idea. He thought I was after his money. Sent us both on our way. I only just found out about him last month. You too."

I took a step back, my skin heating up despite the cold air smacking me in the face. "I'm sorry, but what are you saying?" My throat constricted, and when a little boy came up behind her wearing a fuzzy blue hat that matched his eyes and jacket, and he pointed those big blues at me, my heart jumped from my chest.

"This is your nephew, Chase." With his back to her, she rested her gloved hands on his shoulders. "I'm your sister, Audrey."

I stared at her in shock. I wasn't sure for how long, but long enough that my mother had to intervene and offer for her and her son to come inside.

"What?" I mumbled. As far as I knew, my father had never had another family. Well, I never checked after that day at Princeton, but this woman was too old to be his daughter if he'd had her after I left for the military.

"How old are you?" Mom asked her as I glanced at Seraphina, finding her shocked brown eyes intensely pointed at my sister.

I have a sister? Holy fuck.

"I'm thirty-three. Chase is eight."

I didn't need to be great at math like Seraphina to figure that one out. She was five years younger than me. The math didn't fucking math.

Was I really shocked my father had cheated? And, from the sounds of it, abandoned Audrey's mother, too? How many other siblings did *we* have out there?

"Maybe I shouldn't have come here, either." Shit, there were tears in her eyes. The same color eyes as mine. As *Dad's* eyes.

Fuck that man, though. Fuck him all the way to hell. How could he look at his grandson and send him away?

"No, honey, we're glad you're here." Mom reached for her arm, stopping her from leaving. "Why don't you stay with us for dinner? Unless you have other plans?"

"No, no other plans." Well, that was almost painful to hear. Where was Chase's dad? Audrey's other family? "You're sure we're not imposing?" She smoothed a gloved hand across her cheek, catching a tear.

"You're family. No imposition." Mom didn't even question her story. She believed her, just like I did. I felt it in my gut. We shared not only blood but also the pain of being left behind.

I let go of a deep breath and dropped before her son, taking a knee. "What grade are you in?"

"Third. I'll be nine next week." He smiled, showing two crooked adult teeth that had come in.

"Wow." My heart squeezed. "And what do you like to do for fun?"

His eyes lit up, and his answer did me in. "I love to skate and play hockey."

"I—I had no idea about . . ." Audrey's words trailed off as I looked up at her in surprise. "I probably wouldn't have wanted him to, had I known."

I focused back on my nephew, seeing myself in the kid. *Do not cry. Fucking A. Don't.* "I bet I have some of my old skates in the garage. Maybe you can show me your skills while you're in town? That is, if your mom plans on staying around for Christmas."

"We would love to," Audrey rushed out. "If that's really okay with you?"

All it took was a gentle nod of reassurance from Seraphina to help me make up my mind. I could leave my old man in the past where he belonged, and for this kid, I could pick up a hockey stick again. I could do that for Chase. Maybe I owed it to myself, too.

"I'd like you to stay," I finally said, pushing upright to stand tall. "This is my fiancée, Seraphina."

Audrey removed her gloves and extended her hand, but Seraphina went in for a hug instead, and then my mom did the same.

I startled at the feel of Chase wrapping his arms around my legs to hug me. A chill roped around my spine, and that same bolt of energy continued a path through the rest of my body.

Reed stepped in, offering his hand as he introduced himself. "I'm Jason Reed."

"Wait, how am I just learning *Reed* isn't your first name?" Seraphina folded her arms, shooting Reed an adorable look.

"Well, you never asked," Reed said casually, letting go of my sister's hand, and Alex stepped forward to meet Audrey next.

"Alejandro Rodriguez." I didn't miss the fact he checked her hand for a wedding ring as he greeted her—and nope, there wasn't one there. "I'm his brother from another mother." He closed one eye, shaking his head. "Shit, sorry. Bad joke." But Audrey laughed, and I'd swear the man's whole fucking face lit up at the sound.

"Nice to meet everyone." Audrey unzipped her jacket, and Reed morphed into a gentleman to help her out of it. "Are you sure this is okay? Chase is pretty active, and—"

"It's more than okay." Mom hooked their arms. I was relieved she was so welcoming of a child that'd been from my father's infidelity. "Come on in. You like wine?"

"Absolutely." Audrey smiled, and Mom took hold of Chase's hand with her other, guiding them away from us and into the kitchen.

I remained nailed to the floor in the foyer, not yet ready to move.

"You good, boss?" Alex with the *boss* shit, so help me.

But when I looked around at Seraphina, him, then Reed while hearing my mother chatting away with my sister and nephew, I gulped, realizing I'd never been better.

Seraphina wrapped her arms around me, and I held her back, resting my chin on top of her head.

"Amazing, in fact," I finally answered.

"Well, then"—Alex clapped—"on that note, why don't we give you a moment alone."

I nodded my thanks, and once it was only the two of us, Seraphina pulled back to locate my eyes.

I palmed her cheeks as she stared at me with a mischievous look. "What's on your mind?"

"Nothing." She smirked.

"Liar," I teased.

Her gaze flicked toward the kitchen. "Just wondering if maybe . . ."

Alex and my sister? Yeah, I knew exactly what she was cooking up in that gorgeous mind of hers. "Not happening," I grunted.

"Look at you, stepping into the big-brother role so fast."

I blinked. Processed. Recalibrated. Waited to truly absorb the fact I had a sister and a nephew.

At the sound of laughter coming from Chase in the kitchen, emotion choked me up all over again.

"I'm not sure what Audrey's story is, but I have a feeling it's going to be a novel-length one," she mused.

I held on to her even tighter. "I may have missed out on her whole life, but I'm not like my father, I'll step in and be there for her however I can be."

"Well, she's lucky to have a brother like you." She kissed me.

I swallowed. "I just can't believe my dad sent her and Chase away. I hate him for that, more than I hate him for what he did to me." I hung my head as she rubbed my arm. "I need to close that chapter of my life for good." I was done letting him and what had happened get in my head.

"I'm here for you, for whatever you want to do. And I'm proud of how you're handling the hockey thing with Chase."

Hockey, right. "Been a long time." I sighed. "In a strange way, I'm looking forward to putting on a pair of skates, seeing if I still have it."

"Oh, I have no doubt you do, and you have to promise to do that erotic hip-thrust warm-up thing, too."

I lifted my head, cracking a smile. The woman was beaming. Or, hell, maybe that was me, and she was mirroring my feelings? "If that'll make you happy, I'll do it on top of you, too."

"Maybe if you're good, I'll let you be bad and sneak into my room after everyone's asleep."

Oh, you can count on that happening.

She licked her lips. "A little late-night storm."

I shifted her hair away from her face, hope and a sense of peace dwelling inside me as I murmured, "You are my lightning, beautiful. *Por siempre y para siempre.*"

"Forever and always."

AUTHOR'S NOTE

One of my favorite things to do is to have characters from other series cross over into new books to keep them "alive." Delta Shield Security has quite a few cameos from three different series.

The Costa Family—Italian American "vigilantes" (in private security) who are former military. We had brief cameos from Hudson Ashford from *The Art of You* and Enzo Costa from *Let Me Love You*.

Stealth Ops—Navy SEALs working covert ops for the president of the United States. Cameos included:

- **Stealth Ops: Bravo Team**
- *Finding His Mark* (Luke, Bravo One)
- *Finding Justice* (Owen, Bravo Two)
- *Finding the Fight* (Asher, Bravo Three, Jessica's husband)
- *Finding Her Chance* (Liam, the Aussie, Bravo Four)
- *Finding the Way Back* (Knox, POTUS's son, Bravo Five)

Also mentioned from the **Stealth Ops: Echo Team**: *Chasing the Knight* (Wyatt Pierson, Echo One, Gwen's father).

Falcon Falls Security—features former army operators who work private security. This series is a direct spin-off from the Stealth Ops series. Carter Dominick co-runs Falcon. His book is *The Fallen One*. Gwen Montgomery joins the team later in the series, and her book is not out yet. Martín Gabriel is also a side character from the book *The Guarded One*.

ABOUT THE AUTHOR

Brittney Sahin is the *Wall Street Journal* bestselling author of the Costa Family series, Falcon Falls Security series, Dublin Nights series, and many other novels of romantic suspense. She began writing at an early age with the dream to be a published author before the age of eighteen. Although academic pursuits (and later, a teaching career) interrupted her aspirations, she never stopped writing, never stopped imagining. It wasn't until her students encouraged her to follow her dreams that Brittney said goodbye to Upstate New York in order to start a new adventure in the place she was raised: Charlotte, North Carolina. Here, she decided to take her students' advice and begin to write again. When she's not working on upcoming novels, she spends time with her family. She is the proud mother of two boys, and a lover of suspense novels, coffee, and the outdoors. For more information, visit www.brittneysahin.com.